Y0-BUD-551

9-13-73

THE SEARCH FOR MUSICAL UNDERSTANDING

Robert
W.
Buggert
Northern Illinois University

Charles
B.
Fowler
Music Consultant, Washington, D.C.

THE SEARCH FOR MUSICAL UNDERSTANDING

Wadsworth
Publishing
Company,
Inc.,
Belmont,
California

The Search for Musical Understanding by Robert W. Buggert and Charles B. Fowler

ISBN 0-534-00164-5

L. C. Cat. Card No. 72-86609

Printed in the United States of America

1 2 3 4 5 6 7 8 9 10——77 76 75 74 73

Acknowledgments

Photographs, paintings, musical examples, and poetry are reproduced with permission from the following sources.

Photographs and Paintings

Alverthorpe Gallery: p. 144. Art Reference Bureau: pp. 128, 362, 366, color insert (Watteau); pp. 24, 106, 115, 274 (Alinari). Austrian National Tourist Office: p. 319. Robert Berks: p. 12. Clichés Musées Nationaux, Paris: pp. 8, 200, 390, color insert (Monet). Courtauld Institute Galleries, London: color insert (Cézanne). Fletcher Drake: p. 423. Kenneth B. Dresser: p. 192. Fischbach Gallery: color insert (Davis). The Freer Gallery of Art: p. 406. John Froom: p. 151. Embassy of India: p. 182. The Solomon R. Guggenheim Museum, New York, p. 31. Richard A. Matthews: p. 36. Louis Melancon: pp. 203, 207. The Metropolitan Museum of Art: pp. 20, 44. Museo del Prado: pp. 28, 281. Museum of Fine Arts, Boston: p. 240. The Museum of Modern Art, New York: pp. 2, 19, 64, 166, color insert (Kirchner, Mondrian, Pollock). The National Gallery, London: color insert (Van Gogh). The National Gallery of Art, Washington, D.C.: pp. 148, 283. The New York Times: p. 416 and cover. Pinacoteca di Brera, Milan, Italy: p. 376. Photographic Giraudon: pp. 316, 317. Arthur Tress: p. 426. Vladimir Ussachevsky: p. 54. Bruce White: p. 21.

Musical Examples and Poetry

Boosey and Hawkes, Inc.: Concerto for Orchestra *by Béla Bartók (p. 72). Copyright 1946 by Hawkes & Son (London) Ltd.; String Quartet no. 1, op. 7 by Béla Bartók (p. 214). Reprinted by permission of Boosey & Hawkes, Inc., sole agents for* Kultura *in the U.S.A.;* A Young Person's Guide to the Orchestra, op. 34 *by Benjamin Britten (p. 72). Copyright 1947 by Hawkes & Son (London) Ltd.;* Ceremony of Carols *by Benjamin Britten (p. 162).*

Copyright 1943 by Boosey & Co., Ltd.; The Beggar's Opera *by John Gay/Austin (pp. 284–85). Copyright 1920, 1926 by Boosey & Co., Ltd., renewed 1947, 1953; "Chaconne" from First Suite in E Flat for Military Band by Gustav Holst (p. 139). Copyright 1921 by Boosey & Co., Ltd., renewed 1948; "Love's Stricken 'Why'" and "Stop All the Clocks" from* Poems of Love and the Rain *by Ned Rorem (pp. 229, 230). Copyright 1965 by Boosey & Hawkes, Inc.;* Cantata *by Igor Stravinsky (p. 86). Copyright 1952 by Boosey & Hawkes, Inc.;* Mass *by Igor Stravinsky (pp. 221, 222). Copyright 1948 by Boosey & Hawkes, Inc. William C. Brown Publishers.* The Heritage Songster *by Leon and Lynn Dallin (pp. 108, 109, 111, 113, 114). Copyright 1966 by William C. Brown Publishers, Dubuque, Iowa. Chappell & Co., Inc.: "My Funny Valentine" by Richard Rogers and Lorenz Hart (p. 116). Copyright © 1937 by Chappell & Co., Inc. J. & W. Chester Ltd.:* L'Histoire du Soldat *by Igor Stravinsky (p. 73). Copyright 1924 by J. & W. Chester Ltd. Elkan-Vogel, Inc.* Pelléas et Mélisande *by Claude Debussy (pp. 208, 210). Copyright 1908 by Elkan-Vogel, Inc.;* Prélude to the Afternoon of a Faun *by Claude Debussy (p. 134). Copyright 1908 by Elkan-Vogel, Inc.;* Bolero *by Maurice Ravel (p. 75). Copyright 1929 by Durand and Cie, Paris. Harcourt Brace Jovanovich, Inc.:* Collected Poems 1901–1962 *by T. S. Eliot (p. 108). Copyright 1934, 1936, 1963 by Harcourt Brace and World, Inc. MCA, Inc.: "Polka" from the ballet* L'Age d'or, *op. 22 by Dmitri Shostakovich (p. 85). © Copyright 1944, 1945 by MCA Music, a division of MCA, Inc., 445 Park Avenue, New York, New York 10022, all rights reserved. The Macmillan Company:* Collected Poems *by Vachel Lindsay (p. 110). Copyright 1913 by The Macmillan Company.* motive Magazine: *"In Santa Cruz" by Harry MacCormack (pp. 121–122). Copyright 1968 by the Board of Education of the United Methodist Church, Nashville, Tennessee, reprinted from XXVIII, No. 7, page 25. Music for Percussion, Inc.:* Introduction and Fugue for Percussion and Piano *by Robert W. Buggert (p. 153). Copyright 1957 by Music for Percussion, Inc. New Directions Publishing Corp.:* Selected Poems *by Federico García Lorca, translation by Stephen Spender and J. L. Gili (p. 110). Copyright 1955 by New Directions Publishing Corporation. W. W. Norton & Company, Inc.: "Terzetto" from* Semiramide *by Cesti in* Music in the Baroque Era, from Monteverdi to Bach *by Manfred Bukofzer (p. 138). Copyright 1947 by W. W. Norton & Company, Inc.; Chorale Melody from "Cantata no. 4" by Bach (pp. 142, 293);* Eqo sum panis vivus *by William Byrd (p. 159); Trouvère Song (p. 365) in* Masterpieces of Music Before 1750 *by Carl Parrish and John F. Ohl, editors. Copyright 1952 by W. W. Norton & Company, Inc. Oxford University Press, Inc.:* The Quartets of Beethoven *by Daniel Gregory Mason (p. 32). Copyright 1947 by Oxford University Press; "Etude" and "Scherzo" by Brock McElheran (p. 178). Copyright © Brock McElheran 1965. Princeton University Press:* The Changing Composer–Performer Relationship: A Monologue and a Dialogue *by Lukas Foss (p. 173), in* Perspectives of New Music, *Vol. 1, No. 2 (Spring 1963). Simon & Schuster: "A Mighty Fortress Is Our God" by Martin Luther from* Fireside Book of Favorite American Songs *by Margaret Boni, et al. (p. 112). Copyright 1952 by Simon & Schuster. Universal Edition:* Wozzeck *by Alban Berg (p. 216). Copyright 1926 by Universal A. G. Vienna. University of Nebraska Press: "Two Beers in Argyle, Wisconsin" from* Go Read the River *by David Etter (p. 88). Copyright 1966 by University of Nebraska Press.*

Contents

Part One THE RAW MATERIAL OF MUSICAL MEANING

Part Two THE STRUCTURE OF MUSICAL MEANING

Part Three MUSICAL STLYE

Part Four MUSIC IN THE HUMAN ENVIRONMENT

Preface

This book is designed as an introduction to music and to music appreciation for those wishing to participate in a search for musical understanding. Because musical styles continuously evolve, perspectives on music shift. Music is continually reinterpreted, rediscovered by new generations of listeners, and reevaluated by changing patterns of thought and taste. The authors' purpose is to expose students to all music—the music of many cultures; instrumental, vocal, and electronic music; popular and classical music; traditional and new music; music of the past and music of the present. The authors consider appreciation, however, a by-product of understanding. Conceivably, disliking a piece of music might be as natural a result of understanding as learning to enjoy it. Once the student understands the music he listens to, he will acquire his own set of appreciations. The musical art should be accessible in all its forms, although the choices people make within that selection are personal choices.

The focus of this book is on significant facets of music as an aesthetic auditory experience. Occasional references and analogies to other art forms emphasize that music does not exist in artistic isolation, and that concepts and principles of aesthetic understanding are broadly based. Through directed listening and explanation, the listener is brought into a closer and more sensitive relationship with music. He becomes involved with the composer's creation of musical ideas, the composition of music (the organization of sounds), the performance of music, and the formation of attitudes toward music.

Questions germane to the search for musical understanding are: How does man express himself? What is abstract expression? What expressive ingredients are basic to music? How are these ingredients organized into meaningful musical events? How are musical events structured into compositions? On what bases can the listener make musical judgments?

Part One, "The Raw Material of Musical Meaning," offers insights into aesthetic expression by discussing man's creative potential, the origin and inspiration of musical ideas, and by showing how the creative process finds expression in musical composition. Part Two, "The Structure of Musical Meaning," presents the "architecture" of music: basic elements of design, the use of repetition and contrast, variation, and other techniques of "the craft of musical composition."

Part Three, "Musical Style," allows the listener to compare styles, to find similarities in musical works of different periods and cultures, and to discover the unique aspects of a period. For example, what characterizes Baroque music? Contemporary music? Jazz? The emphasis of this section is on stylistic comparison, setting Modern against Romantic, Classic against Baroque, Renaissance against Medieval, and then discussing stylistic qualities not related to a particular period. In general, this section follows a reverse chronological order, moving from the better known and more striking works of the present to the lesser known works of the past. Chronology is considered in relation to musical style—emphasizing the music itself, not the history of the music.

Part Four, "Music in the Human Environment," focuses attention on musical values, the development of musical taste, and the formation of musical judgments. In this final section, the listener is challenged to evaluate and judge music in the light of an increased knowledge and a broader experience of the creative principles, concepts, and structures of music.

A final word is in order concerning the choices of musical examples. Since this book is not primarily intended as a survey of music literature but instead is intended as a guide to understanding music, little attempt has been made to include the majority of musical masterworks, or, indeed, to include all major composers. The musical examples have been selected on the basis of their pertinence to the specific points under discussion. Other choices might serve as well. For those wishing to expand their listening experiences, a Guide to Additional Listening is included at the end of most chapters.

It would be impossible to acknowledge individually all who have assisted in preparing this text. Students and colleagues have made comments and suggestions on our approach to the subject of understanding music throughout our years of teaching. We extend special appreciation, however, to Paul O. Steg, who originally was a coauthor. We are indebted to him for his contributions to the organization of the book and for portions of Chapters 1 and 3. We would also like to thank the reviewers who made valuable suggestions on the manuscript: Maynard C. Anderson of Wartburg College, Waverly, Iowa; Simon V. Anderson of the University of Cincinnati; Mayer M. Cahn of California State University at San Francisco; Robert Choate of Boston University; Charles Hubbard of California State University at Los Angeles ; and the invaluable assistance of Royal Stanton of De Anza College, Cupertino, California. To all who contributed, specifically or generally, knowingly or unaware, we are grateful.

Robert W. Buggert
Charles B. Fowler

Part One

THE RAW MATERIAL OF MUSICAL MEANING

Musical Understanding

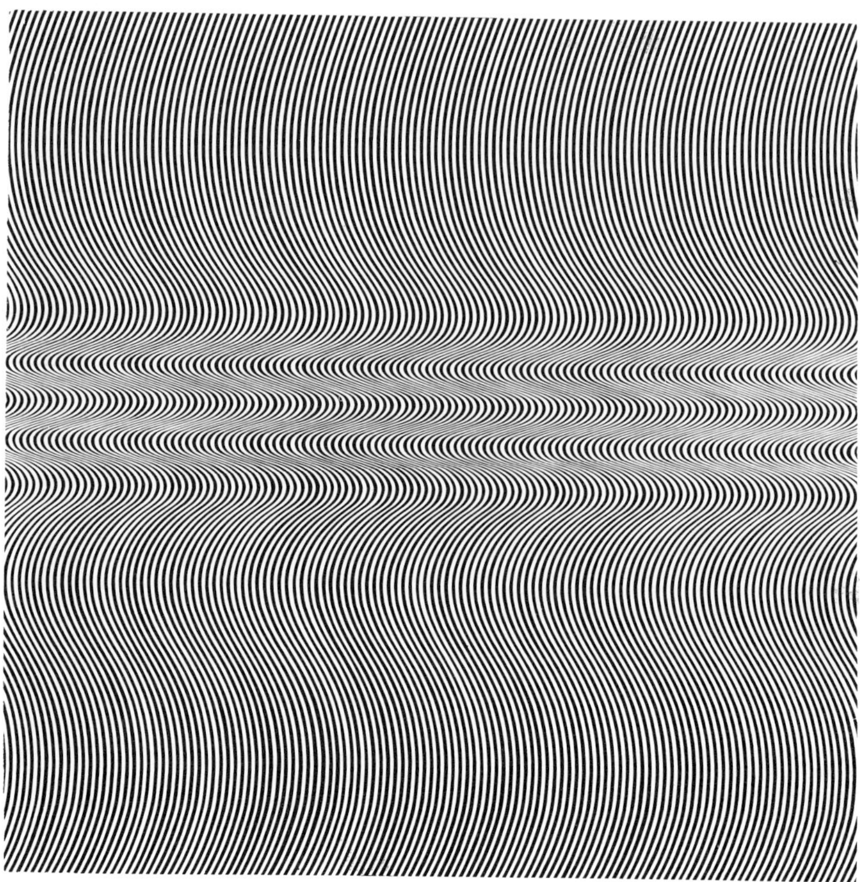

1

A musical composition is an experience in sound that can only be fully understood by being heard. An erudite treatise or an entertaining lecture may communicate musical concepts, but neither can convey or "tell" the sound itself. The search for musical understanding begins and ends with the ear. Whatever music "has to say" can only be realized when it is heard. Whether the listener tries to recognize all the technical components of a score or simply seeks the emotional effect, he must pay attention to every note, following the succession of sounds through to its logical conclusion. Refinement of musical understanding usually depends upon repetition and improved listening techniques.

THE MUSICAL EXPERIENCE

What should a person expect to feel or experience as he listens to music? What kind of response is intended by the composer? How does a person know if he is getting the message? There is no one answer to these questions. Musical response covers the gamut from falling asleep

Bridget Riley: Current *(1964). Collection, The Museum of Modern Art, New York. Philip Johnson Fund.*

The fluid, undulating shapes in Bridget Riley's optical art captivate the eye with their continual rhythmic changes, much as some contemporary music captivates the ear through chance arrangements that make every playing of a piece a completely different experience.

to following the score; from experiencing an emotional tone bath to identifying individual pitches, harmonies, and structural designs; from pleasant unawareness to an intense, moving experience.

Each listener responds in his own way. His taste and knowledge will attract him to one composer's music and not another's, to a blues ballad rather than a dance tune, to a string quartet rather than a concerto, to nineteenth century music rather than contemporary, or to French music rather than American. An individual's preference and level of attention may also vary according to his immediate social activity and frame of mind. Rock 'n' roll or jazz may completely satisfy a person at one time and yet annoy him at another. A classical composition may command his total attention one day and seem disappointingly dull the next. He may be captivated by the exotic sounds of Balinese music in a certain setting and yet be unreceptive to them in another environment.

As in all situations where human behavior is concerned, a number of different personal responses can be expected. Music that stimulates and satisfies one person may offend and bore another. Depending on the circumstances, a piece of music can provoke several equally valid reactions. Generally, people expect their responses to music to differ somewhat from those of others. They are reluctant, however, to admit that other people apparently derive more than they do from the musical experience. No one wants to be robbed of pleasure that might be his. One way a listener can increase his range of musical response and his receptivity to aesthetic experience is to develop his musical understanding.

Aesthetic experience denotes the special realm of human response associated with the arts. While there are levels of aesthetic experience, at its best it represents a total charging of the emotions and the intellect. The musical experience at its height, for example, absorbs a person so completely that he is said "to lose himself in the music." Because it depends upon many factors being precisely right, this intense kind of musical experience does not occur with great frequency. More often, the listener feels pleasantly interested in the music and is transported from the concrete, materialistic world into the realms of imagination and fantasy. Even on this level, music creates certain expectations in the listener, commanding his attention and carrying him towards an ultimate feeling of satisfaction. There is little doubt that a person's degree of absorption in music is one indication of whether he is receiving the message.

There are other indications of the degree of musical communication. Music has become meaningful to the listener when he can reproduce it internally. Sounds that the listener can play in his mind at his own choosing have become his own. Such internalization usually requires repetition and a receptive attitude on the part of the listener. The television advertising jingle is designed to take full advantage of this process. Its catchy simplicity can pierce even the most unwilling ears. When children and adults find themselves humming the tune or singing the lyrics, they have absorbed the message.

Repeated hearings of a musical work are often essential to musical understanding. As a person becomes more familiar with a piece, musical "events" such as rhythm and melody begin to blend into a coherent whole that he can "think" to himself. His ears begin to sort out the sounds, searching for patterns and relationships. The significance of music is largely dependent upon the sense-arrangement of sounds. The logic of the music is generally what makes it satisfying and memorable. Repetition permits the discovery of this logic and assures the retention of a clear sound-image.

Music, like anything in human experience, can also be understood solely on the intellectual level, with no emotional involvement. One can look at it objectively, much as a chemist observes the transformation of substances, and enjoy the sound-structure that fills the silence. Many musicians, for example, listen to music primarily from an analytical viewpoint. Their detailed, highly technical involvement, however, need not serve as a model to be emulated by the general listener, any more than an architect's accumulated knowledge is essential to the general understanding of a building. Ideally, some intellectual understanding can enhance one's total response by reinforcing and substantiating the emotional experience of music.

To a large degree, the accumulated musical experiences of a person's lifetime represent a continual redefinition of music. As a person explores different kinds of music and learns new ideas about the art form, his tastes change and mature. Each new musical experience—each confrontation with a composer's mind—enlarges the scope of what a person understands music to be. In the hands of every new composer, music says something different. This is part of its fascination: it cannot be defined in the finality of language. It continues to evolve, both as an art form and as an idea in the mind of each listener.

These ideas about music take various forms. To a child, music may be the natural accompaniment to playful fantasies. To a teenager, music means rhythm and dance—an expression of sexual and social urges, tensions, and anxieties. It reflects his exhilarating and often disturbing growth toward adulthood. An adult may consider music an expression of beauty that both affirms and develops his maturity, sophistication, sensitivity, taste, and social status. To many concertgoers, music is a ritual, involving a customary form of behavior with prescribed rules of dress, applause, attentiveness, and intermission-conversation. The advent of the phonograph, radio, and television has blurred many of these traditions, however. Now music can be enjoyed in the comfort of familiar surroundings and informal dress and can accompany any activity one chooses, from talking or eating to quiet, absorbed listening. The concertgoer at home evolves his own ritual.

The musical experience can be a pleasant, exciting adventure; it can exalt the human spirit and be an exhilarating affirmation of life; it can be an introspective, contemplative study of serenity; it can be unpleasant, jarring, and emotionally upsetting; it can be an absorbing intellectual exercise. It seems doubtful whether the "good life" to which philosophers have often alluded can be fully realized without aesthetic experience. Like the other arts, music spiritualizes the senses. Music offers people an antidote for boredom, anxiety, materialism, alienation, and the dehumanizing technology of twentieth-century life.

LISTENING

A composer writes music to satisfy a need to create—a need for self-expression. The performer performs for much the same reason. Though the performer's satisfactions are different, music comes alive only through his efforts. The listener, on the other hand, is separated from the initial creation. Necessarily, his expressive experiences are of a more vicarious nature. Because he depends upon the performer's response, he may feel removed from the music itself. Listening is his only means of engaging himself actively with it.

Listening, however, need not be, and should not be, a passive process. Because it requires direction and concentration, it is more than hearing. There are certain listening techniques a person can learn to help him derive more from any musical stimulus. The ear can be trained to penetrate the sounds, distinguishing their special character and the nature of their combinations. Further, the listener can become familiar with various extramusical data—historical facts, analytical studies, philosophical concepts—which can help him establish musical values, modify his musical tastes, and make musical judgments.

Sensitive, discriminating listening is essential to musical understanding and can increase the gratification one derives from music. It is neither expected nor desired, however, that this pleasure be the same for all listeners. Love of music, as of all things, is a personal matter—even for composers, performers, and scholars. One may appreciate music without really understanding it, understand music without enjoying it. Conceivably, familiarity and understanding could lead one to dislike a piece of music as well as increase one's enjoyment. Ideally, understanding does lead to greater musical satisfaction, which is a worthy goal of any education in music. A more logical goal for the listener, however, is to become familiar with, and sensitive to, a wide variety of music. The ability to respond perceptively to music of many types, styles, and cultural derivations may not guarantee equal levels of satisfaction, but it can intensify and extend the range of one's gratification.

How is the capacity for intelligent listening to be developed? Two prerequisites are essential: (1) a clear definition of the objectives of listening and (2) adequate experience in the process of listening. The following chapters will define the objectives and guide the process. It is the individual's responsibility to make sure that listening experiences are frequent, regular, and logical.

Knowing what to listen for in music calls for the ability to analyze—a term more suggestive of science than of art. It implies the necessity of technical knowledge and also raises the question of the ultimate logic of such an approach. Is analytical listening within the grasp of a person with little or no prior musical study? Does repeated emphasis on such listening inevitably stifle the listener's pleasure? Just how far should one go with analysis?

Analysis for the sake of analysis can surely be a dry intellectual exercise, aesthetically self-defeating. On the other hand, analysis that illuminates or clarifies the music can be stimulating and useful. The special skills and technical knowledge essential to rewarding listening are, on the whole, quite accessible to persons with little or no formal music education. Good listening is primarily a process of identifying the significant characteristics of the music, of learning to recognize them through practice, and of perceiving, intellectually and emotionally, their importance in the total composition.

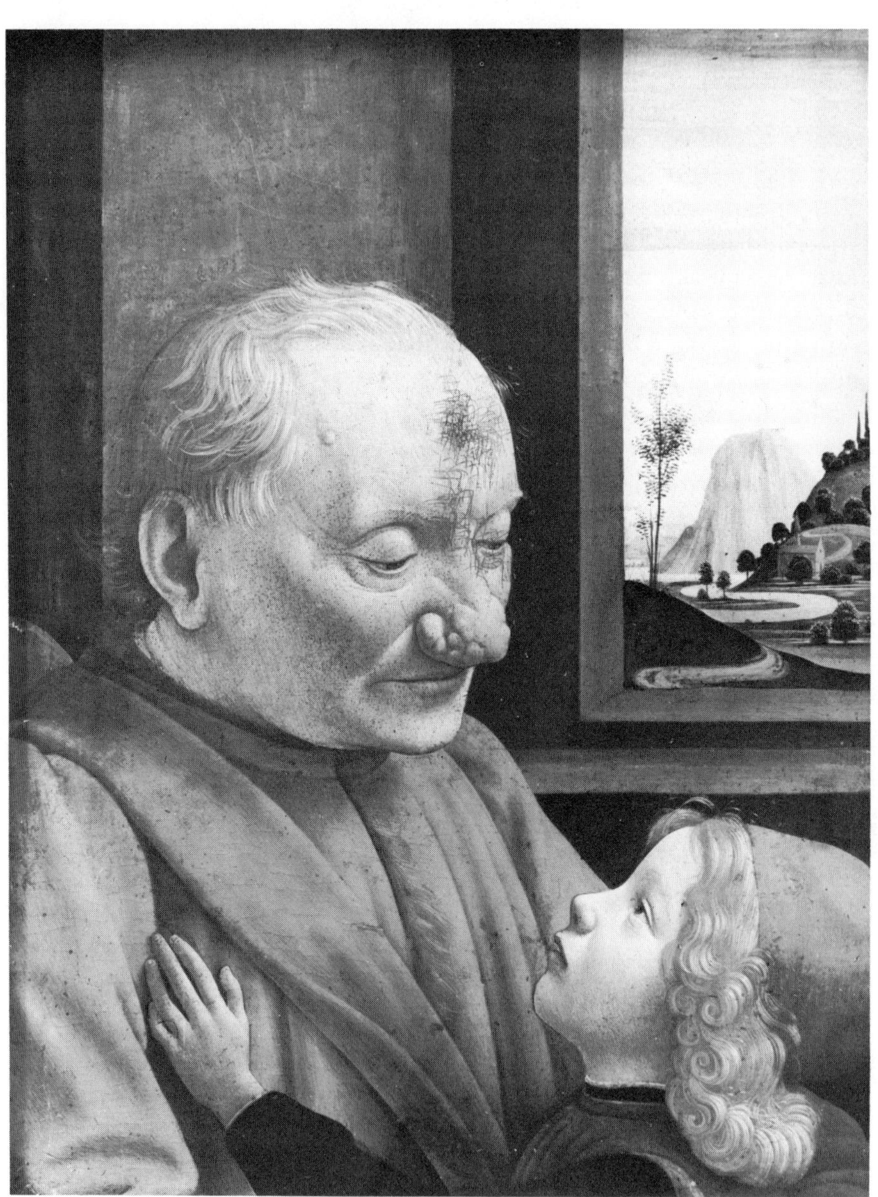

There is a rationale behind how music is put together, and to know it is to understand the music more fully. The overall design of a composition is dependent upon many musical details or events along the way. There is a danger, however, that in identifying these elements, the listener may isolate them from the total context. He may concentrate so much on the melody, for example, that he misses the rhythmic and harmonic events—and the musical conception as a whole. No significant composition is merely a collection of rhythms, motives, melodies, harmonies, or tone colors. Any or all of these aspects gain importance only insofar as they validly represent aesthetic and artistic qualities of the music with which they are associated. The goal of listening is not to recognize a detail here and a detail there, even though some of these might prove to be interesting and effective aspects of the music. Rather the listener must learn to scan aurally, to absorb all the details as they occur and relate them to the unfolding whole. He must learn to hear music in the same way that he views a painting—as a total entity. In the forthcoming discussion of musical details, this point should be kept in mind so that there is no confusion of means with ends.

RECORDED VERSUS LIVE PERFORMANCE

Music comes to the listener in several ways—the live concert hall performance, the "live" radio or television broadcast, and the phonograph or tape recording. Are the differences between these various

---

Domenico Ghirlandaio: An Old Man and His Grandson (*c. 1480*). *Clichés Musées Nationaux, Paris.*

One can look at a painting without really seeing it, just as one can hear a musical composition without really listening to it. There are different levels of perception in the arts, as there are in life. The grandfather's nose in this painting may capture the viewer's attention and repulse him so that he fails to see all that the painter was trying to express. The tender human relationship between the child and his grandfather is wholly unaffected by a physical defect. Ghirlandaio may be suggesting that such genuine, intrinsic affection is unswayed by physical superficialities.

means significant? Is one medium more real or more musical than another? Does one offer more satisfaction—command more aesthetic reaction—than another?

The invention of new electronic mediums makes these questions unique to the twentieth century. Before 1900, barrel organs, music boxes, mechanical pianos, and other reproducing instruments accounted for only a small number of musical performances. The cost of presenting live concerts limited their availability, despite the popularity of music among the rising middle class. Now, however, recordings make all kinds of music readily available. Performed by the world's best artists, they often represent the most polished renderings of various compositions.

If the recording was once considered a substitute for the live performance in the concert hall, it has now assumed a role of its own. Composers create pieces only for recording. Artists create recorded performances that could not be duplicated live. And it can no longer be taken for granted that avid collectors of recordings will automatically be drawn to the concert hall. Recordings work both ways. They can induce people to attend live concerts; but they can also command their own audience. In fact, live performances play only a small part in the musical experience of many people.

Recordings do have certain disadvantages. They lack the spontaneous excitement, the drama, and the controlled listening environment of the concert hall. Also, many musical performers consider the recording unmusical because the interpretation is frozen, forcing the listener to hear the same performance over and over again. In contrast, they maintain, when a performer plays or sings in a live concert, he is often stimulated to alter the interpretation according to his sense of the audience. The audience thus participates in the creative experience. There is no doubt that some artists do respond to an audience in this way, performing with greater emotional intensity. Admittedly, however, there are other performers who fare better before the microphone. Certainly the recorded performance—in terms of numbers of listeners—must be acknowledged as the most significant communication medium for musical experience. A large part of the recorded repertoire could never be encountered by the listener in a lifetime of concert going. Live concerts often repeat standard works rather than provide an extensive variety of selections.

The aspiring listener should seek both kinds of musical experience

—live and recorded. Practically, the recorded performance is more useful to the student because of convenience and cost. Unfortunately, one advantage of recordings may be lost to the student. The personal record library allows one to choose music to suit his momentary mood and surroundings, but listening is assigned to the student and must be carried out at prescribed hours and places. Still, knowledge gained under these conditions can be applied later in the more casual atmosphere of the home or the more formal and exciting atmosphere of the concert hall.

FOR DISCUSSION

1. What are the characteristics of the aesthetic experience that distinguish it from other kinds of experience?
2. Define musical experience. Does it differ from person to person?
3. What is the difference between the recorded concert-hall performance and the recorded studio performance?
4. Have the new performance standards of recordings affected the quality of live performances?
5. Listen to a musical composition in live performance and then on recording. What are the differences in the effect communicated? In convenience? How does environment affect your reaction?
6. Are people capable of closing their ears as well as their eyes? When a person is reading, is he actually hearing the music in the background? Is the movie-goer affected by background music even when he does not listen to it or is unaware of it? Should the study of music change this, or should background music remain background music?

Man and Expression

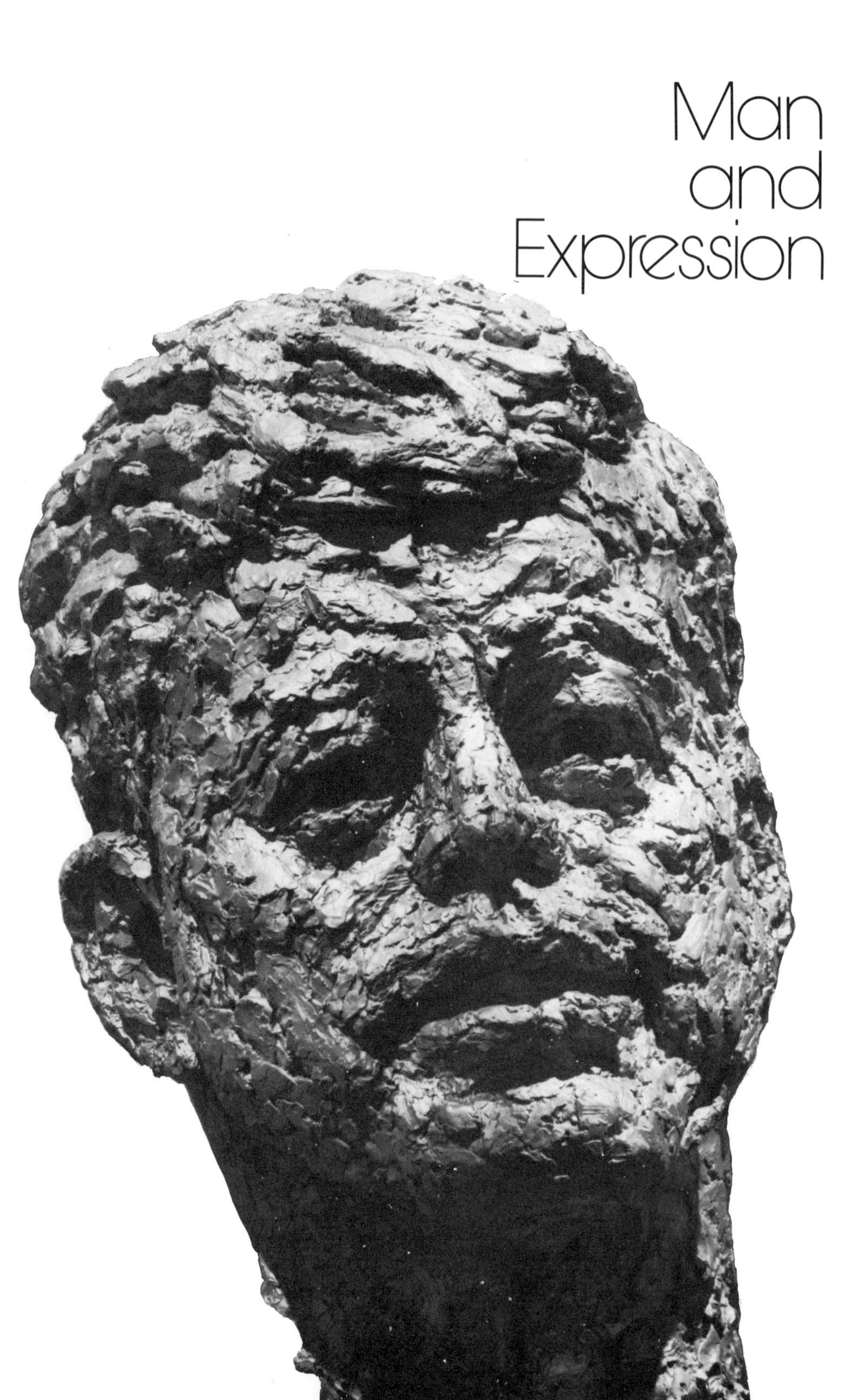

2

Communication in the arts poses numerous questions: What is the nature of artistic expression? What are the means of communication? What does the artist wish to transmit? How does a person perceive and understand creative expressions? What relationships exist among the various arts and between the arts and society?

To understand the arts in general or music in particular, one must become aware of the creative process, the medium of transmission, the technique used to create the expression, and, possibly, the nature of the artist as an expressive being. The study of a specific work in isolation is not enough. To probe the potential meaning of a single artistic expression, it is necessary to survey many works and consider a variety of relationships. The relationship of a work to the mainstream of art, to the historical period in which it was created and to other periods, to the society that produced it and to other societies—all are important dimensions of knowledge about music. Communication also depends upon a person's expectations, which are built up over a long period of time through many encounters with music. One fundamental area of expectations concerns what a listener believes is the function of an art work.

Robert Berks: John F. Kennedy *(1971). The John F. Kennedy Center for the Performing Arts, Washington, D.C.*

Unlike music, an entire painting or sculpture is perceived at a glance. Sculpture is not temporal like a play, a novel, or a musical work, which take time to unfold completely. Seeing a whole work at once does not imply that the viewer immediately apprehends the totality of its meaning. Contemplation may lead to new levels of understanding as one discovers new facets of the work.

The meaning of a work of art depends upon both the nature of the work and the involvement of the observer. Herbert Read describes the interaction in this way:

> . . . man responds to the shape and surface and mass of things present to his senses, and that certain arrangements in the proportion of the shape and surface and mass of things result in a pleasurable sensation, whilst the lack of such arrangement leads to indifference or even to positive discomfort and revulsion.

In music, man reacts to the mass of sounds "present to his senses." These sounds convey meaning according to the same broad patterns reflected in all the arts.

First, art may symbolically represent something quite specific—such as a person, animal, object, event, story, or emotion. In music, these relationships may be exemplified by descriptive titles, such as the "Introduction and Royal March of the Lions" from *The Carnival of the Animals* by Camille Saint-Saëns (1835–1921), the *1812* Overture by Peter Ilyich Tchaikovsky (1840–1893) and the song "David Mourns for Absalom" by David Diamond (1915–). Such music is called "program" or "programmatic" music. The directness of the reference varies considerably. In *The Pines of Rome*, Ottorino Respighi (1879–1936) uses the actual recorded call of a nightingale. In contrast, François Couperin (1668–1733) wrote a more subtle, less direct program music for the clavier, a forerunner of the piano: *Les petits moulins à vent* (*The Little Windmills*) and *Les Barricades mystérieuses* (*The Mysterious Battlements*). Erik Satie (1866–1925) wrote pieces with surrealistic titles: *Trois Morceaux en forme de poire* (*Three Pieces in the Form of a Pear*), and often included similar instructions to the pianist: *avec beaucoup de mal* ("with much illness"), or *leger comme un oeuf* ("light like an egg"). In this case, the descriptive title does not indicate a programmatic content. Satie was caricaturing overly sentimental music and effusive music markings.

Sometimes associations are more symbolic than direct. The chorale "Durch Adams Fall ist ganz ver derbt" ("All Mankind Fell in Adam's Fall"), depicts Adam's fall in a repeated falling figure in the bass:

Ex. 2–1

This same kind of symbolism is often used in the setting of vocal texts. In the "Credo" of the *Missa Solemnis*, for example, Ludwig van Beethoven (1770–1827) sets the text *et ascendit in coelum* ("and ascended into heaven") with a rising melody line:

Ex. 2–2

Treatment such as this is referred to as "tone-painting." Examples are numerous.

Second, an art work may be without apparent symbolism or representational aspects and instead be primarily based on the artist's organization of his material according to formal aesthetic principles. In music, the composer sometimes arranges sounds in a pleasing pattern, in the same way that a person might design a quilt from various pieces of cloth. Such works are termed "absolute music" and are identified by names that refer to their purpose, their organization, and the medium of performance–such as symphony, sonata for cello and piano, theme and variations, fugue for organ, concerto for violin, piano étude, and so on. For example, Étude, op. 10, no. 6 by Frédéric Chopin (1810–1849) is a study that exploits certain piano techniques and at the same time produces pleasurable sounds for the listener. Music like this is not intended to evoke specific visual or literary associations. The statement that it makes is more strictly abstract.

It is impossible to distinguish completely between program and absolute music. Absolute music has emotional content and can evoke various moods and images, while program music obviously contains formal elements of style and organization. Still there is a vast difference between a work that includes an occasional illustrative effect or has ambiguous, general associations and a work that is specifically illustrative throughout. The former may be incidentally descriptive; but in the latter, the "program" or musical description is a major factor of the total expression.

When a person recognizes the meaning or function of an object or an expression, he can readily respond to it. Meaning in the arts, though, is rarely, if ever, precise. This is especially true of music, whether it be a simple tune or a complex work. Even the meaning of program music can be ambiguous. If a person has never heard the "Introduction and Royal March of the Lions," for example, and is unaware of the title, he may not realize that the music is portraying a specific animal. Even though the actual music remains unaltered, it can elicit a vastly different response. Similarly one may enjoy Beethoven's setting of the "Credo" whether or not he is aware of the symbolism the composer employs. Recognition of the symbolism, however, increases his understanding of the work's music and drama. Musical response and meaning are conditioned by knowledge.

Theoretically, when extramusical or symbolic associations are either unintended or undiscovered, objective meaning depends upon a musical title indicating the general structure of the composition. Yet the meaning of absolute music is not totally dependent on form. Composers differ in what they intend to communicate, and musical forms can accommodate a vast range of expressive purposes. Listeners also help to determine the meaning of music by making associations conditioned by knowledge and past experience. Something so subjective as the memory of a friend with whom the listener previously heard the composition, for example, may influence his response to the music. Music is also altered by external circumstances. "Taps" can be a signal for "lights out" when it is played at a military post, but the same sounds played at a military funeral convey a significantly different meaning.

To develop understanding of a composition, it is important to distinguish between the music itself and any extramusical phenomena. To know the story of *Scheherazade* by Nicholas Rimsky-Korsakov (1844–1908) or to be aware of the deafness of Beethoven at the time he composed his Ninth Symphony can affect response to the music. Such knowledge can enrich the musical experience, but if overemphasized it can lead to interpretations that are musically unsound or unrelated to the composer's intentions. The listener need not demand that music portray life in the same manner as words or paint. One of the most valuable aspects of abstract, nonrepresentational music is that it can carry the listener beyond the sphere of the already known into the realm of non-verbal insight. Too much dependence on familiar imagery and elaborate verbalization can distort or confine the meaning of music, and prevent the musical experience from transcending the world of common material experience.

This is not to say that the connotations suggested to various listeners by a piece of music are meaningless or irrelevant. The experience of music, while not dependent upon metaphorical images, is not necessarily thwarted by them either. Music often does arouse connotations in the listener. This is one way that the listener relates to the music. Even when the composer did not intend to be programmatic, Leonard B. Meyer reasons, there is no question of the causal connection between what a composer wrote and what connotations the music evoked. "Had the musical organization been different, the connotation would also have been different."

Regardless of whether music is programmatic or absolute, the study of music *as sound* is essential to complete understanding. Programs, descriptive titles, symbolism, and performance situations all contribute to musical experience. In the final analysis, however, musical sounds—put together by a composer and produced in performance—are the central focus of any search for musical understanding. It is to these sounds that people directly or indirectly react and relate.

MEDIUM, CONTENT, FORM, EXPRESSION

The communication of musical concepts inevitably must rely on words, if for no other reason than to perceive the intangibilities of sounds in some concrete, objective manner. Four general terms used in discussing any art form are medium, content, form, and expression.

The *medium* is the material used by the artist. In music the medium is sound produced by voices, instruments, and mechanical or electronic devices. In sculpture the medium ranges from clay to steel.

Content refers to the specific "events" that the composer fashions from the medium. In music these are melodies, harmonies, textures, rhythms, and tone colors in various combinations. Again, in comparison, sculptural content consists of shapes, colors, and surface textures.

Form is the organization of the events that make up content. It is the factor creating a sense of direction and wholeness in a musical composition. It is determined by the order, effect, treatment, and relative importance of the melodies, harmonies, rhythms, and other musical events that make up the content. In sculpture, form is the resultant arrangement of the shapes, colors, and textures within the total sculpture. In some works of art, form and content may be considered separately; in others, they are indivisible.

Expression refers to how the medium is used, and how the content and form should be conveyed in order for all these elements to work cohesively to achieve a desired meaning. If the composer tells the singer to sing *bravura* (brah-voo′-rah), the performance should be bold and brilliant. The trombone might be given the indication that a passage is to be performed "sweetly." Expression refers to what is done to the sounds—how fast or slowly they are played, how loudly or softly, how angrily or peacefully they are rendered. Expression gives the affective meaning to music. It is the emotive element of music as indicated by the composer, interpreted by the performer, and, hopefully, felt by the listener.

Perhaps some examples from another art form will help clarify what has been said about musical meaning and how medium, content, form, and expression contribute to it.

The medium employed in the sculpture by Robert Berks is bronze. (See p. 12.) The content is determined by the tilt of the head, the inclination of the nose, the attitude of the chin, the expression on the face, and the sweep of the hair. The organization of these events identifies the form as a bust of John F. Kennedy. Although identification is not difficult, the work is not an exact representation—it is more. The texture of the bronze, the focus of the eyes, and the general shape and balance are an expression by the artist of how *he* wished to portray John F. Kennedy. The viewer reacts to what he sees, and his response reinforces the expressive qualities evoked by the artist. While the receptor may not verbalize his reactions, he senses the artist's unique interpretation, and feels the power of the creator's personal vision.

Like Saint-Saëns' "Introduction and Royal March of the Lions," identification of *Bird in Space* by Constantin Brancusi is partially dependent for its meaning upon the title supplied by the artist. Without the title, either concept—bird or space—might not occur to the viewer. The beauty of line, the flawless textural smoothness, the grace, clarity, and balance of shape would all be apparent. Yet if the sculpture is to be understood fully, the viewer must not only recognize the subject matter or idea the artist sought to express, but also have some personal knowledge of it. In short, the insight, imagination, and experience that a person

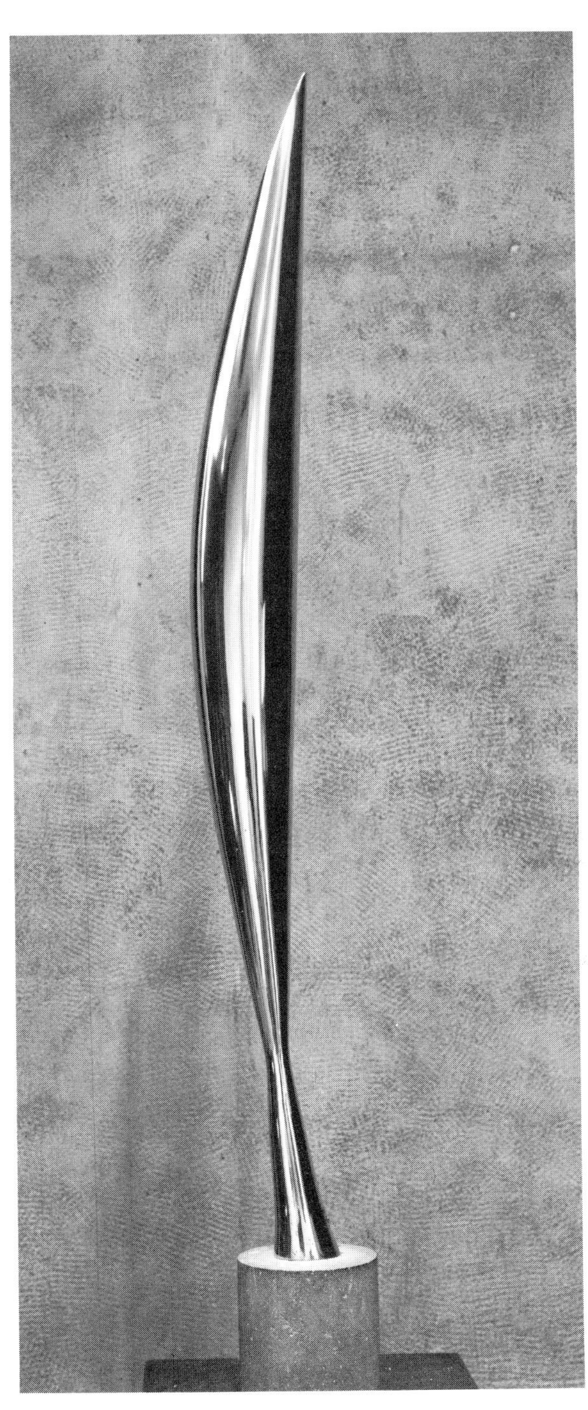

Constantin Brancusi: Bird in Space *(1919–25). Collection, The Museum of Modern Art, New York.*

Ironically, when this work was brought to the United States, customs officials charged duty on it as a piece of metal. (There is no duty on art.) They did not perceive the object as a sculpture. Its gracefully expanding and diminishing curves and highly reflective surface convey a feeling of swift ascent.

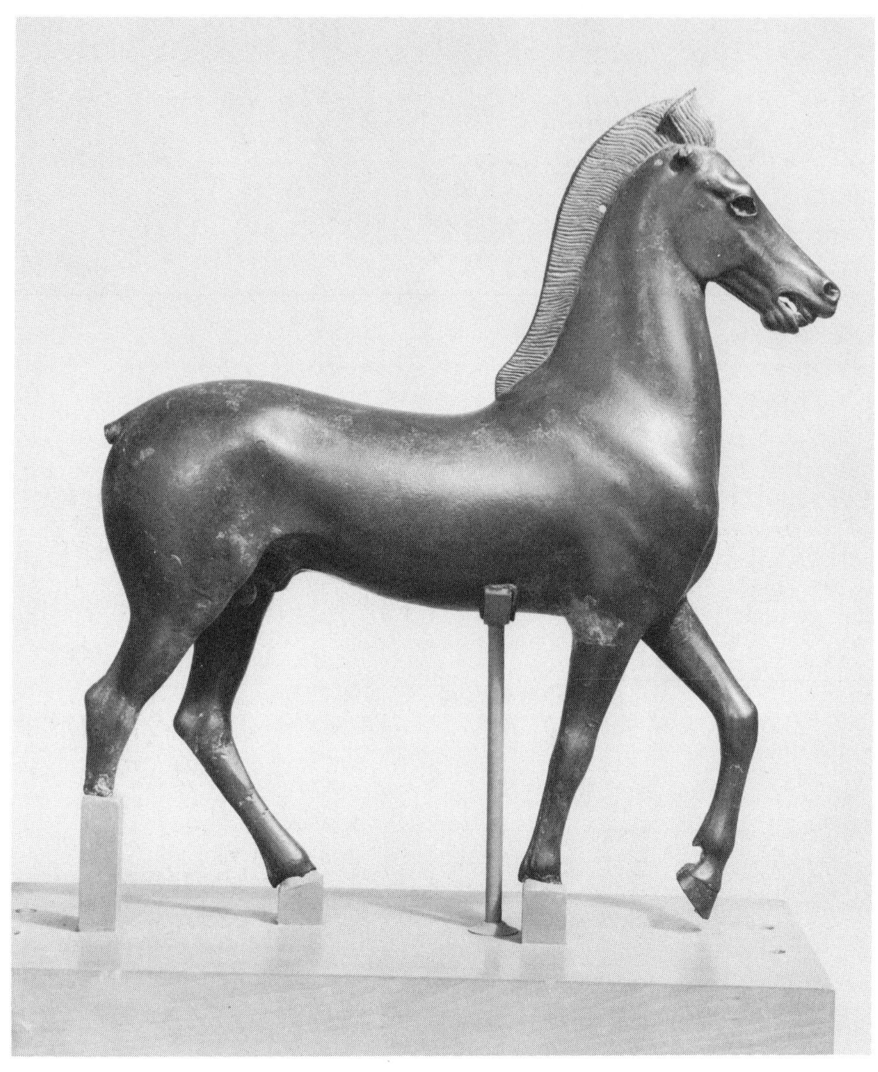

Horse (fifth century B.C. *Greek bronze). The Metropolitan Museum of Art, New York.*

This sculpture represents horses in a generic sense—both the ideal physical and abstract qualities of a beautiful animal.

brings to a work of art become part of it; communication becomes a dialogue between the work and the viewer.

Horse (fifth century B.C.) represents horses in general, idealizing qualities of gracefulness, nobility, and pride. The impression is achieved through skillful control of surface texture, contour, and line. All of these aspects have an intrinsic beauty of their own, quite apart from the idealized qualities that they suggest. While meaning in this work is realized essentially through form (the shape of a horse), form also has a value independent of the specific meaning it may clarify.

This work also demonstrates the fragile qualities of aesthetic communication. Once considered a forgery, the sculpture was destined for the museum basement. Doubt of its authenticity, regardless of whether it had at one time been hailed as a masterpiece of classical Greek culture, influenced the way people reacted to the work. What a person knows about a work changes his sensations, feelings, and perceptions of that work. "Cul-

Bruce White: Untitled sculpture (1970).

This sculpture is nonrepresentational. The viewer is presented with shape, color, and texture. He may experience movement, direction, tension, and repose, but any relationship of the abstract, artistic qualities of the work to concrete reality is left to the viewer. The lack of title and identifiable form frees the viewer to fuse his own thoughts and feelings with the work.

tural beliefs," Meyer says, "not only influence the way in which we perceive, think, and act, but they also condition and modify our emotional and physiological responses . . ." The viewer consequently will alter his attitude and response to a work of art suspected of being a forgery.

The Untitled sculpture by Bruce White presents no object to identify, no representation, no descriptive or associative title. The sculpture suggests only itself. In that sense, meaning and form become one. The meaning of the sculpture is conditioned primarily by the artist's control of unity, variety, symmetry, contour, rhythm, color, and texture, and his shaping of these elements into a cohesive whole.

The experience the individual viewer brings to this sculpture can modify its meaning to the extent that it may conflict with the artist's ideas. Subjectively, individuals make voluntary and involuntary associations when experiencing art works. Objectively, they must try to distinguish between associations that have only personal meaning and associations that have meaning for all viewers. But since White provides no external associations to consider, this distinction is more difficult to make; any *universal* meaning that the sculpture assumes must ultimately depend on the visual effectiveness of the work itself.

MUSICAL MEANING

Chopin's Étude, op. 10, no. 6 provides an analogy with White's sculpture. The title indicates merely that the piece is a technical study. The composer explores the piano for its expressive potential, challenging the pianist to project the separate lines of melody and accompaniment and master the chromatic harmony. There is no attempt at picture or story. The intrinsic "meaning" must be stated, therefore, in terms of the objectives of the study and the pleasures of the music. If listeners find a personal extramusical meaning, they should recognize that this meaning may have validity only for them. For others it may be invalid or irrational.

Finally, returning strictly to music, it is important to reiterate the primacy of sound. Regardless of extramusical associations, *all* music shares this common element: sound is the vehicle for communication. Verbal analyses, descriptions, historical facts, analogies—all are important as means to understanding, not ends. In the search for musical understanding, then, the listener must become familiar with the sounds that make up a composition, grasp the principles upon which they are organized, and seek to respond emotionally as well as intellectually to the work. The listener must adjust to the music. If the sounds were composed in the seventeenth century, he must accept them within the norms of that time. This holds true whether a piece is traditional or avant garde, whether it was composed in the nineteenth century or yesterday. As this kind of communication is pursued in the chapters ahead, remember that regular and repeated exposure to pertinent musical experiences is essential. Few great works of music disclose their deeper meanings on first hearing or through isolated excerpts.

FOR DISCUSSION

1. Can a person "think" music? Does a painter "think" in terms of paint? How do writers and playwrights think? How does this relate to the creative process?
2. Is musical understanding essential to enjoyment? beneficial? detrimental? Discuss this especially in relation to popular music.
3. Music is a temporal art; painting is immediate. How are the other arts related to the aspects of time? How does this relationship affect people's responses to the various arts?
4. Is there such a thing as a forgery in music? Why is authenticity important? Why is painting more prone to forgery?

Musical Ideas: Origin and Inspiration

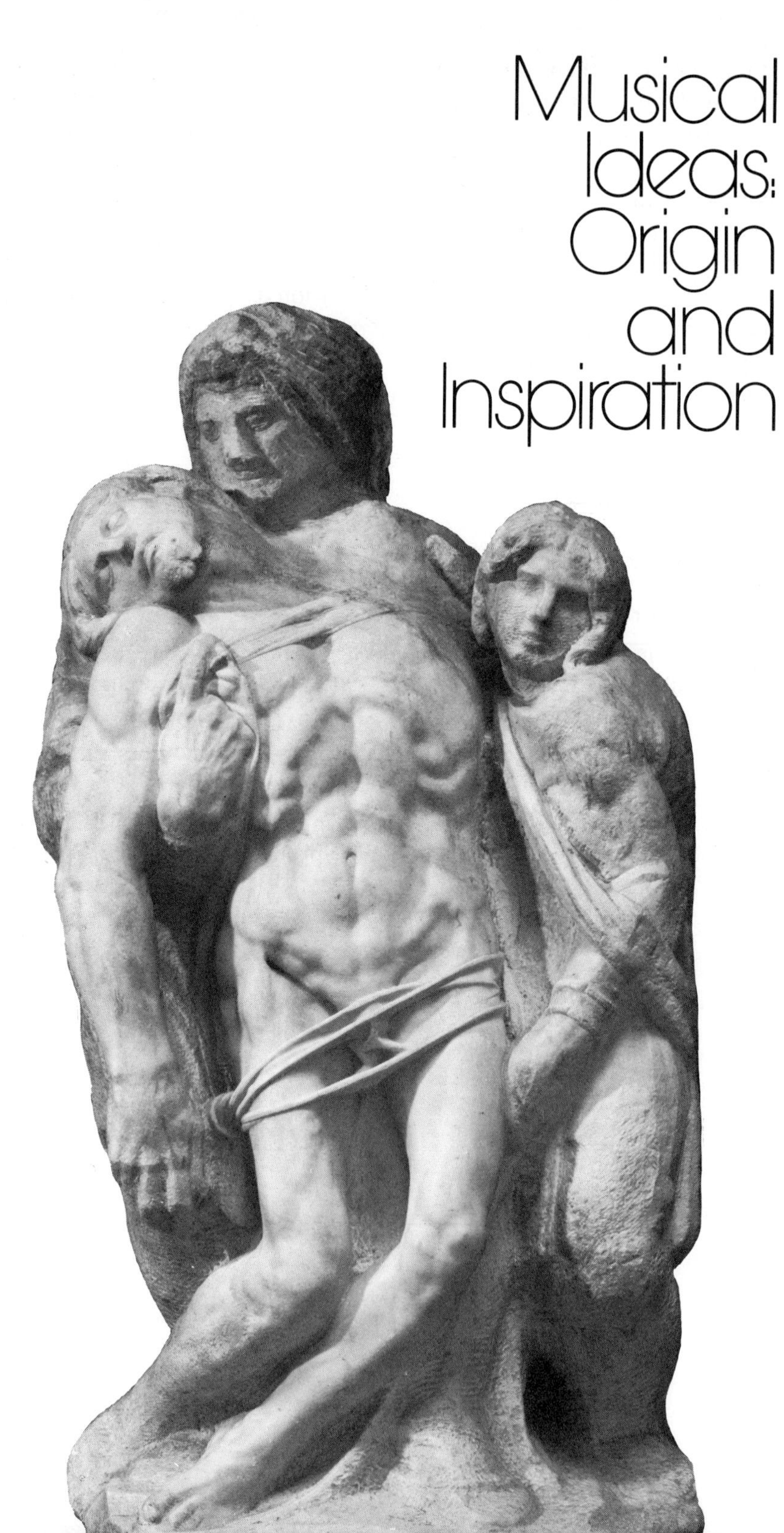

3

One of the great mysteries of music is the source of the composer's ideas—the distinctive melodies, harmonies, rhythms, and tone colors that together form a composition. How does a tune originate? Is it a conscious creation of the composer? Does he manufacture melodies to fit predetermined musical needs? Or is the composer an intermediary, recording sounds freely borrowed from his environment or receiving musical ideas involuntarily from some mystical source?

Many answers, both thoughtful and fanciful, have been given to these questions. The eighteenth-century Italian composer Giuseppe Tartini (1692–1770) reportedly dreamed that he sold his soul to the devil for the price of hearing Satan perform a brilliant violin sonata. When Tartini awoke, he wrote down the entire work from memory. The result was the *Devil's Trill* Sonata. Less mystical, but no less fanci-

Michelangelo: The Palestrina Pietà (c. 1556). Strozzi Palace, Florence.

Religious themes have often been the inspiration for works of art. The serious subject, the massiveness of the stone, and the unfinished, still emerging quality of Michelangelo's carving give this work a dramatic yet quietly sombre feeling. Its expressive, gripping power is due in part to its incompleteness. The viewer is invited to share in the process of the artist's creation and to complete the vision according to his own reality.

ful, is the story of "The Harmonious Blacksmith" by George Frideric Handel (1685–1759), which is a set of variations on a simple tune. According to legend, the tune came to Handel as he listened to the poundings of a blacksmith. Unfortunately, the story is unfounded; the title was conferred on the variations in the nineteenth century, long after Handel's death.

The immediate source of musical ideas has often been puzzling to composers themselves. In one of his letters, Wolfgang Amadeus Mozart (1756–1791) describes an involuntary flow of musical ideas but avoids speculating on their source:

> When I am, as it were, completely myself, entirely alone, and of good cheer . . . my ideas flow best and most abundantly. *Whence* and *how* they come, I know not; nor can I force them.

In a letter to his friend Tobias von Haslinger, Beethoven related how a canon based on a text using Tobias' name "came into his head" while he dozed during a journey to Vienna. When Beethoven awoke, he had "forgotten" the entire melody. The following day, on a return trip in the same carriage, the canon again flashed through his mind. The implication of this experience is that the creative process may be partially subconscious and independent of the will to create. But although modern psychology may explain Beethoven's ability to compose in his sleep and to reconstruct the composition when he returned to the same environment, the nature of musical inspiration itself, whether the composer is asleep or awake, has never been completely clarified. The phenomenon of inspiration resists explanation. Yet certain overt starting points in the creative process can be isolated and studied usefully. When a composer begins to write, he establishes the purpose of the music—a crucial decision that affects the entire flow of musical ideas. Examination of some of these basic decisions can help a listener improve his musical receptivity and understanding.

DANCE MUSIC

The composer may decide to write dance music—one of the oldest forms of musical expression. This choice raises problems and necessitates additional decisions. The dancers' steps and movements require compatible musical counterparts. Will the dance be a folk dance, a classical ballet, or an interpretative dance? Is it to tell a story or convey a mood? Should the music be impassioned, exotic, or stylized? Is the rhythm to follow a traditional pattern, as in a waltz or a polka, or does the dance demand a free and individual rhythmic treatment?

Dance music varies with different cultures. For example, the ballet *Rodeo* by Aaron Copland (1900–   ) captures the flavor of folk songs and dances of the American West. In contrast, Igor Stravinsky's (1882–1971) music for *The Rite of Spring*, which portrays a pagan ritual in ancient Russia, is driven by powerful, primitive rhythms. Both examples are in direct contrast to the elegant, lyrical music of such stylized ballets as Tchaikovsky's *Swan Lake* and *The Sleeping Beauty*.

SETTINGS OF POETRY AND PROSE

Many works of music are inspired by poetry or prose. In this case, the literary source dictates certain musical decisions. The emotive content of the text affects the character of the music. Words and music become interdependent. "General William Booth Enters into Heaven" by Charles Ives (1874–1954), for example, is a rousing setting of Vachel Lindsay's poem that evokes the evangelical fervor of the Salvation Army.

Musical form may be a direct reflection of textual form. Church hymns, folk songs, and some art songs, like "Sugar in the Cane" by Paul Bowles (1910–   ), employ the same music for each stanza of text. These are called *strophic* forms. In other cases, like Diamond's "David Mourns for Absalom," the drama inherent in the poem demands that each stanza or textual unit receive unique, individual treatment. This music is *through-composed*.

The inflections of a language and the accentuation of syllables may also affect the composer's musical ideas. As the composer sets a text, these factors influence the melodic and rhythmic shape of the music. Conceived in this manner, music becomes partially dependent upon the text for its meaning. And since each language has its own indigenous pitch patterns and rhythmic flow, musical "sense" always undergoes some change when a song is translated into another language.

Prose and poetry often gain power when set to music, as, for example, in Arnold Schoenberg's (1874–1951) chilling masterpiece, *A*

Francisco Goya: The Family of Charles IV *(1800). Museo Nacional del Prado, Madrid.*

Goya was a skilled political painter. As court painter to Charles IV, he was forced to work for the establishment, which he strongly opposed. Notice how he portrays the royal family in unflattering realism; he has not attempted to make them look handsome or dignified. The superficial qualities—the detailed, dazzling clothes—managed to distract the court from Goya's scathing commentary. Political commentary is common in art. In music it ranges from political and social satire to popular songs of protest.

Survivor from Warsaw. In the final unison chorus, a Hebrew prayer, Schoenberg treats the text largely as narration, while the principal musical role is delegated to orchestra.

Sometimes, however, the literal meaning of a text is not the source of the composer's inspiration. Ernst Toch (1887–1964), in setting a

Geographical Fugue for speaking chorus, simply uses the rhythms of various geographical names. Ernst Křenek (1900–   ) employs a similar device in his choral work *The Santa Fe Time Table*, based on the names of railway stops from Albuquerque to Los Angeles.

DRAMA

Drama has inspired composers for centuries. The grief of death, the jubilant spirit of a celebration, and the anguish of frustrated love are among the many dramatic emotions that can be intensified through musical realization. Western music has been performed in conjunction with dramatic works since the time of the ancient Greeks; it was a central element in the liturgical plays of the Middle Ages; and its use for dramatic expression has grown steadily since the beginning of opera in about 1600.

Theatrical works provided the basis for the flourishing of opera during the eighteenth and nineteenth centuries. The plays of Shakespeare, for example, inspired three operas by the Italian Giuseppe Verdi (1813–1901), *Macbeth*, *Otello* and *Falstaff*. *Salome* by Richard Strauss (1864–1949) derives its libretto, or text, from a play by Oscar Wilde.

On the other hand, composers—for example, Richard Wagner (1813–1883) and Gian-Carlo Menotti (1911–   )—sometimes write their own librettos.

Plays have also inspired the creation of instrumental music. Called "incidental music," these compositions consist of individual pieces to accompany a dramatic production—including preludes, interludes, dance music, incidental songs, and background music. Some incidental music, such as music to Shakespeare's *A Midsummer Night's Dream* by Felix Mendelssohn (1809–1847) and music to Ibsen's *Peer Gynt* by Edvard Grieg (1843–1907), has attained popularity as independent concert music within the standard orchestral repertoire.

The range of incidental music has expanded in the twentieth century to include music for movies, radio, and television dramas. If such music has often lacked artistic distinction, it is nevertheless indispensable to these mass media. Occasionally, a composer of stature has written music for a film or a television show with impressive results. Especially noteworthy as film scores are Aaron Copland's *The Red Pony*, Virgil Thomson's (1896–   ) *Louisiana Story* and *The Plow that Broke the Plains*, and Serge Prokofiev's (1891–1953) *Lieutenant Kijé*. The best music for television has not been true incidental music but rather independent dramatic or narrative works, such as Menotti's opera *Amahl and the Night Visitors* and Stravinsky's *The Flood.* Nevertheless, much incidental music has been written or adapted to serve as background and theme music for individual television shows. There is no question that this medium serves as a new and important source of inspiration for the composer.

PROGRAM MUSIC AND EXTRAMUSICAL ASSOCIATION

As already discussed, program music attempts to convey a fairly specific extramusical meaning and usually has a descriptive or literary title. Nonmusical events or images have inspired composers for centuries. But their fullest exploitation came in the nineteenth century, as evidenced by works such as Hector Berlioz's (1803–1869) *Symphonie fantastique*, Franz Liszt's (1811–1886) *Les Préludes*, and Claude Debussy's (1862–1918) *Prelude to the Afternoon of a Faun*, written to illustrate a poem by Mallarmé.

Extramusical association continues as an important source of inspiration for twentieth-century music. Richard Strauss's *Ein Heldenleben* (*A Hero's Life*), Prokofiev's *Peter and the Wolf*, Benjamin Britten's (1913–) *War Requiem*, and Ives' *Three Places in New England* are obvious examples. Charles Ives often associated verbally expressed ideas with music. His "Housatonic at Stockbridge" was suggested by a Sunday morning walk with his wife. He reflects upon the mist, the river, the colors of the day, and the sound of a church choir in the distance.

Titles of electronic music, too, often reflect associative connotation. The following are a few examples: *Song of the Second Moon* by Dick Raaijmakers (1930–), *Suite in the Form of a Mushroom* by James Cunningham (1922–), *Hydrogen Jukebox* and *Lemon Drops* by Kenneth Gaburo (1926–).

ABSOLUTE MUSIC

Instrumental music can be self-motivating. Its origin frequently lies in the composer's desire to combine sounds into a unified whole. Music inspired by aesthetic concepts of tonal order usually has no extramusical

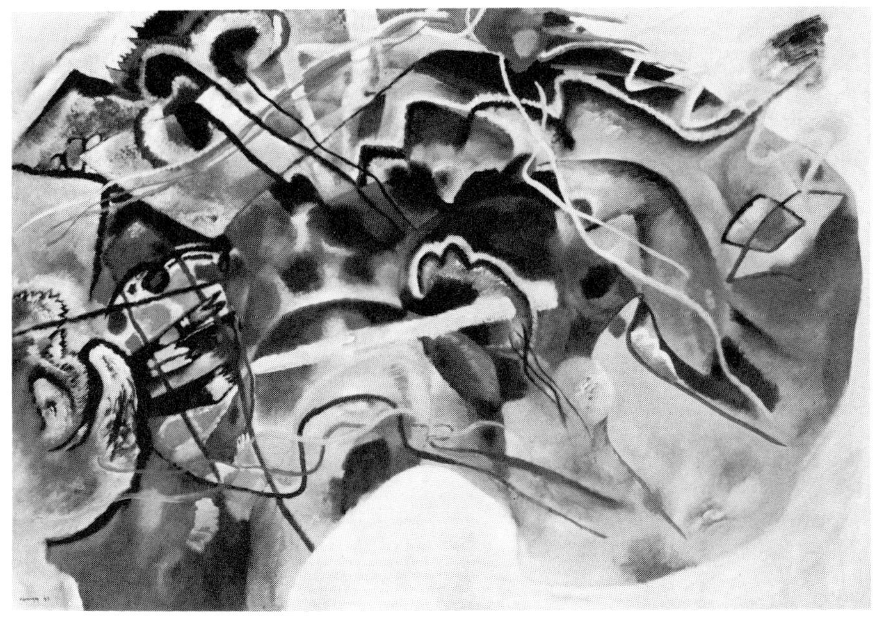

Wassily Kandinsky: Picture with White Edge *(No. 173, 1913). The Solomon R. Guggenheim Museum, New York.*

Kandinsky was one of the first painters to assert that nonrepresentational compositions of colors and shapes were as valid in painting as in absolute music. The viewer follows the intricacies, the recesses, the flow and interplay of hard and soft lines. Tonal changes direct the eye to quickly changing patterns. The white edge presses in on the central mass and vividly contrasts with the emerging tones.

function. Although logically planned and expressive of diverse, abstract emotions, it tells no story and paints no picture. The only function intended is the expression of its musical sound. As mentioned earlier, absolute music is identified by a purely musical designation–sonata, symphony, concerto, trio, quartet, or étude.

The creation of absolute music frequently begins with the invention of a musical idea. A fully realized theme or subject, or even a general concept for an entire piece, represents the intiating step in the composition. Musical ideas might also be shorter, consisting of rhythmic, melodic, or harmonic fragments that occur spontaneously to the composer. Although few composers have provided explanations of how they create, some have kept detailed sketch books illustrating the intellectual growth of a musical idea from its first conception to its final expression. Beethoven's thematic sketches reveal some of the processes of his creative mind. The following example illustrates several steps in the evolution of the opening theme of his Quartet in F Major, op. 18, no. 1.

Ex. 3–1

When a musical idea is short, clearly stated, and has a distinctive character that permits its expansion into larger dimensions, it is called a motive (motif), or germ. Often a motive becomes the germinating idea for a composition. Most of the musical ideas in the first movement of Beethoven's Symphony no. 5 stem directly from the short, four-note opening motive:

Ex. 3–2

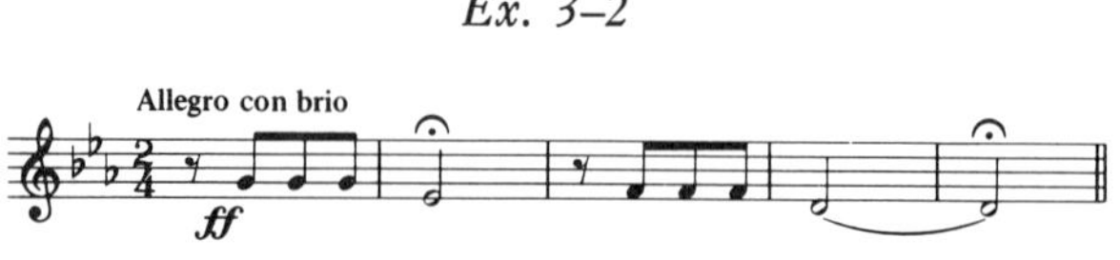

MUSIC USING BORROWED THEMATIC MATERIAL

On occasion a composer may borrow a theme from a piece by another composer and recast it in his own style, somewhat as a playwright might use the plot of an early Greek play to serve as the basis for a modern drama. Johannes Brahms (1833–1897), for instance, uses a borrowed theme for his *Variations on a Theme by Haydn.* The original theme, the "St. Anthony Chorale," is first stated as conceived by Franz Joseph Haydn (1732–1809) and then presented in several modified versions reflecting Brahms' own musical style.

Both the origin of musical ideas and the inspiration for composition spring from many, varied sources. Sometimes these sources are easily discovered, but usually they are obscure or unknown. Unfortunately, many explanations about the origin of musical ideas are legendary, with no direct bearing upon the meaning of the music. Where sources can be identified—a poem, a drama, a dance—a vital clue for understanding the music is clearly established. The person who knows the source of the music to which he is listening has one certainty upon which to build his understanding.

GUIDE TO ADDITIONAL LISTENING

Music and the dance

1. Wolfgang Amadeus Mozart, *Six German Dances with Trios,* K. 509.
2. Johannes Brahms, Hungarian Dance no. 5 in G Minor, Hungarian Dance no. 6 in D Major.

How do the Mozart and the Brahms differ? Which dances seem more unruffled and well-ordered? Which have exaggerated changes of mood? Of action? How does the music express these differences? In what way are the dances similarly expressive?

Settings of poetry and prose

1. Gustav Mahler (1860–1911), "Der Trunkene im Frühling" from *Das Lied von der Erde* ("The Drunkard in Spring" from *The Song of the Earth*).
2. Aaron Copland, *Twelve Poems of Emily Dickinson,* the first poem.

In what ways do the compositions reflect the contents of these poems? Is the musical experience affected by the difference in language? If so, how? Does Mahler's orchestra function differently from Copland's piano?

Music and drama

1. Gian-Carlo Menotti, *The Telephone.*
2. Gian-Carlo Menotti, Magda's aria, "To this we've come," from *The Consul,* Act II, Scene 2.

The Telephone is light-hearted, gay, facetious. Ben, proposing to Lucy, is constantly interrupted by her lengthy incoming phone calls. He retreats to a phone booth, calls her, and successfully proposes. Magda, in the consulate of a European city behind the Iron Curtain, is despondent. Overwhelmed by forms, questions, and red tape, she needs the help of the consul she never sees. Her child is dead, her mother dying, and her husband in danger. Note the contrast between the requirements of the dramas: the frivolity of Lucy, the intensity of Magda.

Program music and extramusical association

1. Claude Debussy, "Voiles" ("Veils or Sails") from *Préludes,* Book 1, and "Ce qu'a vu le vent de l'ouest" ("What the West Wind Saw") from *Préludes,* Book 2.
2. Charles Ives, *Three Places in New England*—"The 'St. Gaudens' in Boston Common"; "Putnam's Camp, Redding, Connecticut"; "The Housatonic at Stockbridge."

Does the music give a cue to action of the wind? How do the pieces by Debussy differ? How does the listener's experience affect his response to Ives' music?

3. The record *Leonard Bernstein Discusses Humor in Music* offers an interesting and informative exposition of this associative possibility.

Absolute music

1. Arcangelo Corelli (1653–1713), Concerto Grosso in D, op. 6, no. 1.

2. Frédéric Chopin, Étude in E Major, op. 10, no. 3.

3. Samuel Barber (1910–   ), *Adagio for Strings*, op. 11.

How does the listener respond when there is no text, no related drama, no association suggested by the composer? In musical terms? Must he? What responses are viable? For the individual? For the universal audience?

Music using borrowed thematic material

1. Charles Ives, *Variations on "America."*
2. Igor Stravinsky, *Chorale Variations on Bach's "Von Himmel hoch."*

How does Ives' version compare with the "America" we usually sing? Can an eighteenth-century chorale successfully be subjected to twentieth-century treatment? How does the music reflect the composer's creativeness?

FOR DISCUSSION

1. Why do church hymns employ the same music for all the verses?
2. Compare a novel, a picture, and a musical composition as mediums for telling a story. Which is apt to be most specific? Least specific? Which conveys sequence most effectively? Least effectively? How have moving pictures altered this?
3. Select a play and begin to plan the musical sounds to accompany its various scenes. How would the drama of each scene dictate the mood, instrumentation, tempo, dynamics, melody, harmony, and form of the music?
4. How do composers distinguish between the villain and the hero in musical comedy and opera? Why is the hero usually a tenor?

Musical Resources: Tone Color and Performing Mediums

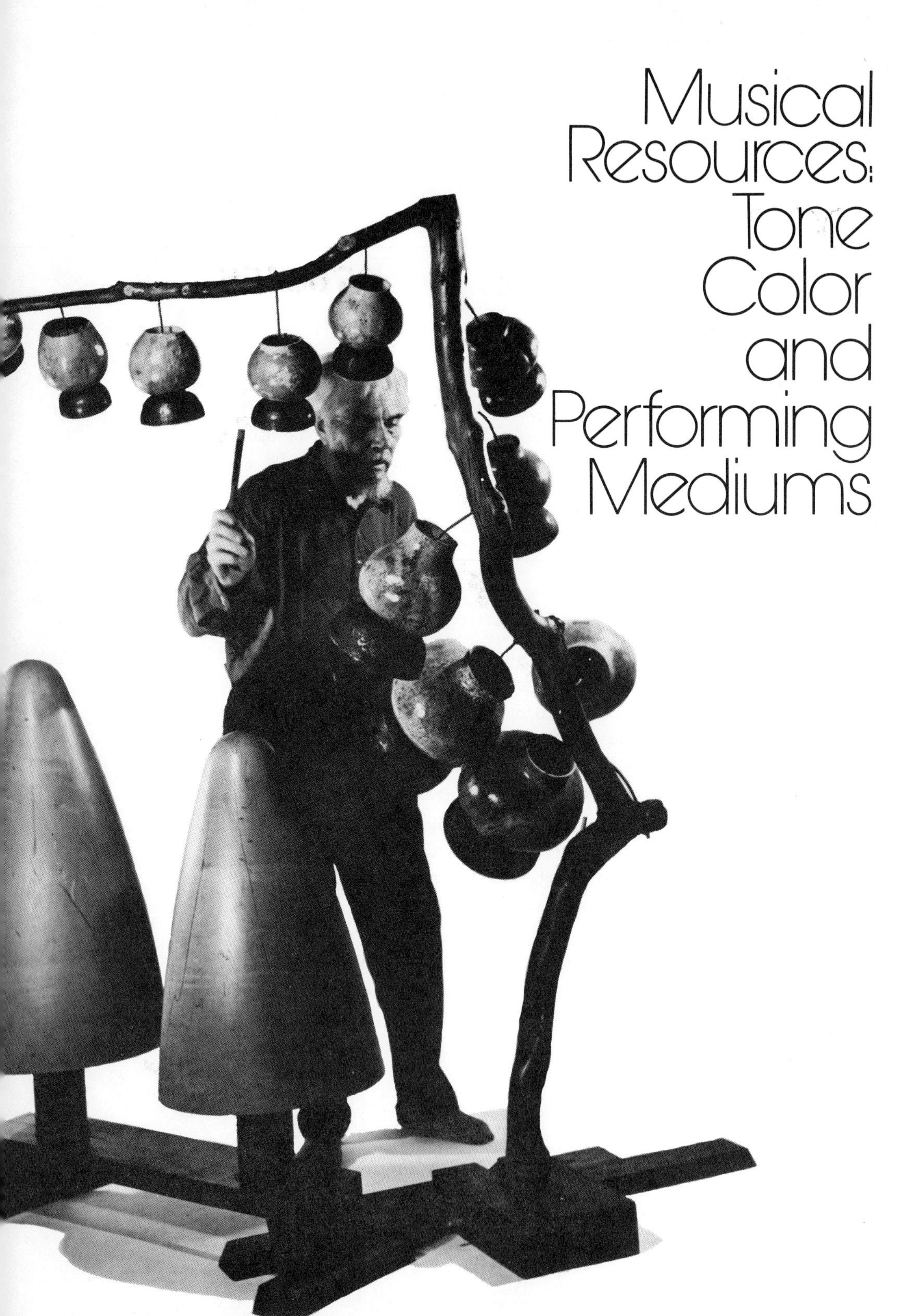

4

Regardless of their origin or inspiration, man does "dream up" ideas. The realization and communication of these ideas necessitate some form of action involving various materials and techniques. In music, the action is composing. The medium (material) is sound. The result is a musical composition, usually communicated by means of a written score and realized through performance.

Chapter 3 explored the origin of musical ideas. Chapters 4 and 5 will focus on the resources that a composer uses to express his ideas. As a means of expression, sound has an infinite number of variables, among which is the performing medium. The ability to distinguish among the sounds produced by the various mediums helps the listener to sense the

Harry Partch, American composer and inventor of musical instruments, playing his gourd tree. His compositions for his instruments borrow elements of many cultures and combine them in a highly personal, primitive, and exotic sound. Photograph by Richard A. Matthews.

special character of each medium, and, consequently, to respond to its expressive potential.

PERFORMING MEDIUMS

Music is communicated to listeners by some medium of performance. The performance may involve one person or several hundred; it may be vocal, instrumental, or a combination of the two. In contemporary music the "performer" might be an electronic medium, such as a prerecorded tape amplified and sounded through a speaker system.

Usually the composer indicates a specific medium of performance for each work he creates. He may compose a solo for soprano with piano accompaniment; he may call for a large orchestra or a limited number of specific instruments; he may indicate that the sound be made by an electronic synthesizer and recorded on magnetic tape. The variables seem endless. Performers—whose responsibility it is to interpret the composer's intentions—follow the specifications of the composer. The printed music serves as a blueprint to be reproduced as precisely as possible.

Composer's scores are sometimes altered to fit prevailing circumstances. Adaptations and arrangements are made when a work, for one reason or another, cannot be performed effectively as the composer conceived it. A composition may be altered to meet the desires of an arranger, to appeal to a special audience, to warrant performance by a certain type of performer, to fit the instrumentation or voice ranges of a particular group, to effect a specific style, and so on. Musical alteration is prevalent in both popular and entertainment music. A song such as "Summertime" from George Gershwin's (1898–1937) *Porgy and Bess* will be performed differently under different circumstances. As Gershwin originally prescribed in his opera, it has one basic sound. Since it is frequently extracted from the opera and performed by various performers, in a number of styles, and under varying circumstances, it undergoes numerous performance changes. Compare the original version, for example, with a rendition by Ella Fitzgerald, Eileen Farrell, or Big Brother and the Holding Company.

Performing mediums differ with historical period, composer, the musical effect desired, and musical function. Historically, however, several performance "units"—ranging from large to small—have become basic. Of the larger variety, the orchestra, chorus, and band are the established "units" that composers have called for again and again.

ORCHESTRA

The techniques and organization of the modern orchestra are rooted in early opera and in the eighteenth-century Mannheim Orchestra. Since then changes have been numerous. Some composers have written works calling for a greatly expanded orchestra, while others compose works playable by a smaller group. Although the requirements for performing a symphony by Mozart vary considerably from those for performing a tone poem by Richard Strauss, certain instruments are common to both.

Four groups of instruments form an orchestra: strings, woodwinds, brass, and percussion. Most instruments can be classified in one of these groups, although there is some ambiguity (the piano, for example, has certain characteristics of both strings and percussion). It should be noted, too, that in a significant amount of contemporary composition, some form of electronic equipment—prerecorded tape, amplifiers, speaker systems, and the like—is incorporated into the orchestra.

The four basic groups consist of the following instruments:

Strings	*Woodwinds*
Violin	Piccolo
Viola	Flute
Violoncello (Cello)	Oboe
Contrabass (Bass)	English horn
	Clarinet
	Bassoon

Brass	*Percussion*	
Trumpet	Timpani	Xylophone
French horn	Snare drum	Bells
Trombone	Bass drum	Chimes
Tuba	Cymbals	Gong
	Triangle	Tambourine

In a symphony orchestra of approximately 100 or more instruments, many of the instruments are doubled. Because of their lighter sound, the strings are usually given the most reinforcement in numbers—normally this means a minimum of 32 violins, 8 violas, 8 cellos, and 6 basses. With the exception of the one piccolo, woodwinds are frequently paired. In the brass section two or three trumpets, two to four French horns, two or three trombones, and one tuba are basic. The percussion section varies widely from the essential pair of timpani to a combination of all the various percussion instruments.

Since it is impossible to describe accurately or completely the sounds of instruments either individually or in combinations, an understanding of the sounds they make can be achieved only by listening.

Examples of orchestral sound exist in infinite variety; therefore, only a very small sampling can be cited. The following examples represent the symphony orchestra as used by three different composers from different eras. Listen to all or portions of each one of these compositions, and note the general differences in sound. Do not attempt to listen for detail, only for the overall, obvious contrasts in total sound.

1. Mozart, Symphony no. 40 in G Minor, K. 550, first movement.

   Notice the predominance of strings, the contrast of the woodwinds, the use of the brass as support and timpani as the only percussion instrument.

2. Tchaikovsky, Symphony no. 4 in F Minor, op. 36, finale.

   Notice the boldness of the overall sound. Observe the solo woodwinds and brasses as well as cymbals, timpani, bass drum, and triangle. Strings do not dominate as in Mozart.

3. Ives, Symphony no. 2, first movement.

   Notice the "thickness" of the texture. Instruments playing solos must project through a veritable web of sound.

Some of the uniqueness evident in these compositions is based upon each composer's use of instruments—his exploitation of the orchestra as a performing medium.

A composer may choose to use additional tonal resources. Several examples suffice to demonstrate the principle:

1. Orchestra with piano: Dmitri Shostakovich (1906–), Symphony no. 5, op. 47, first, third, and fourth movements.
2. Orchestra with additional percussion instruments: Paul Hindemith (1895–1963), *Symphonic Metamorphoses of Themes by Carl Maria von Weber*, second movement, "Turandot" (scherzo).
3. Orchestra with voices as an integral part of the total sound: Claude Debussy, "Sirenes" from *Nocturnes.*
4. Orchestra with electronic tape: Otto Luening (1900–) and Vladimir Ussachevsky (1911–), *Rhapsodic Variations for Tape Recorder and Orchestra.*

THE INDIVIDUAL INSTRUMENTS OF THE ORCHESTRA

Occasionally a composer writes with the sole purpose of "demonstrating" the instruments of the orchestra. One twentieth-century English composer, Benjamin Britten, highlights the full orchestra, each section, and ultimately the individual instruments in *A Young Person's Guide to the Orchestra.* This work is subtitled *Variations and Fugue on a Theme of Purcell.* Britten follows a plan outlined below:

Part I—Theme

Featured instruments

1. Full Orchestra
2. Woodwind Instruments
3. Brass Instruments
4. Stringed Instruments
5. Percussion Instruments
6. Full Orchestra

Part II—Variations

Variations	*Featured instruments*
A	Two Flutes and Piccolo
B	Two Oboes
C	Two Clarinets
D	Two Bassoons
E	Violins (Two sections)
F	Violas (In unison)
G	Cellos (In unison)
H	Basses (In unison)
I	Harp
J	Four French Horns
K	Two Trumpets (Snare drum is also prominent)
L	Three Trombones Followed by Tuba
M	Percussion including timpani, bass drum, cymbals, tambourine, triangle, snare drum, wood block, xylophone, castanets, gong, whip.

Part III—Fugue

The fugue subject is stated by the instruments in the following order:

Piccolo
Flutes
Oboes
Clarinets
Bassoons
Violins (1st section)
Violins (2nd section)
Violas
Cellos
Basses

Harp
French Horns
Trumpets
Trombones and Tuba
Percussion

Part IV—Coda

In the final section of this composition the theme from the beginning, slightly altered, is played by one group of instruments while the fugue subject is superimposed upon it. Percussion instruments provide rhythmical support to the full symphony orchestra as it simultaneously plays both melodies, bringing the work to a rousing close.

The literature for orchestra is abundant. Works are scored for an infinite variety of instrumental combinations. Familiarity with instrumental sounds and their various combinations can help the listener to detect what is going on. Hearing tonal color clearly improves musical understanding.

VOICE

The human voice is man's oldest medium of artistic expression. In music, the voice is emotionally charged through the process of singing, which is merely a form of sustained speech. The singing sound is intensely personal. Voices are classified by range, quality, and sometimes by the type of literature performed.

1. *Soprano:* A female voice in the highest range.
   a. *Coloratura:* A soprano who specializes in executing rapid scale passages, trills, and other vocal pyrotechnics. Example: Léo Delibes (1836–1891), "The Bell Song" from the opera *Lakmé*.
   b. *Lyric:* A bright soprano voice. Example: Giacomo Puccini (1858–1924), "Mi chiamano Mimi" ("They call me Mimi") from the opera *La Bohème*.

c. *Dramatic:* A soprano voice of darker and heavier quality. Example: Richard Wagner, "Brunnhilde's Immolation" from the opera *Die Götterdämmerung.*

2. *Mezzo-soprano:* A female voice in medium range. Example: Georges Bizet (1838–1875), "Habanera" from the opera *Carmen.*
3. *Alto* or *contralto:* A female voice in the lowest range. Example: George Frideric Handel, "He Shall Feed His Flock" from the oratorio *Messiah.*
4. *Countertenor:* The highest adult male voice (in falsetto range). Example: Any recording by Alfred Deller.
5. *Tenor:* The highest natural male voice.
   a. *Lyric:* A bright tenor voice. Example: Giuseppe Verdi, "La donna è mobile" ("Women are frivolous") from the opera *Rigoletto.*
   b. *Dramatic:* A darker quality tenor voice that sings more forceful literature. Example: Ruggiero Leoncavallo (1858–1919), "Vesti la giubba" ("Put on your costume") from the opera *I Pagliacci.*
6. *Baritone:* A male voice of medium range and medium-dark quality. Example: Bizet, "Toreador Song" from the opera *Carmen.*
7. *Bass:* A male voice in the lowest range.
   a. *Bass-baritone:* A male voice with a range between baritone and bass. Example: Modest Moussorgsky (1839–1881), "Death Scene" from the opera *Boris Godunov.*
   b. *Basso:* The lowest range of male voice. Example: Wolfgang Amadeus Mozart, "In These Sacred Halls" from the opera *The Magic Flute.*

Albert Pinkham Ryder: Forest of Arden *(1888–97). The Metropolitan Museum of Art, Bequest of Stephen C. Clark, 1960.*

This nineteenth-century Romantic American painting is nearly monochromatic. Perhaps those who use color the most sparingly are, finally, the greatest colorists. Ryder's simple, expansive forms, and his spare use of color enhance the dark, brooding quality of his paintings. His work stands in direct contrast to the painstaking detail of his contemporaries. The style is symphonic in its strong patterns and its powerful shapes.

CHORAL MUSIC

A "mixed" chorus or choir consists of from twenty to several hundred men's and women's voices usually divided into four parts: soprano, alto, tenor, and bass. Combining voices obviously adds complexity and flexibility to vocal music in terms of harmony, tone color, pitch range, and dynamics.

In contrast to orchestras, which are primarily professional or semiprofessional, amateur choirs and choruses of excellent quality exist throughout the country. Partially because of this fact, the size of singing groups varies more than that of orchestras. Fortunately, much choral composition lends itself to performance by groups of various sizes.

Choral music may be accompanied by piano, organ, or a combination of instruments, or it may be unaccompanied. Performances of the latter type are termed *a cappella.* In some instances, the instrumental accompaniment may be optional, although in many major choral works, the vocal parts are so completely integrated with the instrumental parts that they cannot be performed alone.

Choral music is of necessity closely related to a text. Texts can be liturgical, sacred, or secular; they can derive from poetry or prose; they can be narrative or abstract; they can even be made up of nonsense syllables. Choruses sometimes sing a work in the original language or sometimes use a translation or adaptation.

From the thousands of choral works written over a period of several centuries, representative samples follow. In listening to these, note the various vocal resources used by the composer.

1. *A cappella* choral music
   a. Monophonic sound: Gregorian chant—"Laus Deo Patri" (antiphon) and "Laudate pueri" (Psalm 113), from *Masterpieces of Music before 1750* by Carl Parrish and John F. Ohl.

   Observe the quality of the solo voice, the chorus of men's voices without accompaniment. What is the effect?

   b. Polyphonic sound: two madrigals by Thomas Morley (1557–1603), "Now Is the Gentle Season" and "Clorinda False."

   How does the tone color change when voices are mixed? Observe the dialogue between the contrasting voice sounds.

Some performances of these madrigals will be *a cappella*, while others will be accompanied by instruments.

2. Choral music with instrumental accompaniment
   a. Double chorus with strings, three trumpets, timpani, three oboes, and organ (continuo): Johann Sebastian Bach (1685–1750), Cantata no. 50, *Nun ist das Heil und die Kraft* (*Now Has the Hope and the Strength*).
   b. Chorus and orchestra: Brahms, "How Lovely Is Thy Dwelling Place, O Lord of Hosts!" from *A German Requiem*, op. 45.
   c. Mixed chorus and double wind quintet: "Kyrie" from the Stravinsky *Mass*. The score indicates the descant (soprano) and alto parts should be sung by children. The instruments are two oboes, an English horn, two bassoons, two trumpets, and three trombones.

How do the voices blend with the instruments? Do the instruments sometimes seem to conflict with the voices? Do the instruments merely provide accompaniment, or do they add another expressive dimension to the work?

Composers occasionally score a work for either men's or women's voices. An example of the former is "In Taberna" from *Carmina Burana* by Carl Orff (1895–), which calls for tenor, baritone, and bass solo voices and a men's chorus representing a group of drunken monks. An example of a work written for women's voices is "Sirenes," the third movement of *Nocturnes* by Debussy, which calls for eight sopranos and eight mezzo sopranos.

The greatness of the choral medium as an artistic vehicle of communication rests primarily upon its use for sacred expression. In a sense, choral music grew up with the church. The vocal intoning of the chant mystified the parishioners; the strong hymn tunes solidified the beliefs of the congregation; the imaginative combinations of voices with organ and other instruments strongly conveyed the majesty and the awesomeness of God.

The "Kyrie" of Giovanni da Palestrina's (c. 1525–1594) *Pope Marcellus* Mass, for example, beautifully expresses the hope for a better life that is inherent in the text "Lord, have mercy upon us. Christ, have mercy upon us. Lord, have mercy upon us." Humanity has seldom rejoiced more than in the "Hallelujah" chorus from Handel's *Messiah*.

Nor are there more exquisitely dramatic moments than in Bach's Cantata no. 140, *Wachet auf, ruft uns die Stimme (Sleepers Wake! Loud Sounds the Warning)*. The first verse sets the scene: " 'Wake up!' cries to us the voice of the watchers very high on the battlements: 'Wake up, thou city Jerusalem!' Midnight is this hour: They call us with ringing mouth: 'Where be ye wise virgins? Prepare! The Bridegroom comes, Arise! the lamps seize. Alleluja! Make you ready for the marriage, Ye must to Him go.' " While the sopranos of the chorus join the horn in sounding the broad chorale tune, the lower voices express the confusion and excitement of the people in the streets.

Beethoven added voices to the fourth and final movement of his Ninth Symphony in a powerful ode to the unity of mankind. The joy expressed is profound, and it is the voices that give the work its compelling message and magnitude. Benjamin Britten's *War Requiem* conveys the waste and horror of death in man's war on man. The hope for peace in the midst of despair is presented vividly in Britten's vocal scoring, combined with full symphonic resources of sound. Such works speak in human terms of human conditions. They touch the inner causes of man's outward actions. This spiritual quality is a dominant characteristic of choral music and is reflected, for example, in many folk songs and much protest music.

The chorus also performs a special role in opera. In his first opera, *Orfeo* (1607), Claudio Monteverdi (1567–1643) employed the chorus as it had been used in Greek drama, to comment on the action. In later operas, the chorus became more integral to the plot. In the first act of Verdi's *Otello* (1887), for example, the chorus enters into the drama as townspeople, soldiers, and boatsmen. Used in this manner, the chorus members are not merely articulate spectators who voice the listener's response to the main action, but actors in their own right. Whereas Handel had employed the chorus to divide his operas into parts, similar to the acts and scenes of a drama, here the action flows together. Such continuity is not characteristic of earlier operas, even the early works of Verdi, in which action had often been contrasted with reflection. In *Peter Grimes* (1945) Benjamin Britten realizes the full dramatic potential of the chorus, employing it as a major character: a mass of people acting in direct opposition to the main character.

Of course, not all contemporary operas follow Britten's example. The Argentine composer Alberto Ginastera (1916–   ) returns the chorus to its Greek role of commentators in *Bomarzo* (1966). When the chorus is used this way in contemporary music, it is usually to eliminate the necessity of memorizing extremely difficult scores and rehearsing for long periods of time at considerable expense. The chorus in *Bomarzo* stands with the orchestra and reads the music directly from the printed score just as the instrumentalists do.

Music for chorus exists in abundant quantities, and in almost infinite variety. The interested listener should be able to locate recorded examples from every culture and every historical period from the Middle Ages to the present day.

BAND

The band differs basically from the orchestra in that wind instruments rather than string instruments form its core. Bands vary in size and instrumentation according to their function, ranging from less than 30 to more than 150 members.

A typical concert band would consist of three groups of instruments: woodwinds, brass, and percussion. These instruments are the same as those in the orchestra, although they differ in quantity and some additional instruments are used. In the woodwind section of the band, for example, alto and bass clarinets and a contrabass clarinet are used more extensively. In the brass section, cornets and baritone horns are added as basic instruments. A family of saxophones is added—a minimum of two alto saxophones, a tenor, and a baritone. Percussion instruments remain relatively the same as those in the orchestra.

The distribution of instruments would normally range as follows:

Woodwinds		*Brass*	
1	Piccolo	6–12	Cornets
3–10	Flutes	3–6	Trumpets
12–24	Clarinets	4–10	French horns
2–4	Alto clarinets	4–8	Trombones
2–4	Bass clarinets	2–4	Baritone horns
1–2	Contrabass clarinets	2–6	Tubas
2–4	Oboes		
2–4	Bassoons		
4	Saxophones		

Percussion

3–8 Players

The symphonic wind ensemble is a recent addition to performance organizations in the band field. This is a group of woodwind, brass, and percussion performers used in limited numbers. The usual size varies from approximately forty-eight to sixty members.

Several examples of band literature follow.

1. a. Gustav Holst (1874–1934), Suite no. 1 in E Flat for Military Band, third movement.

   b. John Philip Sousa (1854–1932), "The Thunderer."

   c. William Schuman (1910–), *George Washington Bridge: An Impression.*

   These pieces are all marches. What is the common factor in sound spectrum? Which makes use of greater tonal contrasts? How? Is one more "band-like" than the others? Does one seem more militaristic than the others? If so, does the use of the instruments contribute to this difference in expression? How are the marches similar tonally? Dissimilar?

2. Norman Dello Joio (1913–), *Variants on a Mediaeval Tune.*

   What is the "band" sound? How does it contrast with orchestra? What tonally expressive sounds do they have in common? Notice the greater contrasts in the tonal spectrum in this composition as compared with the marches heard.

3. William Schuman, "Chester."

   How do the sound contrasts of the opening contribute to the composition's expressiveness? What groups of instruments predominate? How are woodwind sounds contrasted with the brass sounds? What part is played by the percussion? "Chester" is based on a song famous during the American Revolution. Does Schuman reflect this? If so, how?

While there is a large quantity of excellent original music for band, much of it dates from recent years. Because it has not always had an abundant literature of its own, the band traditionally has relied on transcriptions or arrangements of music originally composed for orchestra and other performing mediums. In many of these arrangements the clarinets replace the strings. Such changes in timbre alter the aesthetic effect of a composition. The following compositions contrast the sound of the original scoring with that of the adaptation for band.

1. J. S. Bach, Toccata and Fugue in D Minor for Organ.

   Note the similarity of the organ and band sounds, also the choice of instruments in the transcription.
2. Hector Berlioz, *The Roman Carnival* (overture).

   Observe how the band differs.
3. Richard Wagner, *Rienzi* (overture).

   Observe the woodwinds playing the transcribed string parts. Notice the similarity in brass solos and choirs.

CHAMBER MUSIC ENSEMBLES

Often music is written for small groups of performers—from two to about ten. These groups are called small ensembles and perform what is termed chamber music. In some instances a traditional instrumentation or arrangement of voices has become standard. In others the specific use of voices or instruments may be unique. The groups provide a wide variety of sounds and expressive possibilities. The size of these groups dictates a smaller hall and audience and usually conveys a more intimate kind of expression.

Instrumental sonata for an instrument with piano: two performers playing music written for a specific instrument and piano. Most abundant are sonatas for violin and piano and for cello and piano. There are, however, sonatas for virtually all instruments. Since the musical role of both instruments is equally important, the compositions are not categorized as solos with piano accompaniment.

String trio: three performers—violin, viola, and cello.

Piano trio: three performers—piano, violin, and cello.

String quartet: four performers—two violins, viola and cello. The string quartet is one of the most frequently presented forms of chamber music, and there are several internationally known quartets.

Piano quintet: five performers—piano plus string quartet. This grouping is another one for which large quantities of music are available.

Woodwind quintet: five players—flute, oboe, clarinet, bassoon, and French horn. Because of its tone quality, the French horn, although actually a brass instrument, is an important member of the woodwind quintet.

Brass trio: three players—usually trumpet, French horn, and trombone. Other combinations may exist but these three instruments form the most prevalent example.

Brass quintet: five players—a) two trumpets, French horn, trombone, tuba; b) two trumpets, French horn, baritone horn, trombone; c) two trumpets, French horn, two trombones. Other combinations may exist.

Brass choir: ten to fifteen players—most prevalent in high schools and universities. These groups have access to interesting music mostly from the Renaissance, Baroque, and Contemporary periods.

Percussion ensemble: This ensemble varies widely in number and composition. Although an innovation of the twentieth century, its literature is increasing rapidly.

Other small ensembles: Three divisions represent the combinations in this category: big band, jazz combo, and rock groups.

The big band usually has five saxophones, three to five trumpets, three or four trombones, and a rhythm section consisting of piano, bass, guitar, and drums.

Dixieland combos consist of clarinet, saxophone, trumpet (cornet), trombone, bass, piano, and banjo. Other jazz combos include 1) piano, saxophone, bass, and drums; 2) piano, clarinet, vibraphone, and drums; and 3) piano, clarinet, bass, and drums.

The usual rock group consists of electric guitars, electric organ, and drums. Recently some groups include other instruments, such as saxophones and trumpets.

Vocal: Vocal ensembles do not exist in such variety. The most common are those which result from the combination of solo voices in choral or operatic selections.

Vocal duet: two voices—usually one woman and one man, although excerpts from operas might be for two women's voices or two men's voices.

Vocal trio: three voices of almost any combination.

Vocal quartet: four voices—often soprano, contralto, tenor, and bass, but sometimes men's voices only (two tenors, baritone, and bass).

A word is in order regarding texts sung in foreign languages. Listeners should read the text in translation, if possible, since the expressiveness of a song is inevitably tied to verbal meaning. Understanding every word is not always necessary or desirable, however, even when a song is in English. The voice can be approached like an instrument in that tone quality and melodic line help convey the meaning.

SOLO PERFORMANCE

Keyboard instruments (piano, organ, harpsichord), which can be self-sufficient musically, are heard frequently in solo performances. Also, they serve to accompany solo voices and other instruments.

Works for the organ date from the medieval period, and the instrument still commands the attention of many composers today. Organ recitals often feature the works of J. S. Bach, Handel, Jean Langlais (1907–   ), and Oliver Messiaen (1908–   ).

Since its development in the eighteenth century, most composers have written some music for piano. The most frequently performed piano literature includes works of Bach, Haydn, Mozart, Beethoven, Brahms, Franz Schubert (1797–1828), Robert Schumann (1810–1856), Liszt, Chopin, and Debussy.

In the performance of concertos a solo instrument or group of instruments is used in conjunction with an orchestra. There is a solo part, but usually the orchestra and the soloist or solo group are of equal musical importance in the performance.

ELECTRONIC MUSIC

One important development in twentieth-century music is electronic music. A composer may choose sounds that are generated or manipulated electronically as the fundamental raw material for his music. He composes according to the same principles used for other mediums. The difference is that he "performs" his own score, transferring the sounds in his composition directly onto magnetic tape. In some instances the tape is a "solo performer," while in others the sounds prerecorded on tape are used in conjunction with live performers. The sounds used in electronic music vary widely. They may be actual sounds from nature—such as thunder, bird calls, or wind—or sounds from

Vladimir Ussachevsky. Photograph by Rosalee Vogel.

The American composer Vladimir Ussachevsky in the electronic music studio at the Columbia-Princeton Electronic Music Center in New York City. The electronic equipment produces and mixes sounds and records them on magnetic tapes which are reprocessed and combined to form musical compositions, such as his Piece for Tape Recorder *(1955).*

mechanical devices—such as a rifle, a typewriter, or an automobile engine. They may be instrumental and vocal sounds that have been electronically manipulated and transformed or sounds that have been manufactured in a studio by a machine called a synthesizer. All sounds, including noise, have musical potential.

Electronic music should not be regarded as a *kind* or *type* of music. It is simply an extension of sound resources. Composers of electronic music do not intend to supplant traditional instrumental and vocal resources. Nor do they intend to replace the performer. They are interested in extending the variety and range of sounds in much the same way that the instrumental music of the sixteenth and seventeenth centuries supplemented the predominantly vocal music of preceding centuries. Electronic music contains the same events as all music, and its content can be programmatic or absolute.

The following are some examples of electronic music:

1. Edgar Varèse (1883–1965), *Poème Électronique.*

   Created for the 1958 Brussels World's Fair, this piece reshapes the human voice, bells, and electronically generated sounds into a powerful, and dramatic space-oriented world.

2. Vladimir Ussachevsky, *Of Wood and Brass.*

   The expressive limits of brass instruments and the xylophone are extended through electronic modification.

3. Karlheinz Stockhausen (1928–), *Mikrophonie II.*

   Sounds of voices and percussion are distorted electronically to create a grotesque world reminiscent of Kafka.

4. John Cage (1912–), *Variations II.*

   The sound here is the highly amplified scraping of the strings and soundboard of a piano.

PERFORMING MEDIUMS AS A RESOURCE OF THE COMPOSER

Although there are certain more or less standard groups—such as the string trio, string quartet, and woodwind quintet—composers often write for less common instrumental and vocal combinations. The various performing mediums provide sound resources that are virtually inexhaustible. Because of the possibilities for unlimited manipulation and alteration, these mediums permit composers to express infinite shades of expression.

One of the composer's first decisions is to determine what basic sound quality is appropriate to what he wants to convey. Selecting a performing medium that is innately correct for the musical expression desired is an important factor in creating music. One does not choose a string trio to play a Mass or a flute and piano to express the fury of war. The composer must make his music suitable for performance by a particular performing medium.

PERFORMING MEDIUMS AND THE LISTENER

The various mediums of performance produce sounds of different quality; that is, they have different tone colors, or, more technically, different timbres. Many of the striking and subtle effects in music result from the way tone colors are used, alone and in combination.

Usually the mass of sound presented to the listener is quite complex, having many parts and changing constantly. Careful, repeated listening is essential in learning to identify specific sounds and their combinations. Subjectively, most people prefer certain sounds to others; but regardless of one's likes or dislikes, distinguishing among various tone colors can enhance musical understanding and enlarge the scope of listening pleasure.

GUIDE TO ADDITIONAL LISTENING

Orchestra

1. George Frideric Handel, *Water Music.*
2. Hector Berlioz, *The Roman Carnival* (overture).
3. Claude Debussy, *Ibéria.*

Although all three compositions are for orchestra, the orchestral ingredients vary in quantity and treatment. Note the exploitation of tonal color. Observe the different use of solo instruments and families of instruments. Observe similarities and contrasts in tonal expressiveness.

Chorus a cappella

1. Josquin Des Prés (c. 1450–1521), "Gloria" from *Missa Hercules dux Farrariae.*

Observe each tonal color—soprano, alto, tenor, bass. How are contrasts accomplished? What is the effect of the blending of the voices?

2. Clément Jannequin (c.1485–c.1560), *Le Chant des Oiseaux.*

Compare these vocal effects with those of the Des Prés "Gloria." How do the voices reflect *Le Chant des Oiseaux* (*The Chant of the Birds*)?

3. Randall Thompson (1899–), *Alleluija.*

Note the vocal expressiveness possible with a one-word text. Are Thompson's tonal expressions different from those of Des Prés and Jannequin? What similarities exist in the works although 500 years separated them?

Chorus with other sound mediums

1. Ludwig van Beethoven, Symphony no. 9 in D Major, op. 125 (*Choral*), chorale finale on Schiller's "Ode to Joy."
2. Johannes Brahms, "Blessed Are They that Mourn" from *A German Requiem*, op. 45.

The emotional effect is very different from that of Beethoven's work. Composers vary vocal tone color to communicate particular emotional effects.

3. Carl Orff, "Fortune, Empress of the World" from *Carmina Burana.*

This is a contrasting form of choral expression which emphasizes rhythm and text.

Band

1. Felix Mendelssohn, *Overture for Wind Band*, op. 24.

Note the sonority of the introduction, the clarity of the fast section, and the blend of the wind sounds.

2. Vincent Persichetti (1915–), *Divertimento for Band*, op. 42 (a suite of six short movements).

How does Persichetti exploit the sounds of the woodwinds, the brass, the percussion instruments? Observe the muted brass sounds and the piccolo. Does the work seem as interesting as compositions with strings? Do Bernstein's comments on humor, referred to earlier, apply here?

Chamber music ensembles

In the following listing, two compositions are cited for each category. The pairs represent the same instruments used in different styles. The value in listening, at this point, is to observe the sounds, their potential for blending and for contrast.

Sonata for an Instrument and Keyboard

Violin and Piano

1. Johannes Brahms, Sonata for Violin and Piano no. 1, op. 78, first movement ("Vivace ma non troppo").
2. Béla Bartók (1881–1945), Sonata no. 1 for Violin and Piano, third movement ("Allegro").

Clarinet and Piano

1. Johannes Brahms, Sonata in F Minor for Clarinet and Piano, op. 120, no. 1, second movement ("Andante un poco Adagio").
2. Paul Hindemith, *Sonata for Clarinet and Piano*, second movement ("Lively").

Piano Trio (Violin, Cello, and Piano)

1. Ludwig van Beethoven, Trio in B Flat Major, op. 97 (*Archduke*), third movement ("Andante Cantabile, ma pero con moto").
2. Johannes Brahms, Trio no. 2 in C Major for Violin, Cello, and Piano, op. 87, first movement ("Allegro").

String Quartet

1. Wolfgang Amadeus Mozart, Quartet no. 20 in D Major, K. 499, first movement ("Allegretto").
2. Béla Bartók, String Quartet no. 5, first movement ("Allegro").

Piano Quintet

String Quartet and Piano

Johannes Brahms, Quintet in F Minor for Piano and Strings, op. 34, third movement (scherzo: "Allegro").

Violin, Viola, Cello, Bass, and Piano

Franz Schubert, Quintet in A Major for Piano and Strings, op. 114 (*Trout*), fourth movement (theme and variations).

Woodwind Quintet

1. Jacques Ibert (1890–1962), *Trois Pièces brèves (Three Short Pieces)*, first movement ("Allegro").
2. Paul Hindemith, *Quintet for Wind Instruments*, first movement ("Playful").

Brass ensembles

1. Francis Poulenc (1899–1963), *Sonata for Trumpet, Trombone, and Horn*, third movement.
2. Robert Starer (1924–), *Five Miniatures*, first movement ("Fanfare"), third movement ("Canon").
3. Giovanni Gabrieli (1557–1612), Canzona per sonar a Quattro, no. 4.

Percussion ensemble

1. Carlos Chávez (1899–), *Toccata for Percussion*, first movement.
2. Alan Hovhaness (1911–), *October Mountain*, first and second movements.

Jazz and popular

Recordings of jazz and popular music are so numerous that suggestions would be either restrictive or inadequate. The listener is referred to jazz anthologies and current recordings.

Voice: duets, trios, quartets

1. George Frideric Handel, "O death, where is thy sting?" from *Messiah* (duet for alto and tenor).
2. Giacomo Puccini, "O soave fanciulla" ("O lovely girl") from Act I of *La Bohème* (duet for soprano and tenor).

3. Johann Sebastian Bach, "Die Katze lasst das Mausen nicht" ("What's in the bone the flesh will show") from *Coffee Cantata*, no. 211 (trio for soprano, tenor, and baritone).
4. Gian-Carlo Menotti, "From far away, we come" from *Amahl and the Night Visitors* (trio for tenor, baritone, and bass).
5. Wolfgang Amadeus Mozart, "Non ti fidar, a misera" ("Ere thou trust in him, beware") from Act I of *Don Giovanni* (quartet for two sopranos, tenor, baritone).
6. Johannes Brahms, "Rede, Mädchen allzu liebes" ("Oh, give answer, maiden fairest") from Part I of the *Liebeslieder Waltzes*, op. 52 (soprano, alto, tenor, bass, and two pianos).

Notice the statement by the men, followed by the women, followed by all together.

Miscellaneous combinations

The following suggestions represent unique and rare combinations of tone colors. What are the expressive effects of these combinations? Why do you think the composers chose them? How would the music differ if one or more of the tonal ingredients were changed?

1. Igor Stravinsky, *In Memoriam Dylan Thomas* (tenor, four trombones, string quartet).
2. Heitor Villa-Lobos (1887–1959), *Bachianas Brasileiras no. 5*, Part I and Part II (soprano and eight cellos).

Notice that the voice part is wordless except for a brief middle portion.

3. Henry Cowell (1897–1965), *Ostinato Pianissimo* (string piano, eight rice bowls, marimba, xylophone, tambourine, two wood blocks, guiro, bongo drums, three drums, three gongs).

Solo performance

Note the differing capabilities and limitations of the various instruments.

Piano

1. Wolfgang Amadeus Mozart, Sonata in B Flat Major, K. 570, first movement ("Allegro").

2. Johannes Brahms, "Capriccio in F Sharp Minor" from *Eight Piano Pieces*, op. 76.
3. Frédéric Chopin, Polonaise no. 6 in A Flat, op. 53 (*Heroic*).
4. Claude Debussy, "Feux d'artifice" ("Fireworks") from *Préludes*, Book 2.
5. Béla Bartók, *Allegro Barbaro.*

Organ
Not only does organ music differ; organs themselves differ greatly. Note the wide range of their expressive potential.

1. Johann Sebastian Bach, Toccata in D Minor, S. 768.
2. Charles-Marie Widor (1854–1937), Symphony no. 9 in C Minor, op. 70 (*Symphonie Gothique*), fourth movement (toccata: "Allegro").
3. Oliver Messiaen, *L'Ascension* (four meditations).

Harpsichord
1. Johann Sebastian Bach, *Chromatic Fantasia and Fugue.*
2. Johann Kuhnau (1660–1722), *Biblical Sonatas for Harpsichord.*
3. François Couperin, *L'Art de toucher le clavecin.*
4. Daniel Pinkham (1923–   ), *Partita for Harpsichord.*

Other Instruments Unaccompanied
1. Luciano Berio (1925–   ), *"Sequenza" for Solo Flute.*
2. Igor Stravinsky, *Three Pieces for Clarinet.*
3. Béla Bartók, *Sonata for Violin Unaccompanied.*
4. Elliott Carter (1908–   ), *Recitative and Improvisation for Four Kettledrums.*

Electronic music

1. Milton Babbitt (1916–   ), *Ensembles for Synthesizer.*

The synthesizer can move pitches so fast that the changes sometimes surpass human perception.

2. Henri Pousseur (1929–   ), *Trois Visages de Liège* (*Three Views of Liège*).

This haunting portrait of the Belgian city combines electronic sounds with taped sounds of human voices and plucked strings.

3. *The American Metaphysical Circus*, recorded by The United States of America, Columbia CS 9614.

In this piece electronic music creates an atmosphere for a biting social commentary.

4. Yannis Xenakis (1922–   ), *Orient-Occident.*

This film music expresses the reactions of a person confronted by the primordial world. Tone quality is emphasized over melody.

FOR DISCUSSION

1. Why can a chamber music ensemble perform without a conductor? What are the essential differences between the instrumentation of the chamber ensemble and the symphony orchestra?
2. Which are more expressive, instruments or voices? Or is there a difference?
3. Why is an orchestra more appealing in the concert hall than a band? Why is a band more appealing in a parade or on the football field?
4. Can noise be used expressively? How have composers of electronic music extended musical resources?

Musical Resources: Sound Events

5

Sounds become music when they are organized to convey meaning. The composer creates this organization or order as his way of making sound understandable. His musical concepts—musical ideas—are communicated by his exploitation of the characteristics, possible permutations, and effects of the sounds available. The order of music is achieved through the juxaposition of "events"—some of them rhythmic, melodic, and harmonic, others concerned with texture, timbre, and directionality. The various timbres and performing mediums available to the composer were discussed in Chapter 4. The other resources that the composer uses to create musical events will be explored in this chapter.

RHYTHM

Music moves. Sounds always seem to have a certain "going-onness." Listeners are affected by the speed of music, the organization of

Antoni Gaudí (architect): Sagrada Familia (Transept of the Nativity, 1903–26). Barcelona, Spain. Photograph courtesy The Museum of Modern Art, New York.

The surface textures that characterize Gaudí's architecture appeal to one's sense of touch. The powerful character is locked in the sculptured form. In music, texture refers to those particular sounds and their combinations that characterize a piece. As the texture of music might vary in degree from transparent (thinly voiced) to muddy (many voiced), so the texture of a sculptural surface might be heavy, or light and delicate.

sounds into time patterns, and a variety of differences in pulsations. These form rhythmical events, which are among the most important musical resources.

Tempo. The general movement or speed of music is referred to as tempo. The tempo of music ranges from very slow to very fast and has been likened, in its effect, to alterations in the rate of the human heart beat—from the excessive slowness that characterizes the nearness of death to extreme excitement; from steady and reliable to erratic and unpredictable. The composer chooses a tempo on the basis of its expressive impact. As interpreters of the composer's music, the conductor and performer also play a part in determining tempo. Personal expressiveness enters into a musical performance in the same way that an actor interprets a role. Thus individual performances of a composition often vary in tempo.

A few examples suffice to illustrate tempo, enabling the listener to become more aware of its function in music. The tempo of a march is governed by the purpose and intent of the piece. Contrast, in this light, Sousa's "The Stars and Stripes Forever" with the "Triumphal March" from Act II of Verdi's opera *Aida* and also with the second movement of Beethoven's Symphony no. 3 (*Eroica*) in E Flat Major, op. 55, the "Marche funebre." Although each march is different, one primary effect is directly related to the variance in tempo. Sousa's march is a "street-march" tempo enabling paraders to keep step to the music. In Verdi's *Aida* the music accompanies a stately processional—slightly slower, less military, more elegant. "Marche funebre" of Beethoven—slow, somber, and stately—symbolizes the grief of death. Clearly, the pace of the music is determined by the expressive effect the composer desires.

Tempo is highly important in dance music. Dances executed too fast or too slowly tend to lose their character. An eighteenth-century minuet, for example, must be played at a proper tempo if the grace and precision of the dance are to be preserved. The Russian trepak dance in Tchaikovsky's *Nutcracker* Suite evidences the necessity for fluctuating tempos. A rock tune or a jazz work is played in the tempo desired for the particular time, style, and place.

In more abstract music, tempo functions as a device for establishing order and contrast. Many overtures consist of a slow introduction followed by a fast section. The movements of a sonata, a symphony, and a concerto reflect contrasts of tempo that give the work variety. In fact, the movements of these works are usually identified by their tempo: *allegro* (fast), *andante* (moderate), *adagio* (slow), and so on. The tempo of music has a direct effect upon the mood it conveys.

Meter. When music calls for several performers to play or sing together, there is a problem of synchronizing the various parts. Early music, such as Gregorian chant, called for voices to sing a freeflowing melody in unison. With some amount of practice and the development of a sensitivity for ensemble, the singers managed to stay together. As soon as composers attempted to have two groups of singers perform two different sets of sounds simultaneously, they were faced with the problem of coordinating the performers. At first they composed parallel melodies that sometimes began in unison and again converged on a single pitch at the end:

Ex. 5–1. Organum: 9th Century

*Transposed up an octave.

One or two hearings are sufficient for twentieth-century ears to sense the limitations of this device.

Medieval composers continued to search for more expressive means. They began to write what is called "free organum," in which two parts move freely, generally together, note against note, though not necessarily in parallel motion:

Ex. 5–2. Organum: 11th Century

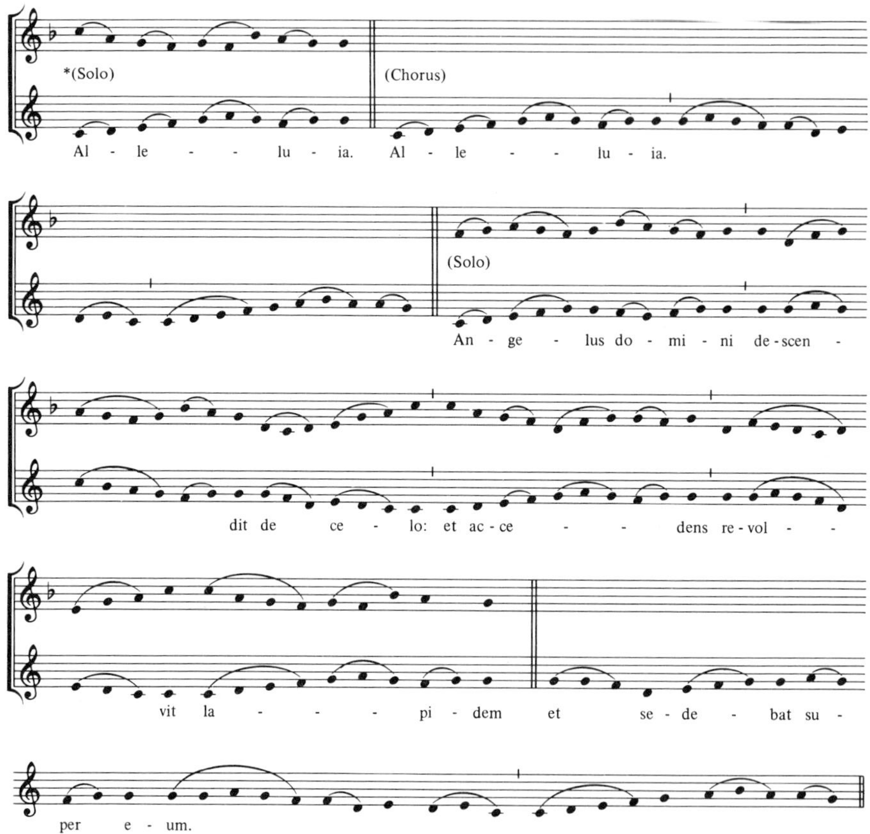

*Both parts transposed up an octave.

The chorus was given the easier monophonic (unison) melody, while the more difficult polyphonic material with its problems of coordination was assigned to soloists.

Later on, composers found that they could have one part sing long sustained tones, while another part sang a florid, "melismatic" series of tones in the same rhythmically free style as Gregorian chant:

Ex. 5–3. Organum: 12th Century

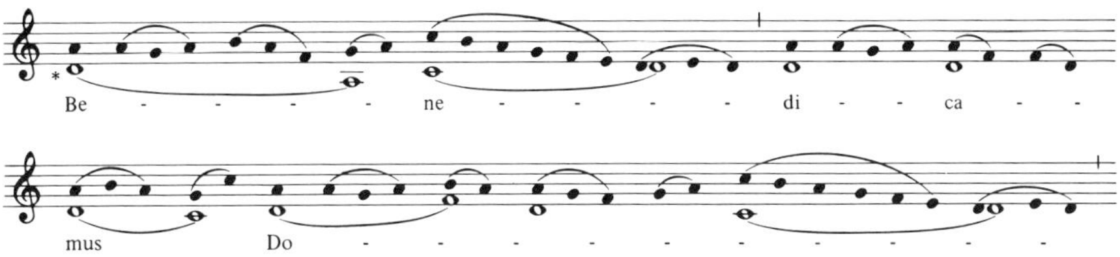

The problem of synchronizing the parts was a matter of signaling the sustaining singers when they were to change to the next pitch. Scores were scarce and usually consisted of each part written out separately.

The expressive potential of sounding two or more melodies simultaneously continued to intrigue composers. Eventually they invented a system of rhythmic "modes"—patterns that were applied to the music by the performers. Although it is not entirely clear today what the exact practice was around the year 1200, it is generally believed that a particular rhythmic mode was applied to all the parts throughout an entire piece. This "measured" style is common in church motets of the twelfth and thirteenth centuries, although the authenticity of modern performances is open to speculation.

Gradually, as scoring became more accurate and more voice parts were added, composers began to adopt a system of steadily recurring beats or pulsations that permitted the various voices great independence but held them together at the same time. Adoption of a basic beat enabled composers to create great rhythmic fluidity with a counterpoint of rhythms between many parts. In the latter part of the Renaissance (1550 onward), composers increasingly moved toward organizing the basic beats into units. The device of organizing music by a system of repeated underlying patterns of pulsation is referred to as meter. All of the music of the Baroque, Classic, and Romantic periods and much of the music in the modern period is ordered metrically. People who tap their foot or clap their hands to music are responding to the basic beat. They are sensing the underlying rhythmical order of the music, usually felt in repeated patterns determined by the meter.

In the majority of compositions heard in concerts and recitals the recurring pulsation is either based on a 1-2, 1-2 pattern called duple meter, or a 1-2-3, 1-2-3 pattern called triple meter. Most other metrical patterns are multiples of these. The conductor illustrates these patterns with his hands so that the performers know where they are in the music in relation to the underlying rhythmic organization.

Ex. 5–4. Conducting Patterns

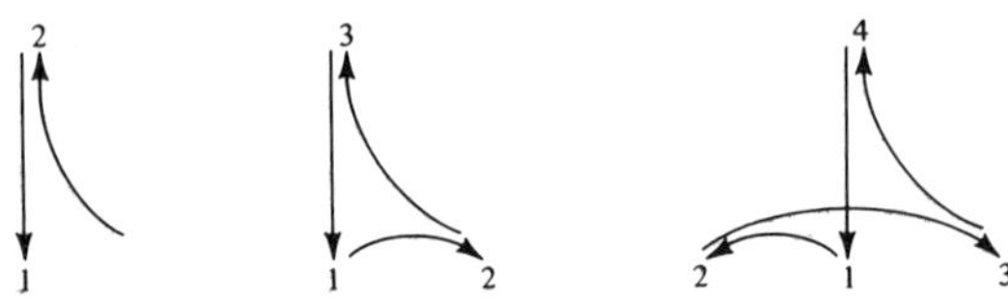

Through communication of these patterns, the conductor can synchronize the playing and singing of a hundred or more performers. The instruments playing melody may move their sounds in a way that is different from the accompanying instruments. The individual rhythms of all the instruments or voices are brought together and ordered through a strict adherence to the basic beat and its metrical divisions.

The difference between a waltz (in triple meter) and a march (in duple meter) is essentially a difference in metrical order. In medieval times, *three* was considered a more perfect meter because it symbolized the Christian trinity. The musical symbol for triple meter was a circle, representing perfection. In later times, when duple meter came into favor, particularly for secular songs, the imperfection (two as opposed to three) was signified by a broken circle or "C"—which is still in use today, although it now signifies a meter of 4:

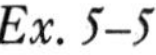

Ex. 5–5

Frequently duple and triple meters are expanded—the duple of two into four and the triple of three into six. The differences between two and four and between three and six are frequently nonexistent or extremely subtle in actual sound.

In the "Triumphal March" from *Aida* by Verdi, a metrical pattern of four pulsations per measure is evident:

Ex. 5–6

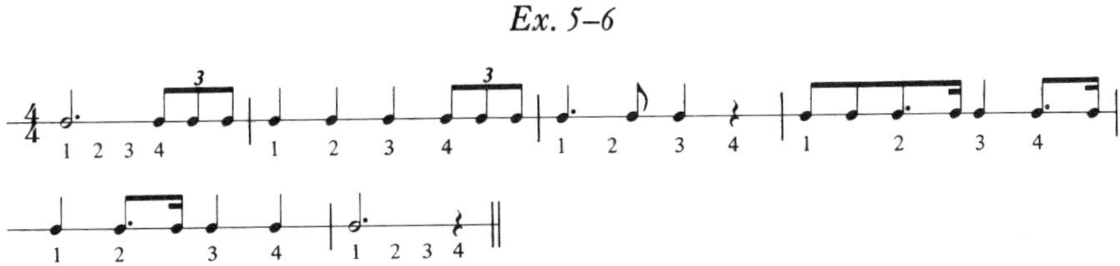

A classical example of six pulsations per measure may be found in the second movement of Mozart's Symphony no. 40, K. 550.

Ex. 5–7

Meter is not restricted to multiples of two and three. Composers might use metrical units of five, seven, nine, or four and one-half, to cite a few. Mixed or unusual meter gives an effect of irregularity. When metrical units are superimposed the result is a conflict of movement similar to actors on a stage moving simultaneously but at different paces, and not necessarily in a coordinated pattern. To experience this, count at a rapid pace: 1 - 2 - 1 - 2 - 1 - 2 / 1 - 2 - 3 - 4 - 5 / 1 - 2 - 1 - 2 / 1 - 2 - 3 / 1 - 2 - 1 - 2. Notice the effect. This might be done by two or more persons simultaneously, but beginning at different points; the varying patterns create a rhythmic tension and excitement.

They may also mix or superimpose metrical units. The following examples illustrate some of these.

Ex. 5–8. Tchaikovsky: Symphony no. 6, op. 74 (Pathétique), *second movement. Metrical unit of 5.*

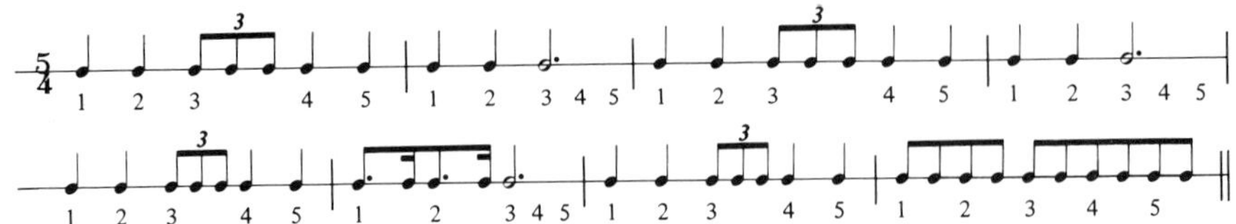

Ex. 5–9. Bartók: Concerto for Orchestra, *fourth movement, "Interrupted Intermezza." Mixed meter.*

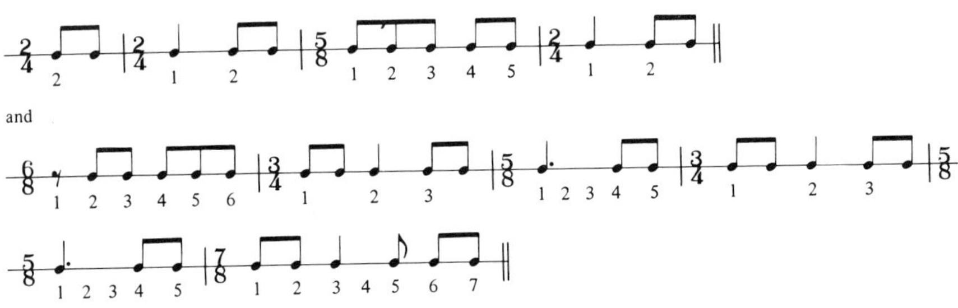

Ex. 5–10. Britten: A Young Person's Guide to the Orchestra, *op. 34. Multiple meters.*

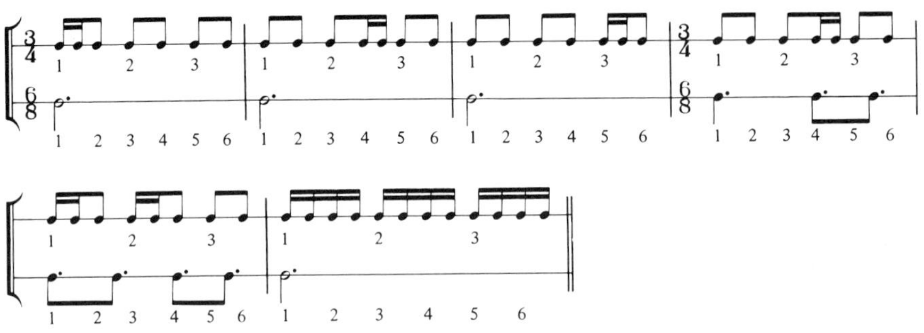

Ex. 5–11. Hindemith: Symphonic metamorphosis, *second movement. Multiple meters.*

Usually the various movements or sections of a large work such as a concerto, suite, cantata, Mass, or symphony are set in different meters for the variety of expression they permit. Much twentieth-century music shifts directly from one pattern to another, sometimes within a single melody and with little or no preparation.

Ex. 5–12. Stravinsky: "Soldier's March" from L'Histoire du soldat. *Clarinet theme.*

The contemporary composer may rely on an unchanging basic beat or pulsation that underlies the entire piece, in spite of the momentary shifts among various meters. New kinds of scoring, new devices for coordinating the performers, and a greater reliance upon the improvisory ability of performers have freed musical conceptions from the constraints of constantly recurring basic meter. The problems of synchronizing prerecorded tape with live performers challenge composers to invent new notational systems and new scoring devices. Some compositions are played by using a stop watch for synchronization. Occasionally a group of notes will be marked, "play as fast as possible." Or, a performer may be given a block of time, say one second, in which to play five notes; he may play these as he wishes rhythmically as long as he performs them all within the one second span of time.

Duration. Although closely related to meter, duration is a more complex rhythmic component. As an expressive device, it is more intricate and subject to greater manipulation by the composer. While meter generally represents a recurrence of pulsations of equal length, duration represents the way in which sounds and silence of different lengths are organized within the metrical framework. Many different rhythmical patterns of long and short tones can occur within the same steadily recurring meter. The person tapping the underlying beat pattern does not attempt to tap all the sounds that he hears.

The use of varied durations of sound is a prime element in the overall rhythmic effect of music. Both "America" and "The Star Spangled Banner" are based upon a recurring pattern of the 1 - 2 - 3: triple meter. The internal relationships of duration, however, are quite different. A few measures indicate this difference:

Ex. 5–13. "America"

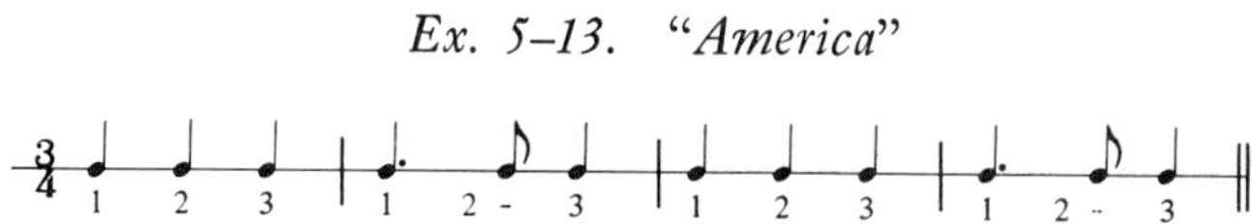

Ex. 5–14. "Star Spangled Banner"

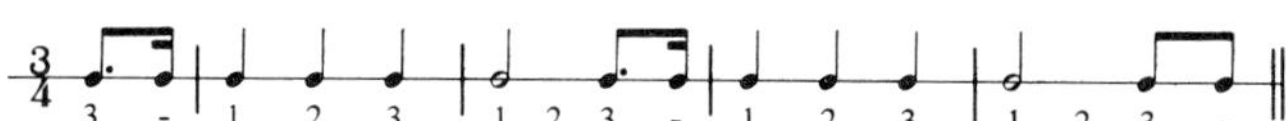

Recite or sing the rhythm to observe the recurring pulsation of 1-2-3. Also observe that the actual patterns of sound—the durations of the various syllables of the text—differ in length. The feeling of meter, the pulsation of 1-2-3, continues even though some of the text is sustained and some of it moves faster than the metrical pulsation. In essence, two rhythms are going on simultaneously, one the melody rhythm with its varied duration pattern, the other the controlling metrical pattern. The example below shows three simple duration patterns possible within triple meters.

Ex. 5–15

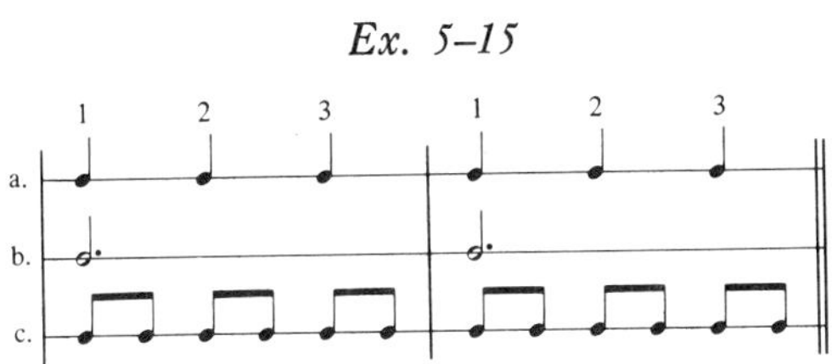

Hundreds of other patterns can be created by the intermixing of many different length sounds and silences. A composer can divide each basic beat into eight or more sounds. Sound can be replaced by a rest; and any mixture of lengths of sounds and silence is possible. The following two examples provide evidence of the variety of rhythmic interest that can be created by the use of more complex duration patterns.

Ex. 5–16. Ravel: Bolero

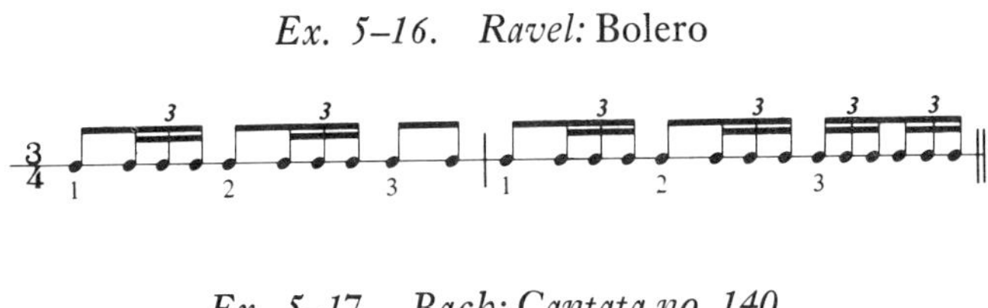

Ex. 5–17. Bach: Cantata no. 140

Whether or not the listener has mastered the technique of reading musical notation, he might imagine from these and other musical examples the rhythmic potential of music, from the very simple to the extremely complex.

The same principles are applicable to duple meter. Referring again to "The Stars and Stripes Forever" by Sousa, a simple rhythmic pattern is evident:

Ex. 5–18

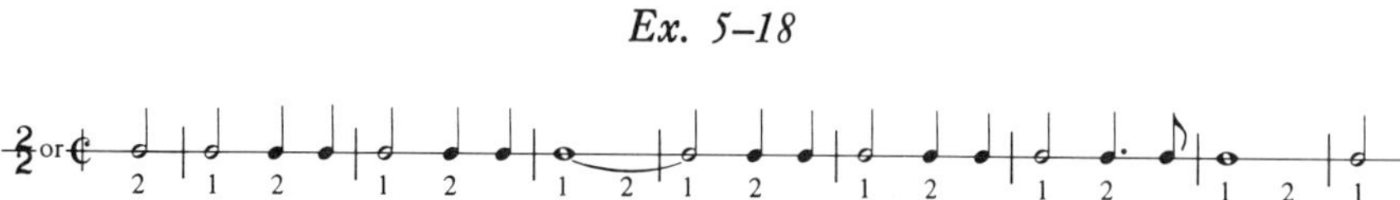

A duration pattern from the first movement of Symphony no. 1 in C Major, op. 21, by Beethoven, demonstrates the latitude of rhythmic expression available to the imaginative composer:

Ex. 5–19

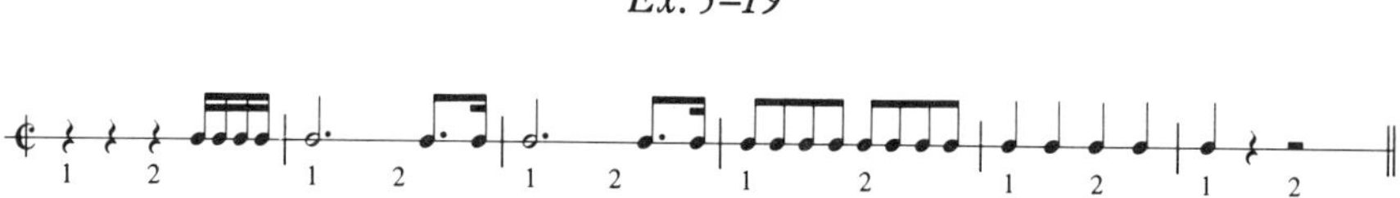

The above discussion and examples represent merely a few relatively uncomplicated duration patterns in simple meters. Each different meter permits the construction of a whole new range of duration patterns. The variety of rhythms is inexhaustible as these are juxtaposed in vocal or orchestral compositions.

Accent. Although the duration pattern (the mixture of diverse lengths of sounds and silence) is a basic ingredient of rhythm, contrast in the strengths of sounds is also important. Accented sounds are those that receive added impetus. Accents are indicated by the symbol >. A simple example illustrates the effect of accent.

The change in accent, without change in the length of any sound, creates a different rhythmical effect. Accent may be realized by several different methods that relate to melody, harmony, orchestration, and other composition techniques.

Ex. 5–20.
a. A series of eight sounds, each sound the same.

b. Every fourth note accented.

c. Every other note accented.

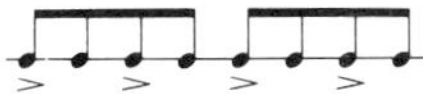

d. A 3+3+2 pattern of accent.

Awareness of tempo, meter, duration patterns, and accent is important in the search for musical understanding. Whether the effects of these rhythmic events in a composition are subtle, delicate, and subordinate to other musical events (melody, tone color, harmony, and so on), or whether they are obvious, bold, and primary, they function as one of the major expressive forces present in all music. The integration of these forces gives rhythmic character to the music. Listeners should identify various rhythmic events primarily in terms of their effect on the overall character of the music. Attention to rhythm, including tempo, accent, meter, and duration, heightens the impact of the music.

DYNAMICS

In listening to music on record or tape the listener controls the volume of sound. In concerts and recitals this volume is controlled by the performers. Changes in sound volume are referred to as "dynamics." A composition may be loud or soft or use many degrees of volume in the dynamic continuum. In a sense dynamics affect the listener's proximity to the sound source. Soft sounds appear to be farther away than sounds that are in a comfortable dynamic range. Soft sounds require greater listening concentration. Loud sounds appear to be closer. They can overwhelm the listener. Sounds that start softly and grow louder appear to move toward the listener, and *vice versa.*

The composer uses different dynamic levels to suit the purpose of his music. A lullaby is set at a dynamic level different from a song of conquest, a serenade different from a triumphal march, and a pastorale different from a hallelujah chorus.

The creation of dynamic contrast is usually accomplished by one of two methods: 1) an indication that the performer put forth more or less sound and 2) an increase or a decrease in the number of performers playing a passage. In the first instance the composer simply indicates his wishes by musical symbols:

fff *fortissississimo*—louder than *ff*
ff *fortissimo*—louder than *f*
f *forte*—loud
mf *mezzo forte*—moderately loud
p *piano*—soft
pp *pianissimo*—softer than *p*
ppp *pianississimo*—softer than *pp*

In the second method the composer may indicate a passage be played by a few instruments and repeated with additional instruments. Additional instruments, however, may not necessarily increase the volume; that is, a passage could be played fff by the string section of an orchestra and repeated softly by the full orchestra. Normally, though, the two go hand-in-hand: a full orchestra means more sound. The beginning of the first movement of Symphony no. 7 in A Major, op. 92, by Beethoven demonstrates how dynamic contrast can serve as a vital expressive factor:

1. *f*—chord sounded by full orchestra
2. *p*—oboe passage
3. *f*—chord—full orchestra
4. *p*—clarinet embellished by oboe
5. *f*—chord—full orchestra
6. *p*—French horn passage embellished by oboe, clarinet and flute

7. *f*—chord—full orchestra
8. *p*—woodwinds plus French horn with soft string accompanient
9. *pp*—short, soft, rapid notes by strings alternating with lyrical passages by clarinets and bassoons
10. *pp* to *ff*—gradual increase in volume from strings, adding flutes and clarinets, then oboes, bassoons and French horns culminating in a loud passage by the full orchestra

The above comments are not a complete analysis, but they focus attention on the element of dynamics. No dynamic markings or other expressive indications appear in manuscripts prior to the seventeenth century, although graduations in loudness were probably evident in performance. The use of contrasts in volume accomplishes several purposes. They punctuate the rhythm, help focus attention on the beginning of each statement of the musical idea, add contrast and variety of expression, give the musical statements interest and life, and focus attention on a forceful statement of the thematic idea.

Dynamic contrasts are sometimes very sudden and can create an element of surprise or suspense. A much referred to example is the "surprise" chord in the second movement of the Symphony no. 94 in C Major by Haydn. The following compositions contain sudden dynamic changes of sound or sudden silence. These contrasts function as significant expressive events.

a. Tchaikovsky, Symphony no. 4, op. 36, finale.
b. Amilcare Ponchielli (1834–1886), "Dance of the Hours" from the opera *La Gioconda.*
c. Modest Moussorgsky, *A Night on Bald Mountain.*
d. Berlioz, *The Roman Carnival* (overture).

Dynamics also refer to gradual changes in sound intensity. A progressive increase in volume is called *crescendo,* and a gradual decrease, *diminuendo* or *decrescendo.*

Dynamics are an important expressive device not only in classical music but in ethnic and popular music as well. The widespread use of electronic amplification in rock-and-roll bands has increased markedly the range of volume on the loudness end of the dynamic spectrum. While not all rock-and-roll music is loud, extreme levels of loudness—even to heights that cause pain—have added to the physical excitement generated by this music. The power of much rock music is due in large measure to its capacity for blotting out everything else in the mind. The loudness of the music seems to rid people of their inhibitions and "hangups" and permits them to dance freely or listen with total absorption. The distortion of sound that occurs at these dynamic levels has become an expressive device in itself. Overamplification and feedback of the guitar, for example, have resulted in distortions that have been explored for their own expressive potential.

MELODY

In addition to the characteristics of tone color, duration, and volume, sounds vary in pitch. People usually refer to "high" and "low" pitches, although in fact pitches differ merely in the number of vibrations per second. The instruments in the four sections of the orchestra range in pitch from high to low as follows: violins to string basses, piccolos to bassoons, trumpets to tubas, bells to timpani. Vocally, sounds range from soprano to bass and on the keyboard instruments, from keys on the right to those on the left.

Sounds are usually organized into logical sequences called scales. The musical scale is simply a convenient way to understand basic relationships in the tonal material one is using.

From the twelve different pitches that make up Western music, many scales can be formed. When, for example, all the different black and white notes on a piano are sounded in consecutive order, the scale formed is called a chromatic, half-step, half-tone, or twelve-tone scale:

Ex. 5–21

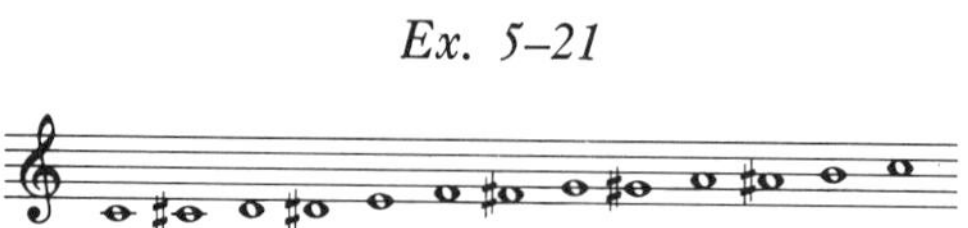

A composer choosing to formulate his music from all these tones is selecting a wide range and variety of pitches. Composers have frequently limited their tonal palette to simpler configurations, often dictated by the prevailing practice of a particular period.

Much folk music, for example, employs the pentatonic or five-tone scale:

Ex. 5–22

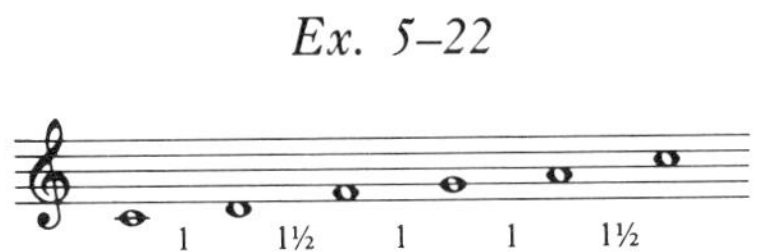

Ex. 5–23. Pentatonic Melody
The melody below is built upon a pentatonic scale consisting of five different tones.

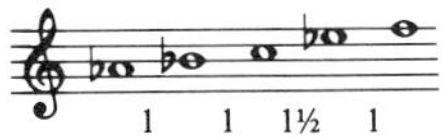

The music of the Middle Ages was built around eight different tonal arrangements called "modes." Each mode was characterized by a particular pattern of steps and half-steps between notes, for example:

Ex. 5–24

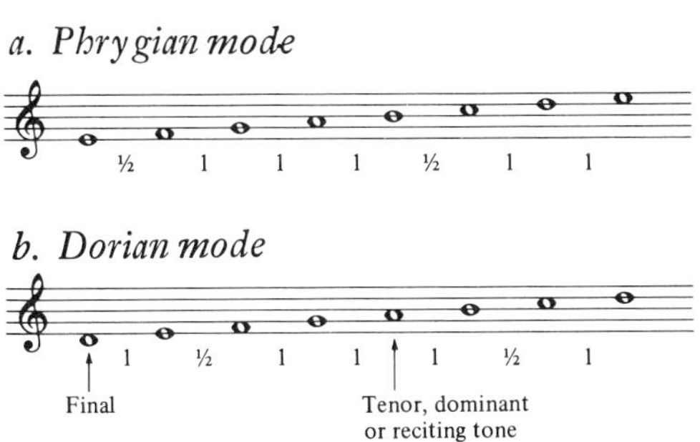

The Gregorian chant is based on the modes, and some twentieth-century composers have written modal music.

Gradually, two of these modes came to be favored over the others. By the end of the Renaissance (around 1600) the major and minor scale systems had asserted their dominance and the system of tonality was used as the basis of music for the next three hundred years.

Ex. 5–25

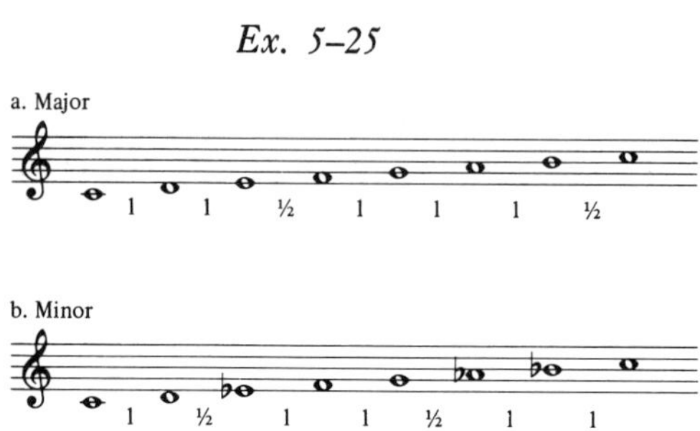

These scales establish a tonal center or "key" tone to which all the others tended to move. They employ both whole and half steps in a set pattern. If a work is called Concerto in A Minor, the A minor refers to the particular tonality, scale, or key in which the piece is written. Many other scales are possible, and, of course, any of the patterns can begin on each of the twelve tones. Scales can be "transposed" to a higher or lower starting pitch, thus enabling instruments or voices with limited ranges to perform the melody. Thus in the key of F the opening of the "Star Spangled Banner" may be too low for some singers:

Ex. 5–26

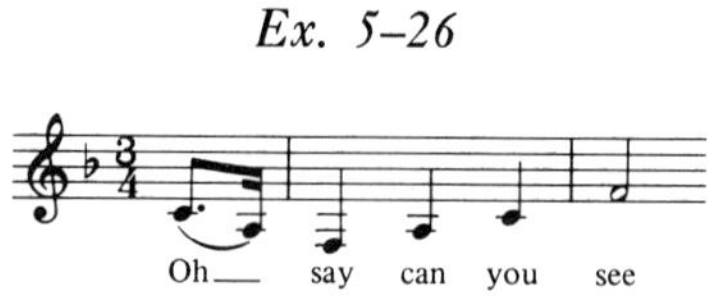

In the key of C it may lie too high:

Ex. 5–27

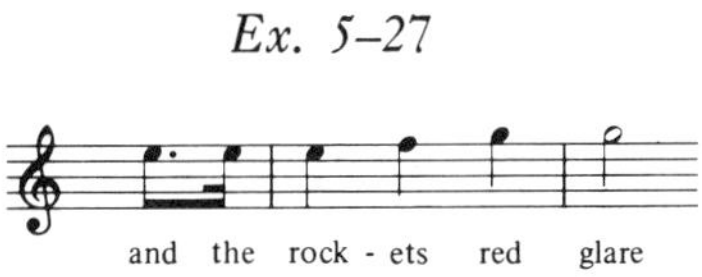
and the rock - ets red glare

The most convenient key is somewhere in the middle—either A♭ or B♭.

The chromatic scale uses all half-steps. Modal, major, or minor scales use a mixture of whole and half-steps. It is also possible to build a scale limited solely to whole steps:

Ex. 5–28

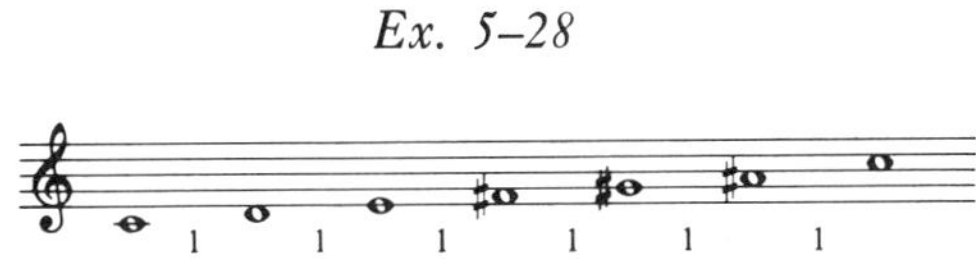
1 1 1 1 1 1

Many composers, particularly in the twentieth century, have invented scales in order to give their musical formulations a new sound. Scales can be fashioned out of larger intervals than whole steps, as well as out of smaller intervals than half-steps such as quarter or microtones that lie between the keys of the piano.

Sounds of various pitches may be extracted from a particular scale and reorganized to form a melody. A melody is simply an arranged series of tones that can convey musical meaning. Music is often considered tuneful. A melody easily sung or whistled is frequently memorable. Simple melodies or tunes may be trite; on the other hand, a melody's attractiveness may be due to its simplicity. Complexity, too, can be a factor in a melody's effectiveness. Defining a good melody is an elusive task. Most melodies make their impression within the framework of their pitch and rhythm, and their associations with tone color, dynamics, and harmony.

The preceding musical examples cited the rhythmic patterns of several well-known melodies. When the necessary pitches are associated with these rhythms, the music becomes familiar:

Ex. 5–29. "Star Spangled Banner"

Ex. 5–30. Verdi: "Triumphal March" from Aida, *Act II*

Melodies, however, are generally more complex than the two cited above and may be extremely difficult to sing. Instrumental melodies often exceed the range of the human voice or shift from one instrument to another. However, a melody that is out of voice range or is suitable solely for instruments can still be recognized and is intellectually and emotionally accessible.

The musical notation of the following examples provides some visual insight into a variety of melodic styles:

Ex. 5–31. Haydn, "Menuetto" from Symphony no. 94. An example of straightforward, unadorned melody written for instruments.

Ex. 5–32. Beethoven, "Adagio," from Sonata no. 1 for Pianoforte, op. 2, no. 1.
A melody written for piano. Notice the wide range of pitches used. This melody is neither unadorned nor florid.

Ex. 5–33. Shostakovich, "Polka," from the ballet L'Age d'or.
An example of a crisp, angular melody orchestrated as a solo for the xylophone.

Ex. 5–34. Stravinsky, "Ricercare II" from Cantata *(1952), tenor solo (1st section).*
An example of complex, florid melody written for voice (anonymous fifteenth or sixteenth century lyrics).

Melodies are constructed from a series of individual sounds, one following the other. They have an internal organization that may be analyzed musically, acoustically, aesthetically, or even psychologically. Within a pattern of pitch organization certain sounds demand that the music continue; others allow it to pause or even stop. The listener becomes aware of this by noting that a melody must continue until it sounds finished.

Usually melodies are organized into four-measure units called *phrases*, which are terminated by a *cadence*. The cadence is similar to the pause in prose or poetry, the half-cadence, like the comma, suggesting a temporary cessation of motion, and the complete cadence or full cadence, like the period, indicating a feeling of finality or repose. This musical punctuation usually occurs at regular intervals so that the ear becomes accustomed to expect it, although melodic phrases of odd lengths are not uncommon.

The melodic content of a composition may be simple or complex. It may be prominent and easily identifiable, or it might be obscure and difficult to hear. While hymns, folk-tunes, popular songs, and patriotic songs use clear, singable melodies as a primary ingredient, melodic content in more sophisticated compositions is frequently subordinate to emphasis upon rhythm, tone color, harmony, or other events. The composer's musical content–his musical ideas–may not always be melodic. Melodic content is, however, a major element in a great proportion of music and one of the elements most memorable and meaningful to the average listener.

FI	FI
Serif Caslon	Sans Serif Gothic

Cooper Black	Barnum	Cicero	Optima
FI	FI	FI	FI

The Printed Letter.

Lettering design falls into two major categories: serif and sans serif (without serif). Serifs are small finishing strokes that give a pleasing and logical ending to the basic lines forming each letter. Originally, the Roman stone carvers added serifs because a single line appeared narrower at the ends than in the middle. To counter this optical illusion the artisan flared the line slightly at each end, which eventually became the serif. These flourishes helped define the form of a letter in much the same way as cadences give definition to musical structure. Cornices of buildings and trim on doors and windows perform the same function architecturally. Lettering has many styles. The Caslon face is elegant, while the Gothic appears strong and functional. In Cooper Black, Barnum, and Cicero, the serif lends character to the type face. In Barnum, for example, the serif is given more stress than the basic strokes of the letter. Cicero is fanciful lettering, while Optima flares only slightly at the ends. Hundreds of lettering styles have been developed and new ones are frequently being designed. As with any art, tastes change and new styles are always in demand.

Melody forms the basic organizational unit of many compositions. Some examples include "America," "The Old Folks at Home," "The Stars and Stripes Forever," Tchaikovsky's Symphony no. 4 (finale), and Britten's *A Young Person's Guide to the Orchestra.* The melodies are of reasonable length, tuneful, comparatively simple, and their carrying power is strong enough to make them easy to recall.

Melodies of this length might be compared to the statement of a complete sentence in the English language. In the following poem by

Dave Etter from *Go Read the River* there are several complete sentences:

"Two Beers in Argyle, Wisconsin"

Birds fly in the broken windows
of the hotel in Argyle.
Their wings are the cobwebs
of abandoned lead mines.

Across the street at Skelly's
the screen door bangs against the bricks
and the card games last all day.

Another beer truck comes to town,
chased by a god on three legs

Batman lies drunk in the weeds.

Most of these words, however, could exist by themselves and create an idea: birds, broken windows, abandoned lead mines, card games, beer truck, Batman, drunk, weeds. Although part of the sentence, these words could be extracted to become a principal idea or germ for other poems. They could exist in an entirely different context from that in which Etter uses them. They are motivic.

Composers frequently use short, clearly-stated, musical ideas that are motivic in nature. Such ideas can be melodic, harmonic, rhythmic, or a combination of these. They are called by various terms—motives (motif), subjects, themes, or germs.

The first part of the principal theme from Mozart's Symphony no. 40 in G Minor shows how a melodic motive can form a part of a more complete musical statement:

Ex. 5–35

If one extracts a motive from this melody it is:

Ex. 5–36

Mozart later reiterates this without the last note:

Ex. 5–37

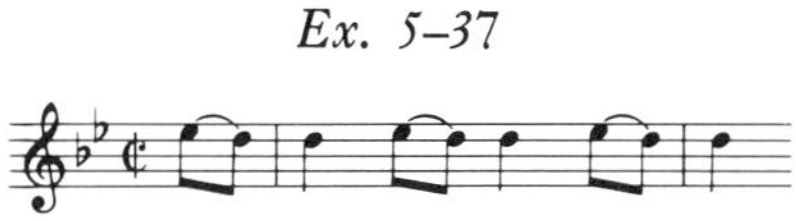

He also reduces it to its smallest motivic element:

Ex. 5–38

Mozart uses similar techniques in the development section of this movement. (Development is discussed in detail in Chapter 9.)

Similarly, the rhythmic and harmonic elements with which Beethoven opens the second movement of his Symphony no. 7 (see example 5–42) form a basis for much of the movement.

In compositions that depend upon imitation (see the section on texture), the melody usually includes motivic characteristics. The main themes, or "subjects," of the Bach *Two-part Inventions* illustrate this use of motive. Two examples follow:

Ex. 5–39. Bach: Two-part Inventions, *no. 1*

Ex. 5–40. Bach: Two-part Inventions, *no. 8*

A motivic idea can be even simpler. In the overture to *Rienzi* by Wagner, a long note by the trumpet is reiterated at different times. This is motivic in nature, demanding the listener's attention to a recurring idea.

Motives are also used extensively in popular, folk, jazz, and rock music. In Gershwin's "I Got Rhythm," for example, the opening rhythmic motive recurs throughout the song.

HARMONY

Different pitches sounding simultaneously form the harmonic events of a musical composition. Harmony, like rhythm and melody, may be easily perceptible, or may be extremely obtuse.

Groups of people singing together often improvise harmony parts to accompany the melody. They "harmonize" in a manner that is compatible with, and complementary to, the tune. This harmonization, seemingly intuitive, frequently derives from sounds heard in folksinging, hymn singing, and in the performance of simple songs.

Chords consist of tones superimposed upon one another. They range in complexity from simple three-note combinations to thick clusters with many different pitches. The movement of the harmony, called harmonic progression, depends upon the changing of the chords, the tonal relationships and the frequency of this change.

"The Old Folks at Home" by Stephen Foster (1826–1864) has infrequent and simple but definitive chord changes. Sing the melody while keeping in mind the changes in the harmonic content indicated by an (X).

Ex. 5–41

There are only three different harmonic sounds:

1. 1, 3, 5, 7 and 9 are basically the same.
2. 2 and 6 are the same.
3. 4 and 8 are the same.

As with melody, some sounds propel the movement, while others retard it; and only certain combinations of sounds form cadences, or logical stopping places.

Harmony is present in almost all music, but in some instances it is especially prominent. Observe and listen to, for example, the beginning of the second movement of Beethoven's Symphony no. 7 in A Major, op. 92 (Ex. 5–42). The top note is stated twelve times without a pitch change. Observe also the reiteration of the rhythmic pattern: $\frac{2}{4}$ ♩ ♫ | ♩ ♩ |. Most change is in the harmonic structure and this gives prominence to the harmonic events. The change is more frequent and more varied than that in the Foster example.

In "Prelude I" from *The Well-Tempered Clavier*, Bach uses interesting harmonic events as a prominent element. Until the very end of the composition there is no rhythmical change. The melodic element, with few exceptions, is based entirely upon sounds which are included in the harmonic structure. In addition, the sounds are sustained in a manner which creates a harmonic effect on a cumulative basis.

Ex. 5–42

Ex. 5–43a

If these were constructed on a purely harmonic basis—that is, the simultaneous projection of sounds—the music would be as follows:

Ex. 5–43b

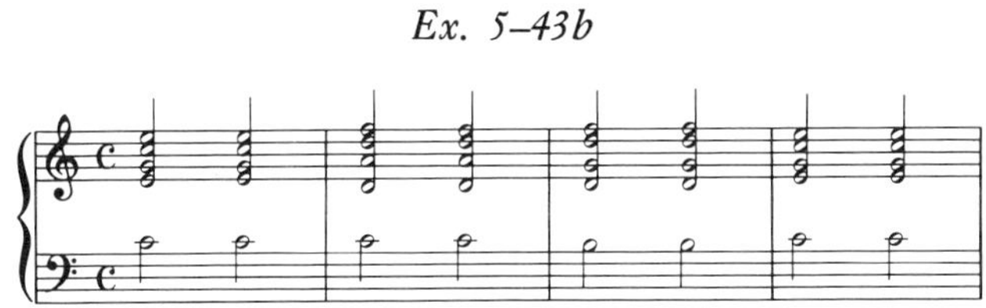

Bartók's "Hommage à J. S. Bach," no. 79 from vol. III of the *Mikrokosmos*, creates the same musical effect in a contemporary musical style.

The two basic functional aspects of harmony are (1) consonance and (2) dissonance. In the broadest musical sense, harmonic consonance refers to compatible combinations of sounds that appear to be inactive and self-resolved. Dissonance relates to conflicting combinations of sounds that require change or resolution. One suggests calm and repose; the other suggests stress and tension.

The techniques for creating consonance or dissonance vary with the historical period. In addition, concepts of consonance and dissonance change with attitudes of society, vary with composers, and may even be uniquely established in terms of a specific composition. Regardless of definition, musical rules and regulations, or scientific analysis, consonance and dissonance are not absolutes. They must be thought of in terms of subjective evaluations and interpretation. They function in relation to the context in which they exist.

The following are examples of different harmonic techniques and degrees of harmonic complexity.

1. Parallel Organum, "Rex caeli," and "Domine."
   Except for the beginning and final notes of each line, the voice movement is parallel. See Example 5–1.
2. Melismatic Organum, "Benedicamus Domino."
   One voice sustains long tones, while the other voice moves more rapidly. See Example 5–3.
3. Hymn tunes. Most hymns change harmonically with each syllable of text.

4. Mozart, Symphony no. 40 in G Minor, K. 550, first movement.

   Harmonic changes are less frequent. They are expressed in terms of rhythmical vitality.

5. Antonin Dvořák (1841–1904), Symphony no. 9 in E Minor, op. 95 (*New World*), second movement.

   Harmonic movement is the musical focus of the introduction. Harmonic support to the ensuing English horn solo plays a secondary role; but immediately after the solo, harmonic events again become prominent.

6. Wagner, "Prelude" to *Tristan and Isolde.*

   There seems to be no harmonic repose; the harmonic content motivates a continuous forward motion of sound.

7. Stravinsky, *L'Histoire du Soldat.*

   In the chorale sections, "A Mighty Fortress Is Our God" is harmonized differently than usual.

8. Ives, Symphony no. 2.

   Note particularly the ending and last chord of the final movement.

9. Jazz or Blues.
   Any jazz or blues tune has harmonic events which support the melodic improvisations of the performers.

10. Oriental or Eastern Music.

    The sounds are based upon a different pitch system.

11. Bartók, String Quartet no. 4, first and fifth movements.

    In the first movement the harmonic events result from melodic movement. In the fifth movement the harmony is basic to the introduction. It joins with rhythm to create the excitement of two "events."

12. Electronic Music.

    Various tone colors are juxtaposed to create consonance and dissonance. The movement of the sound towards the listener causes tension; away from the listener, repose. Directionality of sound and dynamics also usurps the more traditional roles of harmony and melody as expressive and organizational.

TEXTURE

The presentation of a sound or sounds gives rise to contrasting textures. The flow of a melody creates horizontal movement while the simultaneous sounds of harmonic events imply a vertical structure. Texture may be monophonic, homophonic, or polyphonic.

Monophonic texture consists of an unaccompanied melodic line; that is, there is no harmonization and no interweaving of melodies. Gregorian chant and the *Three Unaccompanied Pieces for Clarinet* by Stravinsky are examples of monophonic texture.

Homophonic texture adds harmony to melody, rhythm, and tone color. In music of purely homophonic texture, each note of the melody has harmonic accompaniment. Most hymns are homophonic. Instrumental examples include the first six statements of the theme in Britten's *A Young Person's Guide to the Orchestra* and the beginning of Tchaikovsky's *1812* Overture.

Polyphonic texture occurs when two or more melodic lines are interwoven. These lines can be imitative statements of the same basic melodic idea, or they can be independent melodies. Counterpoint is another term that describes this combination of melodic parts into a single musical work. It primarily involves the horizontal flow of sound, while harmony involves vertical combinations and movement. The "Kyrie" from Bach's Mass in B Minor and the "Kyrie" from Mozart's *Requiem* are excellent examples of polyphonic texture. Fugues exemplify polyphonic texture and contrapuntal compositional technique.

All three types of texture are often used within a composition; for example, a melody could be stated monophonically, then harmonized in choral style, and subsequently treated polyphonically.

The texture of a work can be isolated for study. And although it is perhaps more of a technique of composition than a basic event like melody or rhythm, it should receive the listener's attention in his search for musical understanding.

DIRECTIONALITY

An often neglected expressive aspect of music involves the spacial relationship between the listener and the origin of the sound. In the concert hall, this relationship is fixed by the position of the seats and stage. Stereophonic recordings can give similar directionality to sound in the home. They can simulate the fullness of the sound in the concert hall, where some sounds are received by one ear and some by the other. The placement of the speakers can imitate the concert-hall effect when they are in front of the listener, or they can achieve other effects—as, for example, when one speaker is in front of the listener and the other behind.

Sound does not always come from in front of the listener even in live performance. In ancient times the processing choir carried the chant to all parts of the church. In many churches today, the choir still moves through the congregation. The sounds of a band passing in a parade stir the senses as their proximity changes, first intensifying, then, fading into the distance. The music of various bands overlaps as one disappears and another approaches. The continual flux of sound causes anticipation and excitement.

Many composers have made use of directionality as an integral part of their compositions. St. Mark's Cathedral in Venice has a long history of polychoral music—music that employs choruses stationed in different parts of the church. Brass instruments and portative (portable) organs accompanied the singers as the choruses echoed each other, their sounds overlapping in exciting sequences. It was also at St. Mark's that Giovanni Gabrieli developed the new technique of contrasting instruments and voices—the "concerted" style that led to the idea of the concerto. Gabrieli was also the first composer to contrast the colors of various instruments. His "Sonata pian 'e forte" was the first instrumental work to assign specific instruments to individual parts. He wrote compositions for two organs in which the players rivaled each other in virtuosity.

Both Berlioz and Britten employed directional sounds in their requiems. Berlioz surrounds the listener with four brass bands that bombard the ear with sound in a terrifying effect, especially in the "Dies Irae." It must be experienced live to be believed. In his requiem, Britten places the boys' chorus off from the other performers. Their voices sound even more ethereal because of this separateness.

In electronic music, directionality is often as important as rhythm, melody, harmony, texture, and tone quality. In tape recordings with four or more tracks, speakers send out sounds from every direction. Often sounds appear to move from one side of the room to the other, passing through the listener. Tension and drama are the result. The clear definition of parts and the unexpected direction changes the whole sensory experience of music.

THE SYNTHESIS OF MUSICAL EVENTS

Musical events exist in isolation only when they are extracted for the purpose of study and analysis. Even then, their significance is not fully realized unless their interrelationship is clear. Various events may shift in importance and in prominence throughout a composition. One section may have a beautiful melody with other events subordinate to it. In another section the rhythmic force and drive may be foremost and demand the listener's attention. In some instances an entire composition or a movement from a composition will be centered around one event. Composing, above all, is the craft of combining the separate events into a meaningful whole—a synthesis.

Listening also involves synthesizing. When the listener's aural focus continually migrates toward an obvious and dominating melody, other important aspects of the composition are apt to be overlooked. Where there is no melody in the usual sense the listener must be willing to seek interest in other events.

Visual analogies can assist the listener. The following diagrams show the isolation, change, and synthesis of various musical events. These are presented visually as follows:

Ex. 5–44. Brahms: "Lullaby," a visual representation.
a. Let various lengths of lines indicate the rhythm of the "Lullaby." (- - - = *sound;* / = *silence*)

b. Let high and low placement of these indicate melody.

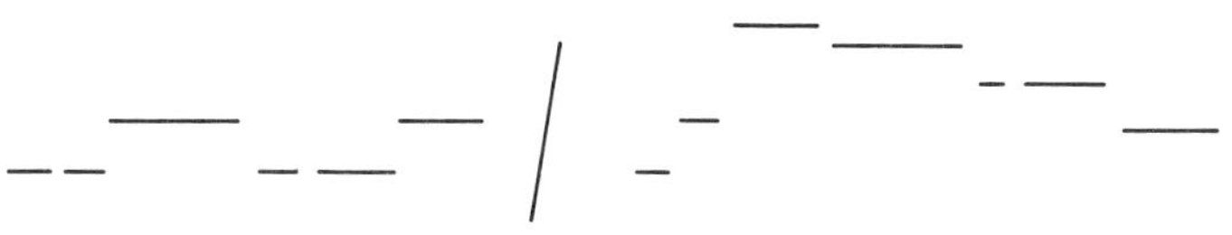

c. Adding several sounds played simultaneously provides the harmony.

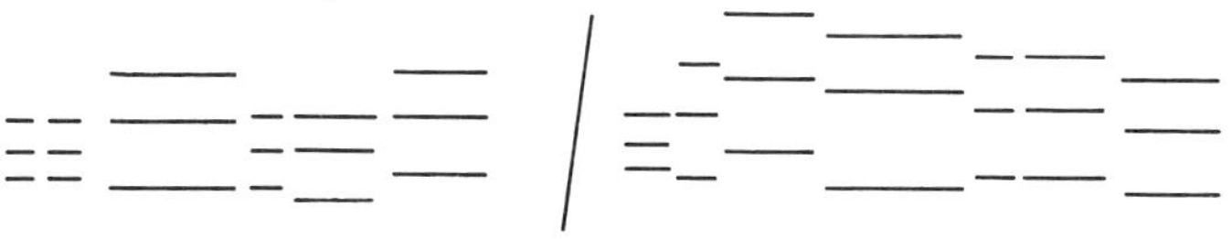

d. Melody, rhythm, and harmony are combined. Played loud, the listener would hear a great volume of sound.

e. It could be performed very slowly or much faster.

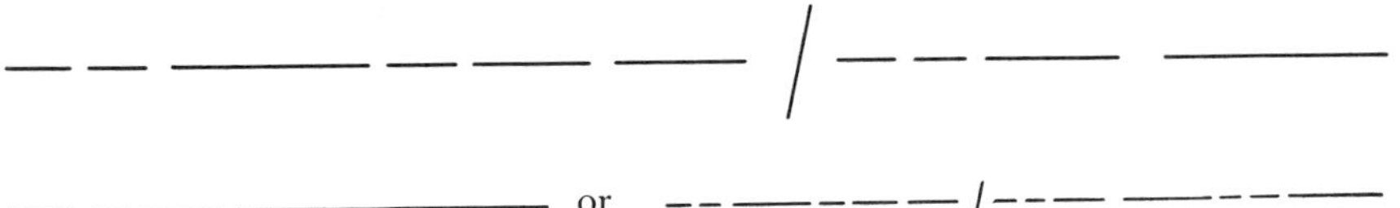

f. Different performing media would produce different tonal color and internal changes of color.

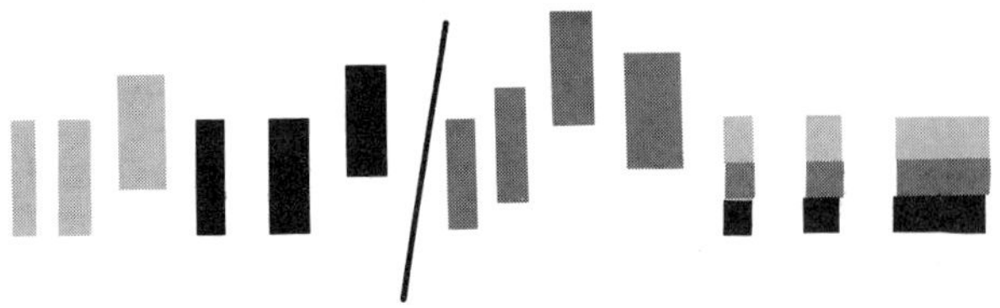

Those elements of sound that a composer uses as his sound resources become the raw material of his composition. Listening and the search for musical understanding do not necessarily depend on the ability to isolate and analyze these factors. However, awareness of their presence or absence, their degree of prominence, their relationships, and their effect, permit the listener to become more intimately acquainted with musical composition. The way in which these raw materials are formed into a musical composition is what gives the music of a specific composer and period its particular identity and meaning.

Tempo

Slow

1. Antonin Dvořák, Symphony no. 9 in E Minor, op. 95 (*New World*), second movement ("Largo").
2. Samuel Barber, *Adagio for Strings.*

Note that the tempo indications—largo and adagio—are part of the title, a characteristic of absolute music. How does the speed of the movement—the tempo—relate to the expressiveness? If the tempo were changed, what would be lost? Gained?

Moderate

1. Wolfgang Amadeus Mozart, Symphony no. 40 in G Minor, K. 550, second movement ("Andante").
2. Béla Bartók, *Concerto for Orchestra,* second movement, "Giuoco delle coppie" ("A Game of Pairs").

The style of Bartók differs from that of Mozart. How does the moderate tempo used in these works create the appropriate feeling? Might a tempo change affect the performers? Does the music seem to have the proper flow at the tempo performed?

Fast

1. Franz Joseph Haydn, Symphony no. 97 in C Major, finale ("Presto assai").
2. Aram Khatchaturian (1903–   ), "Saber Dance," from the ballet *Gayne.*

Is the tempo of this music essential to its spirit? Why? What would be the effect of a slower tempo? Could it be faster? Does a "Saber Dance" have to be "furious"?

Fluctuating

1. Johannes Brahms, Hungarian Dance no. 5.

2. Georges Enesco (1881–1955), Roumanian Rhapsody no. 2, op. 11.

How do these works reflect the nature of Slavic dances? What is the charm, the spirit of these tempo changes?

Meter

Duple

1. John Philip Sousa "King Cotton."
2. Dmitri Kabalevsky (1904–), "Comedians' Gallop," from *The Comedians.*

Note the regularity of the rhythmic pulsation. Even though the Sousa march and the Kabalevsky dance are both duple meters how does the character of the pulsations differ?

Triple

1. Franz Joseph Haydn, Symphony no. 94, third movement (*Surprise*).
2. Johann Strauss, "Emperor Waltz."

Listen to the persistent repetition of the beat, steady in the Haydn, fluctuating in the Strauss. How does Haydn's music give the feeling of an eighteenth-century minuet? How does Strauss's music give the feeling of a Viennese waltz? Observe the non-waltz-like introduction to the Strauss. Observe the beginning of the waltz.

Changing

1. Igor Stravinsky, *L'Histoire du Soldat* (*The Tale of the Soldier*), last movement, "Triumphal March of the Devil."
2. Darius Milhaud (1822–), *Concerto for Percussion and Small Orchestra.*

Note the irregularity of the pulsation. What does this rhythmic "tilt" do to the music? Does this lack of a steady meter challenge the listener? Disturb him? Attract his attention?

No Meter

(metric pulsation is illusive or nonexistent)

1. Mario Davidovsky (1934–), Electronic Study no. 1.
2. Morton Feldman (1926–), *Out of "Last Pieces."*

How does lack of metric order affect the listener? What is the essence of the rhythmic expression? Is there a rhythmic fluidity? Can rhythm (movement) be other than metric or "beat-like"? Contrast the flow of rhythm in earlier examples of chant with the flow of rhythm in Davidovsky's piece.

Accents

1. Morton Gould (1913–), "Rhumba," and "Conga," from *Latin American Symphonette.*
2. Duke Ellington (1899–), "Suddenly It Jumped," from the album *The Indispensable Duke Ellington.*

How do accents create special rhythms? Contrast the rhumba with the conga. In Ellington's music listen for the special accents, the syncopation of the band and the soloists as they contrast with the regularity of the rhythm section.

Dynamics

Few compositions maintain one dynamic level. The following have longer passages in the dynamic levels indicated. Listen for the overall effect.

Loud

1. Peter Ilyich Tchaikovsky, Symphony no. 4 in F Minor, op. 36, finale.
2. Hector Berlioz, *Roman Carnival* Overture, final section and ending.

Moderate

1. Wolfgang Amadeus Mozart, Symphony no. 40 in G Minor, K. 550, second movement ("Andante").
2. Johannes Brahms, *Variations on a Theme by Haydn,* op. 56a, beginning theme and variation 1.

Soft

1. Peter Ilyich Tchaikovsky, "Dance of the Sugar Plum Fairy," from the *Nutcracker* Suite, op. 71.
2. Alan Hovhaness, *October Mountain.*

Melody

Lyrical and Smooth

1. Johann Sebastian Bach, "Sheep May Safely Graze," from Cantata no. 208.
2. Pietro Mascagni (1863–1945), "Intermezzo," from *Cavalleria rusticana.*

What is the musical effect of melodic lyricism? How is it expressed?

Angular and Less Smooth

1. Hector Berlioz, "Witches' Dance," from *Symphonie fantastique*, op. 14, fifth movement.
2. Gunther Schuller (1925–   ), "Twittering Machine," from *Seven Studies on Themes of Paul Klee.*

Does angularity, a lack of smoothness, express a feeling different from Mascagni's "Intermezzo"? How? Do different melodic styles reflect different emotional feelings?

Motivic

1. Ludwig van Beethoven, Symphony no. 9 in C Minor, op. 125, second movement ("Scherzo").
2. César Franck (1822–1890), Symphony in D Minor, first movement ("Lento: Allegro non troppo: Allegro").

The above works present vivid motives. How do these motives differ from melodic events?

Harmony

Clear and Straightforward

1. George Frideric Handel, "All We Like Sheep," from the *Messiah.*
2. Johannes Brahms, *Academic Festival* Overture, op. 80.

Full and Rich

1. Johannes Brahms, Symphony no. 2 in D Major, op. 73, second movement ("Adagio non troppo").
2. Peter Ilyich Tchaikovsky, Symphony no. 5 in E Minor, op. 64, second movement ("Andante cantabile").

Complex and Dissonant

1. Elliott Carter, *Variations for Orchestra.*
2. Oliver Messiaen, *Chronochromie.*

Note the harmonic structure, which ranges from wholly consonant to extremely dissonant. Would different harmonies appeal to different listeners on different occasions? What is the effect of the more complex and dissonant blocks of sound? What is the effect of the comparative noncomplex or the lush blocks of sound?

Texture

Monophonic

1. Gregorian chant: anthologies by the Benedictine Monks of Solesmes.
2. Igor Stravinsky, *Three Pieces for Clarinet.*

Homophonic

1. Frédéric Chopin, Prelude no. 20 in C Minor.
2. Thomas Morley, "Sing We and Chaunt It."

Polyphonic

See listening suggestions at the end of Chapter 8. Observe the variety and effect available to the composer using different textures.

Directionality

1. Giovanni Gabrieli, Canzona prima "La Spiritata" in G Minor for Brass and Organ.

The contrast between the brass and organ gives the work direction. Which sounds seem closer? Which more distant? What is expressed by this contrast?

2. Charles Ives, "Fourth of July," from *A Symphony: Holidays.*

In this work, a marching band seems to enter from afar, arrive on the scene, and proceed on its way. Observe the directionality; the mixture of sounds which seems to come from different places.

Note also the tonal conflict.

FOR DISCUSSION

1. Is musical notation an exact science? Can symbols for rhythm, pitch, harmony, tempo, and dynamics be performed perfectly in classical music? In electronic music?
2. Can a melody be performed without rhythm? Can rhythm be altered without affecting the melody? How does a change in tempo affect the other components of a piece? How does harmony affect melody? Does a change in meter affect expressiveness?
3. How do the various events interact in a musical work?
4. How many different scales can be formed from the twelve different tones within the keyboard octave?
5. Gather several types of melodies. What gives them their particular characteristics?

Part Two

THE STRUCTURE OF MUSICAL MEANING

Repetition, Recurrence, and Contrast

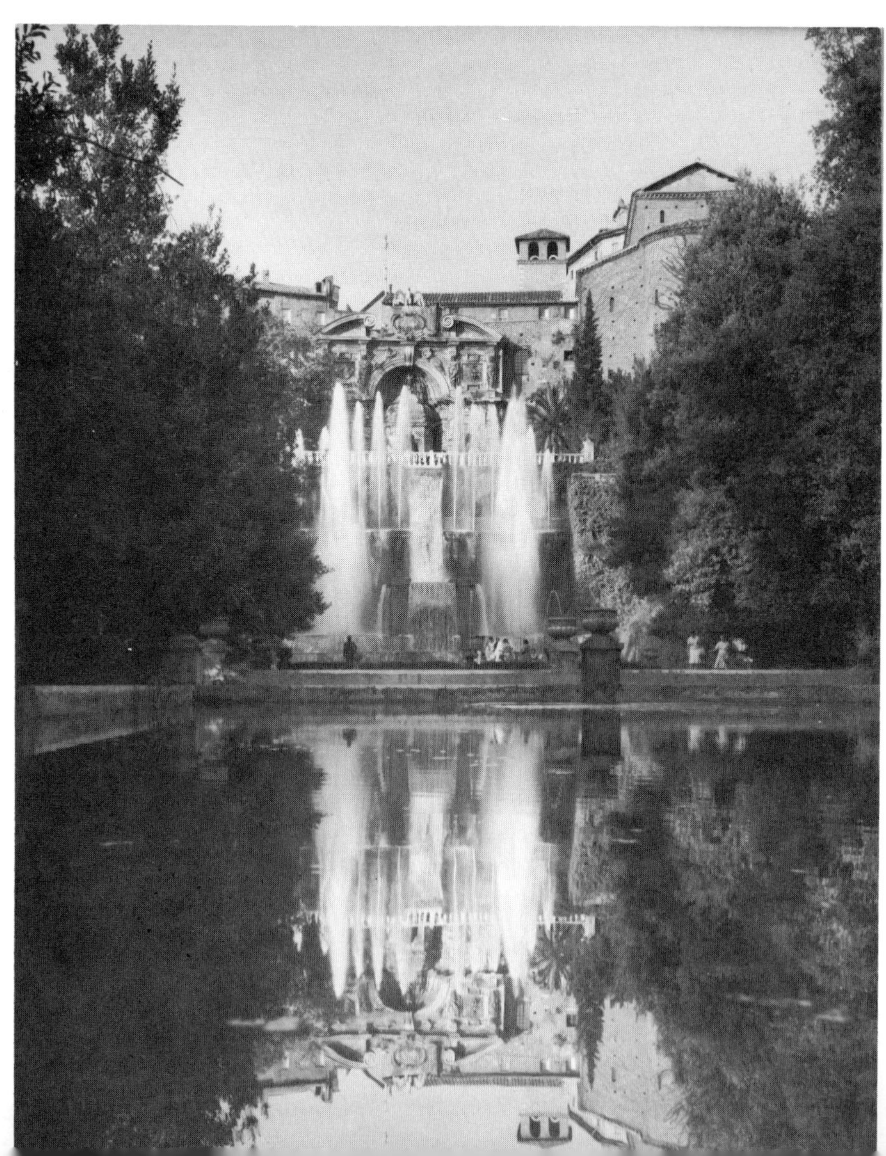

6

After a composer establishes the initial idea for a composition, he is faced with the task of expanding this concept into a meaningful work. In developing his idea, the composer selects from among three options. (1) The original idea may be repeated without change. (2) The idea may be repeated with modification. (3) A new idea may occur. In making his choices, the composer determines the structure most suitable for expressing his idea. The structure or design that evolves is an outline that provides the listener with the feeling that the work has continuity and "makes sense."

REPETITION

Pirro Ligorio (architect): The Hundred Fountains (1550–69). Villa d'Este, Tivoli, Italy.

The rhythmic expansion of a simple idea (a single spray) makes this fountain aesthetically exciting to the eye and the ear. Fountains convey a feeling of time, in part because they express movement and in part because they change continually. In this sense they are musical.

The immediate repetition of a phrase or a pattern is one means of achieving unity and contributing to the rhythmic drive of a work. Consider, for instance, these lines by T. S. Eliot:

> This is the way the world ends
> This is the way the world ends
> This is the way the world ends
> Not with a bang but a whimper.

In simple music, such as folk songs, repetition is fundamental to the organization of the work. It must be clear and obvious, especially when it serves a straightforward, regularly-patterned text. Without some recurrence of a musical idea, the listener tends to "get lost." Like the repetition of petals on a flower, or leaves on a stem, repetition in music gives a composition unity and meaning.

A stanza of the folk song "Wondrous Love" illustrates.

Ex. 6–1

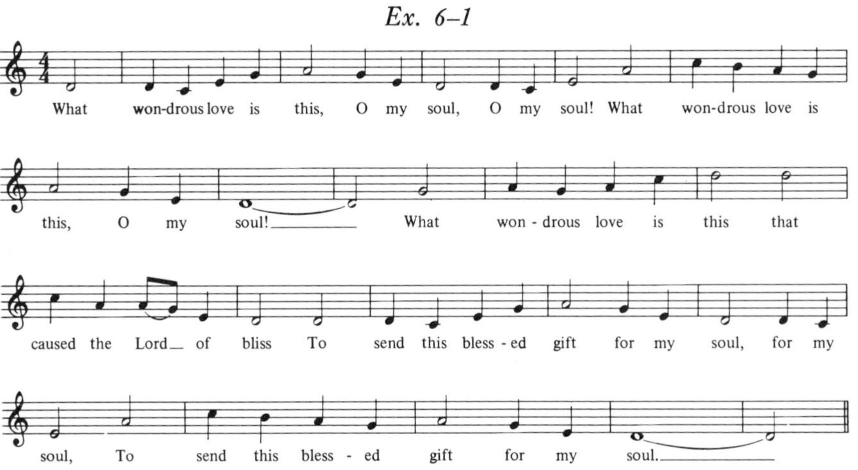
What won-drous love is this, O my soul, O my soul! What won-drous love is
this, O my soul! What won - drous love is this that
caused the Lord of bliss To send this bless - ed gift for my soul, for my
soul, To send this bless - ed gift for my soul.

The text consists of three distinct but related phrases, each expressed in a single line of the verse: (1) "What wondrous love is this, O my soul," (2) "That caused the Lord of bliss," and (3) "To send this blessed gift for my soul." Although the text consists of six lines, subsequent lines are a repetition, or partial repetition, of the three lines quoted.

Similar repetition occurs in the music. Each line of text begins with the same rhythmic pattern, whether or not the words are identical.

Ex. 6–2a

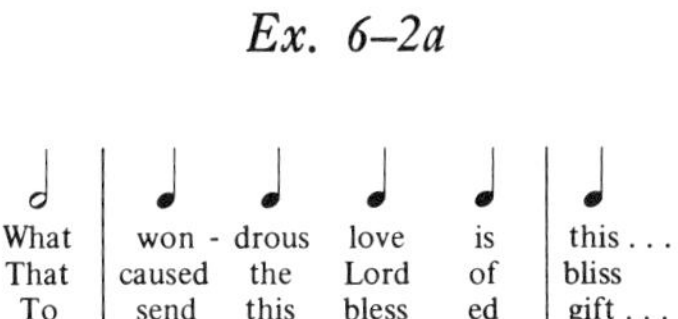

What | won - drous love is | this . . .
That | caused the Lord of | bliss
To | send this bless ed | gift . . .

The song contains two basic rhythmic concepts: long values, indicated by 𝅗𝅥 or 𝅝, and short values, indicated by ♩ or ♫. The whole note (𝅝), though twice as long as the half note (𝅗𝅥), is merely an extension of it, while two eighth notes (♫) are an ornamentation of the quarter note (♩).

A close examination reveals, however, that the principle of repetition is carried out in at least three other ways in this song. 1. The words "O my soul" and "for my soul" have the same rhythmic and melodic setting each time. 2. The fifth and sixth lines are musically and rhythmically identical with the first two, although the text differs. 3. Each verse stanza is sung to the same music as the first stanza.

Ex. 6–2b

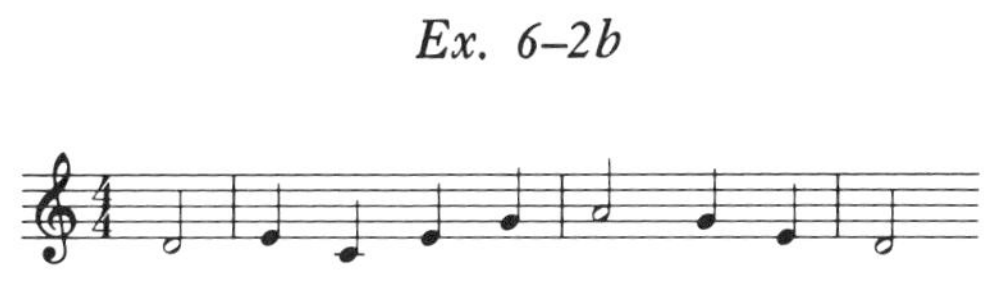

Repetition impresses the message of both text and music upon the mind through *emphasis*. If the initial rhythmic statement is vital, repetition may add to the cumulative effect and drive it toward a climax. This last point is dramatically illustrated by the *Bolero* of Maurice Ravel (1875–1937)—a constant repetition of a melody and an accompanying rhythm, relieved primarily by changes in dynamics and tone color. The effect is hypnotic.

RECURRENCE AFTER CONTRAST

Unity in a work of art may be even more effectively realized if the initial idea recurs after a contrasting idea has intervened. An idea may lose some of its freshness through immediate repetition, while contrast minimizes that loss. Many types of recurrence occur in poetry. Sometimes such recurrences are limited to a single word. Considered in isolation, the word "green" in the phrase "green branches" evokes a simple mental image. In the context of an entire poem, such as the one below by Federico García Lorca, the word acquires new shades of meaning, increasing in power with each recurrence, and heightened by the contrasting elements that intervene:

Green, how much I want you green.
Green wind. Green branches.
The ship upon the sea
and the horse in the mountain.
With the shadow on her waist
she dreams on her balcony,
green flesh, hair of green,
and eyes of cold silver.
Green, how much I want you green.
Beneath the gypsy moon,
all things look at her
but she cannot see them.

The recurrence of the complete phrase, "Green, how much I want you green," is an additional unifying factor. The subtle effect is enhanced by the time span that separates it from its first occurrence. Phrase recurrence after a shorter intervening contrast is also used effectively in the following lines by Vachel Lindsay:

Booth led boldly with his big bass drum—
(Are you washed in the blood of the Lamb?)
The Saints smiled gravely and they said: "He's come."
(Are you washed in the blood of the Lamb?)

In music the recurrence of a musical idea—a motive, a phrase, or a more extended melody—is similarly effective. The familiar song "When Johnny Comes Marching Home" illustrates an interesting pattern of recurrence. Its five phrases are: (1) first phrase (measures 1–4); (2) second phrase (measures 5–8); (3) third phrase (measures 9–10);

(4) fourth phrase (measures 11-12); (5) fifth phrase (measures 13–16).

Ex. 6–3

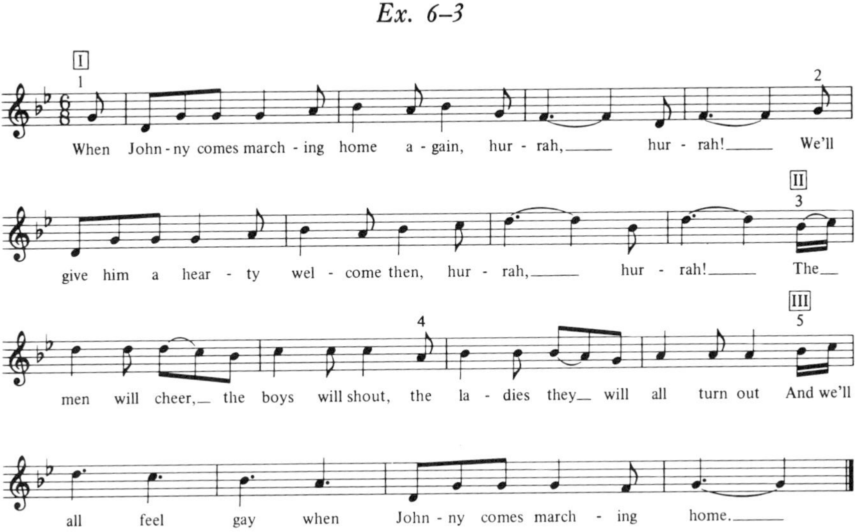
I
1
When John - ny comes march - ing home a - gain, hur - rah, hur - rah! We'll
2
give him a hear - ty wel - come then, hur - rah, hur - rah! The
II
3
men will cheer, the boys will shout, the la - dies they will all turn out And we'll
4
III
5
all feel gay when John - ny comes march - ing home.

Note that phrases one and two both begin with the same motivic ideas and end with the same rhythm but a different melody. Phrases three and four are alike except that four follows three at a lower pitch level. Phrase five begins the same as three, proceeds with a new concept, and then ends with the inclusion of the beginning motive of phrases one and two. Although "When Johnny Comes Marching Home" is a simple short tune, it contains exact repetition, varied repetition, contrast, and recurrence. As a result, the melody commands attention and satisfies the need for order and sense.

Phrase recurrence after contrast is a common element of many folk songs, hymn tunes, and art songs. In Martin Luther's powerful chorale "A Mighty Fortress Is Our God," the initial statement repeats itself—sometimes exactly and sometimes with the alteration of one or more notes in pitch or rhythm. If the alteration is slight, the feeling of recurrence is achieved in spite of the change. Phrases one and two are repeated at the beginning. Phrase two then recurs as the final phrase, altered only by one note (indicated by an X) near the end.

Ex. 6–4

Many popular tunes are based upon a simple structure of repetition, contrast, and recurrence. One common pattern sets a line of text to music, a second line to the same music, a third line to different music, and a fourth line to the same music as the first line (A-A-B-A).

To assure that one hears these recurrences, it is important to be aware of the cadences at the end of each phrase that define these segments of the form. In many hymns and folk songs the first phrase is punctuated by a half-cadence, a temporary pause that leads the ear to expect more. This first phrase, called the *antecedent*, is answered by the second, or *consequent* phrase, which may be terminated by either a half or a full (complete) cadence. These first two phrases form an eight-bar unit called a *period*. The third and fourth phrases again end on first a half, then a full cadence. These second eight bars form another period with antecedent and consequent phrases. The whole piece is in the form of a *double period*, sixteen bars in length, composed of two periods. This structure is typical of many short musical compositions. Recognizing the cadences or pauses helps the ear to grasp the structural units that comprise the form.

When the recurring music has an individual character because of its greater length, or in the case of songs the same text with each repetition, the recurrence is called a *refrain*, *chorus*, or *ritornello*. The refrain is a common element of hymns, folk songs, and popular songs, and provides a unifying factor between verses. The call and response organization of Negro spirituals provides an example of such a format. The call or solo section is followed by a group response on a repeated chorus.

Ex. 6–5. Spiritual: "Michael, Row the Boat Ashore"

The English folk song "Early One Morning" illustrates a song with refrain.

Ex. 6–6

The ritornello (returning section) which occurs in more extended forms of instrumental music of the early eighteenth century will be considered in the final portion of this chapter.

MELODY AS A GUIDE TO SIMPLE FORMS

The structural divisions in songs and other short pieces can be identified by distinguishing musical phrases. Most folk songs and hymns are based upon one of three patterns of organization.

One-part songs are based upon a single melodic idea that is carried from beginning to end before coming to a pause (or cadence). One-part songs are usually short. One example is "The Dying Cowboy," also known as "Bury Me Not on the Lone Prairie" or (with a different text) "Old Texas."

Ex. 6–7

Two-part songs (binary) are composed of two contrasting sections, A and B. The first section comes to a pause before the second is

Ex. 6–8

Paolo Veronese: Christ in the House of Levi *(1573). Academy, Venice.*

This sumptuous banquet might as easily depict a secular party of noblemen as a religious event in the life of Christ. The subject matter here is less important than the form the painter has given to the assembled details. The ABA structure of the architecture provides the basic organization. The larger central arch, presented against a simple background, commands one's attention. The side stairways lead the eye toward the focal point—the figure of Christ. The figures on the right and left balance each other, as do the groups directly to the right and left of Christ. The rhythm and repetition of the arches and balustrades convey a sense of grandeur and excitement.

stated. Sometimes the second part (B) is based on a rhythmic or melodic variation of the first part, but proceeds in a different manner. More commonly, the two parts offer a distinct melodic contrast to each other. "Early One Morning" (Ex. 6–6) is an example of the two-part song. The verse functions as A, the refrain as B. The French folk tune (Ex. 6–8) illustrates another two-part song.

Three-part songs (ternary) employ melodic recurrence after contrast of the form A-B-A, A-A-B-A, or A-B-B-A. The more common pattern is A-A-B-A, as in "Blue Bells of Scotland," "Swanee River," "All Through the Night," and many popular songs. The repeated A sections may not be identical with the first statement. If the divergences are slight, the form is still designated A-A-B-A. Unlike the A-B-B-A pattern, each section of the A-A-B-A form is usually the same length.

Ex. 6–9. "My Funny Valentine"

Songs with the pattern A-A-B-A are sometimes considered two-part (rounded binary) forms, particularly when they do not come to a complete pause—full cadence—after the B section. The recurrence of A at the end, so the logic goes, does not change the two-part organization. For most listeners, however, the three-part form seems a more logical designation because the contrasting melodic line is a more important defining factor than the finality of the cadence.

REPETITION, CONTRAST, AND RECURRENCE IN EXTENDED MUSICAL FORMS

In music of greater length than a folk song or a hymn, repetition and recurrence are even more important in clarifying the musical structure for the listener, particularly in unfamiliar music. The beginning of the repetition of a musical unit marks the end of the first hearing of that unit. Recurrence of a musical unit marks the end of the contrasting unit. Repetition differs from recurrence only by its position.

Composers develop the larger structure of a work by "pyramiding" smaller units. For example, a simple melody may have several units: A-A-B-A. Instead of comprising a complete piece, this melody might serve as one larger section (A) of a longer composition. Additional musical material (arbitrarily called c-d-c) might be the B section in what is then an extended binary form:

A	*B*		*A*	*B*[x]
a a b a	*c d c*	or	*a a b a*	*a a b a*

[x] (Similar material at a contrasting pitch level.)

Sometimes in specialized types of binary forms, both sections are repeated in turn. The resulting form may be symbolized A-A-B-B. In actual practice, however, performers sometimes ignore the composer's instructions to repeat sections, and the listener may hear A-A-B, A-B-B, or A-B, instead. Binary form is the principal design employed in suites for keyboard instruments by many late seventeenth-century and early eighteenth-century composers such as Bach. These suites consist of short pieces, most of which are in the meter and rhythm of a stylized dance, with such names as *Allemande*, *Courante*, *Sarabande*, *Minuet*, *Gavotte*, and *Gigue*. Each dance is in binary form. The A and B sections are usually based on the same melodic and rhythmic ideas. The contrast between A and B is achieved in the following ways.

1. The two sections focus on contrasting pitch centers; A comes to rest on the pitch center where B begins and B comes to rest on the center where A began.
2. The melodic and rhythmic ideas of A are modified in B.
3. The length of the two sections differs.

Pieces in which A and B are based on different themes, possibly in different meters, are also considered binary. Although examples are less common, this form is illustrated by a harpsichord piece, *La Drollerie*, by Jacques Champion de Chambonnières (1602–c. 1672). In this piece the A is repeated, but the B is not, resulting in the pattern A-A-B.

"Pyramiding" of parts may also result in a more complex ternary form if the first section recurs:

A	*B*	*A*		*A*	*A*	*B*	*A*
a a b a	*c d c*	*a a b a*	or	*a a b a*	*a a b a*	*c d c*	*a a b a*

United States Capitol Building, Washington, D.C. Views of the building before 1855 (left) and as it stands today.

Before 1855, the United States Capitol building was a simple ABA structure that later became the central section of the larger and more complex building that stands today. The Capitol still retains the symmetry of the ABA form, even though its parts may be analyzed as ABCDCBA. Architecture often provides clear and striking examples of ABA form. The formality and dignity of this arrangement make it suitable for government buildings. The simplicity and repetition of the forms reassure, while the variety exhilarates. The ABA scheme provides both security and liveliness, expressing the concept of an institution that, ideally, maintains stability at the same time that it alters its course according to the current needs of the people it serves.

The ternary form A-B-A occurs in extended compositions in both vocal and instrumental music. Many operatic arias (solo songs in operas), particularly in the seventeenth and eighteenth centuries, illustrate the A-B-A structure, as do the third movements of many symphonies and piano sonatas of the late eighteenth and early nineteenth centuries. Bach's "Da capo aria" is an example of the A-B-A form that represents the perfect musical fulfillment of the late Baroque (1725–1750). Handel also composed arias of this form, and in the nineteenth century it was a favorite form in the short piano compositions of Chopin and Schumann. When the A-B-A form is used in extended compositions the need for variety often requires that the B section differ radically from the A sections. Chopin's Nocturne in F Major, op. 15, no. 1 demonstrates how dramatically the B section may contrast with the A sections.

Short and distinctive musical ideas lend themselves to frequent recurrence, usually with intervening contrasting phrases and sections. In the eighteenth century frequent recurrence was a significant feature of the *concerto grosso*, a multimovement piece for instruments. A soloist or a small group of soloists called the *concertino* alternated with the ensemble called the *ripieno*, somewhat in the manner of question and answer. The recurring ensemble phrase is known as a *ritornello*. As a rule, the fast (*allegro*) movements of concerti grossi by such composers as Bach, Giuseppe Torelli (1658–1709), and Antonio Vivaldi (1675–1741) use the ritornello.

A common musical form of the seventeenth century was the *rondeau* (French for rondo), an instrumental piece in which the refrains (A) were separated by varied contrasting "couplets" (B, C, D). Both refrain and couplet were short and concise resulting in a form with numerous brief sections, for instance A-B-A-C-A-D-A. The rondeau was a favorite of French keyboard composers and was also employed in the eighteenth century by Bach in the "Gavotte en rondeau" movement of his Sonata no. 3 for Unaccompanied Violin.

In the classical period of the eighteenth century the rondo was expanded into five and seven part forms which might be represented as follows:

Five-part forms

A B A B A

A	*B*	*A*	*C*	*A*

Seven-part forms

A	*B*	*A*	*C*	*A*	*B*	*A*

A	*B*	*A*	*C*	*A*	*D*	*A*

The contrasting sections B, C, and D were mostly in a related key or pitch level. The recurrence of the A section was usually at the same pitch level but often modified in some way.

Although contemporary and slightly variant the following poem by Harry MacCormack represents the idea. However, MacCormack repeats the third line of his poem.

"In Santa Cruz"

They've got warrants to kill
The green we are planting,
They'll transplant us in Santa Cruz.
They've hammered Japanese gardens
Into masques for detention,
They'll transplant us in Santa Cruz.
Chained with words of sedition,
They'll transplant us in Santa Cruz.
Strawberries behind barbed wire,
They'll transplant us in Santa Cruz.
They chew our sweet flesh,
They'll transplant us in Santa Cruz.
They swallow our seeds,

They'll transplant us in Santa Cruz.
Together we'll flower in Santa Cruz.
Together we'll die in Santa Cruz.

The rondo form is sometimes used for the final movement of a symphony or a sonata. The final movements of the Haydn Symphony no. 94 (*Surprise*) and no. 101 (*Clock*) are rondo form; other movements in rondo form are the final movements of the Beethoven Piano Sonatas op. 2, no. 2, op. 14, no. 1, and op. 53.

Occasionally, in multimovement works such as sonatas, symphonies, and Masses, the same musical idea may be heard in more than one movement. When this occurs, the work is called "cyclic." This device is used for the same purpose as all other kinds of musical redundancy: it assures unity and cohesiveness. In the fifteenth and sixteenth centuries cyclic structure was a common feature of one type of Mass in which each movement began with the same melodic pattern. Cyclic structure is also apparent in several nineteenth-century symphonies, including Symphonies no. 4 and 6 by Tchaikovsky, no. 9 by Dvořák and Franck's Symphony in D Minor. Although the term is not commonly used in opera, cyclic structure is evident in musical-dramatic works, particularly when a distinctive musical theme accompanies an important character each time he appears.

The search for musical understanding is enhanced by an aural awareness of the design, structure, and logic in the composition of sounds.

GUIDE TO ADDITIONAL LISTENING

Repetition

1. Franz Joseph Haydn, Symphony no. 94 in G (*Surprise*), second movement.

First eight measures repeated; repeat is softer than first statement.

2. Ludwig van Beethoven, Sonata for Piano, op. 2, no. 2, third movement.

First eight measures repeated; exact repetition.

3. Johannes Brahms, *Variations on a Theme by Haydn*, op. 56a, theme.

First ten measures repeated; exact repetition.

4. John Philip Sousa, most marches.

Introduction, first section repeated, second section repeated, trio (third section) repeated twice, often with interlude.

Recurrence after contrast

1. Wolfgang Amadeus Mozart, Symphony no. 40 in G Minor, K. 550, third movement.

A	*B*	*A*
aababa	*ccdcdc*	*aba*

Although the A sections do not appear to be exact repetitions, they are traditionally performed so; aababa becomes aba.

2. Ludwig van Beethoven, Sonata for Piano, op. 2, no. 2, fourth movement ("Grazioso").

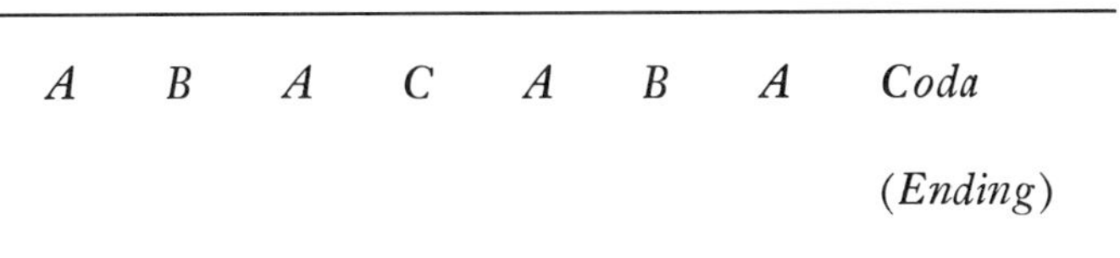

Note the unity created by the repetition of the A section even though it reappears slightly changed. The second B section is also varied. Observe the fragments of the A and C sections in the ending (coda).

3. Béla Bartók, *Concerto for Orchestra*, fourth movement ("Interrupted Intermezzo").

Introduction	*A*	*B*	*C*	*B*	*A*	*Coda*

Note the short introduction, the spritely character of A, the smoothness of B, C as an interruption, the transitional return of B and then A in reverse order.

Two-part forms

1. Johann Sebastian Bach, Suite in B Minor, no. 2 for Flute and Strings, part IV.

Bourée I	*A*	*B*
	a a	*b b*

Bourée II	*A*	*B*
	a a	*b b*

Bourée I is often repeated after Bourée II creating a larger three-part form.

2. Wolfgang Amadeus Mozart, "Minuet" from *Don Giovanni.*

A	*B*
a a	*b b*

3. Béla Bartók, *Mikrokosmos,* vol. II, nos. 43a, 65.

Three-part forms

1. Wolfgang Amadeus Mozart, Symphony no. 41, third movement.

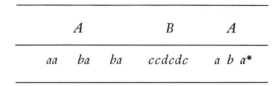

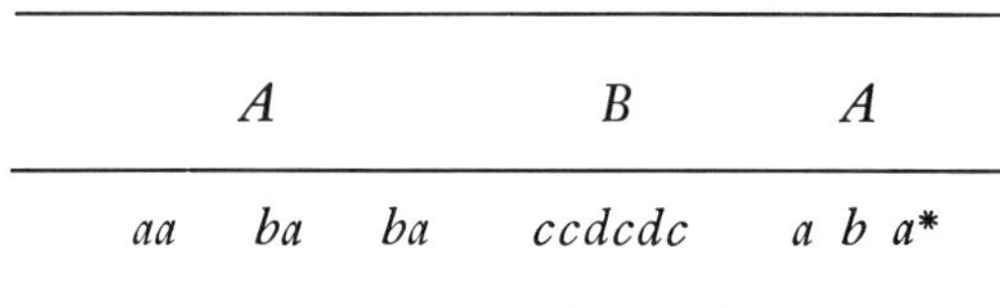

A	*B*	*A*
aa ba ba	*ccdcdc*	*a b a**

* Note extensive elongation of the "a" section.

2. Ludwig van Beethoven, Sonata for Piano, op. 2, no. 2, third movement ("Scherzo").

A	*B*	*A*
a a b a b a	*c c d c d c*	*a b* a*

* Note the similarity between "a" and the beginning of "b."

3. Frédéric Chopin, "Valse," op. 64, no. 1.
   Often referred to as the "Minute Waltz."

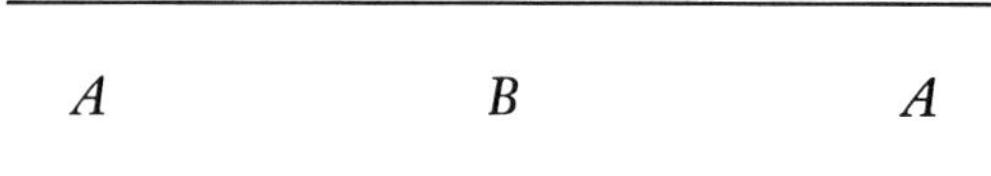

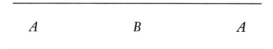

A	*B*	*A*

Note the contrast between A and B: the rhythm of A, the song-like quality of B, the transition to and return of A.

Other works based upon repetition–contrast–recurrence

1. Johannes Brahms, Symphony no. 2 in D Major, op. 73, third movement ("Allegretto grazioso").
2. Peter Ilyich Tchaikovsky, *Nutcracker* Suite, op. 71, "Marche," "Russian Trepak Dance," "Waltz of the Flowers."
3. Peter Ilyich Tchaikovsky, Symphony no. 4 in F Minor, second movement ("Andantino in modo di canzone") and third movement (Scherzo: "Pizzicato ostinato").

FOR DISCUSSION

1. Locate examples of A-B-A form in painting and architecture. Do local public buildings use this form?
2. Plot the color relationships in a piece of electronic music. Is there a pattern?
3. Draw some simple A-B-A designs. How does this method of organization aid the artist? Hinder him?
4. Give some examples of repetition in nature among both plants and animals. Is there such a thing as A-B-A form in nature? Symmetry? Why do humans find the A-B-A form satisfying or beautiful?
5. One musical theory equates the A-B-A form with the form of the human body and maintains that the satisfaction it holds for humans stems directly from its indigenous quality. Discuss.
6. Why don't composers just write what sounds good and forget about structure? What does structure do for the creator? The listener?
7. Listen to a current popular tune. How does the composition maintain unity? What kinds of contrast are employed to maintain interest? Does classical music use more or less contrast? Why?

Variation

7

Inventiveness is difficult to suppress. Simple repetition for the sake of unity makes too much of constancy to satisfy some musical situations. A new turn of the melody, a different twist of rhythmic flow, a change of tone color or harmony, a contrast in the dynamic level, or a simple alteration of texture or tonality can add fresh zest to a composition.

In Chapter 6, repetition, and recurrence after digression were introduced. This repetition or recurrence may be an exact restatement but more often it is altered. "Pop" singers and instrumentalists often embellish a tune by adding notes. Sometimes they go so far afield that they in effect spin a web around the melody. Jazz musicians and church organists improvise on a well-known melody, extemporizing flourishes that give it new life and color.

Variation is mostly an ornamentation of the melodic idea as, for example, in the second movement, "Adagio," of Beethoven's Sonata for

Andy Warhol: Flowers *(1964). Photo courtesy of Leo Castelli Gallery, New York.*

Like many pop art works, this painting reveals the artificiality of modern life. Warhol uses multiples of flat, simple forms. The mechanical repetition of the advertising illustration of a flower on each panel, with only slight variation provided by the lifeless colorations, creates a feeling of nonindividuality, sapped vitality. The artist is passive and indifferent toward this devitalized quality in American life. We sense an emptiness in this insipid world, about which the artist remains apathetic. Warhol simply portrays; he does not become personally involved, but leaves the interpretation to the viewer.

Piano, op. 2, no. 1. The melody begins:

Ex. 7–1

After some digression the melody recurs slightly changed.

Ex. 7–2

The second statement is varied by the addition of tones in the melody and also by the repetition of tones, a rhythmic variation. Example 7–1 shows six tones between "a" and "b," seven between "c" and "d," and four between "e" and "f." Example 7–2, a repetition of the same basic melody, shows twelve tones between "a" and "b," nine between "c" and "d," and eight between "e" and "f." The melody has been made more active by the variation.

Another example is Beethoven's Sonata for Piano, op. 2, no. 2, last movement ("Rondo"). The first measures of the four opening statements of the theme are as follows:

Ex. 7–3

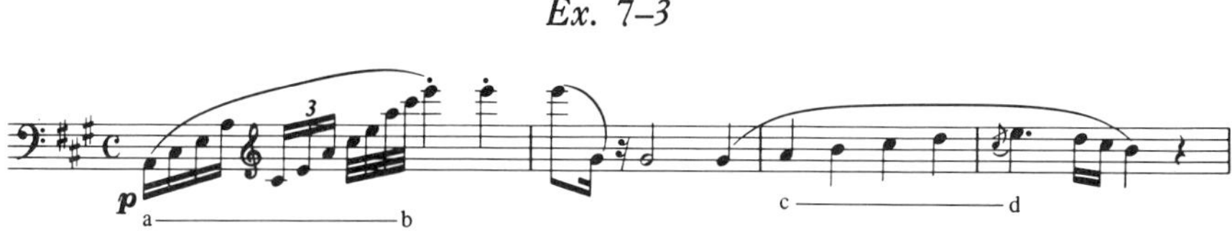

The equivalent in the second statement, after an extended digression, is slightly more elaborate.

Ex. 7–4

The melody at the beginning of the third entrance:

Ex. 7–5

And a florid last statement extended to the conclusion of the work:

Ex. 7–6

The melody in its original form, Example 7–3, undergoes changes in successive statements:

> Ex. 7–3. "a" through "b," 11 notes;
>
> Ex. 7–4. "a" through "b," 14 notes beginning on a lower pitch but arriving at the same top pitch;
>
> Ex. 7–5. "a" through "b," 32 notes;
>
> Ex. 7–6. "a" through "b," 14 notes—same as Ex. 7–4.

Compare the passage from "c" to "d" in each example.

Beethoven uses this technique to refresh the melody upon each restatement. Variety does not cancel the unity that results from repetition and recurrence. It simply adds interest. The technique of melodic ornamentation is often used in compositions of the theme-digression-recurrence structure.

Another form of modification may be achieved through the instrumentation. Debussy's *Prelude to the Afternoon of a Faun* begins with a melody played by one flute—a monophonic statement. A few measures later it is repeated accompanied by two clarinets and strings and subsequently two French horns. Note the flute melody at A, and the same passage with other instruments at B.

The final movement of Beethoven's Symphony no. 3 in E Flat Major (*Eroica*) is based on a four-note motive. If the listener can mentally recall these four tones, they serve as a sign-post in the music. Subsequent statements are recognized then in light of the changed accompanying events. In these examples (Ex. 7–7a and 7–7b) of Debussy and

Ex. 7–7a

A
Molto moderato
Solo
3
p dolce, espress.
Unaccompanied flute
3 Flutes
2 Oboes
p
English Horn
2 Clarinets in A
p
2 Bassoons
4 Horns in F
1.
p
Ancient Cymbals
2 Harps
1. glissando
Molto moderato
Violin I
Violin II
Viola
Violoncello
Bass

Ex. 7–7b

B
Solo
Fl.
p
Flute with accompaniment
Ob.
Oboe
p
espressivo
Clarinets
Cl.
pp
pp
Bn.
p
1. French Horn
p
Hn.
3. French Horn
p
Vn. I
Strings
div.
sulla tastiera
Vn. II
pp
sulla tastiera
Vla.
pp
sulla tastiera
Vc.
pp
Cb.
pp

Beethoven, the repetition unifies while the modification varies. Predicted repetition is thus balanced by change.

A third technique of variation superimposes a new musical idea on the original theme and conveys a fresh supplementary melodic concept—the countermelody. Haydn uses such a countermelody in the second movement of his Symphony no. 94 in C Major (*Surprise*), as does Beethoven in the second movement of his Symphony no. 7 in A Major. Haydn uses the additional melody as a decorative polyphonic interweaving, whereas Beethoven's melodic addition is a more basic component of the composition.

Ex. 7–8. Haydn: Symphony no. 94, second movement.

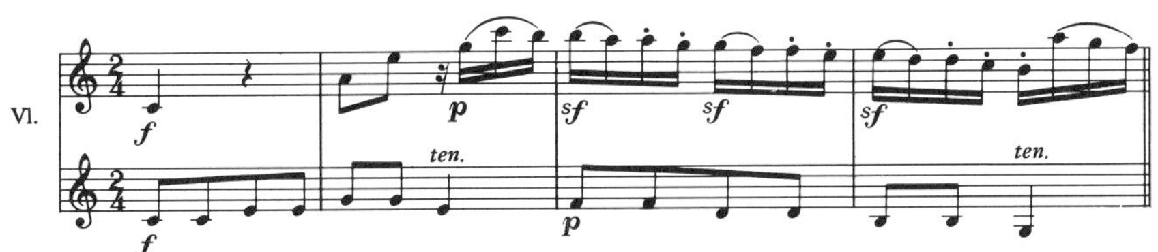

Ex. 7–9. Beethoven: Symphony no. 7, second movement.

Another variation technique is change of tone color. The examples in the performing mediums section of Chapter 4 demonstrate this. Recall the statements of Purcell's theme in Britten's *A Young Person's Guide to the Orchestra* (p. 41) as played by full orchestra, brass, woodwinds, strings, and percussion.

The possibilities for variation are limitless. A composer may vary rhythm, harmony, texture, tonality (a change in the pitch level or system), and dynamics. Since such variations rarely occur in isolation, it is more meaningful to study them in context.

The following musical works demonstrate a number of variation techniques.

1. Joseph Haydn, Symphony no. 94 (*Surprise*), second movement ("Andante").

   Form of the movement: Theme and Variation.

   Theme: Two-part (A-B).
   1st Variation: decorative melody added (change in tone color); change of dynamic level.
   2nd Variation: change in tone color; change in dynamic level; change of tonality.
   3rd Variation: rhythmic change in oboe passage; change in tone color; change in accompaniment; decorative melody in oboe and flute; change in dynamic level.
   4th Variation: full orchestra sound; heavy harmonic accompaniment; change in dynamic level; embellishment by violins.

2. Peter Ilyich Tchaikovsky, Symphony no. 4 in F Minor, op. 36, second movement ("Andantino in modo di canzona").

   Form of the Movement: Rondo.
   Variations in the first 97 measures.

   Opening: Theme (part A) stated as an oboe solo, accompanied by pizzicato strings; very soft.
   Repetition: Theme stated by cellos, accompanied by pizzicato strings and decorative parts in clarinet, French horns, flutes, and bassoons; remains soft.

Recurrence: Theme stated by violas and bassoon, accompanied by pizzicato strings and a light, rapid, decorative embellishment by violins; decorative passage changes to cello.

Repetition: Theme stated by violins and violas, accompanied by pizzicato strings, passages for French horn, embellishment by short, rapid decorative tones of flutes and clarinets.

3. Johannes Brahms, *Variations on a Theme by Haydn*, op. 56a.

Theme: Begins with woodwinds, French horns, cellos and basses. Three-part form ends with full sound; tempo moderate.

Variation 1: Strings predominate by weaving a web of embellishment around the original theme which does not appear, but is left for the listener to imagine.

Variation 2: Spirited; pitch orientation changes; first three notes of the original theme used in a motivic fashion; emphasis on dynamic contrast.

Variation 6: Variation of a fanfare-like nature developed around the theme, emphasis on French horns; spirited.

PASSACAGLIA AND CHACONNE

Variation sometimes functions as a primary structural element rather than a limited ornamental recasting of the theme. Entire compositions are based upon the principle of variation. Foremost among these forms are the passacaglia, chaconne, chorale prelude, and the theme and variations.

The passacaglia and chaconne are forms which are both probably derived from early Italian or Spanish dances. Both consist of many variations set upon a recurring chord pattern or melody. The two forms resemble each other to such a degree that they cannot be clearly differentiated by definition. Manfred Bukofzer states: "Although it seems certain that the chaconne was an exotic dance of the Spanish colonies, its musical origin and its name have not yet been satisfactorily elucidated."

John Gillespie establishes some distinction between these forms:

Chaconne—a keyboard form that employs a type of continuous variation. The only apparent "theme" is the harmonic pattern established by the initial chords.

Passacaglia—A form consisting of continuous variations based on a repeated melodic pattern. It belongs to the category of the ostinato.

Ostinato—A short melodic phrase that is repeated, usually in the bass, and accompanied by changing superstructures. The terms *ground* and *ground bass* are interchangeable with ostinato.

Composers of the seventeenth and eighteenth centuries made extensive use of these variation techniques in both vocal and instrumental music. The following example from the opera *Semiramide* (1667) by Marcantonio Cesti (1623–1669) illustrates two different solo voices superimposed over the repeated bass melody.

Ex. 7–10. Cesti: "Terzetto" from Semiramide.

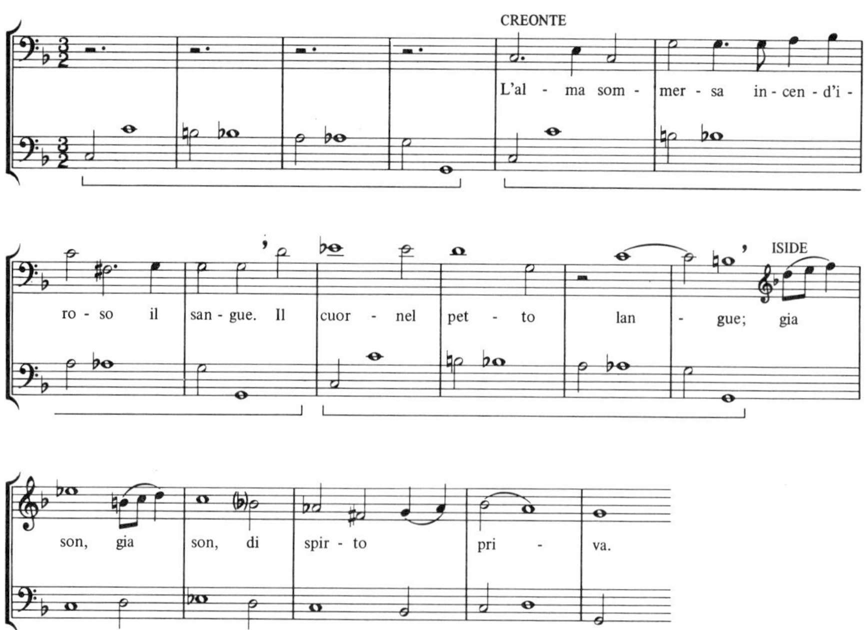

The following examples are representative of the passacaglia and chaconne:

1. Bach, Passacaglia in C Minor.
2. Bach, "Chaconne" from Partita no. 2 in D Minor for violin alone.
3. Handel, *Suite de Pièces*, vol. II, no. 9 (chaconne and variations).
4. Brahms, Symphony in E Minor, no. 4, fourth movement ("Allegro energico e passionato").

The "Chaconne" from First Suite in E Flat for Military Band by Gustav Holst illustrates variation beginning with a ground bass (ostinato) melody. The melody and a design for listening follow:

a. Original statement:

Ex. 7–11a

b. Inverted statement:

Ex. 7–11b

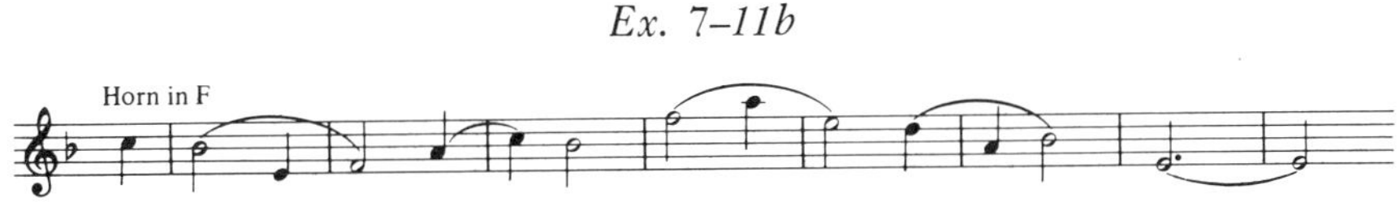

First statement:	Melody softly stated by tuba, euphonium and contra-bass clarinet; monophonic.
Second statement:	Melody in lowest voice (softly) by trombone; harmony by other trombones and cornets.
Third statement:	Melody in lowest woodwinds (very soft); harmony by other woodwind instruments with a contrasting melody in one clarinet part.
Fourth statement:	Stylistic change; melody in lowest brass and woodwinds; slightly louder and in a less smooth style; embellished by fanfare-like passage in higher woodwinds; gradually increasing in dynamic level.
Fifth statement:	Melody loud in lower voices with stylistic embellishment from fourth statement assumed by trumpets and cornets; increasing volume.
Sixth statement:	Melody very loud by brasses in very short rhythmical style with elaborately embellished woodwind passages; percussion added; gradually decreasing in intensity.
Seventh statement:	Melody in top voice with full brass harmonization and embellished by moving parts in bass line; diminishing.
Eighth statement:	Melody soft; French horn solo accompanied by embellishing clarinet.
Ninth statement:	Melody soft; alto saxophone with embellishments by flutes; one oboe and an E-flat clarinet.
Tenth statement:	Inverted melody (slightly louder); French horns, saxophone and some clarinets; embellished by other clarinets, oboes and flutes.
Eleventh statement:	Inverted melody by euphonium, cornets and baritone saxophone with

quiet but slightly arhythmical bass accompaniment.

Twelfth statement: Melody, as originally stated, played by trombones; accompaniment similar to that in eleventh statement continues; instruments added gradually giving effect of increasing intensity.

Thirteenth statement: Melody stated by euphonium and cornets; instruments gradually added.

Fourteenth statement: Full band playing; melody by French horns, fluegel horn, cornets, some clarinets, flutes and piccolo; percussion which entered earlier continues to build volume; other instruments embellish and harmonize; end of melody altered.

Fifteenth statement: Climactic statement; full band with the exception of percussion.

Sixteenth statement: Continuation of style of statement fifteen with melody prominently stated by trombones leading to the ending based on a slight extension of the melodic line; loud, fully harmonized, not ornamentally embellished; full resources of the band including percussion.

The technique of variations on a ground bass may stand by itself as the principal structural element of a one movement work, or it may comprise only a portion of a composition.

Almost any recording of Louis Armstrong's trumpet playing provides an example of the ground bass variation as applied to jazz. His rendition of "St. Louis Blues" or "When the Saints Come Marching In" illustrates how Armstrong superimposes improvised melodies over the harmonic pattern underlying the original tune. While the harmonic pattern of the piece is repeated again and again, other members of the band take turns improvising a solo chorus.

CHORALE PRELUDE

In seventeenth-century Germany it was the custom in the Lutheran church "to play on the organ an introduction to the hymn (or chorale) to be sung by the congregation." The chorale prelude is usually considered a contrapuntal form, although the listener may find it more helpful to think of it as a variation form. It is simply an embellished organ performance or organ composition based upon a hymn tune.

The examples that follow demonstrate the chorale melody (a), its harmonization (b), and its embellishment as a chorale prelude for organ (c).

Ex. 7–12a. Bach: Christ lag in Todesbanden, *Chorale from Canata no. 4. Melody.*

Ex. 7–12b. "Christ lag in Todesbanden," *Harmonized Chorale*

Ex. 7–12c. Christ lag in Todesbanden, *Embellished Chorale*

THEME AND VARIATIONS

The theme and variations form is usually more expanded than the passacaglia, chaconne, or chorale prelude. The passacaglia and chaconne are based on a short melodic ground bass, whereas the theme upon which the variations are based is a full-blown melody, often in binary or ternary form. This melody serves much the same function as the ground bass of the passacaglia. It operates as the structural basis upon which the whole composition—in this case a set of variations—is spun. In contrast to the ground bass of the passacaglia and chaconne, however, the first statement of the melody (theme) is usually in the upper voice.

Frequently, the form theme and variations can be identified from a title: Brahms' *Variations on a Theme by Haydn*, op. 56a; Tchaikovsky's *Variations on a Rococo Theme for Cello and Orchestra;* Bach's *Goldberg Variations;* Carter's *Variations for Orchestra.* However, a work may be of the theme and variations form even though the title or subtitle does not so indicate, for instance the second movements of Beethoven's Symphony no. 5 in C Minor, op. 67, and Haydn's Symphony no. 94 (*Surprise*).

The theme and its successive variations are sometimes interlocked in a continuous musical flow, without breaks between the individual variations. The *Goldberg Variations* and the variations in the *Surprise*

Antonio del Pollaiuolo: Battle of the Nudes (*c. 1465–70*). *Rosenwald Collection, The National Gallery of Art, Washington, D.C.*

The subject of ten vigorously fighting figures provides the engraver Pollaiuolo with a theme and variations: different views permit the artist to explore in depth his interest in the anatomical stresses involved in human action. The similarity between the stylized background foliage and the stylized hair of the figures unifies the composition while the variation of the poses provides diversion and interest. The precariously leaning figures create a tension that is balanced by the counter-motion of opposing figures. Cover the fourth figure from the right and his opponent appears to topple backward. The individual details are unified by the perfect balance of the composition.

Symphony and Beethoven's Symphony no. 5 are of this type. Other works such as Brahms' *Variations on a Theme by Haydn* and *Enigma Variations* by Sir Edward Elgar (1857–1934) observe a slight pause between most of the variations. Variations are usually identified by number—"variation one," "variation two," and so on.

The theme may be treated in several ways. In the first few variations it may appear unchanged, while the context is varied around it. Successive changes may lead to extensive alteration that makes identification more difficult. Sometimes the theme is only implied—that is, the "theme" may be retained only by harmonic outline. Understanding this form does not depend alone upon a continual awareness of the theme. It depends upon an awareness of what happens to it. It also depends upon the ability to supply the essence of the theme in its absence. The theme in the second movement of Haydn's Symphony no. 94 (*Surprise*) endures and is obvious regardless of the variations. The theme in Brahms' *Variations on a Theme by Haydn* is frequently left to the imagination of the listener—only the variation is present.

A visual illustration using horizontal lines for theme and vertical lines for variation may clarify this principle:

Ex. 7–13

a. Theme:

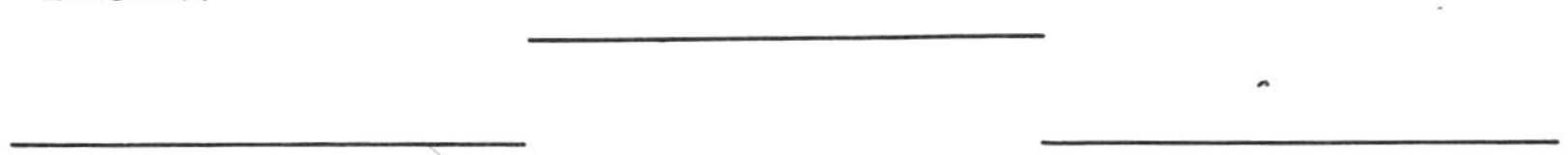

b. Theme with some change:

c. Original theme with variation added:

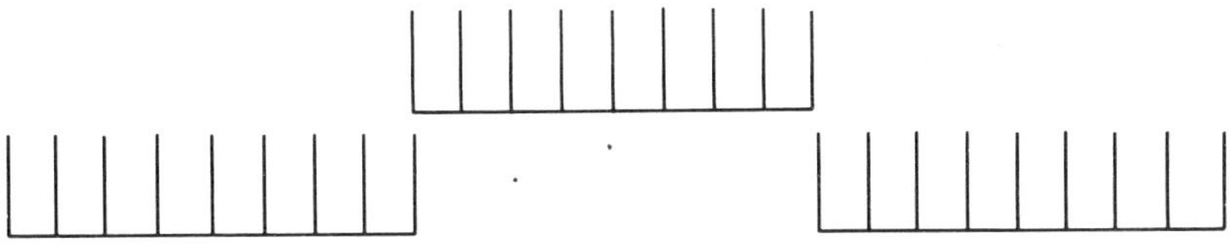

d. Theme from b with same variation:

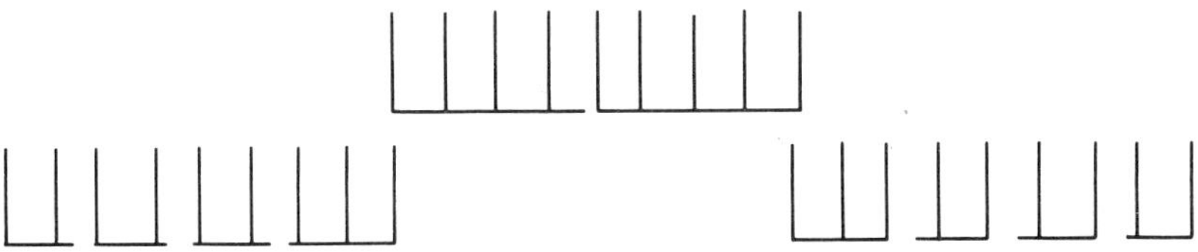

e. Variation alone:

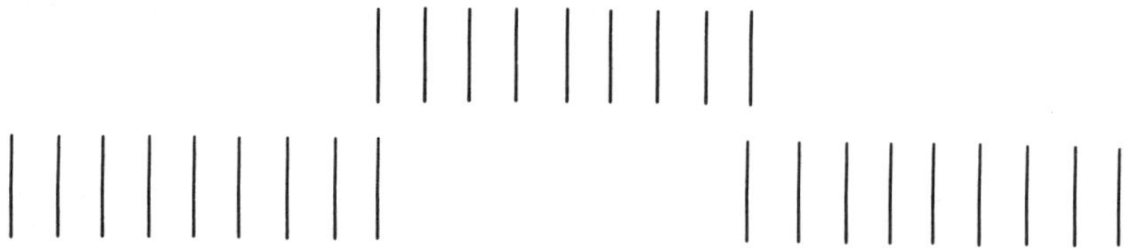

Versions "a" or "b" of the theme can be visually superimposed upon variation "e." The listener can do the same aurally. In listening to a variation in which the theme is implied, the listener can recall the theme and fill it out mentally.

The total pulse of a composition depends upon the various contrasts in degrees of tension created by successive variations. Like the ebb and flow of tension and repose in a play, changes in intensity and the introduction of elements of surprise give life and vigor to musical forms based upon variation. Like the new arrangement of an old popular song, variation forms challenge the innovative capacities of the composer. How many moods can be extracted from one melody? In answering that question, composers draw on all their musical resources and imagination.

GUIDE TO ADDITIONAL LISTENING

Passacaglia and chaconne

1. Johann Sebastian Bach, Passacaglia and Fugue in C for Organ, S. 582 (passacaglia only).
2. Paul Pisk (1893–), *Passacaglia* (1944).

Contrast Bach's use of the ostinato idea with that of Pisk; Bach's organ with Pisk's orchestra.

Chorale prelude

1. Johann Sebastian Bach, "Jesu, Meine Freude," S. 610, from *Orgelbuchlein.*
2. Igor Stravinsky, *Chorale Variations on Bach's "Von Himmel hoch."*

Contrast Bach's chorale prelude with Stravinsky's composition based on a Bach chorale. What elements of the Stravinsky are "Bach-like"? What is contemporary? Does each one express a musical religious experience? How?

Theme and variations

1. Charles Ives, *Variations on "America."*
2. Ulysses Kay (1917–   ), *Fantasy Variations.*

How does Ives vary a familiar tune? How does he express "America"? How does Kay weave a set of variations around the opening theme? How do these vary in style? In technique? How do the themes vary?

3. Listen to the theme of Brahms' *Variations on a Theme by Haydn*, op. 56a. Sing it with the record. When the theme becomes familiar, try singing it while the orchestra is playing variation 1, variation 2, and variation 6.
4. Listen to a record of a Dixieland group playing a well-known tune. Sing the tune in its straightforward version while the performers are playing their variations.
5. Sing "America." Repeat it. Change the rhythm, the tempo, the style. Sing it in a different key.

FOR DISCUSSION

1. Compare one set of variations with another. What does the composer vary each time? Which displays the greater imagination? Which appears to go further afield from the original theme and why?
2. What is the difference between irregularity and variation?
3. How does Truman Capote's novel *In Cold Blood* use the technique of variation? How do row houses in contemporary architecture use variation? When does it succeed? Fail?
4. Why do composers generally choose relatively simple melodies upon which to build their sets of variations?
5. How do theme and variations test the creative powers of the composer?

Imitation and Counterpoint

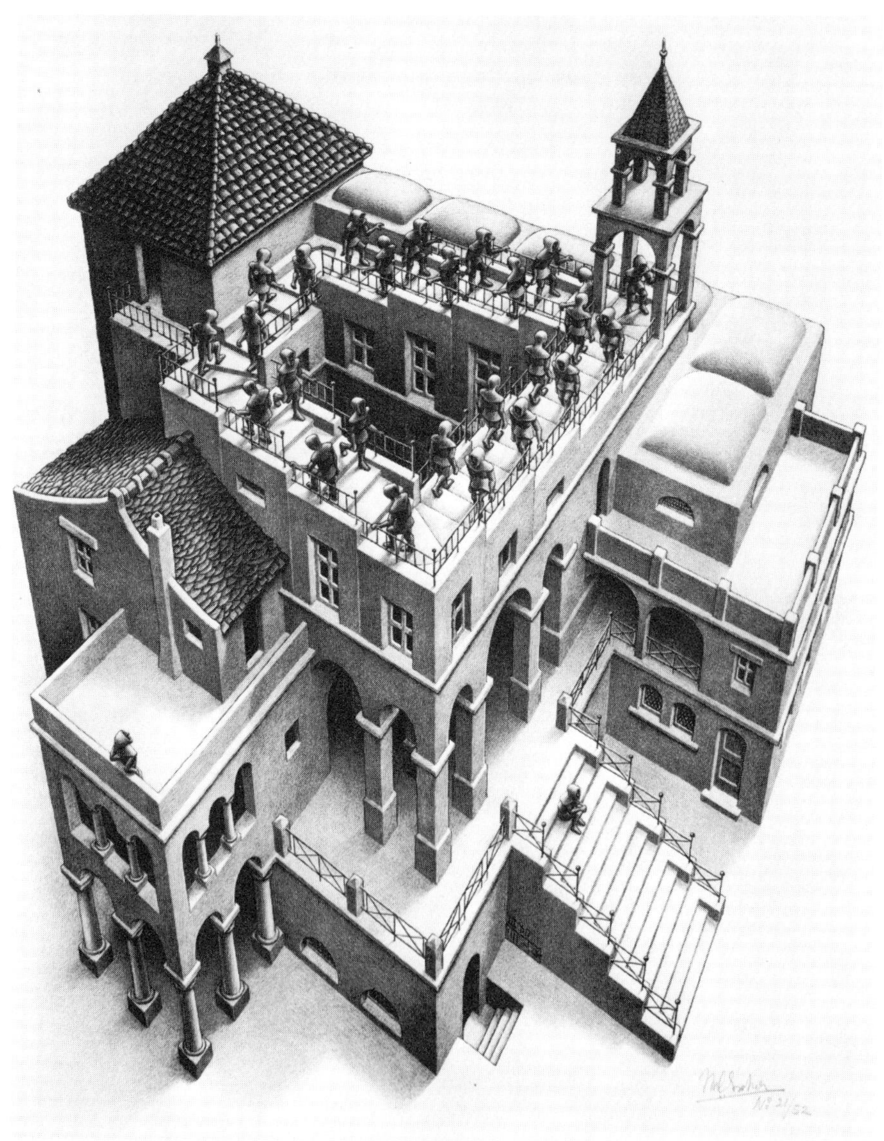

IMITATION

8

Imitation is a type of repetition. It differs from the repetition referred to in Chapter 5 in that the initial statement of the musical idea, called the subject, and subsequent restatements, called answers, are more interconnected. The first answer usually follows immediately at the end of the subject and subsequent answers immediately upon the ending of previous answers, even overlapping. The first statement of the subject is usually monophonic and the answers are of the same musical substance as the subject. The answer or answers and the first statement are usually by different voices, for instance soprano answered by tenor, answered by alto, followed by bass, or flute, answered by clarinet, followed by bassoon. Two or more pitch levels and different keys may be used. The initial subject and its answers form a unit and, in effect, comprise a section of a composition.

M. C. Escher: Ascending and Descending *(1960). Rosenwald Collection, The National Gallery of Art, Washington, D.C.*

Escher, master of his graphic technique, deceives the eye of the viewer. Here the roof is constructed of a continuous stairway with no entrance or exist. One group of monk-like characters follow each other in a continuous procession ascending the stairs, while another group performs the same useless ritual continuously descending the stairs. From one perspective, the stairs themselves appear to be continuously ascending, while from another perspective the stairs appear to be continuously descending. A lone observer (perhaps the artist himself) watches the senseless procession with curiosity.

Imitation as a compositional technique may be used in a relatively small portion of a composition, or comprise the composer's basic structural ingredient. In the following diagram "a," "b," and "c" illustrate the repetition of an idea.

Ex. 8–1

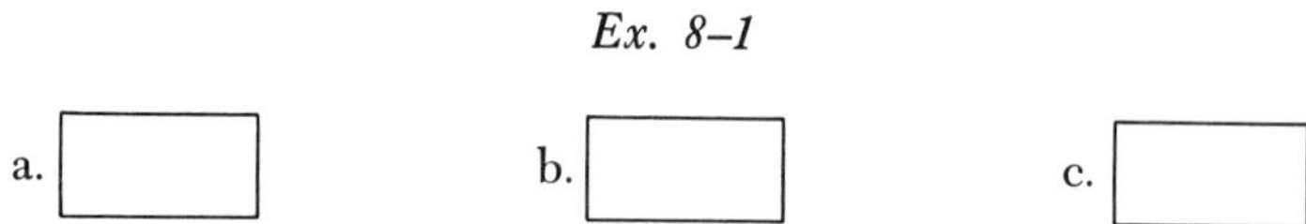

The three parts are alike. They are on the same pitch level, represent the same tone color, and follow one another in follow-the-leader fashion. In the visual illustration of imitation, "a," "b," and "c" are related differently.

Ex. 8–2a

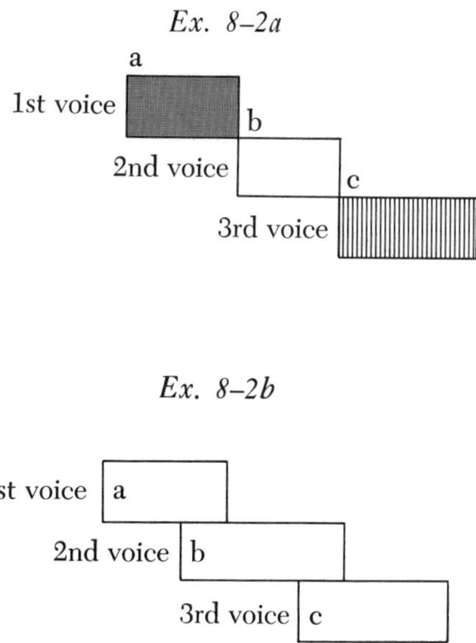

Ex. 8–2b

As one ends, the other begins; they are at different pitch levels and have different tone colors. Note that in Example 8–2b "b" and "c" begin before the subject or previous answer ends, a "telescoping" idea called stretto.

"Three Blind Mice" and "Frère Jacques" are examples of a special type of imitation called a round. All the voices sing the same melody, but their entrances are spaced:

Ex. 8–3

1st voice	A	B	C			
	2nd voice	A	B	C		
		3rd voice	A	B	C	

This round could be repeated *ad infinitum* unless the voices stop as they began: one by one. The example explains why the word round was derived from the Latin word *rota*, meaning wheel. As the various parts of the round overlap, harmony results. Singing the following round will clarify the idea of imitation and demonstrate the melodic interplay and resultant harmony. Superimposing the three lines gives the piece a polyphonic texture.

Round *by Charles Hamm. Photograph by John Froom.*

Students at Northern Illinois University rehearse Round *by Charles Hamm. The music is on a revolving wheel. Each performer plays his part as the music comes into his line of vision.*

Ex. 8–4. English Round: "Hey, Ho! Anybody Home?"

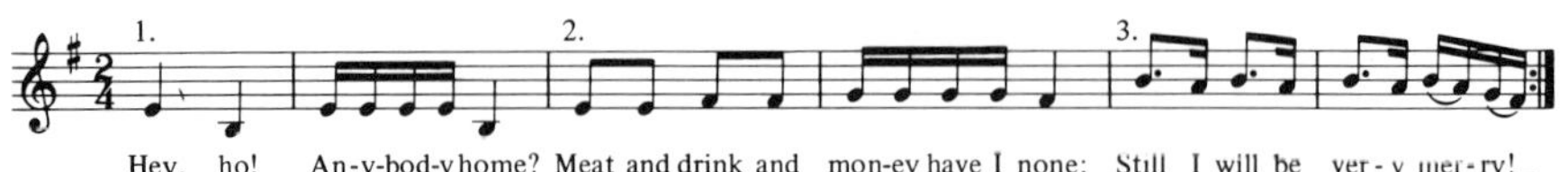

As explained earlier, the term repetition or recurrence refers to blocks of sounds which are separated. Contrasting material may be interjected between theme and subsequent restatements.

Ex. 8–5

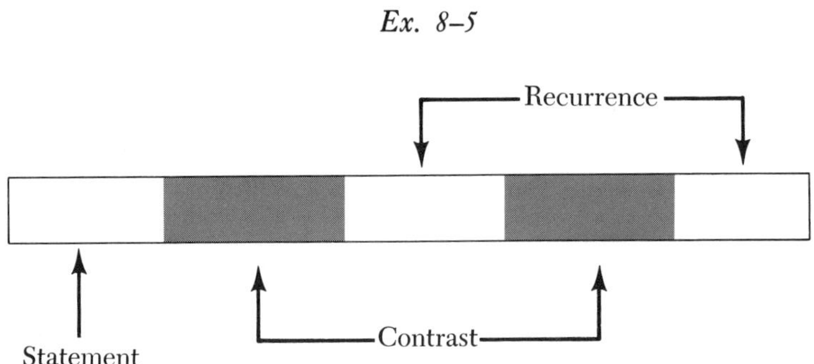

Imitation, however, occurs when the contrasting material appears simultaneously with the subsequent answer. It must, therefore, be related to, or, at least, be tonally compatible with it. The listener can immediately see and hear the unifying effect of this device:

Ex. 8–6

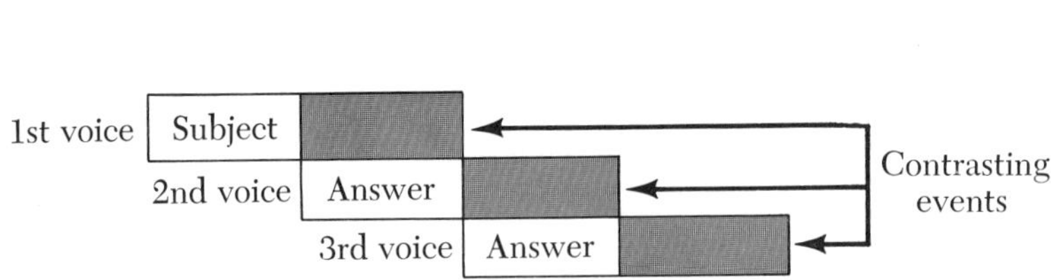

Even with a subject and only two answers the possibilities for variation are already extensive. One possibility follows.

Ex. 8–7

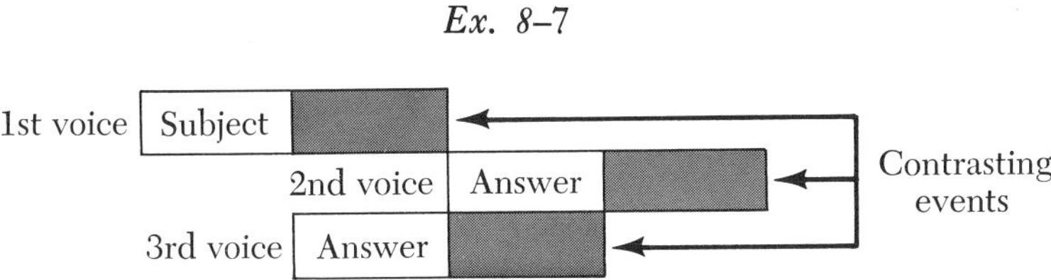

Imitation as a form offers both unity and variety. The only changes in the examples thus far have been in the arrangement. No substantive variation techniques have been used. Imitation, therefore, is a most effective resource; it generates its own variation.

A clear example of imitation resulting from rhythm alone appears in Buggert's *Introduction and Fugue for Percussion and Piano.* A rhythmic subject is stated by the snare drum, answered by the same rhythm on bongo, then by small tom-tom, and finally by large tom-tom.

Ex. 8–8

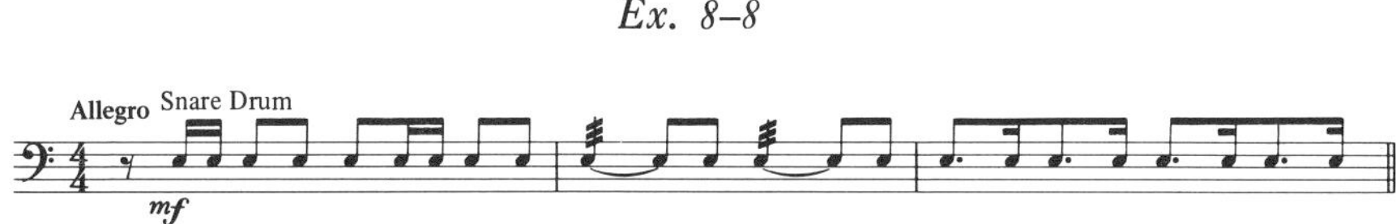

This piece illustrates exact imitation. Except for the changing of instruments the answer is the same as the subject.

Another example of imitation occurs in the beginning of Bach's Two-part Invention no. 8 in F Major:

Ex. 8–9

The pitch level is constant and the imitation exact (although an octave below the original melody) until a break (starting at X and ending at Y in the example) brings the first section of the composition to an end. The original melody then reappears at a new but related pitch level.

Many composers use exact imitation as a unifying device in their compositions. In the second movement of his Symphony no. 7, op. 92, Beethoven rather suddenly introduces a fragment of the first theme in an imitative manner. The subject (see Ex. 5–42) is presented by the first violins (a), answered by the second violins (b), followed by cellos and basses (c), and finally by violas (d).

Ex. 8–10

(a)
Vl. I
pp
Vl. II
pp
Vla.
Vlc.
e Cb.
pp
Vl. I
sempre pp
(b)
Vl. II
sempre pp
Vl. I
sempre pp
Vl. II
Vla.
pp
(c)
arco
Vlc.
e Cb.
pp
Vl. I
Vl. II
(d)
Vla.
sempre pp
Vlc.
e Cb.
sempre pp

The compositions referred to thus far give evidence of exact imitation. However, imitation also encompasses the devices of inversion and retrogression. These two compositional techniques, like other forms of imitation, create cohesion between the parts of a musical composition.

To invert a melody, subject, or motive means to play it upside down: that is, reversing the direction of the pitches used. A short visual example should clarify this technique. Let "a" be the contour of a melodic line; then "b" is its inversion.

Ex. 8–11

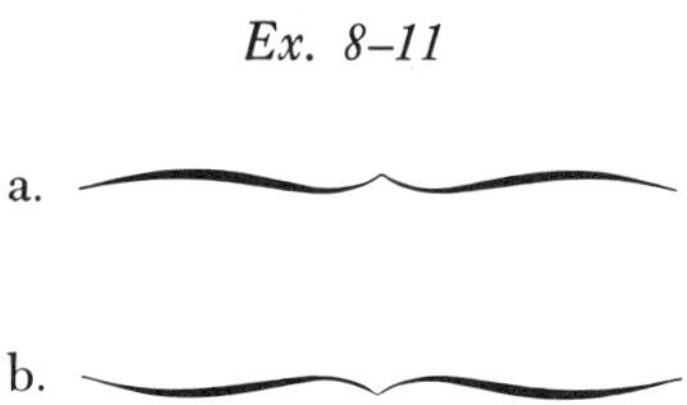

Similarly, "a" is the first phrase of "America"; "b" is its inversion.

Ex. 8–12

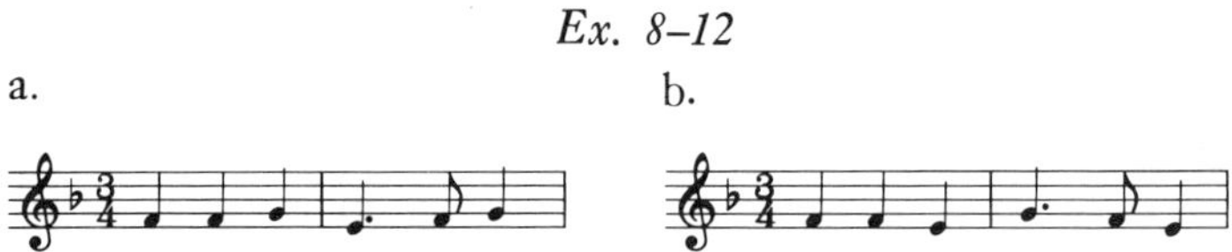

Bach's Two-part Invention no. 1 in C Major demonstrates frequent inversion of the subject.

Ex. 8–13

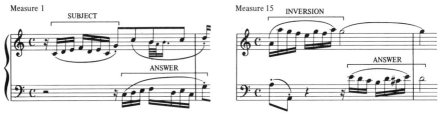

Retrogression is a reversal of order: playing the notes of a melody backwards. Usually only the pitches retrogress and not the rhythmic content, although both may do so.

Ex. 8–14a. "America"

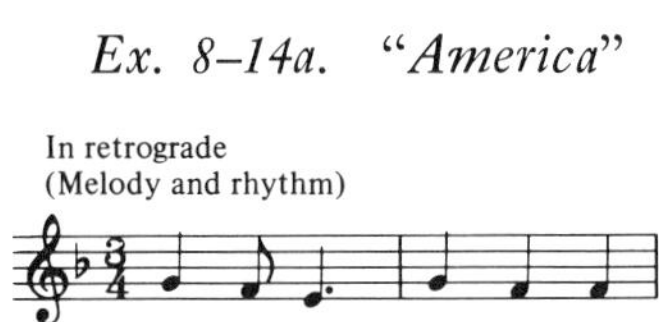

Example 5–34 (Chapter 5) is an example of Stravinsky's use of retrograde (retrogressing) motion. The first eleven notes of this melody are e, c, d, e, f, e♭, d, e♮, c, d, and b; the next eleven (using the last "b" as common to both units) are b, d, c, e, d, e♭, f, e♮, d, c, and e—an exact reversal.

Inversion and retrogression often are not easily recognizable even to the most sophisticated listener. They are, however, a subtle, ingenious, psychological device, unifying and at the same time creating variety. Inversion and retrogression are sometimes used simultaneously. A theme may then occur both upside down and backwards.

Ex. 8–14b. "America"

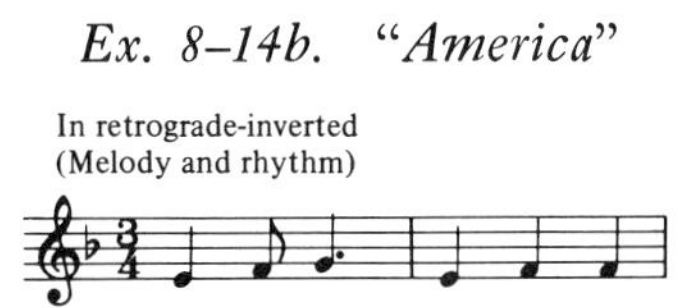

COUNTERPOINT

Counterpoint is the combination of two or more independently moving parts. This independence is usually in terms of melody and rhythm. Although imitation is necessarily contrapuntal, not all counterpoint is imitative. In the coda of Britten's *A Young Person's Guide to the Orchestra* (Chapter 4), Purcell's theme and Britten's fugue subject are played simultaneously, an example of counterpoint without imitation.

One of the most elementary forms of contrapuntal writing is the descant—the addition of a second melody sung or played above the principal melody. Although the descant is usually decorative, it is more than a variation of the principal melody. Sometimes the descant is a reiteration of the melody at a higher pitch level but frequently it amounts to a new supplementary musical idea. Occasionally in solo music for voice, the accompanying medium plays the principal melody while the solo voice presents the descant.

The countermelody is another contrapuntal technique. Countermelodies usually sound below the principal melody. Sousa's "The Stars and Stripes Forever" offers us an excellent example of these techniques. The melody of the trio (the last part of the march) is well known: the piccolo part in the second statement of the melody gives a descant-like effect, and is played above the melody. In the third playing, a strong countermelody is stated by the trombones and baritones. The relationship of the three melodies is illustrated in the following diagram.

Ex. 8–15

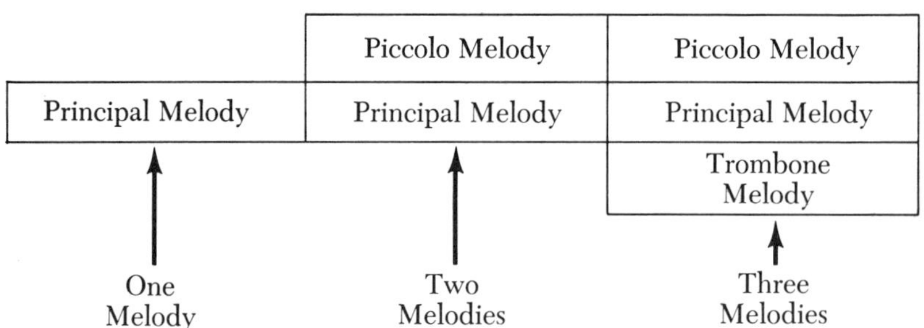

Beethoven's Symphony no. 7, op. 92 (second movement) provides an interesting example of contrapuntal writing, although it is not usually thought of in these terms. The melody that appears after the first complete statement of the opening idea never reappears without the original theme. (See Ex. 7–9.) These themes relate to each other in a contrapuntal manner. The second theme is sometimes subordinate to the first. At other times it assumes primary importance. The themes compete, complement each other, and interact in a manner that makes both of them vital to the movement. This example demonstrates counterpoint in the broader sense: contrasting but compatible forces.

Another less obvious (but possibly more characteristic) technique of counterpoint occurs in much choral writing of the sixteenth century. The motet *Ego sum panis vivus* by William Byrd (1542–1623) demonstrates this technique in which imitation dissolves into a multiple melody.

Ex. 8–16

Each voice has a quality of independence. Collectively, however, the voices produce a coherent whole.

In the following example let ▭ equal an opening imitative figure and 〰 equal a continuing, but independent, melodic line. The beginning of the Byrd work might then be represented:

Ex. 8–17

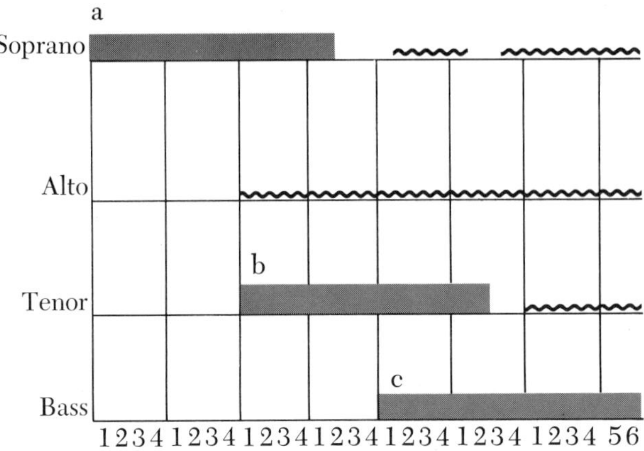

Notice the order of entrance of the voices. Notice also which voices state the opening subject, which voices rest, and which voices are continuous.

CANON AND FUGUE

The two most common musical forms based on imitation are the canon and the fugue. A canon is a contrapuntal form in which all the answers are identical to the subject. The melody is stated by one voice and subsequently imitated (perhaps at a different pitch level) by others. A canon and a round are essentially the same. Rounds, however, are usually simpler, and imitate in unison or at the octave, whereas canons may imitate at the fourth, fifth, or other intervals above or below the original melody.

A canon may be subject to a variety of techniques. A visual design illustrates. Let "a" (blocks 1 through 5) represent a canon melody of five units. Let "b" and "c" represent two additional (but identical) melodies beginning at 3 and 5. The players may repeat each part a number of times and end one by one, or they may break away from the strictness of the imitation in a special coda and end together. The answer parts may also vary. One answer may be inverted, another in retrograde. Or

Ex. 8–18

a.	1	2	3	4	5						
b.			1	2	3	4	5				
c.							1	2	3	4	5

an answer might be in augmentation or in diminution:

Ex. 8–19

<table>
<tr><td>a.</td><td colspan="5">1</td><td colspan="5">2</td><td colspan="5">3</td><td colspan="5">4</td><td colspan="5">5</td><td colspan="5">1</td><td colspan="5">2</td><td colspan="5">3</td><td colspan="5">4</td><td colspan="5">5</td><td></td></tr>
<tr><td>b.</td><td colspan="10">1</td><td colspan="10">2</td><td colspan="10">3</td><td colspan="10">4</td><td colspan="10">5</td><td>½ as fast as (a)</td></tr>
<tr><td>c.</td><td colspan="2">1</td><td colspan="2">2</td><td colspan="2">3</td><td colspan="2">4</td><td colspan="2">5</td><td colspan="2">1</td><td colspan="2">2</td><td colspan="2">3</td><td colspan="2">4</td><td colspan="2">5</td><td colspan="2">1</td><td colspan="2">2</td><td colspan="2">3</td><td colspan="2">4</td><td colspan="2">5</td><td colspan="2">1</td><td colspan="2">2</td><td colspan="2">3</td><td colspan="2">4</td><td colspan="2">5</td><td colspan="2">1</td><td colspan="2">2</td><td colspan="2">3</td><td colspan="2">4</td><td colspan="2">5</td><td>2½ times faster than (a)</td></tr>
</table>

Note that while "a" plays the melody twice,"b" plays it once, and "c" five times.

Benjamin Britten's "This Little Babe" from the *Ceremony of Carols* is an excellent example of canonic writing. The three parts follow each other in such close succession that they give the effect of a multiple echo. (See Ex. 8–20.)

The term canon comes from the fifteenth century when it meant the rule for determining how the second or third parts were to be derived from the first. For example: "Sing the melody an octave lower, entering when the first voice reaches the fifth measure." The technique has fascinated composers and performers for centuries and will probably continue to do so.

The essence of the fugue is the elaboration of a basic musical idea or subject, which is sometimes referred to as the "question." Imitations of the subject are called answers. A contrasting melody juxtaposed against the subject is known as a countersubject. In general these parts form a series of expositions that are connected by "episodes " and finally culmi-

Ex. 8–20

nate in a coda. The expositions are those sections of the composition in which the subject, countersubject, and answers are stated, the episodes are the sections between the expositions, the coda is the closing material. The subject and its answers appear at different related pitch levels or keys in the expositions. When several expositions occur, the pitch levels usually form a contrasting but compatible relationship. The episodes sometimes contain development-like material. They build a transition from one exposition to another. (Development is further discussed in Chapter 9.)

Fugues have been written for almost every medium: chorus, keyboard, orchestra, band, string quartet, and even percussion instruments (rhythmic fugues). Imitation and all the other techniques of contrapuntal writing are used in the fugue.

The design of the statements of the subject and the principal sections of Bach's Fugue in G Minor are shown in Ex. 8–21.

Other fugues often follow a similar structure. No two, however, even by the same composer, follow the same structure exactly. Fugues seem complicated; however, they are not as difficult to hear and under-

Ex. 8–21

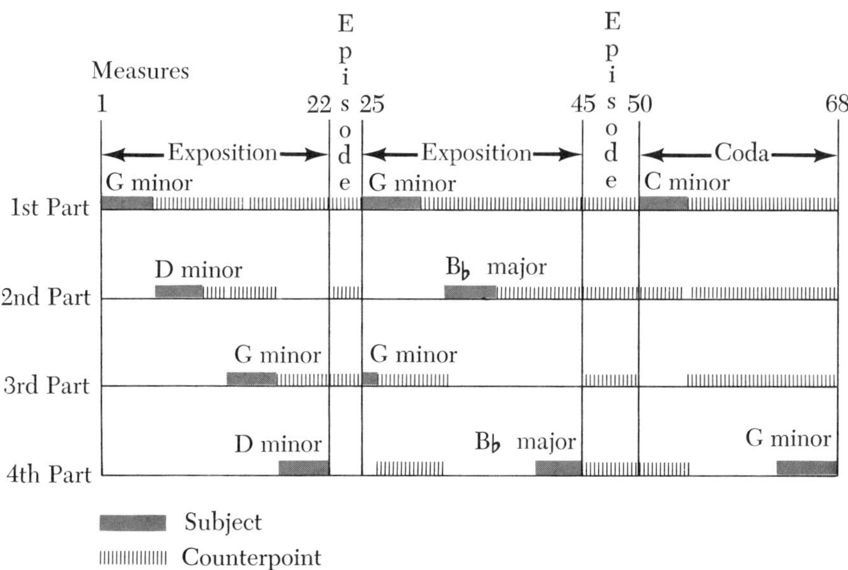

Typical Fugue Structure

Exposition	*E P*	*Exposition*	*E P*	*Exposition and/or Coda*
Principal Pitch Level	*I S O D E*	*Related Pitch Levels*	*I S O D E*	*Principal Pitch Level*

stand as may initially appear. The interweaving of the horizontal melodies requires that the listener know the original subject well in order to identify its entrance in each voice. The richness and inventiveness of the fugue make it one of the most satisfying polyphonic designs. J. S. Bach is the unexcelled champion of the form. His forty-eight preludes and fugues of the *Well-Tempered Clavier* and his *Art of the Fugue* are among his major works and demonstrate his mastery. For the listener they provide endless hours of intrigue for ear and mind. In Bach's fugues interrelationships and coherence triumph.

GUIDE TO ADDITIONAL LISTENING

Canzona

1. Giovanni Gabrieli, Canzona per sonar a Quattro, no. 4.
2. Girolamo Frescobaldi (1583–1643), (a) "Canzona prima," (b) "Canzona seconda," (c) "Canzona terza," for brass, harpsichord, and organ.

Observe the different sections of the Gabrieli canzona. Each begins with an imitation. How many voices enter? Contrast with the more sophisticated fugue form. Note also the nature of the contrapuntal writing where imitation is not prevalent. How does the style of Gabrieli differ from that of Frescobaldi?

Two-part and three-part inventions

1. Johann Sebastian Bach, Invention no. 1 from *Fifteen Two-part Inventions.*
2. Johann Sebastian Bach, Invention no. 1 from *Three-part Inventions* (sinfonias).

Observe the similarities and differences of these two works. Recordings on both harpsichord and piano are available. Compare the expression on each.

Fugue

1. Johann Sebastian Bach, Chromatic Fantasia and Fugue in D Minor.

2. Franz Liszt, Fantasia and Fugue on B.A.C.H.
3. Wolfgang Amadeus Mozart, "Introit and Kyrie," from Requiem Mass in D Minor.
4. Jaromir Weinberger (1896–1967), "Polka and Fugue," from *Schwanda the Bagpiper.*

Observe the length of the subject in the Bach. Liszt's subject is based on the tones B flat, A, C, and B natural. (The Germans call B Flat "B", and B Natural "H".) Compare the freedom of the fantasia sections with the structural formality of the fugue sections. The Mozart "Kyrie" is a fugue based on two themes. Note the vitality of Weinberger's fugue subject.

Canon

1. Johann Sebastian Bach, *A Canonic Variation-Series on the Christmas Tune "Von Himmel hoch, da komm' ich her,"* S. 769.
2. César Franck, Sonata in A Major for Violin and Piano, fourth movement ("Allegretto poco mosso").
3. Wallingford Riegger (1885–1961), Canon and Fugue in D Minor for Strings.

Listen to the sequence of events. Notice the reversals in Franck. At the beginning the piano precedes the violin—later the piano answers the violin.

FOR DISCUSSION

1. How does imitation structure a composition?
2. An early form of the canon in France is called a *chace* (chasse). The term is derived from the word for hunt, or chase. Discuss.
3. The word canon also means a law or rule. Discuss.
4. Construct a visual canon; a visual fugue.
5. Sing several rounds with a group. Alter some of the answers by augmentation, diminution.

Improvisation and Contrast

9

Improvisation and chance are forms of musical variation in which some creative decisions are left to the performer. They depend upon spontaneity in performance. Composers may indicate guidelines or give instructions, but the final choice is made by the performer. Although improvisation and chance are designed to be spontaneous, some decisions may be the result of previous planning and study by the performer. For example, in an improvisation which requires the performer to choose an instrument, the need for planning is obvious. Improvisation and chance allow deviation from a stereotyped reproduction and permit each performance to be, at least in part, an original creation. It is unlikely that any two performances will be the same. They may be similar but are often markedly different.

IMPROVISATION IN JAZZ AND POPULAR MUSIC

Improvisation is most apparent and accessible, for the majority of listeners, in jazz, popular dance music, and folk music.

The term jazz, in the broad generic sense, includes music of the early part of the century called ragtime and blues, styles originating in

Alexander Calder: Lobster Trap and Fish Tail *(1939). The Museum of Modern Art, New York.*

Balance is the essential element of the mobile. The form is calculated to change with the breeze in the room. These fish appear to float. Their shapes are repeated with slight variation. Both the repetition of the basic forms and the movement of these forms in time constitute the rhythm of the sculpture. The work is not just three-dimensional like most sculpture, but four. It undergoes continual alteration within the dimension of time. Calder's mobiles demonstrate chance rhythms and chance forms. The shadow play of Lobster Trap and Fish Tail *permits an infinite number of arrangements. Like chance music, one's interest in such works never becomes static. This unpredictable quality is an essential part of a mobile's perpetual fascination.*

Chicago and New Orleans called Dixieland, "big band" renditions of the 1930s usually referred to as swing, the music of the small jazz combos, popular dance music, and the stylized development referred to as progressive jazz. The influence of jazz is also apparent in some of the longer works of such composers as Gershwin, Copland, Stravinsky, Hindemith, and Gunther Schuller.

Ragtime, popular in the early 1900s, was performed by a small ensemble of instruments, most often piano, banjo, trumpet or cornet, clarinet, and drums. Although many groups frequently played the same tunes, each group sounded different because of the individual style of the performers. Given a basic rhythmic pattern, harmonic pattern, and an original melody, the players improvised. Ragtime was also performed by soloists, principally on piano and banjo. Typical of the syncopated style is "Maple Leaf Rag" by the American composer Scott Joplin (1868–1917), whose music is presently commanding a long-deserved revival.

Dixieland jazz is another style in which improvisation plays an important, if not a major, role. A Dixieland combo is usually composed of piano, banjo, clarinet, trumpet (cornet), trombone, tuba or string-bass, and drums. The music, again based upon rhythmic, melodic, and harmonic guidelines, allows the players a broad range of improvisation. Typically, a composition begins with an introduction followed by a chorus (one complete statement of the melody). One instrument plays the "lead" while the others improvise a subordinate accompaniment. In subsequent choruses each player improvises his own "solo version" for a portion or all of a chorus. After all of the players have had their "solo," they all join in a final chorus. This final chorus, in which everyone improvises, is a sort of "grand finale" and, with good performers, becomes an example of intricate contrapuntal improvisation. Following are several representative long play recordings including ragtime, blues, and Dixieland jazz:*

1. Jelly Roll Morton: *Hot Jazz, Stomps & Joys.*
2. Pearl Bailey: *Birth of the Blues.*
3. Eddy Peabody: *On Stage* (a two-volume album).

* For detailed information refer to the current *Schwann Long Playing Record Catalog.* Editions are available in most libraries, music stores, and record shops.

4. Dukes of Dixieland: *Live at Bourbon Street.*
5. Pete Fountain: *New Orleans at Midnight.*

In the 1930s and 40s the "big band" and "swing" sound became popular. Bands were typically composed of five saxophones, four or five trumpets, three or four trombones, one or two pianos, a string bass, guitar, and drums. Each band usually included two solo singers—one male and one female. Each group developed its own unique style. These bands used complex, highly stylized arrangements, and improvisation was not as much a part of their music as it was of Dixieland music. The soloist, however, did improvise for a chorus or portion of a chorus or, in some instances, for longer periods. These improvisations became part of the style of the band. Performers became well known for their particular style of improvisation. They extemporaneously applied unique rhythmic devices, offered their own melodic embellishments, or employed their individual patterns of harmonization. Listen to the individual sound of the group and the improvisatory quality of the soloists.

1. Duke Ellington: *Ellington Era*, vol. 1 & 2.
2. Benny Goodman: *Carnegie Hall Jazz Concert.*
3. Louis Armstrong: *Satchmo at Symphony Hall.*
4. Gene Krupa: *Let Me Off Uptown.*
5. Glenn Miller: *Carnegie Hall Concert.*

Small combos developed either independently or within the framework of the big band. The small bands improvised more than the big bands, and their success was more directly related to the performance style of each individual. Trios, quartets, and quintets of many different instrumental combinations came into existence. They played the most popular dance tunes, but always in their own style.

The following provide examples of such combos.

1. Dave Brubeck: *At Carnegie Hall, Countdown.*
2. Art Van Damme: *Septet.*

"King" Oliver's Creole Jazz Band. Chicago (c. 1923).

"King" Oliver center front; Louis Armstrong, center rear; Lil Hardin (Armstrong) at the piano. The group played an improvised New Orleans style of jazz. Armstrong's artistry on trumpet helped legitimatize jazz as a popular art form.

3. Gene Krupa: *Great New Quartet.*
4. Miles Davis Quintet: *Miles Smiles.*
5. Herbie Mann: *Bonga (sic), Conga, and Flute, Standing Ovation at Newport.*
6. The Modern Jazz Quartet: *Under the Jasmine Tree.*

To sense the originality that improvisation requires, compare familiar songs with the different interpretations in these albums:

1. Mills Brothers: *Ten Years of Hits.*
2. Nat "King" Cole: *This Is Nat "King" Cole.*
3. Ella Fitzgerald: *Best of Ella.*
4. Diahann Carroll: *Nobody Sees Me.*
5. Leslie Uggams: *Time to Love.*

Popular dance music varies in style from the arrangements of Lawrence Welk to the ever changing innovations of rock-and-roll. Improvisation is used in most of these performances. In many of the recorded performances of groups such as the Beatles, the "arrangements" are improvised in the recording studio.

Less well known to most listeners are the improvisatory techniques of non-Western music. Indian music is currently better known in the United States because of the popularity of Ravi Shankar and Ali Akbar Khan. Three instruments are usually used in Indian music: the *sitar* or *sarod* (stringed instruments), the *tamboura* (a drone instrument), and the *tabla* (a pair of tuned drums). The music is based on *raga*, a framework for generating melody, and *tala*, a framework for generating rhythm. The alternation accelerates until an exciting climax is developed by improvisatory dialogue.

Improvisation in the popular idiom offers an opportunity to the performer for virtuoso display. Because the musician is both performer and composer, the vocal technique of a Sarah Vaughn or the instrumental pyrotechnics of a Jimi Hendrix are exploited to the fullest. For the listener, the result is a spontaneous, exciting communication tailored to the moment. The musicianship required for such expression demands an originality and creative immediacy often lacking in the classical realm, where the performer is generally restricted to the notes printed on the page.

IMPROVISATION IN THE CONCERT HALL

Present-day performances of Baroque music include little or no spontaneous improvisation. However, in performances of the period (1600–1750) both keyboard performers and soloists improvised. Accompaniments for keyboard instruments were left incomplete but were suggested by a series of numbers called "figured" or "thoroughbass." Bass and melody were outlined and the harpsichord player completed the accompaniment on the basis of the harmonic indications provided by numbers. Melodic lines were often written in an unembellished manner and the keyboard soloist was expected to improvise a pattern of ornamentation.

Like much of the jazz, popular, and rock-and-roll music of the twentieth century, the notated score and the performance score in Baroque music did not coincide. "The notation," Bukofzer says, "presented merely a skeletal outline of the composition; its structural contour had to be filled in, realized, and possibly ornamented by an extemporizing performer." Soloists singing lead roles in operatic performances were afforded the opportunity to display their technical facility by improvising on repeated melodic passages. They also improvised flourishes just before the end of an aria. These penultimate improvisations were called *cadenzas*. Cadenzas became common for instrumental soloists as well.

Bach's *Musical Offering* is an example of the major role played by improvisation in Baroque music. This group of pieces, which includes two fugues, several canons, and a sonata for flute, violin, and harpsichord, was composed around a theme written by Frederick the Great of Prussia. Bach's elaboration of the theme originated as a spontaneous improvisation in Potsdam. Upon his return to Leipzig, Bach wrote down and revised his improvisations, dedicating the finished work to the king.

"Practical" editions have eliminated the need for present-day performers to improvise Baroque music. Editors have "completed" the works left "incomplete" by the composers. A detailed discussion of the values and shortcomings of these editions is, however, beyond the scope of this book.

Improvised cadenzas in instrumental concertos continued for some time, but other forms of improvisation fell into disuse during the eighteenth and nineteenth centuries. However, as improvisation became prominent in jazz and other associated forms, it attracted the attention of twentieth-century composers of concert music. The revitalization of improvisation brought with it greater performer freedom. Composer and performer become more closely interrelated. Performers are called upon to create in addition to recreating, while composers are becoming more involved with performance. In his article "The Changing Composer-Performer Relationship," the contemporary American composer

Lukas Foss, in whose works improvisation sometimes plays an important role, cites several composer-performer teams experimenting in what he calls "a joint enterprise in new music."

Foss also discusses "essential" and "nonessential" notation. In a fast run of notes that moves from low to high and back again, the outermost notes may be essential, while the "intermediate notes may, under certain circumstances (tempo, style) be unessential:"

Ex. 9–1

Foss believes that in this variety of notation "there is immediate clarity regarding the important low and high notes." The intermediary notes need not be carefully delineated. Foss maintains that this type of sketchy notation "actually clarifies."

In the example above the performer is given the responsibility for the final formulation of the run. Nevertheless, the end result is to a large degree controlled by the composer. Sometimes composers leave even more to chance. In his *Tempi Concertati*, Luciano Berio uses the term "tutta" to indicate that the percussionist is to strike all his instruments as fast as possible. If such an effect were to be notated, it would lose its spontaneous feeling and become studied and pedantic. The element of chance permits the effect to be one of abandonment, of eruption.

Improvisation is a challenge to the performer, and not merely the freedom to do anything he wishes. The improvisation must be compatible with the overall composition. The adept improviser will use one criterion for ragtime, another for "big-band" jazz, and still another for Dixieland. Concert hall improvisation is not the "cup of tea" of the majority of present-day professional musicians in symphony orchestras, string quartets, and other classical performing mediums. Younger musicians, for instance those associated with performing groups at Columbia University, the University of Illinois, and University of Chicago, are, however, adept in performing music in this contemporary idiom.

CHANCE MUSIC

Chance or aleatory music is music in which some element of a "happening" takes place. The result is not predetermined but depends upon what "happens" during the performance. For example, some modern music may call for a radio as one of the instruments. If so, whatever is being broadcast at the time of performance becomes part of the composition. Audience participation may also be part of a performance and each audience will respond differently. As in improvised performances, decisions are relegated to the performer. Chance music and improvisation may overlap and exist simultaneously. Chance music may also, however, include no elements of improvisation.

Chance music may give the performer a choice of instruments. This technique is seen in a number of percussion compositions, for example Feldman's *King of Denmark* (for solo percussionist). No instruments are specifically indicated. Feldman's first statement in the performance instructions is:

> Graphed High, Middle and Low . . . The top line or slightly above the top line, very high.
>
> The bottom line or slightly beneath, very low.

With the quantity of percussion instruments available the number of options given the performer is obvious.

The notation is graph-like rather than traditional.

Ex. 9–2

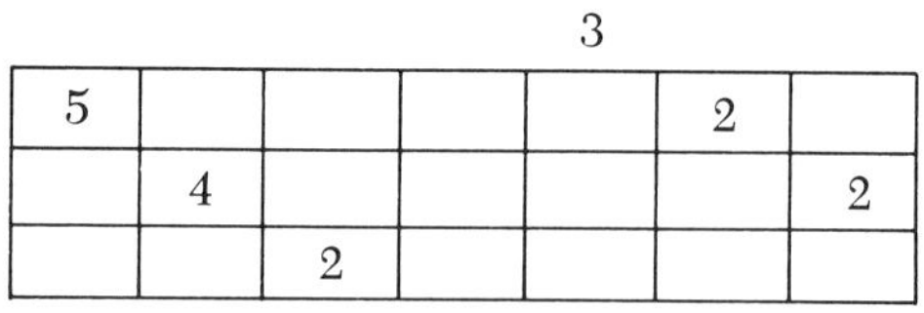

				3		
5					2	
	4					2
		2				

(This illustration is not directly from Feldman's work. It does, nevertheless, demonstrate the principle.) The vertical lines represent a span of time, in this case, somewhat less than a second. The horizontal lines represent the relative pitch of the instruments. The numbers represent the number of notes to be played in that span of time on the instrument selected. The above notation would be interpreted:

5 notes on a high sounding percussion instrument;

4 notes on a medium sounding percussion instrument;

2 notes on a low sounding percussion instrument;
a short silence;

3 notes on a very high sounding percussion instrument;

2 notes on a high sounding percussion instrument;

2 notes on a medium sounding percussion instrument.

No specific rhythm is indicated. The relationship of the 5 to the 4 to the 2 are left for the performer to decide.

Another form of chance music gives the performer the choice of selecting the order of the sections in a multisectional work. Let the following represent a composition with five parts:

Ex. 9–3a

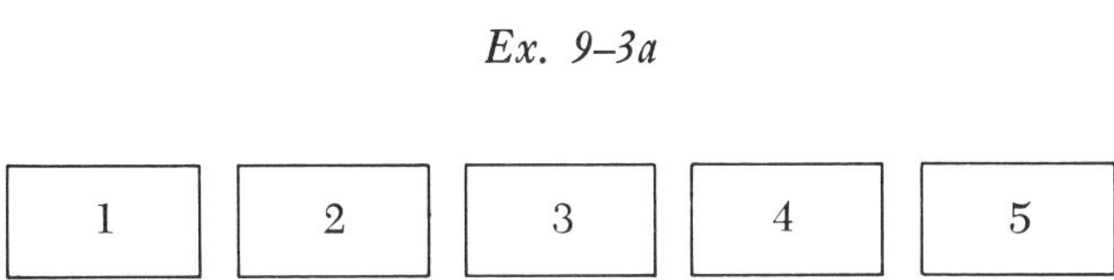

The composer indicates that the performer may begin with any section and proceed in either direction. He may, for example, begin with three, play four, five, one, and end with two: or, he may play three, two, one, five, and end with four.

Ex. 9–3b

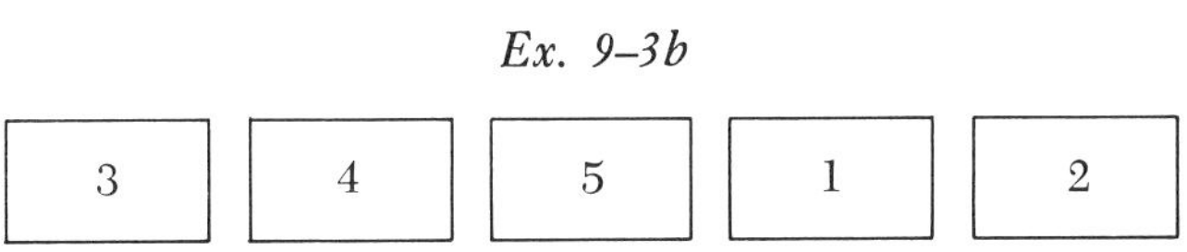

Ex. 9–3c

3	2	1	5	4

The tempo in sectional pieces may also be left to chance, or partly to chance. For instance the performer may receive instructions to begin in the style, speed, dynamics of his choice. Following the first section are the instructions, "loud, very slow, rugged," which apply to the next section. This process of instructions continues. The following example illustrates.

Section 1: Play in style of your choice.
Play next section loud, very slow, rugged.

Section 2: Played loud, very slow, rugged.
Next section soft, moderate speed, delicate.

Section 3: Played soft, moderate speed, delicate.
Next section as fast and furious as possible.

Section 4: Played as fast and furious as possible.
Next section calm.

Section 5: Played calm.
Next section performer's choice.

In general, the composer does not expect the order of such works to be preplanned. It should be spontaneous and extemporaneous at the time of performance. Suppose then, the performer plays section one, followed by three, five, two, and ends with four. The order chosen by the performer affects the style with which any portion of the work will be performed.

The following chart illustrates the different styles which result from a particular order of sequence. Notice that the two performances are different—unlike traditional music, where tempo and expressive markings remain unchanged.

Improvisation and chance imply experimentation. Many contemporary artists wish to try something new. New sounds are gathered and explored for their expression. Harry Partch (1901–   ) (see page 37)

Performance 1	*Performance 2*
1. Performer's choice	*1. Performer's choice*
2. Loud, very slow, rugged	*3. Loud, very slow, rugged*
3. Soft, moderate speed, delicate	*5. As fast and furious as possible*
4. As fast and furious as possible	*2. Performer's choice*
5. Calm	*4. Soft, moderate speed, delicate*

is foremost among these experimenters. Partch has divided the octave minutely into 43 intervals, and invented many instruments to play all these pitches. Among his instruments are marimba-like giant bamboo reeds called boos, 72-string kitharas, an altered organ called a chormelodeon, "bloboys" which employ bellows, a "marimba eroica" made from sawed off glass vats, and a 1912 auto exhaust pipe. According to Martin Bernheimer of the Los Angeles *Times*, Partch easily justifies his unorthodox approach: "The notion that there must be a standard pattern of tonal belief (the piano scale), of behavioral belief (the concert), even of dress belief (tie and tails), without which music would cease to exist, is a crag so monstrous that it blots out vision."

The combinations of sounds available to imaginative composers with notated music are almost limitless. However, when the composer and performer combine as a team and add improvisation and chance, the potential is even further expanded.

As with most creative endeavors, old or new, redundant or innovative, arguments have been made for and against the uses of improvisation and chance. The final evaluation, however, lies in the quality of the final product. When the composer "abdicates" certain responsibilities and gives these to the performer, the creativeness of the performer may become as important as the creativeness of the composer.

Aleatory music opens up new possibilities for musical expression. The performer is asked to enter into the composition in a highly personal way. Brock McElheran's *Patterns in Sound* is a good example.

Ex. 9–4. McElheran: "Etude" and "Scherzo" from Patterns in Sound.

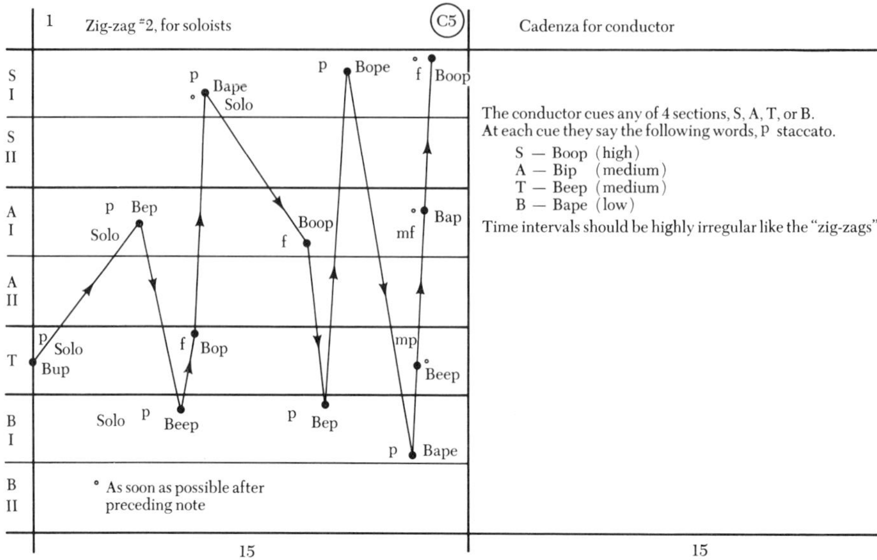

1
Zig-zag #2, for soloists
C5
Cadenza for conductor
S I
S II
A I
A II
T
B I
B II
p Bape Solo
p Bope
f Boop
p Bep Solo
Boop f
mf Bap
p Solo Bup
f Bop
mp
Beep
Solo p Beep
p Bep
p Bape
° As soon as possible after preceding note
The conductor cues any of 4 sections, S, A, T, or B.
At each cue they say the following words, p staccato.
S — Boop (high)
A — Bip (medium)
T — Beep (medium)
B — Bape (low)
Time intervals should be highly irregular like the "zig-zags"
15
15

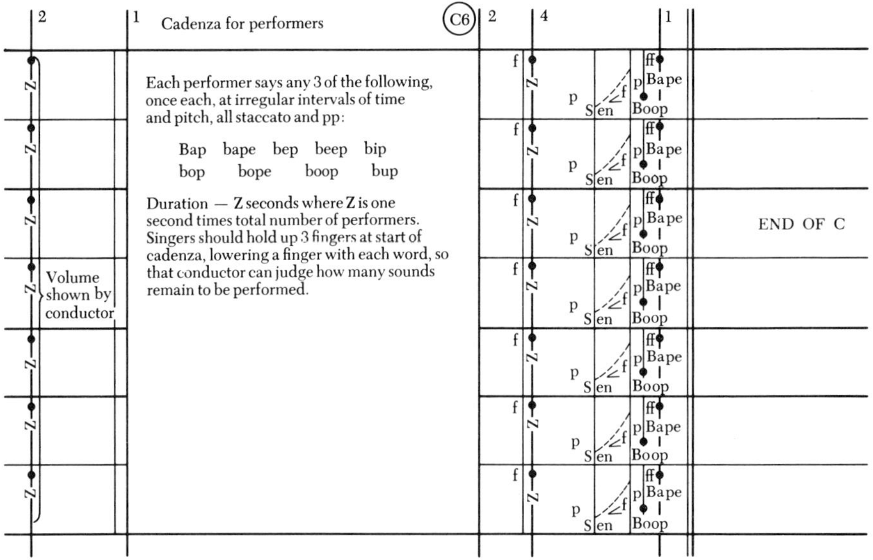

2
1
Cadenza for performers
C6
2
4
1
Volume shown by conductor
Each performer says any 3 of the following, once each, at irregular intervals of time and pitch, all staccato and pp:
Bap bape bep beep bip
bop bope boop bup
Duration — Z seconds where Z is one second times total number of performers. Singers should hold up 3 fingers at start of cadenza, lowering a finger with each word, so that conductor can judge how many sounds remain to be performed.
f
p
Sen
ff
p Bape
Boop
END OF C

In making new demands, composers have had to invent new symbols to indicate to performers the nature and bounds of their inventiveness. Each piece of aleatory music must be viewed on its own terms. The musical symbols are often original and, therefore, nonstandardized. Once the symbols are understood, the performer can begin to invent according to the outlines and suggestions of the composer. The freshness and challenge of this approach to musical expression provide unique rewards to both performer and listener.

GUIDE TO ADDITIONAL LISTENING

Improvisation

Group A

1. Lukas Foss (1922–), Improvised Interlude no. 1, from *Time Cycle.*
2. Gunther Schuller, *Concertino for Jazz Quartet and Orchestra,* second movement (passacaglia).
3. Leonard Bernstein (1918–), Improvisation no. 1, from *Four Improvisations for Orchestra.*

How do the styles differ? Compare the small combo in *Time Cycle* with the quartet plus orchestra in Schuller's concertino, and Bernstein's full symphony orchestra.

Group B

1. Fletcher Henderson's recording of "Copenhagen," from the album *Big Bands Before 1935* (Folkways Records #2808).
2. Duke Ellington's recording of "Don't Get Around Much Anymore," from the album *The Indispensable Duke Ellington.*
3. Coleman Hawkins' recording of "How Deep Is the Ocean," from the album *Encyclopedia of Jazz on Records,* vol. 2.

Compare the overall sound, and contrast the divergent improvisatory styles.

Group C

1. John Mayall's Blues Breakers, *Bare Wires.*
2. The Beatles, *Sergeant Pepper's Lonely Hearts Club Band.*

3. Cream, *Wheels of Fire.*

How do these groups achieve an individuality of style? A uniqueness?

Chance

1. Morton Feldman, *The King of Denmark.*

Rhythms and instruments are not specifically notated. Is it possible to be certain of this by listening?

2. Luciano Berio, *Circles.*

This piece is based on a poem by e. e. cummings and is composed for voice, harp, and percussion.

3. John Cage, *Aria with Fontana Mix.*

This work is actually two compositions, one superimposed on the other. The final recording is synthesized from several tapes. The instructions are read from transparency overlays.

Each of the above three works sounds different with each performance.

FOR DISCUSSION

1. Listen to several jazz groups perform the same selection. Compare their manner of improvisation.
2. Compare the vocal style of Nat "King" Cole to Frank Sinatra's. Considering the improvisatory character, interpretation, and rhythmic feeling.
3. Listen to Leonard Bernstein's record *What Is Jazz?* Discuss.
4. Compare the improvisatory solo drumming styles of Gene Krupa, Buddy Rich, Joe Morello, and Ginger Baker.
5. Form a group of four people. Carry out an improvisatory conversation and record it. Then, with one person at the piano, one with some percussion instruments, one using his voice and one narrating, improvise music to reflect the conversation.
6. Record on tape several divergent sounds at different speeds (for example, laughing, brushing teeth, air drill, dog barking). Rerecord them on another tape recorder using a faster or

slower playback speed. By splicing the tapes, construct a single tape demonstrating how these sounds might be mixed and altered by such recording/playback devices.

7. What problems result when a composer allows a performer some freedom? What benefits result?
8. A chance composition could be developed by using calendar dates, dice, playing cards, or license plate numbers. Experiment with the possibilities.
9. Discuss the innovations of new performing personalities as they become popular in concert, on television, or on record.

Development and the Sonata-Allegro Form

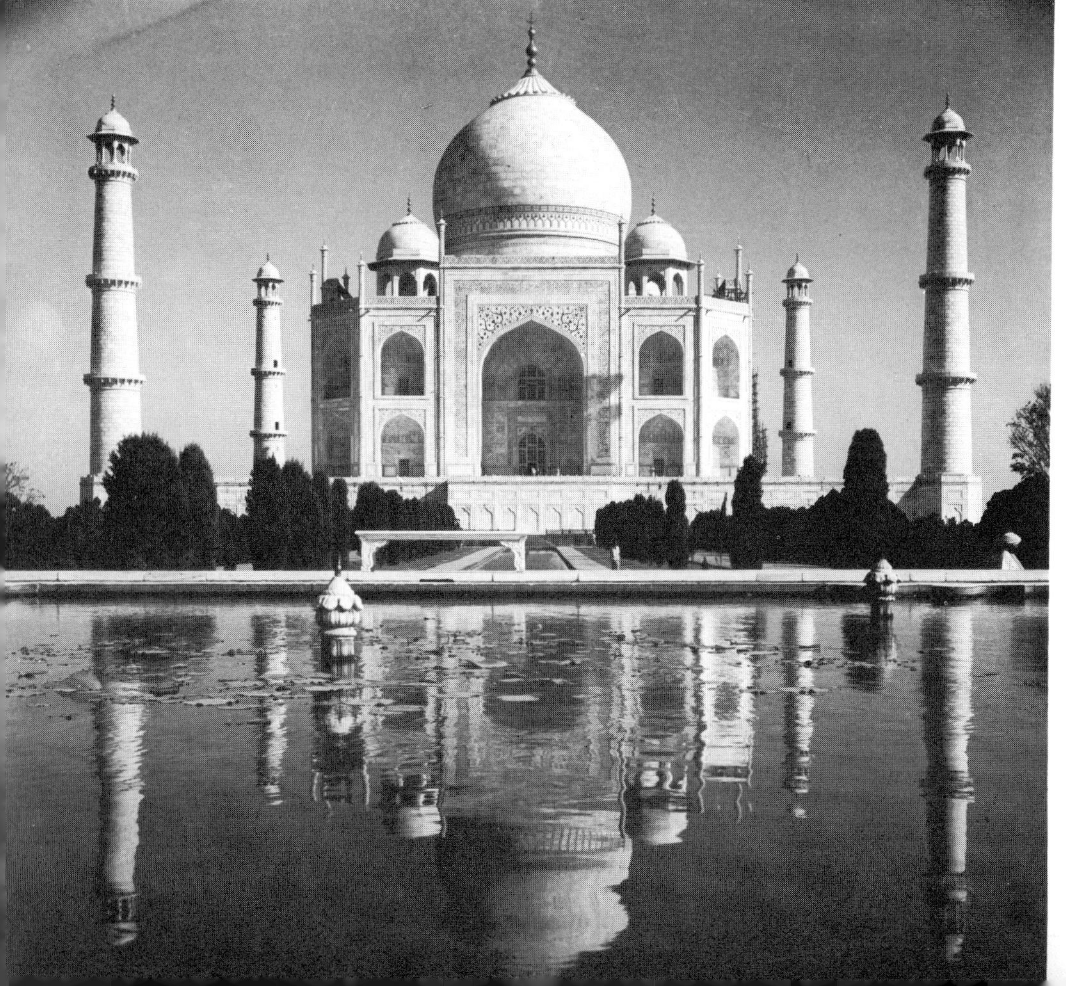

10

The importance of an initial musical statement often depends upon its subsequent treatment. Like an historical event, the musical idea takes on meaning as its effect on other events becomes known. As more is revealed about it, the musical idea assumes greater authority. If it is repeated or if it recurs after digression, its significance is increased by the process of reinforcement. If it is subjected to variation and imitation, its significance is increased by providing a new context or musical environment.

A composer may wish to treat his initial musical ideas in further ways. He could find himself in a role similar to a novelist or playwright. Through the actions and reactions of a character revealed in different contexts and situations, the playwright develops his character, until at the end of the play, the audience feels they know him thoroughly and have sympathy for his behavior. This expanded treatment of various personality characteristics is similar to the way a composer may wish to develop his musical ideas, the principal "characters" in his "play." Such exploitation of thematic material requires more than the techniques of repetition, recurrence, imitation, and variation. It demands a process called development.

DEVELOPMENT

A number of terms are used to define the process of development: "exploitation," "working-out," "motivic play," "manipulation," "transformation," and "fragmentation" are some of these. However, development defies accurate and thorough definition by words alone. It must be heard to be understood.

The Taj Mahal (c. 1634). Agra, India.

Called the most exquisite tomb in the world, the Taj Mahal is basically a simple, symmetrical design enhanced by intricate ornamentation. Balance is integral to the design. The relationship of the parts is imaginative yet ordered. The central dome presents a dynamic contrast to the whole, yet it is carefully controlled in relation to the other, smaller domes that repeat each other on the sides. The vast central arch is also repeated in miniature. Unity disciplines each individualization.

Development depends on several composition techniques, many of which relate to variation and are already familiar to the listener. However, the exploitation of thematic material is different. Alterations are compounded and substantive, affecting the structure as well as the rhythmic and tonal stability of a musical idea. Themes may be restructured and rebuilt, or divided into motivic components that are presented in a variety of instrumental textures and keys. The listener's ability to predict is challenged. Examples 10–1 to 10–6 demonstrate some basic techniques of development.

1. *Fragmentation of motives:* Frequently a composer will use only a portion of a motive or melody. Recall a familiar melody. Think of it in terms of its first few notes, and then recall a different group of notes from some other portion of the melody. A dialogue between these two units gives the essence of a development.

Ex. 10–1a. "America," measure 1

Ex. 10–1b. "America," measure 11

Ex. 10–1c. "America," dialogue between measures 1 and 11

2. *Alteration of pitch:* Constant pitch change is frequently a characteristic of development. Again, recall a familiar melody. Extract a motive and repeat this motive at differ-

ent pitch levels. The result gives the feeling of development.

Ex. 10–2. "America," measure 1

Development: Pitch Alteration

3. *Alteration of rhythm:* Rhythmic alteration is frequently employed though it is usually not as dominating an effect as fragmentation and pitch change. Recreate a portion of a motive using different rhythmic effects. The rhythmic pattern, for example, might be stated in values that might double the length of the notes in the usual statement. Or the pattern might call for note values half the length of the original. Augmentation creates the effect of spreading out, diminution the effect of contracting.

Ex. 10–3. "America," measure 1

Development: Rhythmic Change

4. *Alteration of harmony:* Alteration of pitch is usually accompanied by a recasting of the harmonic background. The development effect is then felt in the constantly changing harmonic structure.

Ex. 10–4. "America," measure 1

Development: Harmonic Change

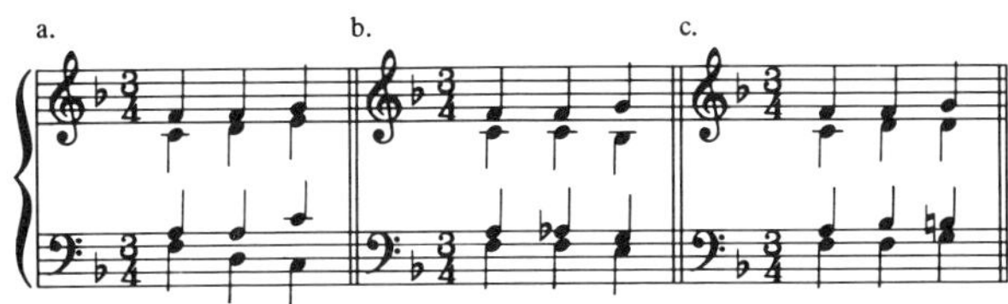

5. *Alteration of color and dynamics:* Contrasts in tone color and dynamic level are also elements of development. Such changes, from one instrument or group of instruments to another, are present in most instrumental development sections. In a solo, the performer will initiate different color contrasts on the same instrument.

Ex. 10–5. "America," measures 1 and 11

Themes or portions of themes in a development may appear in several ways. Two or more may appear in the nature of a dialogue: a musical conversation presenting one idea at a time. They may appear simultaneously, one superimposed on the other: a dialogue presenting more than one idea at a time.

Let ◯ represent one musical idea and ▭ a contrasting musical idea. In a musical composition they might appear as follows:

Ex. 10–6a

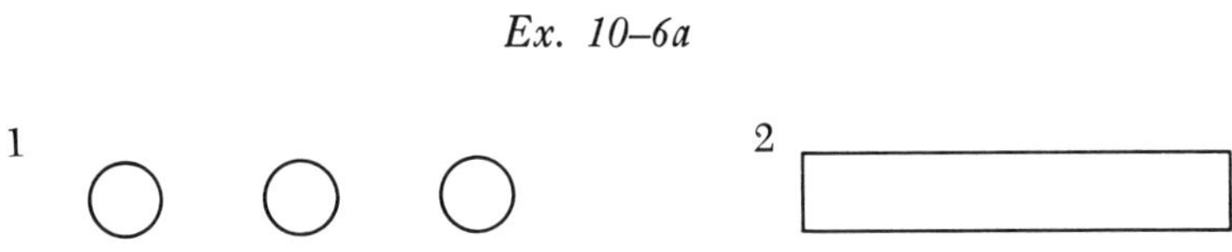

If these same themes are partially presented, repeated as fragments, mixed, and presented at continually changing pitch levels, they might be represented:

Ex. 10–6b

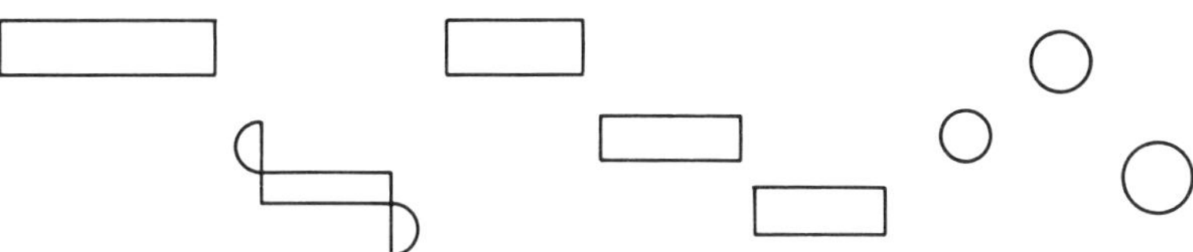

If they were rhythmically or dynamically changed, altered in tone color and superimposed on each other they might appear:

Ex. 10–6c

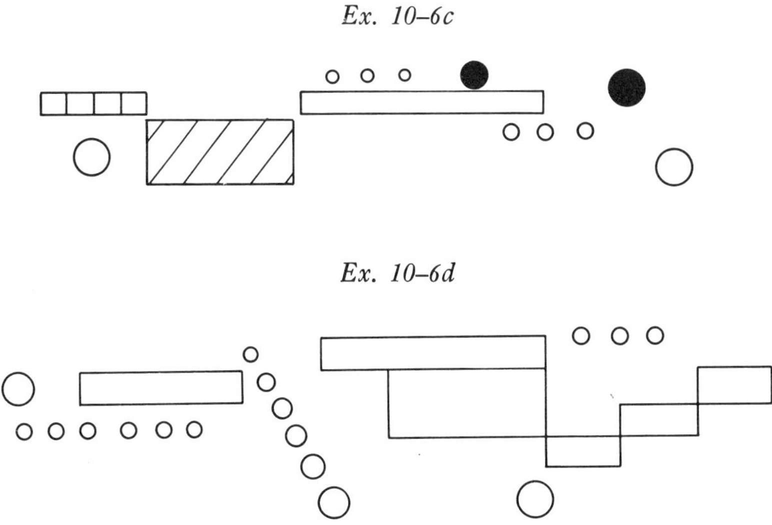

Ex. 10–6d

Notice the types of manipulation available. The themes are sounded at a higher or lower pitch level, presented in diminution or in augmentation, extended by new material, or made shorter by subtraction. They appear in different tone colors, are larger, smaller, bolder, lighter, fragmented, or mixed in various ways. Themes or motives are presented in different textures: homophonic and polyphonic, solo and ensemble. These techniques expose the innermost character of the themes. The extensive alteration creates a feeling of turmoil and uncertainty as new facets are revealed. This "embroiling" character of development is similar to the complexities of a plot in a play. The audience is held in a state of suspense, uncertain of where the new events are going or what the outcome will be. In music, the listener becomes caught up by the "musical plot"—activity created by the alteration of the original events. Movement away from established pitch centers, rhythmic regularity, harmonic security, and into a state of agitation is the essence of development. Involvement should increase until the mounting tension demands a solution. Most music leaves little doubt about its resolution. Endings are usually definite and convincing.

Any subject, musical or otherwise, may be developed from different points of view. No two development sections are alike. Listen to the development sections of the following symphonies.

1. Mozart, Symphony no. 40 in G Minor, first movement.
2. Tchaikovsky, Symphony no. 4 in F Minor, first movement.
3. Bartók, *Concerto for Orchestra*, first movement.

Mozart develops only one thematic idea. Tchaikovsky devotes most of the development to one idea, but also interjects thematic material from the introduction of the work. Bartók uses a greater variety of themes and techniques of development. Notice also the difference in feeling. Development can encompass a wide range of moods from defiant to pleading, lively to ponderous, festal to foreboding, friendly to ominous, and from heroic to mysterious.

SONATA-ALLEGRO FORM

Development has an important place in musical form. It is used in some contrapuntal writing; in the orchestral parts of Wagner's operas (see Chapter 11); in the structure of some tone poems; and is a principal part of the sonata-allegro form.

Sonata-allegro form is a general structural outline that permits a composer considerable latitude in treatment. No two compositions in this form are internally the same. Although it is one of the most important concepts of musical organization, sonata-allegro form should not be thought of as a ready-made mold into which a composer pours his notes.

Roughly, sonata-allegro form has three principal sections: (1) exposition, (2) development, and (3) recapitulation. The first section states the thematic ideas, the second develops one or more of them, and the third restates the original ideas. An introduction is optional. The coda is also optional but is generally included. The following represents the usual design of the sonata-allegro form.

Introduction	*Exposition*	*Development*	*Recapitulation*	*Coda*
(Optional)	*Presentation of Themes*	*Development of One or More Themes*	*Restatement of Themes*	*Closing Material*

The purpose of the introduction is to give impetus to the beginning of the work and bring into focus the first theme of the exposition that follows. An introduction may be short or extensive. Its thematic material may or may not recur later.

The exposition of the sonata-allegro form exposes the listener to the principal ideas which form the core of the work. The themes (there are usually more than one) may be extended melodies, but they may also be motivic ideas or groups of musical ideas. The exposition itself also generally follows a format: (1) first theme—often called principal theme, (2) material leading to the next theme or themes—called transition or episode, (3) second theme or group of themes—called subordinate theme or themes, (4) thematic material bringing the section to a close—called closing theme or codetta. The exposition is sometimes repeated. The following illustrates the principal ingredients of an exposition.

Theme one

Principal theme in principal pitch level or key.

Episode, transition, or bridge

Material, usually of a contrasting nature, modulating from the key of theme one to the key of theme two or the key of the subordinate group of themes.

Theme two

Usually a theme in contrast with theme one, and at a related pitch level. Additional themes may make this theme a subordinate group of themes.

Closing material (codetta)

The ending of the exposition. Usually a briefer close as compared to the more extensive closing material at the end of the entire form, which is called a coda.

Even though the themes of the exposition serve as the musical material for the development and the recapitulation, the listener should be forewarned that too much can be made of the identification of themes to the detriment of the overall musical flow and effect of the sonata-allegro form. The continuity and inevitability are evident only when the form is experienced in its entirety. The composer who uses this form is striving to express coherency, consistency, and *imbalance*. The development section alters and distorts. It suspends the listener's ability to predict. This musical suspense is similar to the anxiety and insecurity experienced in real life when the future is impending but unknown. Blocking expectations causes emotions to be aroused. The development section often contains surprise events that evolve in such a way that they delay gratification. At the same time, the impact of these events increases interest and excitement. Delaying gratification produces sustained animation and forward movement that give the climax dramatic thrust and the listener a feeling of complete fulfillment.

Following the development section, the sonata-allegro form levels off. Fulfillment is assured in the recapitulation and the return of the thematic ideas of the exposition. In general terms, the exposition states the musical ideas, the development section exploits them, and the recapitulation recalls them. If the exposition begs the question, "What does this musical material have to say?" the development astonishes the listener, exclaiming a destiny that is both inevitable and compelling. The recapitulation affords the listener a reacquaintance with the original materials, now enhanced by the knowledge of their unlocked and fully-realized potentials. The coda might be equated with "the moral of the story." In other words, there is a statement of circumstances, a dramatic happening, and a summation of meaning that parallels good fiction. As with Shakespeare, or a satisfying novel, the drama is unfolded with a sense of unity and deliberateness.

Although the recapitulation is similar to the exposition, it varies in some ways:

1. The second theme or group of themes is stated at the principal pitch level or key rather than at the related pitch level as in the exposition because most compositions end on the principal pitch level.
2. The transitional or episodic material is different because of the varying pitch levels. The key relationship of the first and second themes is different than in the exposition.
3. The orchestration is usually different.

The first movements of solo sonatas, symphonies, concertos, and string quartets are usually based on sonata-allegro form. The Mozart, Tchaikovsky, and Bartók compositions mentioned in the discussion of development are examples of sonata-allegro form. Each is from a different century; eighteenth, nineteenth, and twentieth, respectively, and illustrates the range of expression and treatment possible within the outlines of this form. In earlier works, such as movements in sonata form by Carl Philipp Emanuel Bach (1714–1788), there is a similarity of mood and character between the two themes of the exposition. Haydn and Mozart contrast these themes. By using crescendos, accents, pauses, and unexpected changes from *forte* to *piano*, they create a dramatic tension not heard in earlier works. With Beethoven, the well-defined sections heard in Haydn and Mozart tend to become blurred, and the progress of musical unfolding becomes continuous. Richer harmonies and modulations are introduced and the development becomes longer and more complex. Sometimes codas are extended, almost assuming the dimensions of a second development section. Sonata-allegro form has attracted composers for almost two hundred years because it has the flexibility to accommodate the stylistic idiosyncrasies of many periods and composers.

The search for musical understanding depends upon the listener's awareness of the composer's presentation, development, and resolution of his musical ideas. Crucial to this is the ability to become involved in the working-out of the musical ideas. In addition to study, listening is mandatory. Perception depends on questioning, "What is happening? Where is the music going? What is its route back?"

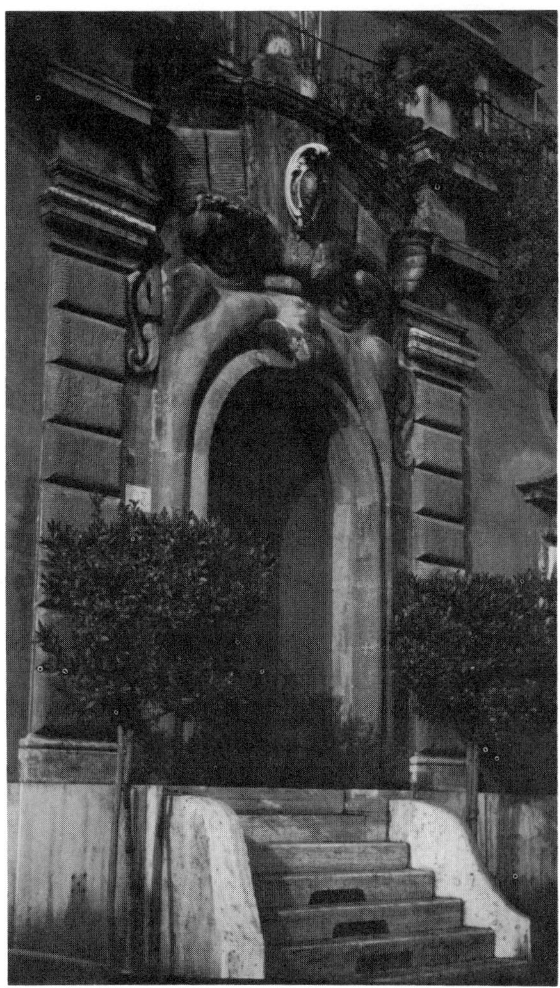

Federico Zuccaro: Portal of the Palazzetto Zuccaro (1593). Via Gregoriana, Rome.

The artist has found a new use for the caricature. The form is accommodated to its function. The result is at once grotesque and whimsical. Like Jacques Offenbach's Gaieté Parisienne, *such aesthetic expressions do not require laborious analysis for their effect. Artistic mastery does not always come in a serious package.*

THE LOGIC OF MUSICAL COMPOSITION

Although their perspectives may differ, the composer and society both search for music that has meaning. Such music is more than a pretty melody, a captivating rhythm, a lush harmony, and an imaginative orchestration. The composer must be able to compose music that as a whole is more meaningful than the mere content of the basic events. It is in creating this whole that the composer expresses himself. Musical logic is related to aesthetic principles—unity, variety and contrast, balance, symmetry, tension, climax, resolution or repose. It is upon the form or structure of the complete entity that logic in musical composition depends.

Logic in musical creation implies selectivity and order. In the fitting-together of all the parts there must be a feeling of reasoned rightness, like the perfection one senses when surveying a favorite painting. The listener can learn to admire this craftsmanship when he begins to distinguish the choices of sounds made by the composer and the ways in which he combines them.

The craft of musical composition is the composer's technique, learned or intuitive, which is applied to the formulation of all these musical events into some meaningful form or structure. The form or structure may or may not have an historic precedent. Certain forms and structures are traditional and may be defined in terms of the past; some may be slight alterations of these; some may deviate to a great extent; some are new. There are, however, from the consideration of all available perspectives, no formless compositions.

The essence of a musical composition rests in the composer's selection and development of his raw materials. Repetition, recurrence, variation, imitation, counterpoint, development, improvisation, and chance are all techniques that the composer uses to create structure for his musical statement. The expressiveness or perfection he seeks depends upon the logic of his choices. When the logic projected by the composer elicits a sympathetic response in the listener, a rapport and musical understanding takes place.

Listener attention is only the first step in this understanding. Sorting out the essential events and hearing them in relation to one another requires perception. Recognizing the melody every time it enters is to perceive one part of the essential organization of the music. By coordinating details, the mind recreates and reinterprets the music on an individual basis. The listener recodes the music in his own terms. Each event acts like a landmark along a highway. As the musical events relate to one another, the landmarks help the listener know where the music is going. As a result, the listener senses the coherence of the music. As his expectations are frustrated, delayed, then ultimately fulfilled, he derives a sense of satisfaction from the musical experience.

GUIDE TO ADDITIONAL LISTENING

Sonata-allegro form

The first movements of most symphonies, concertos, sonatas, and string quartets as well as many overtures and other instrumental works are in sonata-allegro form. The following first movements from compositions of different periods demonstrate the wide range of the form.

1. Wolfgang Amadeus Mozart, Symphony in G Minor, K. 550.

Mozart develops only the principal theme of the exposition. Note the constant change of pitch level.

2. Ludwig van Beethoven, Symphony no. 3 in E Flat Major, op. 55 (*Eroica*).

In contrast to the Mozart, more of the thematic material is developed. The development section plays a more forceful role in the composition.

3. Johannes Brahms, Symphony no. 2 in D Major, op. 73.

The main theme is partly motivic, partly a longer melody. Listen for this duality in the development section.

4. Antonin Dvořák, Symphony no. 9 in E Minor (*New World*).

Listen for the variety of themes used in the development section; also, the motivic development of the principal theme.

5. Béla Bartók, *Concerto for Orchestra.*

Observe the variety of musical expressiveness in the development section, the imitation used, and the different concept in the return to the recapitulation.

FOR DISCUSSION

1. Consider the relationships of the characters in a play. Can parallels be drawn to the development section of a symphony or concerto?
2. When musical events undergo development, they function differently. Discuss.
3. Does listener involvement in the development of a work intensify the work for him?
4. Development differs from simple repetition, variation, digression. How?
5. What techniques are employed in blues to give coherence to the musical structure?
6. Does rock-and-roll use repetition? Recurrence? Contrast? Discuss rock-and-roll in terms of rhythm, melody, and harmony.
7. What effect might chance techniques have on the longevity of a piece of music?
8. Can chance music have a definite form?

Part Three

MUSICAL STLYE

INTRODUCTION

The year and make of an automobile may be guessed from its distinctive appearance. During World War II, spotters could distinguish different kinds of aircraft by their sounds. The difference between silk and velvet can be determined by the texture. Objects, their source, and their age are identifiable through a set of distinguishing characteristics. These features constitute the object's nature—its style.

Chapters 11 through 16 are concerned with musical style. The study of style should enable the listener to identify the historical and cultural origins of a piece of music by ear. What makes a composition sound Baroque? Romantic? Modern? What makes a piece of music sound Russian? American? African? Style is personality—those features that set one piece off from another. For the listener, the study of style can give definition to a particular composition, the works of a particular composer, or the music of a particular period or culture.

MUSICAL STYLE

Musical style is the manner in which the musical resources are presented. Out of the millions of choices and combinations possible, which does the composer prefer? Style reflects the musical taste and selectivity of the artist.

The searching listener becomes acquainted with musical style by listening to the particular nature of several works. What instruments are used? What is the nature of the melody and harmony? Is the texture unique? What are the rhythmic characteristics? What dynamic levels are used? How? How does the composer use repetition, digression, recurrence, variation, imitation, or development? What is the formal structure? Has the composer allowed for improvisation? Chance?

The listener must be aware, however, of the atypical. For example, the musical style of the late Renaissance may be considerably different from the style of the early Renaissance. To think in terms of one Renaissance style may be misleading. Some vocal music may seem instrumental in style. Contemporary music envelops many different styles and is constantly embracing new ones. The style of a composer may change radically within his lifetime. Despite all the variables which the study of style discloses, such study can also reveal the general aesthetic values of a composer, a period, or a people.

The study of musical style ranges from broad generalizations to detailed analysis of the most obscure characteristics of the music. Neither is adequate by itself. Ideally, detailed analysis provides the substantiation for any generalities that emerge. Because the study of musical detail requires years of preparation, this text treats only the most characteristic detail. The composers and compositions selected provide a representative survey of historical styles.

STYLISTIC CHANGE

Communication is a never-ending concern to man. New means of expression are sought, established, perfected, depleted, and eventually, discarded. No one style can suffice to convey for all people at all times what they need to communicate.

Styles sometimes change gradually through evolution and metamorphosis. At other times they become exhausted and die. When styles lose their capacity to evolve, become static, or are pushed to their limits, a new style is apt to spring up. The new style is not necessarily a more sophisticated artistic development. The developmental view of art is not substantiated by historic evidence. The polyphonic and contrapuntal rhythms of so-called "primitive" African music and their harmonic approach to percussion instruments surpass in sophistication most rhythmic expression in Western music. The melodic sophistication of early Greek and Indian music is more "developed" than some music of more recent vintage.

Stylistic change in music can be evolutionary or revolutionary in much the same manner as women's clothing styles or automobile styles. Some automobiles are evolutionary in stylistic alterations (Volkswagen, Rolls Royce); others change more radically, at least in outward appearance (Ford Mustang, Chevrolet Camaro). Identifying the year of a Volkswagen is more difficult than identifying the year of a Camaro.

Stylistic change in music can be evolutionary or revolutionary in each individual style, and provides a basis for understanding developments within a style. The stylistic similarities and differences between two major musical periods, or between two composers, should be understood before the listener seeks to distinguish the stylistic similarities and differences between one composer's early and late works, or between two performances of a single composition. Listeners progress from recognizing broad fundamental stylistic differences to recognizing more subtle variations.

Romantic and Modern Styles: Vocal Music

11

Chapters 11 and 12 will contrast the Romantic style of the nineteenth century with the Modern style of the twentieth century. Can a listener detect the fundamental differences between the music of the Romantic period and the music of the Modern period, when examples of both are juxtaposed? Listen to the opening five minutes of the following pieces and try to characterize and compare the composers' general approaches to expression, melody, rhythm, tone color, harmony, dynamics, structure, medium, and texture.

Théodore Géricault: Raft of the Medusa *(1818–19).*
Clichés Musées Nationaux, Paris.

As David's The Oath of the Horatii *exemplified Classicism, this work is typical of Romanticism. The turbulent, anguished forms of starving, half-crazed men are depicted in a desperate, futile effort to attract the rescue ship in the far distance. The painting depicts in startling reality the true story of the survivors of the ship* Medusa *that sank on July 2, 1816. One hundred and forty-nine passengers and crew members crowded onto*

A. Peter Ilyich Tchaikovsky, Concerto no. 1 in B Flat Minor for Piano and Orchestra (1875).

   Elliott Carter, *Concerto for Piano* (1964–1965).

B. Hector Berlioz, *Nuits d'été* (*Summer Nights*) (1832).

   Arnold Schoenberg, *Pierrot Lunaire* (*Moonstruck Pierrot*) (1912).

How did musical style come to change so radically from the Romanticism of the nineteenth century to the Modern music of the twentieth century? By the end of the nineteenth century, musical expression seems to have reached its maximum potential. Many composers sought new patterns of tonal expression, new bases for harmonic and contrapuntal exploitation, new rhythmic freedom, and new structural designs. They craved a freshness that would free them from the expressive excesses and restrictions of the nineteenth-century establishment. Richard Wagner, the towering figure of German Romantic opera, carried nineteenth-century music to the brink of perfection—and exhaustion.

OPERA

One of the dominant characteristics of Wagner's aesthetic philosophy was coalescence. To Wagner, this meant the unification and internal solidification of action, scenery, singing, and orchestral accompaniment. Everything was to meld into one. Wagner called his ideal a

---

a makeshift raft. Only fifteen men survived the ordeal of thirst, insanity, and cannibalism. There is no symmetry or feeling of control here, as there is in Classic style. There is, however, a kind of dynamic balance, for the mast and lines of the figures tend to reverse the left to right movement by their counter-movement. Emotion is intensified by exaggeration of the contours of the bodies. Light and dark are contrasted with maximum intensity, and dark, ominous colors help express the horror. The people are not idealized types, but real persons living a real drama.

Gesamtkunstwerk, a universal composition in which the inner and outer being of each character was expressed and all elements of the opera unified. To achieve this complete synthesis, Wagner employed the *leitmotiv*, a musical theme or subject that symbolizes a character, an object, or an idea in the opera.

Act 1 of the Metropolitan Opera's 1971 production of Wagner's Tristan und Isolde.

Wagner's leitmotivs number in the hundreds and each is ingeniously formulated to symbolize the essence of what it represents. For example, the opera *Tristan und Isolde* has a leitmotiv for Tristan, the ring, love, gold, Wotan, and many other essential elements of the opera plot. The motives are often made to function suggestively, foreshadowing or representing the subconscious origin of an event. These leitmotivs may be developed to convey the particular emotion of new events surrounding the object or idea that they reflect. They are occasionally sung, but more often are instrumental. In Wagner's operas, the orchestra does not function as mere accompaniment but enters into the drama as an equal partner with the scenery, the lighting, the costumes, and the action on stage.

Ex. 11–1. Wagner: Tristan und Isolde. *Motives*

A listener does not have to memorize all of the leitmotivs to understand Wagnerian opera. On the contrary, the motives exert their influence purely on their own strength. As they are introduced, repeated, and developed, the listener becomes absorbed with the symbolic meaning and is drawn in by their psychological power and dramatic rightness. Wagner's approach, however, did result in a static stage. "When you come to see my Tristan, leave your glasses home," Wagner said. He sought to create "the invisible stage." The music and text were to convey the meaning with only a suggestion of action on stage.

Wagner termed his work "music-drama" in contradistinction to the music-theater of former times and the grand opera of his own day. The differences are basic. In pre-Wagnerian opera, the recitative, a wordy or speech-like interlude, conveyed the action of the story, while the arias or ensembles expressed the feelings evoked by these happenings. In contrast, Wagner's vocal parts are continuously spun melodic lines that follow the natural declamation of the text. The orchestral parts form a harmonic accompaniment, but simultaneously inject a polyphonic interweaving of the leitmotivs with the voice.

Wagner's later operas are not readily divided into set pieces as are the grand operas of the nineteenth century. The flow of the music is continuous. Musical forms are, however, present even though they are not distinctly separable. They are fused with the drama in a continuously interwoven manner.

Early Romantic operas often had rescue plots. They had touches of suspense, escape, danger, and rescue by friends or servants. They often expressed concern for humanity and the triumph of justice. Wagner extracted his plots from history, folklore, and mythology. Ancient Norse mythology was the basis of the story told in the four operas comprising his *Der Ring des Nibelungen*, which was 28 years in the making. *Tristan und Isolde*, a story of erotic love, is based on a medieval legend. *Die Meistersinger von Nürnberg*, a comic opera of great pageantry and vividness of characterization, was based on historical events. *Parsifal*, a colossal religious work, was based on an epic poem. Wagner's penchant for giganticism can be seen in the length of these works. *Die Meistersinger* is four and a half hours long, the *Ring* more than twelve hours, and the first act of *Parsifal* alone, two hours.

German symphonic developments during the nineteenth century are given some of their finest statements in Wagner's orchestration. One need only listen to the "Liebestod" ("Love Death") from *Tristan und Isolde* to feel the expressive and sustained power of his music. The "Liebestod" ends the opera. Tristan, Isolde's great love, is dead. For a moment it seems to her that he has come to life again. She is enveloped by the presence of his being, gazing transfigured at his body until she dies of anguished longing and grief. Wagner pushed the long, surging melodic line to its furthest extent. His music continually unfolds and rarely arrives at a resting point. Each climax surges toward another and still another climax. The "longing" quality of Wagner's music is in large part due to his continuing changes from one scale to another and his continual thematic transformations. The frustration of unfulfilled romantic love is captured by sounds that are rarely permitted to pause at home base. The chord that opens *Tristan* (Ex. 11–1—"Longing") and is used throughout, is finally resolved only at the end of the opera. Wagner conditions the listener to expect the music to settle somewhere and invariably confuses him and thwarts his expectation by taking him somewhere else. His masterful manipulation of instrumental color is integrated in his continuous stream of music. Phrases overlap in such a way that the sounds of one set of instruments fade into another, and coloration subtly melts into coloration so that all the elements are thoroughly fused.

The music of Claude Debussy contains the first signs of movement away from the usual practices of the nineteenth century. Debussy rejected the all-encompassing Romantic forces that had been brought to such full flower by Wagner. As a student in the Paris Conservatory, Debussy fought the constraints of the "discipline of musical composition" taught by his teachers: he refused to obey the rules.

His sounds jelled into a new style called Impressionism. Philosophically the orchestral music remained linked to the nineteenth century. It was symphonic. It was programmatic. But musically, it was different. Debussy strongly resisted the extreme coalescence and continuous development that characterized Wagner's music. In order to assure that his music would not string on and on, Debussy did not utilize chords on the basis of their "function"—their tendencies to move in certain directions, and their relationship to each other. Harmonic sounds, especially those considered dissonant, were allowed to stand alone. Progressions of harmonies did not have to move from someplace to someplace; they could just "be." In addition he found his own new paths for harmonic progressions. In the eighteenth and nineteenth centuries there was a more or less "correct" flow of harmonic sound. Debussy's harmony moved in the direction he dictated without reference to established practice. He emphasized the separateness of chords by adding extraneous notes in order to increase their individual color effect.

Debussy also made use of different scale systems: the whole-tone and the pentatonic scales. A different tonal system changed the melodic sounds and refocused the harmonic content. As a result, tonalities tended to become less fixed, more fluent. This fluency created a delicacy in the movement of sound. Rhythm and color took on new meaning. Rhythms could be more subtle, less punctuated, less obvious. Color for the sake of color became musically useful.

The Balcony Scene from the Metropolitan Opera's 1971 production of Debussy's Pelléas et Mélisande. *Judith Blegen as Mélisande; Barry McDaniel as Pelléas.*

Debussy's opera *Pelléas et Mélisande* is characteristic of Debussy and typically French. Language, for the French, has always held great fascination. Above all, the French insist on the natural declamation of the text, with proper enunciation and inflection. The heart of the opera is in the words; music is a secondary consideration. Debussy's orchestration is transparent, shimmering, elegant, and discreet. He introduces none of the ponderous, heroic qualities of Wagner's opera. Debussy would not subject an audience to one opera four evenings in length, such as Wagner's *Der Ring des Nibelungen.* The voice line does not soar, but adheres to a narrow range, closely resembling spoken French. The orchestral sonority is veiled, and individual instruments emerge with delicate clarity. Fragmentary phrases replace the broadly tooled melodies of Romantic style. The fluidity of the sound is in part due to

Ex. 11–2. Debussy: Pelléas et Mélisande.
The death of Mélisande, Act V

Ex. 11–3. Wagner: Tristan und Isolde.
Isolde's death at the end of the "Liebestod"

Debussy's deemphasis of the meter, steady accent, and bar line. Only in the interludes does Debussy use the full symphonic resources. In these, the music summarizes the action and prepares the listener for what is to follow. The story is vague, not full of the cumbersome detail of Wagner's operas. It seeks to capture the mysterious and magical character of Maeterlinck's fictitious medieval land. Everything is in simple, good taste. There are no histrionics or high Cs. Compare, for example, the death of Mélisande in Act V with the death of Isolde in the "Liebestod" (Exs. 11–2 and 11–3) or the meeting of Pelléas and Mélisande in Scene 1 of Act IV with Tristan and Isolde's hearty greeting in Act II (Exs. 11–4 and 11–5). A quiet eloquence creates an otherworldly, poetic spell in Debussy's work.

Ex. 11–4. Debussy: Pelléas et Mélisande.
The meeting of Pelléas and Mélisande, Act IV, Scene 1

Ex. 11–5. Wagner: Tristan und Isolde.
The meeting of Tristan and Isolde, Act II, Scene 2

Debussy deliberately interrupts the sequence of events, breaks up the musical substance, and introduces restrained and objective expression in the place of a flowing outpouring of emotion. *Pelléas et Mélisande* has no set arias, duets, or quartets such as in Wagner's early operas or in the usual grand operas of the nineteenth century. In Romantic music one could ask of a sound from where it came, where is it going, to what is it related and how. In Debussy's music one might say, "This is the sound. Enjoy it while it is here for what it is."

Debussy was an innovator. He was interested in the colors of sound, not harmonic traditions. This is evident in the bell-like effects he often employs. His distinctive style was translucent. He became the counterpart to the impressionistic painters such as Claude Monet, Camille Pissaro, Edgar Dégas, and Auguste Renoir, in that he could create an atmosphere without employing harsh clashes and sharp contrasts. Debussy's music appears vague and less dramatic than Wagner's, but is far more subtle and poetic.

Impressionism was short-lived. It was an entity unto itself and did not allow for expansion. Although this style did not provide a base upon which a new system could develop, it did help to end the long period of German dominance over music that characterized the nineteenth century. Debussy's modification of tradition helped others to do likewise. The 1880s gave birth to numerous composers who were innovators. They produced the nucleus and spirit for twentieth-century developments. Among these were Igor Stravinsky, Béla Bartók, Edgar Varèse, Arnold Schoenberg, Anton Webern (1883–1945), and Alban Berg (1885–1935). These composers believed that the survival of music as a vital art form depended upon setting out in a new direction. While much nineteenth-century style music continued to be composed in the twentieth century, this new generation of composers felt that retaining the same old styles would be musical suicide.

For over three hundred years most European music had been based upon tonality. Fixed scale patterns of seven tones and a key center were used. In this system some pitches were of primary, others of secondary importance. Certain tones in the system afforded the listener repose, others created motion. Schoenberg, Webern, and Berg brought a new approach to composition. Like Debussy, they took issue with their immediate heritage. In their early works they drove the tonal system inherited from Wagner to atonality. So many extraneous tones were added to the basic scale that the feeling for key was obliterated altogether. A new system was needed. In the 1920s Schoenberg devised a compositional technique called serialization. Webern and Berg, disciples of Schoenberg, adopted serial technique and helped to establish it as a new system replacing the tonal systems of the past.

Serial music freed the composer to use pitch materials in a new way. Traditional tonal music centers around a limited number of basic pitches, which are repeated with considerable frequency. Other tones are introduced as a supplement to the basic scale in order to enrich the fundamental tonal relationships. These nonscale tones (accidentals) lend variety and tension as they exercise a pull away from the established tonal center. Tonal music often employs all twelve tones of the octave, but the magnetic attraction of the basic scale continues to function and maintain its dominance. Serialization also uses all the twelve tones of the octave, but as a scale system in itself. The pull, instead of being fixed on a tonal center, is dependent upon the logical ordering of the sounds as they are used to create a melody.

Ex. 11–6. Twelve tones for serial composition

Ex. 11–7. Resulting tone row

Ex. 11–8.

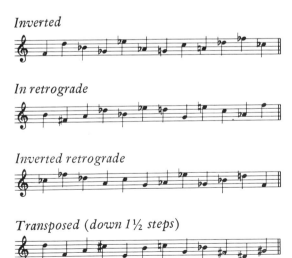

Inverted

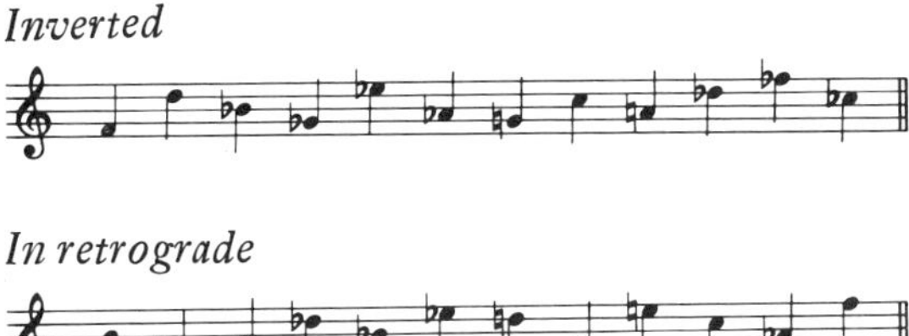

In retrograde

Inverted retrograde

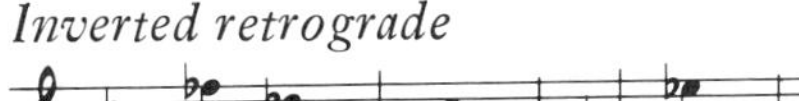

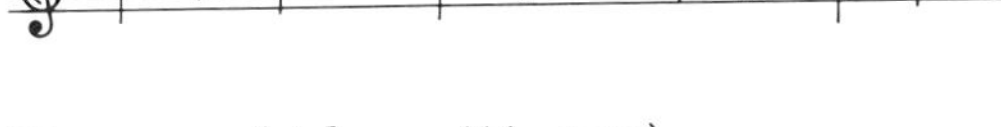

Transposed (down 1½ steps)

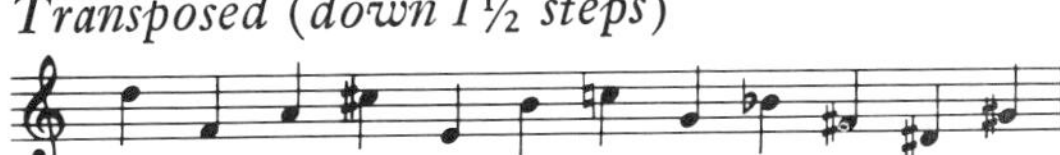

Ex. 11–9. Bartók: String Quartet no. 1, op. 7. In the first movement Bartók distributes this tone row between the first and second violin parts.

In its strictest sense, serialization means that every note of the twelve tones within the octave is used before any one of them is repeated. The composer sets up an order, called the tone row, in which these notes appear. His technique depends on a variety of ways of using the particular tone row that he creates.

Bartók departs from strict serialization by repeating four tones (X) before stating all twelve tones of the row. The example illustrates that composers can exercise freedom even within what appears to be a restrictive formula. Bartók also uses the tones 4, 7, and 11 in different octaves than indicated in the original tone row.

Many modifications have evolved from this system. Listeners should not despair if they cannot identify the tone row, particularly in all its guises. It may be no more evident than the rhythm and rhyme scheme of a Shakespearean play, when spoken by a fine actor. The tone row system is far more obvious on the printed page than when it is heard. Its function is organizational, and from that standpoint it does have psychological power.

Another technique fostered primarily by Schoenberg is that of *Sprechstimme* or "singing" in a speaking manner. In a sense this is a combination of speaking and recitative. The result is neither singing nor speaking but a kind of speech-song. An example of this, Schoenberg's *Pierrot Lunaire*, has already been referred to earlier.

Debussy's revolt against Romantic tradition appears less bold and complete when compared with the innovations of Schoenberg, Webern, and Berg. Impressionism still embraced beauty of sound, sensuous mood-painting, and a fondness for programmatic music.

Berg's opera *Wozzeck*, composed from 1914–1922, signals a new era of sound. The significance of the text is translated into the music and intensified by it. Sound is exploited for its meaning. Like Debussy, Berg uses the full orchestra primarily in the interludes. But the chamber groups that accompany the various scenes are employed with adroit intensity. Tone color, melody, rhythm, and harmony capture the emotional sense of the plot. Berg unified the opera with Wagnerian leitmotivs. These melodic profiles have a psychomusical thrust, helping to create a stream of relentlessly emotional outpourings.

Berg's style contains elements of Wagnerian lyric melody, the *Sprechstimme* that Schoenberg used in *Pierrot Lunaire*, and even spoken passages. The amalgamation is unique. The voice parts, which use angular melodies, are often more instrumental than vocal. The music is largely atonal, adhering to no one scale but exploiting all the available sounds. Berg borrows many older forms to organize the scenes: fugues, inventions, suites, variations, passacaglias, and sonata movements.

Berg, like Wagner, wrote his own libretto, basing *Wozzeck* upon a play written a century earlier by Georg Büchner. Wozzeck is a dull-witted soldier who is deluded into believing he is going crazy. His mistress Marie has an encounter with a drum major which becomes the source of anguished jealousy for Wozzeck, who already shares with Marie the burden of their illegitimate child. The plot centers on the psychological torture and breakdown of Wozzeck that leads him to murder Marie and commit suicide.

Compare Marie's death in Act III, Scene 2 with the death of Mélisande and with the death of Isolde (Exs. 11–3 and 11–10). Berg's work is tight and economical. The form is an invention on a single tone. No sound or word is wasted. The repeated timpani stroke whispers, then pounds the death note. The dramatic sustained tone in the interlude that follows is unforgettable for its terrifying crescendo. The savage rhythm symbolizes the brutal murder. The example shows the complex scoring as Marie sings her last note.

Wozzeck, the person, is a prototype, the universal poor man imprisoned within his social order. He is an eternal symbol of the human condition. The opera is the product of World War I, of Freud, Kafka, and the uncertainties of that period. The work marks a historical departure in music. It represents a major breakthrough, toward new expressive possibilities. Alban Berg and Schoenberg were the foremost exponents of a movement called "Expressionism." While Impressionism

Ex. 11–10. Berg: Wozzeck, *Act III, Scene 2*

had sought to express the outer world of objects, Expressionism sought to express the inner world of human experience. Expressionism, too, contained elements of Romanticism, but the subject matter was man in the modern world described in psychological terms.

Tristan und Isolde, *Pelléas et Mélisande*, and *Wozzeck* exemplify in a general way Romantic, Impressionistic, and Expressionistic styles. The following chart presents these styles as they emerge from these works.

Comparative Styles: Opera

	Romantic	*Impressionistic*	*Expressionistic*
	Wagner (1813–1883), Tristan und Isolde	*Debussy (1862–1918)*, Pelléas et Mélisande	*Berg (1885–1935)*, Wozzeck
Expression	*Supercharged emotionalism, heroic, ponderous. Drama is central.*	*Sensuous mood-painting, elegant, discreet. Story vague. Drama secondary.*	*Intense and violent, swiftly-paced realism. Drama psychological.*
Melody	*Long-flowing, surging. Tonal. Taxing the power of the singer.*	*Natural declamation of text. Singing with human proportions.*	*Instrumental in character. Some* Sprechstimme, *some spoken; angular, atonal.*
Rhythm	*Largely square cut, 3 or 4 beats per measure.*	*Subtle, not punctuated. De-emphasis of meter, accent, and steady beat.*	*Much variety, freedom, and experimentation.*
Tone Color	*Variety of instrumental coloration.*	*Sounds used for exotic coloration.*	*Sound colors evoke meanings.*
Harmony	*Rich, ornate, much modulation. Chords move according to function.*	*Chords used as independent entities.*	*Tonal combinations chosen for dramatic qualities of expressiveness.*

	Wagner	*Debussy*	*Berg*
Dynamics	*Music builds from one climax to another.*	*Restrained.*	*Extreme contrasts.*
Structure	*Few divisions between sections. Orchestra molds singing, scenery, and drama into one. Leitmotivs unify.*	*Fluid.*	*Older forms such as fugues, inventions, suites, and variations used. Clear divisions. Concise.*
Medium and Texture	*Orchestra and voice. Thick sonorities. Mass of sounds. Theatricality often in the music and not on stage.*	*Orchestra and voice. Individual instruments emerge with delicate clarity.*	*Orchestra and voice. Use of chamber groups rather than full orchestra lends economy and tightness. No sound is wasted. Theatricality as much in the action and visual elements as in the music.*

SACRED MUSIC

By 1800, sacred music had assumed an independent status in the concert hall, quite apart from the church. The settings of the Mass were often concert works that could not be performed within the confines of the liturgical service. The works were lengthy and demanded the resources of many singers and instrumentalists. Stylistically, the Mass, the oratorio, and the requiem appropriated the musical characteristics of symphonic and opera music of the nineteenth century.

Although religious music represented the major output of many composers before the nineteenth century, it dwindled to a small part of the music produced by the composers of the Romantic and Modern periods. Even the most religious music took on a secular cast. Secular and sacred styles differed primarily in text. Sacred choral music, particularly in the twentieth century, has been slow to absorb the newest techniques of musical composition. Church music tends to be conservative, especially when designed for liturgical use.

The oratorio of the nineteenth century continued to reflect the models of earlier composers. The leading oratorio writer was Felix Mendelssohn with his work, *Elijah*. The text is a mixture of history and religion. The musical format includes recitatives, arias, and choruses, more typical of early opera than the grand opera of the period. Its musical style, melody, harmony, rhythm, and tone are, however, of the nineteenth century.

Two Masses representative of nineteenth-century developments are *A German Requiem* by Johannes Brahms and the *Manzoni Requiem* by Giuseppe Verdi. The Brahms work represents a departure in that it is in German rather than Latin and is not based upon the liturgy of the Catholic Church. It is set for solo voices, chorus, and orchestra. Verdi's *Requiem*, composed in 1874, is based upon liturgical text but is operatic in character. It is composed for solo voices, large chorus, full orchestra, and off-stage trumpets. The "Dies Irae" is a *tour de force*. A rush of instruments and voices announce the day of judgment. (See Ex. 11–11.) The setting is typically Romantic: a full-blown musical embodiment of the damnation.

The "Sanctus" ("Holy, holy, holy") is set in a double fugue. The chorus sings one subject, while the soloists simultaneously sing another. The fast (*allegro*) tempo gives the "Sanctus" a light, happy feeling, quite a different interpretation of the text than is customary. The effect is not reverent and liturgical, but expressive of individual religious conviction. (See Ex. 11–12.)

Unlike the musically excessive Masses of the nineteenth century, Stravinsky's *Mass* of 1948 is relatively short and compressed and has no repetition of text. The melodies are forthright and the harmonies crisp. The work is scored for chorus and ten wind instruments. In comparison with nineteenth-century Masses, Stravinsky's is a simpler, more objective statement. Religious belief is not shouted or imposed. For Stravinsky, the mind is the primary repository for religious belief. A perfection of musical statement—logical and ordered—is a more reverent religious expression than an emotional outpouring.

Ex. 11–11

Allegro agitato
Soprano
Contralto
Tenor
Bass
Chorus
Allegro agitato (𝅗𝅥 = 80)
Piano
(Orchestra)
Day of an - ger, day of an - - -
Di - es i - rae, Di - es i - - -
Day of an - - -
Di - es i - - -

Paul Cézanne: Lac d'Annecy *(1896). Courtauld Institute Galleries, London.*

Water—fountains, lakes and sea—has often inspired musicians, poets, and painters. La Mer *by Debussy,* The Fountains of Rome *by Respighi, and* Seadrift *by Delius are a few musical examples. Here Cézanne captures the rich but fragile, quiet but commanding, calm of the lake.*

Gene Davis: Dr. Peppercorn *(1967). Fischbach Gallery, New York.*

When people are unfamiliar with the style of an artist, they want to know what he's trying to say. In this case, the painter employs a simple geometric pattern and makes no attempt to represent literal subject matter. He juxtaposes even vertical bands of vivid color with precise hard edges. The stripes of color react with one another—some of them appear to step forward, while others seem to move back. His "meaning" is in the titillation of the eye provoked by the apparent mobility of the surface, though the title is no more revealing than "etude" or "concerto."

Claude Monet: Rouen Cathedral *(1894). Clichés Musées Nationaux, Paris.*

Impressionists preserved the transient beauty of everyday events. Monet painted 26 canvases of Rouen Cathedral; each one caught and fixed it in a different light, a different season. Form is shattered by the play of light. Similarly, Debussy used free forms and the special colorations of various scales and chordal effects.

Vincent Van Gogh: Wheat Field and Cypress Trees *(1889). The National Gallery, London.*

One feels the wind in this painting. The repeated rhythm of the brush strokes creates an overpowering turbulence. The quick beat of the wheat field combines with the more deliberate background rhythm and then merges with the larger, deeper rhythms of mountains and sky. Rhythms are repeated and combined in rich counterpoint, as in the African tribal chant.

Ernst Kirchner: The Street *(1913). The Museum of Modern Art, New York.*

Expressionism represents sensations and emotions by freely distorting color and form. The subject is often morbid, tragic, or violent and induces spontaneous empathy in the viewer. Kirchner's angular figures express the alienation, tension, and sinister hypocrisy of city life. The architectural organization and the social commentary are similar to the expression in Alban Berg's opera, Wozzeck.

Piet Mondrian: Broadway Boogie-Woogie *(1942–43). Collection, The Museum of Modern Art, New York.*

Mondrian uses geometric horizontals and verticals and the three primary colors plus black and white to create "the balance of unequal but equivalent opposition"—a nonsymmetrical balance. Boogie-woogie—a steady rolling bass and a rhythmic melody—is analogous to the relationship of his rectangles and squares.

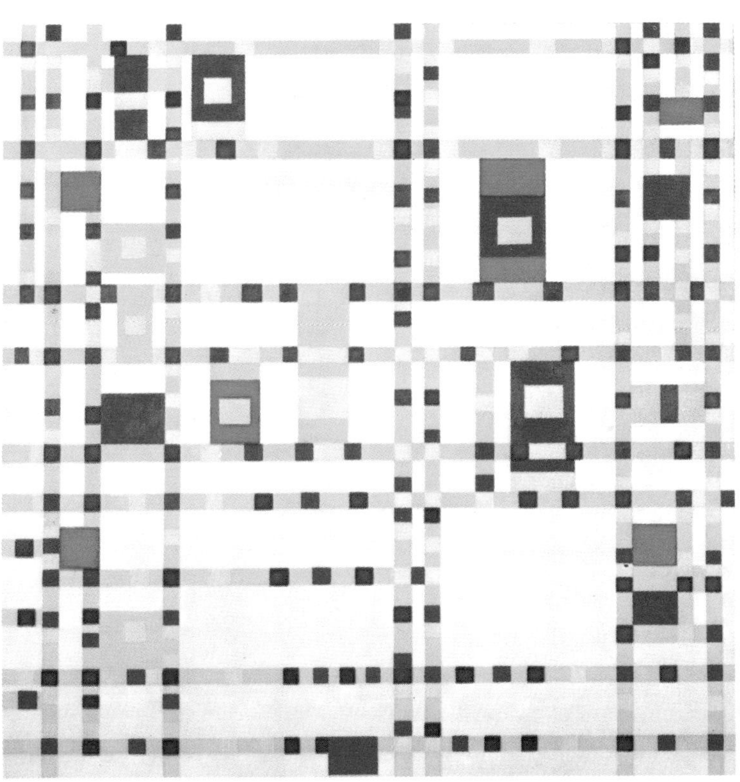

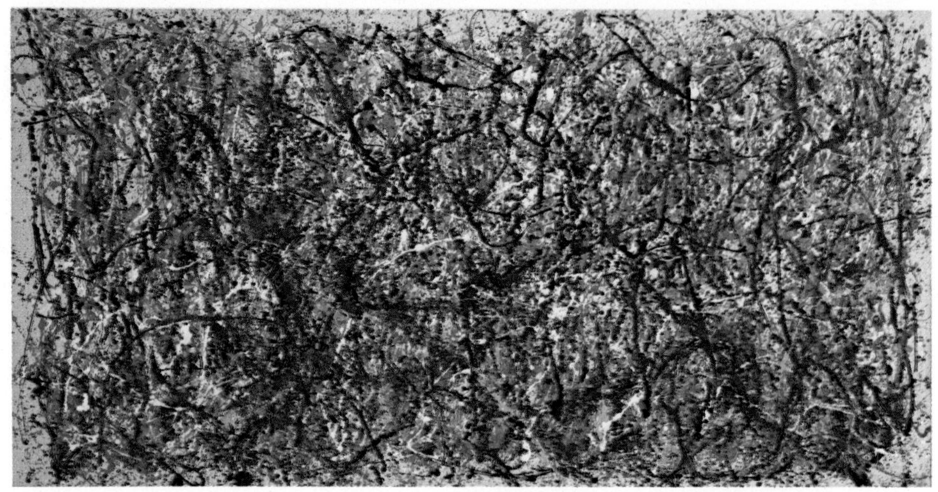

Jackson Pollock: One (*Number 31, 1950*). *Collection, The Museum of Modern Art, New York. Gift of Sidney Janis.*

Jackson Pollock established abstract expressionism. Like John Cage in music, Pollock freed the artist to use any technique for expressive purposes. He created focuses of intensity by dripping the paint in swirls that varied in brilliance and weight, effectively gathering and dispersing energy. Chance events were integral to the creative process.

Antoine Watteau: Embarkation for Cythera (*1717*). *National Gallery, Berlin.*

Watteau, master of Rococo painting, depicts couples leaving for the legendary "isle of love." The embellishment and elegant stances, gestures, and clothing seem frivolous at first. But on closer examination, wistfulness belies the surface prettiness—the lovers' anticipation seems doomed to disappointment; each figure seems isolated in loneliness. Watteau's psychological insight is reminiscent of Mozart's.

Ex. 11–12

Allegro
SOPRANO
Chorus
mf A
Ho - ly, ho - ly, ho - ly, ho - ly, Lord God of Sa - ba - oth,
San - ctus, san - ctus, san - ctus, Do - mi - nus De - us Sa - ba - oth,
CONTRALTO
mf A1
Ho - ly, ho - ly,
San - ctus, san - ctus,
SOPRANO
Solo
B p
Ho - ly, ho - ly, ho - ly, ho -
San - ctus, san - ctus, san - ctus, Do -
Allegro (♩ = 112)
Piano (Orch.)
mf
Heav - en and earth are full of the ma - jes - ty
Ple - ni sunt coe - li et ter - ra glo -
A1
ho - ly, ho - ly, Lord God of Sa - ba - oth, Heav - en
san - ctus Do - mi - nus De - us Sa - ba - oth, Ple - ni
TENOR
mf A
Ho - ly, ho - ly, ho - ly,
San - ctus, san - ctus, san - ctus,
- ly, Lord God of Sa - ba - oth,
- mi - nus De - us Sa - ba - oth,
B1 mf CONTRALTO
Ho - ly, ho - ly, ho - ly, ho - ly,
San - ctus, san - ctus, san - ctus Do - mi -
TENOR
B p
Ho - ly,
San - ctus,

Ex. 11–13. Stravinsky: "Sanctus" from Mass

In comparison with Verdi's warm, joyous setting of the "Sanctus," Stravinsky's is coolly impersonal. He elevates the text beyond the personal and gives it an air of permanency. His *Mass* is not one man's confession but a search for universal truth. Toulouse-Lautrec and Modigliani present this same polarity in painting. Toulouse-Lautrec gives his own individual interpretation to each character, while Modigliani creates the classic prototype.

Stravinsky's earlier work, *Symphonie de Psaumes* (*Symphony of Psalms*, 1930), is probably more expressive in the emotive sense. In spite of the absence of violins and violas in the orchestration, it cultivates warm, rich sonorities. The work is not a symphony in the Romantic sense. Like many other twentieth-century works, it has no development. The work, by comparison to Romantic traditions, might even be said to be antidevelopmental and antithematic. Stravinsky uses his resources with careful order, restraint, refinement, and economy. The psalms chosen for the text express various ways to praise the Lord. At the end, over an ostinato bass, Stravinsky creates with the simplest materials a mystical feeling of exultation.

Comparative Styles: Sacred Music

	Romantic	*Modern*
	Verdi (1813–1901) Requiem Mass	*Stravinsky (1882–1971)*, Mass
Expression	*Warmly sentimental, operatic, personal.*	*Clean and strong, impersonal.*
Melody	*Highly singable, stays with the listener.*	*Carefully constructed, cool, instrumental in character.*
Rhythm	*Simple. Repeated patterns help to unify movements.*	*Follows language at times. Of equal importance to melody as an expressive device.*
Tone Color	*Sectional effects predominate over individual instruments.*	*Clear and simple.*
Harmony	*Warm, rich.*	*Terse, pungent, dissonant.*
Dynamics	*Exaggerated softs and louds. Every range of variation is exploited.*	*Restrained.*

	Romantic	Modern
Structure	*Massive. Much use of repetition in melodies. Clear-cut sections. Extensive development.*	*Short movements. Little development or repetition.*
Medium and Texture	*Full orchestra, chorus, four soloists. Thick-textured use of orchestral, choral, and solo resources.*	*Chorus and ten winds. Well defined. Clear use of a limited number of instruments and tone colors.*

OTHER VOCAL MUSIC

In addition to opera and sacred music, vocal literature includes a large body of secular music. The solo song was a widely-exploited form in the nineteenth century. It reached maturity in the compositions of Schubert, Schumann, Brahms, and Hugo Wolf (1860–1903). Composers set to music the poems of the great German poets such as Goethe, Schiller, Heine, and Wilhelm Müller. Poetry, in many ways, became the central expressive focus of the Romantic spirit.

The Romantic *lied* was more than a poem sung with accompaniment. The piano parts reflected the dramatic content of the poetry. Schubert was a master at creating piano parts that enhanced the mood of the text. The "galloping" accompaniment of his "Erlkönig" ("The Erl King") depicts both the onrushing horse, and the desperation of the father as he rides through the night clutching his frightened child in his arms. (See Ex. 11–14.) Another example is "Gretchen am Spinnrade" ("Gretchen at the Spinning Wheel"). Here the accompaniment whirls and creates a mood of anxiety as Gretchen sings of her lover. Such accompaniments can be viewed as characterizations, a kind of tone painting. (See Ex. 11–15.)

More important, however, is Schubert's genius for creating beautiful melodies. His more than six hundred songs represent almost every shade and nuance of feeling. They are tailored so naturally to their text

Ex. 11–14

that they often belie the artistic sophistication that produced them. His forms include through-composed, strophic, and organizations that contrast recitative or declamatory sections with lyrical passages. Schubert's songs are always melodic and never mundane. For example, he usually

Ex. 11–15

alters a phrase length in a song so that all the phrases do not reflect the usual four-bar squareness typical of less imaginative composers. For instance, in "Du bist die Ruh" ("Thou Art Rest"), Schubert stretches the last phrase to six bars. (See Ex. 11–16.)

A group of poems by a single poet was sometimes set to music in a sequence forming a song cycle. The complete cycle comprised a unified poetic drama and musical experience. Schubert's *Winterreise* (*Winter Journey*) is one such cycle based on 24 poems by Wilhelm Müller. Schubert never made the mistake of elevating poetry above the music. Instead, he created music of great harmonic, rhythmic, and melodic imagination, to balance with the poetry.

Winterreise tells a story of unrequited love. The singer tells the tale in first person. As a stranger he comes to a village, falls in love, but finds that, because of his class, his love is not returned. The girl of the cycle is already a lost love, a shadowy figure, when the cycle begins. She is mentioned in only eight of the songs and never after the thirteenth. The singer appears to walk away from his listeners from the first to the last song, gradually becoming obscured by the ever-falling snow. As he leaves, he passes landmarks symbolic of his situation: a weather vane tells him that he should have never looked for love in that house; a linden tree reminds him of happier days when he dreamt sweet dreams in its shade; a swirling torrent under the ice reminds him of his own inner torment; a crow hovers around him and he wonders if it is waiting to use his body for its prey.

One of the ways Schubert gave unity to the cycle was to incorporate the rhythm ♫ ♪ into many of the songs. In fourteen of the songs the figure is used enough to affect the character of the melody. It is used to a lesser degree in six others, leaving only four without it. Schubert had been greatly stirred by Beethoven's Seventh Symphony and borrowed this figure, which is so predominant in that work.

The Romantic composer wrenched every drop of emotion from poetry. Through harmonic intensity, rhythmic coloration, melodic expressiveness, and dynamic contrasts, he could create a wide variety of emotional shadings. Hugo Wolf and Gustav Mahler carried Romantic expression in song to its height. They applied many of Wagner's means in the last stage of Romanticism.

Few composers in the twentieth century have composed many songs. Debussy and Ravel both used the solo voice as an expressive

Ex. 11–16

Langsam (Lento)
Piano
pp
4 bars
Du bist die Ruh, der Frie - de mild,
4 bars
die Sehn - sucht
du, und was sie stillt.
4 bars
Ich wei - he dir
voll_ Lust_ und_ Schmerz
6 bars
zur Woh - nung hier_____ mein_ Aug_ und_
Herz,_____ mein_ Aug_ und_ Herz._____

medium, but as music became more atonal the singer found it difficult to perform contemporary scores. The technical problems of singing atonal and tone-row music make it desirable for singers to possess absolute pitch in order to execute the difficult leaps accurately. The singer agonizes over technical hurdles that the instrumentalists perform with less difficulty.

Modern composers have written many fine isolated songs, and some have composed song cycles, usually on commission. American composer Ned Rorem (1923–   ) has achieved a command of the vocal medium that is notable. Among his many songs and song cycles, *Poems of Love and the Rain* (1963) (seventeen songs with texts by American poets, for mezzo-soprano) demonstrates his deft use of the voice and piano to express the subtle meanings of the poems. Every note of the accompaniment is choicely placed to create the precise shading that fits the words.

The form of the work is remarkable. Unity is no longer achieved by melodic repetitions within the songs. Rorem sets each poem to music twice, contrasting the two as much as possible. The pivot of the cycle is an interlude for unaccompanied voice. A short prologue and epilogue, nearly identical, round out the form on either end.

1 | *Prologue* from "The Rain"
2 | "Stop All the Clocks"
3 | "The Air Is the Only"
4 | "Love's Stricken 'Why' "
5 | "The Apparition"
6 | "Do I Love You"—Part 1
7 | "in the rain"
8 | "Song for Lying in Bed During a Night Rain"
9 | Interlude
10 | "Song for Lying in Bed During a Night Rain" (Conclusion)
11 | "in the rain"
12 | "Do I Love You"—Part 2
13 | "The Apparition"
14 | "Love's Stricken 'Why' "
15 | "The Air Is the Only"
16 | "Stop All the Clocks"
17 | *Epilogue* from "The Rain"

The music is not repeated; the words are. As in Schubert's *Winterreise,* however, one motive does recur throughout:

Ex. 11–17. Rorem: The Motive from Poems of Love and the Rain

Similarly, the mood creates a kind of unity.

Rorem uses the piano to its fullest extent, from one end to the other, in all its dynamic range and all its technical capacity. Less repeti-

Ex. 11–18. Rorem: "Love's Stricken 'Why'"

Ex. 11–19. Rorem: "Stop All the Clocks"

tion of melody has the effect of creating more urgency of subject. Melodic repetition in twentieth-century works is suspect of boredom, and, therefore, used more cautiously as an organizing device. Imitation and repetition are not completely absent, but are used with greater discretion (see Ex. 11–18). Phrases are generally of irregular length. Melody is freed from the constraint of dependence on tonality. The motive is played a great variety of ways.

Excitement is generated through the free use of metrical groupings ($\frac{7}{8}$ $\frac{5}{8}$ $\frac{7}{8}$ $\frac{8}{8}$ $\frac{6}{8}$ $\frac{7}{8}$ $\frac{6}{8}$ $\frac{6}{4}$ $\frac{11}{8}$ $\frac{7}{8}$).

Off-beat accents with a definite jazz flavor also add to the interest and vitality of the expression.

Comparative Styles:
Song Cycles

	Romantic	*Modern*
	Schubert (1797–1828), Der Winterreise	*Rorem (1923–)*, Poems of Love and the Rain
Expression	*The subject of unrequited love is viewed with anguish and remorse. Symbolic and dreamlike.*	*The subject of unrequited love is viewed with objective disappointment and intense resolve.*
Melody	*Tonal. Phrases generally balanced, with occasional extensions.*	*Not dependent upon tonality. Irregular phrases. Melody is motivic throughout.*
Rhythm	*Metrical patterns are predictable. Much repetition of rhythmic patterns.*	*Metrical patterns are unpredictable. Much variety of patterns with little repetition. Jazz elements.*

	Romantic	*Modern*
Tone color	*Often dark and brooding. The baritone voice sinks into despair. Many of the songs are in minor tonalities.*	*Warmth is generated by the dark quality of the mezzo-soprano voice. The piano is explored for bright, light, fast, contemplative, and angry sounds that allow the singer to command the situation. Wider voice range.*
Harmony	*Reliance on established, functional harmonies.*	*Freedom of choice for expressive needs.*
Dynamics	*Varied within each song.*	*Many gradations within each phrase.*
Structure	*Songs organized independently mainly according to binary and ternary patterns.*	*Text repetition creates a mirror form. Songs are less independent, more reliant upon their place in the cycle.*
Medium and Texture	*Baritone and piano. Poems of one poet give a consistency.*	*Mezzo soprano and piano. Poems of eight poets lend variety. Resources of piano are explored for their coloration.*

The English composer Benjamin Britten and the French composer Francis Poulenc produced a considerable amount of music for voice in the twentieth century. Britten's *Les Illuminations* and Poulenc's *Chansons villageoises* (*Songs of the Villagers*) are song cycles that clearly show the expressive possibilities of twentieth-century techniques. Electronic media have also been employed together with the voice. Luciano Berio's *Visage* (1961) uses the voice to express erotic metaphors. These few exceptions aside, the medium of voice is not widely used by classical composers in the present century. In addition to the technical limitations already mentioned, the natural warmth and intimacy of the human voice may offend the present penchant for intellectual reserve. Younger composers may feel that the aura of the ancient art of singing too often intervenes between his message and his listeners. This is not the case of course in popular music, in which the voice maintains a supremacy among expressive instruments.

Nineteenth-century composers wrote few large secular choral works. When the twentieth-century composer was moved to compose a large-scale choral work, it was often to a secular text. Carl Orff's *Carmina Burana* (*Songs of Beuren*, 1936) is an example. This robust and ribald setting of thirteenth-century songs and poems plays earthy humor against sober thoughts of nature and love. The simplicity and vitality of the melodies and rhythms help to convey the air of the bawdy folk ways that are the focus of the student writings that serve as the text.

Randall Thompson wrote *The Testament of Freedom* for chorus and orchestra in 1943. There have been many other secular American works. Among them are *A Lincoln Portrait* (1942) by Aaron Copland, *The Prairie* (1944) by Lukas Foss, and *Dover Beach*, op. 3 (1931) by Samuel Barber, a setting of Matthew Arnold's poem for solo voice and string quartet.

GUIDE TO ADDITIONAL LISTENING

Romantic opera

1. Giuseppe Verdi, *Il Trovatore*, "Ah! si, ben mio," and "Di quella pira," from Act III, Scene 2.

In "Ah! si, ben mio," Manrico (who is about to marry Leonora) sings to her of his devotion and tries to calm her fears, even though an enemy attack on the fortress is imminent.

The "Di quella pira" scene comes while Manrico is leading her to the chapel. They receive news that Azucena, Manrico's mother, has been captured by besiegers and is about to be burned at the stake.

Does the musical expression reflect the different situations? How? Contrast the melody, rhythms, voices, orchestra, and dynamics in terms of reassuring love, interruption and alarm, the hastening to rescue Azucena. How does grand opera as represented by *Il Trovatore* differ from Wagner's *Tristan und Isolde?* Berg's *Wozzeck?*

2. Georges Bizet, *Carmen,* Act II (opening).

The scene is in an inn full of gypsies, townspeople, and soldiers. The gypsies dance. The crowd drinks. Carmen sings "Chanson Boheme," a song describing the colorful scene of a gypsy dance. The excitement grows as the pace of the dance increases.

How do the rhythm and instrumental color create a dancing mood? What effects do the contrasts in dynamics have? Notice the gradual increase in speed, and the added musical role of the percussion.

3. Richard Wagner, *Die Götterdämmerung,* "Siegfried's Funeral March."

Note the undulating aspects of tension, release, tension. Note also the alternation of approach to climax, fall, and approach to another climax.

Observe the varying dramatic qualities reflected in the music of these excerpts. How do these three excerpts reflect the essence of Romanticism?

Modern opera

1. Benjamin Britten, *Peter Grimes.*

The opera *Peter Grimes* has been referred to as an essay in compassion and understanding. Is this reflected in the text? The action? The music? How? Is the listener's attitude affected by knowing that English is the original language of the opera?

The opera opens with a prologue followed by an orchestral interlude leading to Act I. What is the effect of such a beginning compared with an overture or orchestral prelude? Observe the musical variety in the prologue; the orchestral texture, the songlike quality of some of the singing, the declamatory style of other passages, the use of the chorus as a creator of hubub, and the closing unaccompanied duet. Contrast Interlude I with Interlude II.

Follow the libretto while listening to Act I, Scene 1. What is the dramatic effect of the orchestra at the following places:

1. Peter: Then home
   Among fishing nets
   Alone, alone, alone
   With a childless death!

2. Peter: I'll marry Ellen
   I'll marry Ellen
   I'll marry Ellen!

3. Balstrode: The storm is here. O come away.
   Peter: The storm is here and I shall stay.
   What harbour shelters peace?

2. Aaron Copland, *The Tender Land.*

Listen to the short orchestral introduction, the quintet-finale of Act I, "The Promise of Living," and Ma Moss's song of acceptance at the conclusion of the opera.

The setting of *The Tender Land* is the rural midwest United States. The plot is not as complex and intricate as are those of most large-scale operas, nor the range of emotion as great. How are these conditions reflected in the music? Does Copland's music reflect the essence of the title? If so, how?

3. Alberto Ginastera, *Bomarzo.*

Two acts and fifteen scenes tell the life story of the Duke of Bomarzo. Sometimes the sixteenth-century flavor of the story is evoked by the viola d'amore, mandolin, and harpsichord, but the music is severely modern, using every device, including the rattling of woodwind keys, to convey the story of this psychotic hunchback.

Ginastera has the following to say of the opera: "I see Bomarzo not as a man of the Renaissance, but as a man of our time. We live nowadays in an age of anxiety, an age of sex, an age of violence. Bomarzo struggles with sex, submits to violence, and is tortured by anxiety, the metaphysical anxiety of death."

How is this music different in sound from that of Romantic opera of the nineteenth century? Contrast the orchestral passages of

Bomarzo with those of *Peter Grimes* and those of *The Tender Land*. How does Ginastera's music project anxiety, violence? What sounds seem "new" for an opera orchestra? How is the chorus used?

Sacred music

Romantic

1. Hector Berlioz, *Requiem*.

If this piece were a painting, it would require a large canvas and glaring colors. In the "Dies Irae" the *tuba mirum*, calling for four brass choirs, four tam-tams, ten pairs of cymbals, sixteen kettledrums, full orchestra of 140, plus large chorus, creates all the terror of the text: "The trumpets, sounding rich harmonies through the tombs of the lands, shall compel all to come before the judgment seat." Berlioz's mastery of orchestration is also evident in the "Hostias," where the men's chorus alternates with flutes and trombones. Compare the "Dies Irae" with Verdi's "Dies Irae."

2. Felix Mendelssohn, *Elijah*.

The story of the oratorio concerns the search for the true God. The people who believe in Baal are pitted against Elijah whose God is Jehovah. How does Mendelssohn use tempo and orchestration to increase intensity during the three "Baal" choruses? Note the dramatic use of silence. How does Mendelssohn finally picture God in "Behold, God the Lord"?

Modern

1. Benjamin Britten, *War Requiem*, op. 66.

The text is unique. Britten mixes the Latin of the Requiem Mass with the English war poems of Wilfred Owen. The *War Requiem* was composed after the Second World War. The poetry is from the period of the First World War.

Listen particularly to "Requiem Aeternam" followed by "What Passing Bells for Those Who Die as Cattle?" and "Sanctus" followed by "After the Blast of Lightning from the East."

What is the effect of the contrasting alternation of liturgical-sacred text with secular poetry? What changes of musical style accompany the textual changes? How does Britten accompany the words, "Sanctus, Sanctus, Sanctus"? The words, "Hosanna in excelsis"? "Benedictus qui venit . . ."?

2. Krzysztof Penderecki (1933–), *Passion According to St. Luke* (1966).

The interpretive range of instruments and voices is stretched to new dimensions. Quarter-tones, chance techniques, vocal howls, hisses, glissandi, and whispers paint the drama in florescent terms. Compare the intensity, fervor, and violence of the setting of the crucifixion with the drama Mendelssohn achieves in the three "Baal" choruses.

3. Dave Brubeck (1920–), *The Light in the Wilderness* (1968).

An oratorio for orchestra, chorus, baritone soloist, and jazz ensemble. The temptations of Christ are reinterpreted to speak to the contemporary spirit. Jazz improvisation and syncopation move beside and within choral tone-rows to bring the ancient messages of peace and love into the twentieth century. Is the juxtaposition of jazz and classical orchestration effective?

Other vocal music

Romantic

1. Robert Schumann, *Five Poems of Mary Stuart*, op. 135.
2. Franz Schubert, "Der Wandrer an den Mond" ("The Traveller to the Moon"), op. 80, no. 1.
3. Hugo Wolf, "Verschwiegene Liebe" ("Secret Love"), from *Eichendorff Lieder*.
4. Johannes Brahms, "Dein blaues Auge" ("Your Blue Eyes"), op. 59, no. 8.

Note the variety of poetic subjects. Does the music reflect these poetic contrasts? How? Listen and follow the text. Listen without following the text. How does the music augment the expression of the poetry?

Five Poems of Mary Stuart was originally written in English, and later translated and set to music with German text. What makes these songs German?

Modern

1. Maurice Ravel, *Chants populaires* (1910).

These popular songs include "Spanish Song," "French Song," "Italian Song," and "Hebrew Song." Each is in its vernacular language. Do these songs give the flavor of the country they represent? How? What is the effect of the variety of language?

2. Francis Poulenc, "Hotel" and "Trip to Paris," from *Banalités* (1940).

"Hotel" as a poem seems banal. The music seems serious. What is the effect of this contrast? Is this contrast also true of "Trip to Paris"?

3. Paul Reif (1910–), *Five Finger Exercises.*

4. John Koch (1928–), "An Immortality," and "The Tea Shop."

Read the poetry of T. S. Eliot used as the text for *Five Finger Exercises* and Ezra Pound's "An Immortality" and "The Tea Shop." Listen to the songs. How do the musical settings complement the poems? Are the poems more effective with or without the music?

5. Serge Prokofiev, *Alexander Nevsky*, op. 78 (1939).

What gives this work its Russian character? How does Prokofiev convey the feeling of great strength in the first chorus?

FOR DISCUSSION

1. Is there any evidence among recorded rock music that songs have been strung together into cycles and cantatas? What factors are helping to break down the three-minute length barrier in popular songs?
2. Why do people express such strong opinions about opera? What factors contribute towards its limited audience? How might the audience for opera be enlarged?
3. Listen to the opening of Verdi's opera *Otello*. How does the orchestra add to the drama? How does this opening differ from standard openings? What makes the use of the chorus effective?
4. What made nineteenth-century grand opera "grand"?

5. Listen to a jazz Mass. What does the jazz style bring to the text? Does such a setting make the church more contemporary? Does it have an effect on the makeup of the congregation?
6. What kind of music is available to local churches? Are any of the performers paid? Do amateurs participate? What instruments are used? What kind of music is performed?

Romantic and Modern Styles: Instrumental Music

12

As an expressive medium the human voice has limitations. Composers in the nineteenth and twentieth centuries found that they could expand the range of expressive possibilities through instrumental means. While the voice seems bound to concrete images, instrumental combinations provide a means of expressing not only programmatic content but more abstract realms as well. Composers turned increasingly toward instrumental music, developing its forms and tonal colors for maximum effect.

Albert Bierstadt: Storm in the Mountains *(c. 1870–80). Courtesy, Museum of Fine Arts, Boston. M. and M. Karolik Collection.*

Albert Bierstadt, a nineteenth-century American painter, "orchestrated" his paintings. This work captures the grandeur and drama of nature. Bierstadt, who often painted from memory, exaggerated the natural world, giving it a loftiness and a majesty beyond reality.

THE SYMPHONY

The symphony reached a new maturity in the nineteenth century. Composers found that this form could incorporate every known technique of composition, making it unsurpassed as an all-encompassing expressive vehicle of instrumental music.

By May 7, 1824, Beethoven's nine symphonies had been composed and performed. Many of his innovations of musical expression set the pattern of the Romantic symphony for the rest of the century. These innovations included: expansion of dynamic contrasts, caustic dissonance, use of rhythmic devices to create both surprise and driving forward motion, extensive development of the thematic material, alteration of form to serve expression, and exploitation of tonal resources. In the case of tonal resources, Beethoven was the first to use trombones in a symphony (no. 5), the first to add voices to the orchestral language (no. 9), and the first to use timpani as thematic-motivic instruments (no. 9).

In the hands of nineteenth-century composers structural freedom, emphasis on lyricism, and a desire for an emotional expressiveness became the foundation of Romantic symphonies.

Imaginative structure and the development of thematic material, although basic to Beethoven, play a secondary role to the flowing, lyrical melody, the rich sounding harmonic progressions and the exploitation of orchestral color.

Hector Berlioz adopted and expanded these trends. His *Symphonie fantastique* is a synthesis of symphonic and programmatic music. Lizst defines programmatic music in terms of a "preface added to a piece of instrumental music, by means of which the composer intends to guard the listener against a wrong poetical interpretation and to direct his attention to the poetical idea of the whole or to a particular part of it." Berlioz' symphony is subtitled "Episode in the life of an artist." It has five movements: "Reveries-Passions," "A Ball," "Scene in the Country," "March to the Scaffold," "Dream of a Witches' Sabbath."

In a detailed explanation Berlioz describes a sensitive musician who, unable to refrain from thoughts of his beloved, turns to opium. Under the effects of opium, he dreams that he kills his beloved and is himself executed. Finally, his reverie takes him to a witches' sabbath. To sound the funeral knell, Berlioz parodies the "Dies Irae" from the Requiem Mass, and combines it with a grotesque round-dance.

Stylistically, the composition suggests the vivid moods, spirit, and reflections of the artist (thought by some to be Berlioz). Each movement has its own musically independent structure. Berlioz includes the theme of the loved one in all movements. This cyclical recall creates unity, binding the movements together. The program, too, ensured the artistic unity of the whole—a difficult achievement in a work of this length.

Perhaps more important than the expanded form and the variety of compositional devices that Berlioz used are his new techniques of orchestration. He uses the small, high-pitched E-flat clarinet to express eerieness in the "Witches' Sabbath." He uses the English horn in the third movement to simulate the sound of a shepherd's horn. He uses several timpani simultaneously, requiring two timpanists, and off-stage chimes in the "Dies Irae." Through the force of his originality, Berlioz could create with instrumental color and harmony a drama that the symphony had not known before.

Nineteenth-century Romantic music continued to develop in the symphonies of Johannes Brahms.

Brahms' symphonies express a compatible blend of melodic, harmonic and tonal events. The sound is fluid, homogeneous, sonorous. As the music progresses, changes from one melodic idea to another are accomplished by smooth transition. Even the unexpected appears with an element of preparation. Harmonic events blend and all progressions are prepared and resolved. The rhythmic flow is uninterrupted; the sound is continuous; even very short silences rarely exist. Any dissonance that occurs seems to evolve and dissolve. All events abide and subside in a complete and consistent "oneness."

The nineteenth-century symphony absorbed and expressed a wide range of dramatic content. Systems of tonality, harmony, and rhythm did not basically change. They evolved, and were subjected to the maximum exploitation these techniques could bear.

Twentieth-century composers have not been as kind to the symphony as a compositional form. Changes in tonality, experimentation with chromaticism, polytonality, atonality, tonal colors, serial techniques, and electronic devices have caused them to turn to shorter musical forms and smaller, less traditional combinations of instruments.

Igor Stravinsky looked to principles of balance and intellectual control that were the antithesis of the Romantic tradition. He, as well as other composers, generally abandoned the emphasis on programmatic music that marked the Romantic period. In place of the voluminous Romantic forms, the overblown emotionalism, and the thick-textured orchestral resources, twentieth-century composers preferred a re-

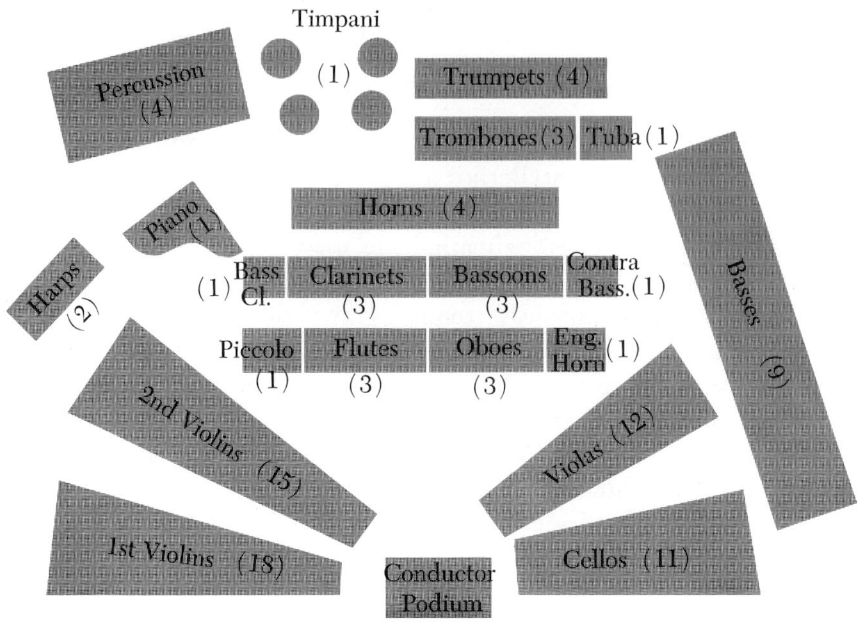

The Modern Symphony Orchestra.

The seating arrangement and instrumentation of the Boston Symphony Orchestra (shown here) is only one of several possibilities. Other large orchestras sometimes seat the violas or second violins in front on the right, with the cellos behind them. Acoustics in the concert hall often dictate the arrangement of the instruments. In addition to the 101 instrumentalists in the orchestra, there is a musical director, an associate and an assistant conductor, and an administrative staff including librarians, a stage manager, a personnel manager, and a press director.

strained, economical use of sound. They sought musical rather than poetic significance. Stravinsky's *Symphony in Three Movements* demonstrates one modern approach to the symphony. In the first movement, "Overture," Stravinsky uses a three-part form: tutti, solo, tutti. The second movement, "Andante," contrasts flute, strings and harp in a serene and restrained manner. The third movement, "Con moto," follows the second immediately after a short interlude and has five carefully balanced sections.

The contrasts between contrapuntal and chordal writing, movement and rest, and loud and soft are clearly planned. Rhythms are often irregular, obliterating the feeling of steadily recurring meter. Stravinsky uses rhythm with great imagination and expressive power. He creates tension, movement, climax, and release through calculated patterns of silence. Tonality and atonality are juxtaposed in the same work. Stravinsky uses unusual groups of instruments but rarely sounds all of them or the full orchestra simultaneously. In his *Symphony in Three Movements*, he includes the piano as an orchestral instrument. In several works, such as *Symphonies of Wind Instruments*, he does not use stringed instruments, perhaps to avoid their Romantic warm and sentimental qualities.

In contrast to Brahms' style, the musical events in Stravinsky's symphonies act more independently and individualistically, creating a greater heterogeneity in the total sound. The melodic events are set in relief to dissonant harmonic events; florid embellishments vie with melody and harmony rather than accommodate them. Rhythmic force is primary and commands the listener's attention. Rather than hearing the orchestra as a total entity, as with Brahms, one is more likely to hear simultaneous musical events in a grid of conflict, the attention shifting from one event to another. Stravinsky's works emphasize harmonic dissonance, rhythmic irregularity, and stark contrasts. While both composers' music is glorious and fulfilling, Stravinsky's has an unresolved tension that is not found in Brahms'. Brahms' music flows, while Stravinsky's seems to be driven.

Charles Ives, representative of the American experience, explored musical expression with different sounds. His principal works include four symphonies, many songs, choral pieces, and works for piano. As one listens to his music, tunes such as "Columbia, the Gem of the Ocean," "What a Friend We Have in Jesus," "Bringing in the Sheaves," or even the principal motive of Beethoven's Fifth Symphony emerge from the complex texture. He was known to attach the names of prominent Americans such as Emerson, Hawthorne, and Thoreau to movements of his compositions, and frequently "teased" those who could not tolerate his music by offering them ironic program notes to his music.

The following style chart highlights and contrasts two symphonies, one Romantic, one Modern.

Comparative Styles:
The Symphony

	Romantic	*Modern*
	Brahms (1833–1897), Symphony no. 2	*Stravinsky (1882–1971),* Symphony in Three Movements
Expression	*Warm, gentle, conversational. Secure, dramatic power. Ranges from somber to joyous.*	*Wide range of expressive events with frequent shifts, in a manner similar to dialogue. The drama is tightly controlled.*
Melody	*Lyrical and fluid. Range from sorrowful and sensuous to joyous, sometimes playful. Flows beautifully, even when motivic.*	*Fragmentary but not elusive. Dependent upon frequently-changing dialogue. Themes not lyrical or connected as in Brahms.*
Rhythm	*Subtle. Sometimes forceful but supportive of other events.*	*Prominent. Often primary, overshadowing melody, harmony, and tone color. Often driving and pungent.*
Tone Color	*Full orchestra; rich in strings and woodwinds. Contrasting colors presented in a blending field.*	*Less a blend of tonal resources; more of a conflict of individual colors. More emphasis on winds, brass, percussion, and piano.*
Harmony	*Full, rich, luscious. Tensions resolved. Pungent dissonance is immediately resolved. Supportive.*	*Not functional in the Romantic sense. A basic event in its own right. Pungent, unresolved dissonance.*

	Romantic	*Modern*
Dynamics	*Wide range. Some sudden changes but mostly gradual. Dramatically used.*	*Wide range. Forceful. Related to rhythm and structure. Sudden changes. An independently expressive event.*
Structure	*Rather formal, meaningful. Degree of delineation of sections varies. Much development.*	*Shorter than usual nineteenth-century symphony. Form not traditional. Continual evolving organic force. Less dependent on repetition, recurrence, development, and so on.*
Medium and Texture	*Romantic orchestra. Much melody with harmonic accompaniment. Some imitation. Counterpoint not prominent. Rich solo passages. Use of partial as well as full orchestra.*	*Orchestra plus harp, piano, and bass-clarinet. Equally dependent upon winds, piano, and instruments other than strings. Instruments used as independent speakers, not members of a homogenized group. Some counterpoint.*

THE CONCERTO

With few exceptions the symphony composers were also the principal composers of concertos. A concerto is a work in which two compatible but contrasting performing mediums (usually the full orchestra and a solo instrument) are combined in a unified presentation in spite of the musical competition that is an essential ingredient. Themes are exchanged. The soloist is sometimes accompanied by the orchestra, and sometimes accompanies the orchestra. Each medium is of equal importance. A "virtuoso" violin may be set off against the entire orchestra; a cello may be first set off against the string section and then against the winds; a piano might mingle with and emerge from the orchestra, alternately frustrating and gratifying the listener. Reconciliation of this conflict is the essence of the concerto.

The violin and the piano concerto were prominent forms in the nineteenth century, reflecting the musical characteristics of Romantic symphonic writing: lyrical melodies, rich harmonies, and brilliant orchestral color. They did not, however, reflect the nineteenth-century practice of extramusical titles and programmatic descriptions. Solo parts are extremely difficult to perform. A performer's virtuosity could be measured by his performance in a solo concerto.

The nineteenth-century concerto is a three-movement form. The first movement is in sonata-allegro form, with the soloist and the orchestra often joining together for the opening exposition. A fully scored (not improvised) cadenza usually concludes the development section and serves as the transition to the recapitulation. The second movement is generally slower and more lyrical, and the third movement faster and often in rondo or sonata-allegro form.

In the twentieth century, concerto form has remained a mainstay. In Bartók's *Concerto for Orchestra* (1943), instruments of the orchestra play both the role of soloist and the role of contrasting group. The work is divided into five movements that follow a modified classical pattern.

1. First movement—modified sonata-allegro form.
2. Second movement—sectional form:

	A	*B*	*C*	
Introduction	*a b c d e*	*chorale*	*a′ b′ c′ d′ e′*	*Coda*

3. Third movement—slow, dramatic.
4. Fourth movement—interrupted intermezzo:

A B Interruption B A

5. Fifth movement—elements of sonata-allegro, rondo, and rhapsody.

The second movement—"Giuoco delle Coppie" ("Game of Pairs")—reveals a variety of expressive qualities. The introduction is stated by a muffled snare drum. The first section consists of a series of duets by bassoons, oboes, clarinets, flutes, and muted trumpets. Strings are used for accompaniment, rhythmic interest, and transitional passages. A chorale section follows—all brass accompanied by drum. The third section is an expanded, more elaborate and intense statement of the earlier duets, which no longer remain duets. The coda is a reiteration and fading out of the rhythm stated in the introduction. The expressiveness of this movement lies in the integration of the rhythmic, tonal, and melodic events which are introduced, characterized, changed, and eventually dissolved.

The music of Béla Bartók represents a remarkable synthesis of Classic, Romantic-Nationalist, and contemporary influences. The external formal structures found in his music are closely allied to the forms of the Classic period and Beethoven. The creative way in which he uses Roumanian and Slavic folk music gives a unique characteristic to much of his music. The expansion of forms, the tonal systems, the new mediums, the rhythmic forces, and the new coloration bring all of his music into an alliance with twentieth-century change.

Bartók was fond of irregular rhythms and offbeat accents. He juxtaposed homophonic (chordal) style with polyphonic style, combining melody with melody in a full and complex texture. His fertile imagination showed that pungently dissonant tonality still offered expressive potential.

In 1965, Elliott Carter, one of the most original and talented living American composers, finished his *Piano Concerto* and dedicated it to Stravinsky. Carter has indicated that he thinks of his compositions as auditory scenarios with the performers being individuals as they participate in the ensemble. His concerto reflects this. Many musical events happen simultaneously, carrying the listener along in the momentum and power of the work. The complicated counterpoint and complex rhythmic passages do not appear cohesive upon first hearing. Each part remains distinct, even though ultimately fused into a concerted whole.

Comparative Styles:
The Concerto

	Romantic	*Modern*	
	Tchaikovsky (1840–1893), Concerto no. 1 in B Flat Minor for Piano and Orchestra	*Bartók (1881–1945),* Concerto for Orchestra	*Carter (1908–),* Piano Concerto
Expression	*Bold, rich, commanding of full attention. Almost pompous, grandiose.*	*Mixture of classic, romantic, contemporary, and Slavic folk moods.*	*Fragmented. Many events to listen to at one time. Constantly evolving.*
Melody	*Lyrical, flowing, fluid. Sectional alternation with orchestra and piano.*	*Varied: motivic, lyrical, folk-like.*	*Fragmentary. Based on dialog. Frequent but subtle, lyrical passages.*
Rhythm	*Steady. No surprises. Supportive.*	*Important, sometimes primary. Mixed meter, seemingly erratic at times.*	*Evolving and seemingly erratic. Frequently a primary event.*
Tone Color	*Contrasts between solo piano, solo instruments, and the orchestra. Compatible use of color.*	*Full exploitation of orchestra, solo instruments, and sections.*	*Changing. No one color persists for long. Constant dialog.*
Harmony	*Supportive of other events. Rich and full. Traditional.*	*Sometimes dissonant as a result of counterpoint. At times folk-like.*	*A result of dialog and counterpoint. Very dissonant.*

	Romantic	*Modern*	
Dynamics	*Full range. Surging toward climax.*	*Full range, but changes and variation used with discretion.*	*Wide range. Frequent changes and surprises. Dramatic and innovative.*
Structure	*Traditional concerto design.*	*Modified traditional form.*	*Evolving. Nontraditional.*
Medium and Texture	*Orchestra plus piano; melody with accompanient. Homophonic.*	*Orchestra featured as its own "virtuoso"; competes with itself. Wide range of textures: sometimes homophonic, solo with accompaniment, duets, solo percussion, and complex counterpoint.*	*Orchestra and piano. Constant dialog. Piano functions as important member of orchestra.*

THE SUITE

Music originally composed for the theatre sometimes finds its way into the concert hall. Music incidental to a play, or from various parts of an opera or ballet is sometimes excerpted and presented in the form of a suite. The sectional structure of a suite permits the various musical selections to retain their individual character and their literary or theatrical associations. The music, however, still must be able to succeed independently of its relationships to other art forms. The suite became a vehicle for bringing the music of the opera, ballet, or theatre to the concert stage without producing the whole work.

Bizet wrote the incidental music to the play *L'Arlésienne* in 1872. The two suites extracted from it are excellent examples of the Romantic suite. No. 2, the better known, exemplifies the colorfulness of French orchestration. Throughout the four movements, lyrical melody predominates. Since the harmony is straightforward, contrasts in dynamics and tone color are the suite's other primary musical resources.

The suite has also been used by modern composers. It has, however, changed shape and character and has also been called by different names. Stravinsky's *The Tale of the Soldier* (1918) is such a work. It is written for narrator, violin, string bass, clarinet, bassoon, trumpet, trombone, and various percussion instruments. The composition utilizes the solo potential of the instruments, as well as their ensemble qualities. The influence of early jazz is found in this work in the movement titled "Ragtime." Ragtime music has a base rhythm of: $\frac{2}{4}$ ♪♩♪ ♫ while the tango (used in another movement) uses $\frac{2}{4}$ ♩. ♬ ♫ at a slightly slower tempo. The rhythms of ragtime give a feeling of joyousness and frivolity, while those of the tango appear more formal and stately.

Comparative Styles: The Suite

	Romantic	*Modern*
	Bizet (1838–1875), L'Arlésienne *Suite no. 2*	*Stravinsky (1882–1971)*, The Tale of the Soldier
Expression	*Pastoral, dance-like. Generally pleasant, reassuring, colorful.*	*Suggestive of the titles of each section of the music. Contrast from quiet and pastoral to march-like and raucous.*
Melody	*Singable, flowing. Range from lyrical to joyous and danceable; sometimes playful.*	*Singable but less lyrical and fluid; more dialog-like. Much contrast in the melodies.*

	Romantic	*Modern*
Rhythm	*Steady, constant meter; supportive of other events.*	*Mixed meter. Frequent change even when there seems to be a steady ostinato figure. Related to forms in the suite: tango, ragtime, waltz, march, chorale.*
Tone Color	*Orchestral. Pleasant blend of solo, sections, and full orchestra. Generally a compatible synthesis of contrasting colors.*	*Small ensemble. Exciting contrasts and combinations.*
Harmony	*Supportive of melody. Nondissonant. Neither unique, surprising nor innovative.*	*Nontraditional; more a result of melodic and rhythmic events. Dissonant. Unique and innovative when a primary event.*
Dynamics	*Some contrast. Soft to pleasantly moderate. No overbearing loud levels or dramatic surprises. Secondary in function.*	*Wide range. Expressive. Sometimes used as structural element. Sudden contrasts.*
Structure	*Standard suite structure.*	*Follows standard structure.*
Medium and Texture	*Full orchestra, sections, and solos. Mostly melody with accompaniment. Infrequent innovation.*	*Limited ensemble. Contrapuntal texture. Independence of instruments creates ever-changing textural innovations. Each event of primary importance.*

Stylistic contrasts are apparent in these two works. Notice how differently the two composers treat the pastorale. In the Bizet suite the "Pastorale" is sonorous, making use of the full orchestra as well as a flute solo accompanied by the orchestra. Observe the richness, the homogenization of the sound—the Romantic expression of a peaceful country life. Conversely, the Stravinsky "Pastorale" lacks this fullness, the sense of harmony, the impression of a peaceful countryside. The Stravinsky is calm but more "haunting." The sonorities occur individually rather than in unison, as a "chorus." One pastorale is sonorous, a combination of blended sounds, the other more a number of independent musical events.

SYMPHONIC POEM

The tone poem or symphonic poem is an extension of program music into the realm of the symphony. The symphonic poem was invented by Liszt, who sought to break away from the strict dictates of sonata form. The score of *Les Préludes*, one of Liszt's most familiar symphonic poems, includes a reference to Lamartine's *Méditations poétiques*, which suggest that life is a series of preludes to death. Liszt's musical style is the epitome of Romanticism. The extremely somber beginning of the one-movement composition contrasts with its glorious ending. Light pastoral themes are set in contrast to noble, brilliant, powerful musical statements. A coherent story line provided a new way to achieve musical unity, while permitting freedom of expression. The many contrasts in life—its sorrows, glories, frustrations, calms—all find enhanced reflection in Liszt's music. His use of brass instruments, particularly horns, his slowing down of harmonic changes, his emphasis of the single chord and the progression of one chord to the next, and the nobility of his themes, give a grandness and an opulence to his orchestral sound. It is no wonder that this style of music has been adopted as sound tracks for romantic movies.

The symphonic poem continued with the works of Richard Strauss and Jean Sibelius (1865–1957) and into the twentieth-century works of Ottorino Respighi and Claude Debussy. Although some style changes occurred, the Romanticism of the nineteenth century persists in most twentieth-century symphonic poems; it was shattered, however, by programmatic music that turned to the imagery of the machine and the city in such works as Arthur Honegger's (1892–1955) *Pacific 231*,

John Carpenter's (1876–1951) *Skyscrapers*, and Alexander Mossolov's (1900–) *Iron Foundry*.

Liszt's *Les Préludes* represents the Romanticism of the nineteenth century. A somber introduction is followed by a lyrical theme that finds fulfillment in full orchestra—rich, full-bodied, completely homogeneous. Next a pastoral, lyrical melodic line passes from cellos to French horns. Throughout, Liszt's musical events encompass the rise and fall of the melodic line, the complementary use of tonal colors, a wide range of dynamic levels, and fluid rhythmic events. Liszt has expressed Lamartine's poetic thought with the melodic, harmonic, and tonal resources of the orchestra.

Debussy's *La Mer* describes the sea programmatically. The third movement, "The Dialogue of the Wind and the Sea," contrasts in style to Liszt's *Les Préludes*. Melodic ideas are fragmentary; harmonic events play a more primary than supportive role; dynamics are extremely important. The sense of fulfillment expressed in the more noble and glorious themes of *Les Préludes* is absent here. Tonal colors are more directly contrasting and frequently changing, more sudden, and more surprising. There is more use of motives and the long themes that evolve from the motives. Rhythmic events are ever present; melodic events result from motivic culmination; harmonic events lack the resolution of those of Liszt. The entire movement is an organic growth rather than a series of vignettes.

In *Pacific 231*, Honegger uses the orchestra to pay homage to the twentieth-century's mechanical giant—the railroad. Honegger does not imitate the steam engine; he uses musical events to reflect its massiveness and strength, its sluggishness, its impressive speed, its starting, its stopping. He transcends sheer imitation to a spiritual celebration in sound of the machine.

Honegger combines musical events for their total effect. Melody, at first, does not exist; harmonic events are caustic and forceful; rhythmic events are of major importance; unresolved dissonance is basic. The emphasis is on creating a gradually increasing forward motion. Once the appropriate acceleration is achieved melodic ideas enter—motivic at first and eventually in longer spans. The bassoon melody with snare drum accentuation is particularly effective. Dissonant harmony, motivic melody, lyrical melody, and exciting rhythm describe the train's motion. At the climax, melodies and other events mesh as if they were large numbers of coordinate but independent moving parts. Each part joins another, but each remains distinct in its musical function and its strength —the whole becomes more than the sum of its parts.

OTHER ORCHESTRAL MUSIC

In addition to the symphonies, concertos, suites, and programmatic music, orchestral music also includes extracts from opera and ballet, incidental music, orchestral variations, and other miscellaneous forms.

Ballet has provided a particularly fertile field for musical creation. Stravinsky's ballet *Le Sacre du Printemps* (*The Rite of Spring*), for instance, reflects a complete break with prevalent practices of the nineteenth century. Its primitive-sounding rhythms evoke images of fertility rites and tribal dances. Its driving, forceful, rhythmic activity is reinforced by harsh dissonance. Stravinsky rejected the rhythmic regularity of nineteenth-century style in favor of an unprecedented irregularity. He used instruments in unique ways. Performers were challenged by his bizarre combinations of instruments and technical demands. Although Stravinsky wrote *The Rite of Spring* as a ballet he never let the demands of the ballet interfere with the musical integrity of the composition. His entire approach to composition was that of solving musical problems.

In the American style, musical comedy and music for the theater inspired the use of contemporary American music for the dance. Consequently jazz and rock found their places on the stage. Representative are dance scenes from Bernstein's *West Side Story*, George Antheil's (1900–1959) *Ballet mécanique*, the folk-rock musical *Hair* and the religious musical *Godspell*.

Other Works. The twentieth century has produced works in which the form is created to answer the specific needs of the individual piece. Samuel Barber's *Adagio for Strings* and his *Essay for Orchestra* (1938) are examples. Schoenberg wrote a *Fantasy for Violin and Piano* (1949), and Milton Babbitt wrote *Ensembles for Synthesizer*.

CHAMBER MUSIC

Chamber music from any period is largely an art of the performer. It is often far more exciting for the performers than for most listeners. Like tasting fine wine, chamber music requires a specialized taste that must be developed through listening. Since the scoring is limited to a has a clarity of texture that permits the listener to hear every note. But even in a small hall, where it is meant to be performed, the sounds rarely flood the listener.

The string quartet and the piano quintet, although by no means the only chamber-music mediums of the nineteenth century, reflect best the Romantic spirit. Schubert wrote fifteen quartets. However, quartets did not flow as profusely from the pens of other nineteenth-century composers. Mendelssohn wrote six, Schumann three, Brahms three, and Tchaikovsky three.

The quartet medium did not satisfy the nineteenth-century demand for expanding color combinations and "bigness" of sound. The quartets of this period do reflect the new Romantic lyricism and harmonic content. In some instances they reflect folk-nationalism. They do not, however, represent the bold and brilliant musical characteristics of nineteenth-century orchestral Romanticism. The string quartet is an intellectual exercise demanding the composer to summon his highest powers of creativity in order to fully exploit the four instruments. The limitations of tone color and number of tones that can be sounded simultaneously challenge the composer to find the means to express a broad range of moods.

Quartets by Debussy and Ravel, one each, usher in the innovative spirit of the twentieth century. Both quartets reflect new sounds. Debussy moves away from the traditional harmonic and rhythmic pat-

Comparative Styles: String Quartet

	Romantic	*Modern*	
	Schubert (1797–1828), Quartet no. 14, "Death and the Maiden"	*Ravel (1875–1937), Quartet in F Major*	*Bartók (1881–1945), Quartet no. 4*
Expression	*Straightforward. Warm, personal. Traditional.*	*Impressionistic. Emphasis on change, variety of tonal color.*	*Intellectual, innovative. Less melodic, more percussive.*

	Romantic	*Modern*	
Melody	*Lyrical, fluid, clear. Ranges from song-like, dramatic, and mournful to joyous, happy and zealous.*	*Lyrical. Variety of expressions. Song-like but also motivic.*	*Wide range, from lyric to motivic.*
Rhythm	*Straightforward, steady meters. Supportive of other events. Solid and unified.*	*Exciting contrasts as well as subtle inflections.*	*A primary event. Exciting use of both obvious and subtle rhythmic devices. Irregular.*
Tone Color	*Traditional sound of string quartet.*	*Emphasis on new colors. Not based on simple major scale. Less homogeneous.*	*Explorative.*
Harmony	*Rich and full. Little dissonance. Supportive of melodic events.*	*Impressionistic. Less traditional. More counterpoint and dissonance.*	*Dissonant; often the result of emphasized counterpoint.*
Dynamics	*Full range.*	*Wide range. Contrasts with pizzicato and bowed techniques.*	*Wide range of dynamic contrast. Use of pizzicato. Sometimes bombastic.*
Structure	*Traditional (four movements).*	*Nontraditional (although still in four movements).*	*Nontraditional (five movements). Evolving.*

	Romantic		Modern
Texture	*Melody with accompaniment; homophonic.*	*More exploitation.*	*Still more exploitation. Use of counterpoint and new performance techniques: glissando, pizzicato, and Bartók pizzicato.*

terns of the nineteenth century. Ravel expands the total extent of color available from the string quartet. Quartets by Bartók, Schoenberg, Weber, and Berg follow. The musical events and the elements of sound exploitation in the six Bartók quartets place them among the most significant in the twentieth century. Bartók brings together new harmonic and rhythmic devices, contrapuntal and harmonic events, but couches them in an architectural structure derived from the late Beethoven quartets.

SOLO MUSIC

PIANO

In the nineteenth century the piano became the foremost solo instrument. In his later years, Beethoven is joined and followed by a succession of piano composers so monumental as to be almost legendary.

The solo sonata was a widely used form but other new forms for piano appeared as well. Romanticism found elegant expression in the piano keyboard. Among the new and newly adapted forms created during this period were intermezzos, impromptus, songs without words, études, fantasies, independent rondos, variations, preludes, character-pieces, suites, studies, program music for piano, nocturnes, waltzes, mazurkas, polonaises, ballades, independent scherzos, rhapsodies, and on occasion transcriptions of major orchestral works.

Nineteenth-century pianists developed an unheard of virtuosity.

The instrument, its music, and the performers captured the attention of audiences everywhere. The piano became a household instrument. A giant among these giants was Franz Liszt. Liszt composed many character pieces, usually in collections. His *Années de pèlerinage* (*Years of Pilgrimage*) contains many piano works inspired by leading Romantic writers and poets. Birds sing in *St. François d'Assise* (*St. Francis of Assisi*); and a fountain is described in *Les jeux d'eaux à la Villa d'Este* (*The Fountain of the Villa d'Este*). Melodies are often accompanied by virtuoso figurations.

The music of Chopin is also representative of the majestic and heroic Romantic style. His music was emotionally expressive and filled with the spirit of song-like lyricism. His sonatas were fantasy-like. Some forms took on a nationalist flavor: the polonaise, the mazurka. Others were free from the rigidity of architectural design: scherzos, intermezzos, waltzes, impromptus, fantasies, études.

Embellishments were highly elaborate, breaking out of the metrical framework of the music. This characteristic created a freedom from metrical regularity and gave the music a colorful, improvisatory nature. The beat had to wait for the lyrical flow of the music.

In many ways the impressionistic character of the works of Debussy and Ravel are due to the impressionism in Liszt's works and the improvisatory embellishments in the works of Chopin. Ravel's impressionistic techniques do not function with as much flexibility as those of Debussy. Ravel's harmonies remain more conventional and his rhythms less abstract.

Both Debussy and Ravel, although Debussy to the greater extent, explored new realms of sound for the piano. The use of whole-tone scales, pentatonic scales, unresolved dissonance and the exploitation of the exquisitely soft, veiled possibilities of piano sound led to new styles. Debussy also depended to a great extent on titles: "Veils," "The Wind on the Plain," "The Girl With the Flaxen Hair."

In the twentieth century, Prokofiev composed a number of conventional piano sonatas and concertos. But few other modern composers have been preoccupied with the piano.

There are apparent stylistic differences between Chopin, Debussy, and Prokofiev. In the Chopin *Fantaisie-Impromptu*, op. 66, written in the Romantic style, the melody, harmony, and rhythm form a unified, sonorous whole. The dominant melody is accompanied by lush, rippling harmonies. As the work progresses the melody becomes florid, but is always supported by complementary harmonic and rhythmic events. Chopin uses the piano's dynamic resources fully.

Debussy's second prelude, "Voiles" ("Veils or Sails"), from *Préludes*, Book I, is in contrast to Chopin's *Fantaisie*. Melody is more fragile, more fragmentary. The harmonies are more prominent and less supportive of the melody. Debussy's rhythms are subtle, vague, and expressive. The piano is used delicately. There is no great splendor, there are no ponderous chords; the rhythm is gentle, the effect is delicate and sensitive.

Prokofiev, in his Sonata in B Flat Major, emphasizes rhythmic percussiveness and caustic harmonic events. The beginning of the sonata presents a fascinating interplay of melodic, harmonic, and rhythmic events. Fragments of melody are interrupted by chordal-rhythmic passages. Poignant harmonic events accompany effective, straightforward melodies. Percussive, harmonic passages reach a forceful climax.

Comparative Styles:
The Piano Solo

	Romantic	*Modern*	
	Chopin (1810–1849), Fantaisie in F Minor, op. 49	*Debussy (1862–1918), Selections from* Préludes, *Book 1*	*Prokofiev (1891–1953), Sonata in B Flat Major, op. 83*
Expression	*Lyrical, fluid, warm. Some nationalistic flavor. Idealistic. Gives feeling of beauty beyond man.*	*Mystic, reticent, calm. Not forceful.*	*Spirited. Forceful in a percussive manner. Changing. Domineering. Not always singable. Essence of realism. Restless and surprising.*

	Romantic	*Modern*	
Melody	*Extremely lyrical. Dominates. Range from somber to joyous, clear and concise to highly elaborate. Formal.*	*More fragmentary, fragile. Less formal structure.*	*Strongly integrated with harmonic and rhythmic events. Sometimes not the primary event.*
Rhythm	*Steady, but flexible. Unifying.*	*Free. Expressive of titles.*	*Forceful and dynamic. Percussive. An important, primary event.*
Tone Color	*Reflecting total expressive sentiments of the piano. The piano used as a "singing" instrument.*	*Veiled. The piano becomes less a singing, more a conversational instrument. Less ponderous. More gentle, sensitive.*	*Percussive. Changes frequently with the spirit of the musical dialogue.*
Harmony	*Rich, full, supportive. Some homophonic sections. Harmony important. Use of full-chordal sounds.*	*Break from tradition. More prominent. Based more on whole-tone, pentatonic scales. No use of the full scope of Romantic expression.*	*Surprising. At times calm, relaxed, reassuring, but often dissonant, vital, and full of tension.*
Dynamics	*Wide range. Use of crescendo and diminuendo.*	*More quiet. Some brief loud percussive sounds. Reserved.*	*Full range.*

	Romantic	*Modern*	
Structure	*Reasonably free. However, with a general dependence on repetition and recurrence. No development of musical ideas.*	*Free. More rambling. Decreased emphasis on repetition, variation, recurrence, and development.*	*Rhapsodic. Nontraditional.*
Texture	*Melody with accompaniment or homophonic. No reliance on counterpoint.*	*More counterpoint but not in a formal structural sense.*	*Mixed. Melody with accompaniment. Some passages primarily harmonic and rhythmic. Frequent counterpoint.*

ORGAN MUSIC

The organ had the potential to express fully the spirit of Romanticism. Nineteenth-century composers wrote large works in an effort to glorify the instrument. Louis Vierne (1870–1937) even wrote six large-scale "symphonies" for organ. Composers also composed "Masses" for the organ.

Worthy of mention is the great variety in the construction of the instruments themselves. Organs of different historical periods vary, as do organs of different churches and different organ builders.

The nineteenth-century organ was capable of the widest variety and maximum expressiveness man could devise. Twentieth-century composers tend to be satisfied with a more concise, classic instrument, limited to less flamboyant colorations. The relationship of organ music to religion has become fixed, since most organs are found in religious houses. For this reason much of contemporary organ music is sectarian. Since the organ as an instrument is given to the bombast and pyrotechnics of the virtuoso performer, even modern music for organ reflects the grandiose style associated with the nineteenth century. The tonal language, however, is frequently contemporary: massive tonal clusters, crashing dissonances, and wild rhythmic counterpoint are characteristic of the compositions.

ELECTRONIC MUSIC AND OTHER NEW MUSIC

Twentieth-century composers have sought new tonal resources to enrich their palates. One of the new sound sources is the sophisticated electronic sound-generating equipment which permits the composer to plug-in or program a full range of possible sounds, from city noises to simulations of the violin and voice. To be able to push the human soundscape to the infinite—to produce pitches far lower and higher, faster and longer, than are possible in the symphony orchestra—lends a new vitality to this music.

Unlike the pitched melody of the nineteenth century, electronic melody might consist of a sweep of sound or a tone approaching from far off. Rarely are there chords or harmony as such (although composers can simulate these electronically), but more often, combinations of tone colors in general pitch ranges.

The growing interest in the use of electronic synthesizers and computers for composing is a dominant factor in present-day music. Electronic music centers were established in Toronto, New York, and Cologne, and are also mushrooming elsewhere. New electronic instruments have been and are continually being developed. Currently large numbers of composers are working in the electronic field. Eminent among these are Ussachevsky and Luening (already mentioned), Luciano Berio, Pierre Boulez (1925–), Milton Babbitt, Mario Davidovsky, and Karlheinz Stockhausen. Their music includes electronically produced sounds, manipulated prerecorded sounds, sounds being modulated during a performance, and combinations of these in conjunction with traditional instruments. The techniques of composition range from highly structured patterns to unstructured, random arrangements of sound.

Electronic music by its very nature instigates new concepts of musical language and measurement. Pitches can be established in terms of frequency, rhythms in terms of stop-watch timing, tonal color in terms of wave form, and volume in terms of decibels. The composer can conceive of patterns that a musician probably could not perform. For example, the electronic medium makes available usable sounds (microtones) between the notes on the piano. Time can be divided into split-second accuracy. (There may be 24 sounds in one voice accurately accompanied by twenty-nine other sounds in an equal time space.) Dynamic levels which are suggested by the vague markings *ff*, *p*, *mf*, etc., can now be measured in exact decibels of sound.

"Isn't this a dehumanizing of music?" "Are machines gaining control of our lives?" Not necessarily. Man has created the machine to do only what it is programmed to do. It may automatically combine, synthesize, fragmentize, transpose, and modulate—but it cannot, ultimately, create. Further, all musical instruments, including the human voice, are physical machines. The synthesizer is simply another of man's tools—permitting a greater range of sound resources and combinations, and an enlarged capacity for expression.

Electronic music has long been used as background in film and television. Now it has come into a realm of indigenous expressiveness. The limitless range of possibilities in electronic music is inspiration to those desiring "all possible sounds" at their command.

Not all twentieth-century composers have written electronic music. The search for new sounds has lead some experimental composers to invent new instruments or to tap natural sound sources for their expressive potential.

Edgar Varèse pioneered in electronic music as early as 1927. He never stopped searching for new sound possibilities. His composition, *Ionisation*, was the first composition scored for what was to become a new medium in the twentieth century—the percussion ensemble.

The influence of technology also finds expression in the music of George Antheil. His music for *Ballet mécanique* required a new group of "instruments." Principal among the instruments are numerous percussion sounds, eight pianos, doorbells, and airplane motors. *Ballet mécanique* was a striking new venture into the expansion of possible musical sounds.

Although Tchaikovsky called for cannons in the *1812* Overture and Verdi anvils in *Il Trovatore*, their use was more for dramatic effect than musical sound. The *Ballet mécanique* raises the nebulous issue of "where noise stops and music begins"; composers John Cage and Harry Partch explore the question in depth. They have investigated the idea of sound as it occupies space, silence as a musical entity, and natural sounds as music. They have modified instruments, as well as created new ones.

Cage believes in music as the "organization of sound." He would include all sounds—sounds organized by the listener as well as the composer and sounds organized by chance as well as by plan.

> Music is, for him, not the restricted art form that our civilization has always assumed, but a vastly enlarged area of speculation that emerges as both a branch of theatre and a branch of philosophy.

Cage is one of the most controversial contemporary composers. He has written music for prepared piano—a piano in which the strings and hammers are modified to produce different sounds. He has written for an ensemble of radios, composed electronic music, and even music for silence. Except when asleep, people seldom experience absolute silence. In his *Sonata for Silence* a "performer" walks on stage, sits at the piano, and does nothing for approximately three minutes. The audience listens to and organizes what they hear during the silence—program rattles, coughs, air-conditioning (heating) fans, shuffling of feet, and other sounds. Such experimentation is characteristic of twentieth-century music.

THE PERCUSSION SOLOIST

This exploration of electronic sound, newly conceived instruments, utilitarian objects to produce musical sound (brake drums, steel pipes), and the combination of these with traditional percussion instruments, has brought the percussionist to the fore as a soloist. The number of instruments and artifacts used for instruments seems infinite. The performer may use a variety of mallets: wood, metal, yarn, rubber. He may use his hands, fingers, elbows, and may strike, scrape, flip (with fingers) or rattle the instruments. The musical literature available for such performances is rapidly increasing. There are representative pieces in the Guide to Additional Listening to acquaint the listener with this style.

SUMMARY
ROMANTIC AND MODERN STYLES

No style is assimilated so completely that every composer in a period expresses it in pure form. Individual personalities always produce contradictions and exceptions. To acknowledge that style exists, however, is to accept the notion that certain general characteristics can be identified.

Romanticism is a movement of transformation. It transforms the experiences of the real world into a new idealistic world. It seeks to transcend the limited sphere of one's own time and existence, and reach out beyond it. It relies on symbolism, mystery, suggestion, and impression. The Romantic composer searched for new sounds to express this world. He used more complex harmonies and textures. Instrumental tone color became highly developed as new instruments joined the orchestra and color combinations became more flexible. These techniques helped give expression to the boundless, free, searching, dramatic, and emotional feelings of the Romantics.

Romantic art reached for the infinite and in so doing gathered many stylistic devices together in a grand amalgamation of feeling and thought. It is the art of the heroic, of masses, of volumes, of sound complexes. Distinctions break down and individual entities merge.

The Romantic composers did not invent forms, they exploited them. They were often more successful with the shorter forms, such as the song, depending on a story or poetry for continuity. They often turned to nature for inspiration. Beethoven wrote a *Pastoral* Symphony; Schumann, a *Spring* Symphony, Mendelssohn, *A Midsummer Night's Dream*, Liszt, the *Transcendental Études* with descriptive titles such as "Feuxfollets" ("Fireflies"), "Chasse-neige" ("Snow Storm"), and "Harmonies du soir" ("Evening Harmonies").

In contrast, the music of the twentieth century has a Classic tendency. Intellect appears to control emotion. Emphasis has shifted from the melody to the rhythm, or even to the tone color. Composers are interested in new internal organization, even going beyond the atonal and twelve-tone scale systems. They are interested in articulation of all the sounds. They explore distinctness and explicitness, and a balance of clearly defined elements. Theirs is a less pretentious and more objective music. Experimentation is a basic element. The composer has come back to earth to react to and to express the real world of which he is a part. If the audience is not always with him, it may be because many people prefer to escape into the subjective realm of the Romantic rather than face the somewhat cooler, intellectual reflection of their own time.

GUIDE TO ADDITIONAL LISTENING

The symphony

Romantic

1. Peter Ilyich Tchaikovsky, Symphony no. 5 in E Minor, op. 64.
2. Robert Schumann, Symphony no. 4 in D Minor, op. 120.

Observe the effect of the cyclic form of the Tchaikovsky symphony. (The same themes appear in the first and last movements.) Contrast the orchestral sound of Tchaikovsky with that of Schumann. Do the symphonies contain operatic elements? In what ways do they reflect the idealism of Romanticism?

Modern

1. Igor Stravinsky, *Symphonies of Wind Instruments.*
2. Aaron Copland, Symphony no. 3.

Contrast the melody, rhythm, instrumentation, overall sound, and expression of these nineteenth- and twentieth-century symphonies. Is one more emotional? Does one appear more intellectually controlled? Why?

The concerto

Romantic

1. Felix Mendelssohn, Violin Concerto in E Minor.
2. Franz Liszt, Concerto no. 1 in E Flat for Piano and Orchestra.

Modern

1. Serge Prokofiev, Piano Concerto no. 5 in G Major, op. 55.
2. Béla Bartók, *Concerto for Violin and Orchestra.*

Compare the "solo" instrument. Note the numbers of movements and the titles of the movements.

The suite

Romantic

1. Edvard Grieg, *Peer Gynt*, Suite 1.
2. Felix Mendelssohn, *A Midsummer Night's Dream.*

Modern

1. Igor Stravinsky, *The Firebird* (from the ballet).
2. Ralph Vaughan Williams (1872–1958), *Suite for Viola and Orchestra.*

The tone poem and other programmatic music

Romantic

1. Franz Liszt, *Les Préludes.*
2. Peter Ilyich Tchaikovsky, *Romeo and Juliet.*

Modern

1. William Schuman, *George Washington Bridge: An Impression.*
2. Claude Debussy, *La Mer.*

Compare the story or idea lying behind these works. What problems did the composer have relating the music to the titles? Was he successful in solving these problems? Imagine the same music without the programmatic titles. Suggest different titles. Do they change the piece for the listener?

Other instrumental music

Romantic

1. Serge Prokofiev, *Lieutenant Kijé.*
2. Nicholas Rimsky-Korsakov, *Russian Easter* Overture.
3. Mikhail Glinka (1804–1857), *Ruslan and Liudmila* (Overture).

Modern

1. Béla Bartók, *Music for Strings, Percussion and Celeste.*
2. Igor Stravinsky, *Dumbarton Oaks.*
3. Charles Ives, *Holidays.*

Observe the unlimited range of sound available to the composer.

Chamber music

Romantic

1. Franz Schubert, Quintet in A Major, op. 114 (*The Trout*) (violin, viola, cello, double bass, and piano).
2. Johannes Brahms, *Clarinet Quintet,* op. 115 (clarinet and string quartet).

Modern

1. Maurice Ravel, *Introduction and Allegro for Harp, Flute, Clarinet, and String Quartet.*
2. Henry Cowell, *Ostinato Pianissimo* (string piano, 8 rice bowls, marimba, xylophone, tambourine, wood blocks, guiro, bongo drums, 3 drums, 3 gongs).
3. Béla Bartók, *Sonata for Two Pianos and Percussion.*
4. Modern Jazz Quartet, "The Blue Necklace" (vibes, piano, double bass, drums). From *Under the Jasmine Tree* (Apple Records).

Each chamber group above uses different instruments. Comment on the variety and expressive nature of a particular group. How are the instruments able to blend, or to assert their independent qualities? Discuss the qualities of jazz combos which place them in the category of chamber ensembles.

Unaccompanied solo

Romantic (Piano selections)

1. Robert Schumann, *Album for the Young,* op. 68.
2. Johannes Brahms, Rhapsody in G Minor, op. 79, no. 2.
3. Franz Liszt, Hungarian Rhapsody no. 2.
4. Frédéric Chopin, *Préludes,* op. 28.

Modern: Piano

1. Samuel Barber, *Piano Sonata,* op. 26.
2. John Cage, *Amores* (Movements I and IV for prepared piano).
3. Arnold Schoenberg, *Sechs Kleine Klavierstücke,* op. 19.

4. Béla Bartók, *Mikrokosmos.*

(Six volumes containing a total of 153 pieces, all short. Many of these can be played by students who have a minimal amount of musical instruction.)

Other Instruments

1. Luciano Berio, *Sequenza* (solo flute).
2. Béla Bartók, *Sonata for Solo Violin.*
3. Igor Stravinsky, *Three Pieces for Clarinet Solo.*
4. Morton Feldman, *King of Denmark* (solo percussion).

The use of instruments as solo mediums, especially nonkeyboard instruments, poses special problems for the composer, the performer, and the listener. Discuss. Comment on the expressive qualities of these solo mediums.

Electronic music

1. John Cage and David Tudor, *Indeterminancy.* New aspect of form in instrumental and electronic music.
2. *Images fantastiques.* Electronic experimental music by Berio, Maderna, Ferrari, Xenakis, Dufrène-Baronnet.
3. Mario Davidovsky, Electronic Study no. 1.
4. Milton Babbitt, *Ensembles for Synthesizer.*
5. Luciano Berio, *Visage.* Electronic sounds with modulated voice.
6. Ilhan Mimaroglu (1926–), *Agony.*
7. Karlheinz Stockhausen, *Mikrophonie II for Choir, Hammond Organ and Ring Modulators.*
8. Walter Carlos, *Switched-on Bach.*

Discuss electronic sounds as a medium of musical expression. Discuss the synthesizer as an instrument. Compare with traditional performances of the same Bach compositions. Observe the contrast between music which is totally instigated electronically and that of a voice or other sounds electronically modulated.

FOR DISCUSSION

1. Compare the instrumentation of Berlioz's *Symphonie fantastique* with Stravinsky's *Symphonies of Wind Instruments.* Has

the use of strings, woodwinds, brass, and percussion changed in the twentieth century?

2. Why is the conductor's job such a difficult one? What qualities make a great conductor? Have conductors always used a baton? Is there a difference between choral and instrumental conducting?

3. Listen to Howard Hanson's (1896–) Second Symphony, (*The Romantic*). What elements mark it as a twentieth-century work?

4. Is instrumental music more expressive than vocal music? Discuss considering range, tone color, volume, and versatility.

5. How does a particular ensemble of instruments affect a piece of music? For instance, orchestra vs. string quartet or piano solo vs. percussion solo.

6. Discuss the effect of music with descriptive titles or commentary as opposed to absolute music. Do these titles pose problems for the listener? Do some titles give false impressions? Do titles get in the way? Does music without a descriptive title leave too much to the listener?

7. Electronic music is a twentieth-century phenomenon. Is there any Romanticism in it?

Baroque and Classic Styles: Vocal Music

13

"Baroque" was originally an uncomplimentary designation. The word referred to imperfect pearls which used to be considered ugly, defective gems. Applied to music, Baroque meant music that was inferior to, and a distortion of, the earlier Renaissance music. The derogatory connotation no longer remains. To contemporary ears, it does not sound weird, grotesque, or overly elaborate.

"Classic," too, is a term that is not entirely satisfactory. The word has been overworked, having been applied to the music and art of several periods. Classic generally signifies the principles and qualities of the "Golden Age." It should not be confused with "classical," which generally refers to so-called "serious" music in contradistinction to "popular" music.

Francesco Borromini (architect): Façade and floor plan of the Church of San Carlo alle Quattro Fontane (1638–67). Rome.

The effects of Baroque architecture are rich and varied. The irregularity, recesses, and curved forms of the façade of San Carlo give a feeling of undulating movement. The floor plan is based on the oval, a less stable and more dynamic form than the circle, which dominated Classic and Renaissance architecture. Instead of the clearly defined units typical of Renaissance buildings, space flows and fuses, alternately compressed and exploded. The tightly integrated complexity of arches, columns, and interweaving lines and spaces lend Baroque architecture an expressive force akin to a fugue.

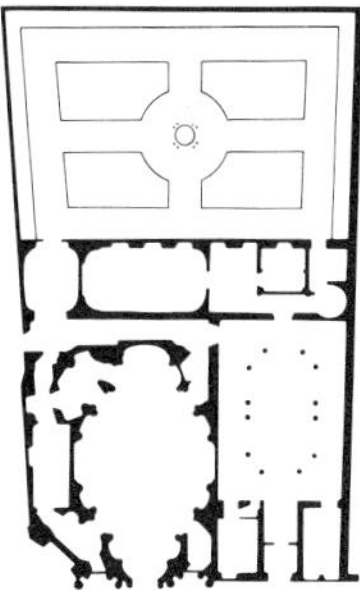

Much of the design is nonfunctional and deliberately illogical. The columns are applied to the walls and serve no structural function. Spaces appear to be of different proportions than they actually are. Ornamentation became increasingly luxurious: decorative sculpture fills the designs; leaves and scrolls abound; painted ceilings present heavenly scenes that create the illusion of vast space. The swirling forms, elaborate decoration, and sweeping, dynamic organization gave a grand, operatic exuberance to Baroque architecture.

The Baroque period began about 1600 with the birth of the opera and ended with the death of J. S. Bach in 1750. The Classic period is associated with Haydn, Mozart, and Beethoven, and ranges from about 1725 to 1825. Beethoven's style contains both Classic and Romantic elements and represents a bridge between those periods.

Distinguishing the differences between Baroque and Classic musical style requires the same kind of listening exercised in the previous chapters. In order to get a preliminary impression, compare the overtures, a recitative, and an aria from the following two operas:

> Claudio Monteverdi, *L'incoronazione di Poppea* (*The Coronation of Poppea*).
>
> Wolfgang Amadeus Mozart, *Die Zauberflöte* (*The Magic Flute*).

Look for similarities as well as differences and try to grasp the overall effect of each style.

Early Baroque style developed as a reaction to the prevailing style which had become overripe and had failed to satisfy new tastes and demands. Significant innovations took place during the Baroque era including the development of the opera, the recitative, the solo song, and certain forms of Protestant sacred music. There was a synthesis of contrapuntal and harmonic writing, an equalizing of the importance of instrumental and vocal music, and a formulation and shaping of instrumental forms that are basic components of the present-day concert repertory. Pitch systems, harmonic practices, and rhythmic concepts established in the Baroque era persisted until the early twentieth century.

During the second half of the sixteenth century, counterpoint had become so involved that it provoked reaction. The Florentine *Camerata*, a group of scholars who met during the last decade of the century, called for musical reform. Their basic complaints were that the music was too complex, the expression of the poetry was lost in a texture that distorted the meaning, and the music was pedantic. The climate was right for a new and simpler style in which music became subordinate to text, and counterpoint was abandoned, at least temporarily. In the new style, melody was to be supported by chords. What had been completely linear or horizontal texture became more vertical. Composers concentrated on the meaning of the text and the expression of this meaning.

In 1602 Giulio Caccini (c. 1550–1618), an Italian composer and writer, published a collection of songs. These songs were based upon the new style called monody. The publication was called *La Nuove Musiche* (*The New Music*). The change is also seen in the later works of Claudio Monteverdi. In these he moves away from contrapuntal style to solos and duets with accompaniment. These works, which reflect the style of the early Baroque, coupled with the *Camerata's* desire to revive ancient Greek drama, lead to the beginning of opera.

OPERA

The earliest known surviving opera is Jacopo Peri's (1561–1633) *Euridice*, first performed in 1600. Peri's melodies, supported by simple harmonies, follow the natural speech rhythms of the text. Each verse closes with what sounds like a final cadence. The free, speech-like "recitative" sections are relieved by songs in regular measure which generally fall at the ends of the scenes. Alternating with these solo parts are choruses which also favor the simple note-against-note style. Peri includes instrumental interludes and even suggests an introduction, although he wrote no overture as such. Early operas provide a good example of the monotony that results from overstylization, lack of variety (especially in the recitatives with their continually recurring cadences), and absence of significant characterization and musical organization. Still there are beautiful moments, such as the "Lament of Arianna" from the opera *Orfeo* by Monteverdi. (See Ex. 13–1.)

To be successful an opera must sustain dramatic excitement. Plot, characterization, costumes, scenery, and music must support each other in a way that assures communication. This synthesis is so complex that opera remains one of the most demanding musical forms, comparable, when it "comes off," to organizing a voyage to the moon.

In spite of its shortcomings, Florentine opera spread throughout Europe and England. Although Italian opera did not become popular in France, it was popular in London in the early part of the eighteenth

Ex. 13–1

Lento
La - scia - te - mi mo - ri - re la - scia - te - mi mo -
Lento
Piano
ri - re e chi vo - le - te voi che mi con - for - te
in co - si du - ra sor - te in co - si gran mar - ti - re la - scia - te -
mi mo - ri - re la - scia - te - mi mo - ri - re

century. Later Italian operas consisted of recitatives, arias, duets, and other small ensembles, choruses, and dances. The recitative tells the story. The aria responds melodically, expressing the emotions engendered by the action. Group emotions are given voice in duets, trios, small ensembles, and choruses. Dances were often added for color and interest and provided relief from the tension of the plot.

The Baroque style in opera culminated in the works of Handel. His forty operas, even though they are not widely known or admired today, do offer some of the finest moments in opera during that period. *Giulio Cesare* (*Julius Caesar*, 1724) is a good example. Listen to Cleopatra's aria "Se pieta di me non senti" ("If Thou Hast No Pity for Me") from Act II, Scene 8. The recitative, accompanied by orchestra, is notable for its expressive string writing. The aria contains, as part of the accompaniment, a violin obbligato melody based on a "weeping" motive:

Ex. 13–2

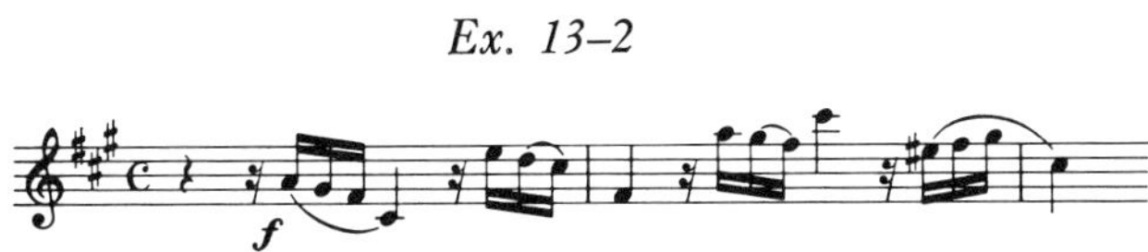

Harmonic changes are rich, varied, and moving. The combination of voice line, violin melody, and chord changes gives eloquent expression to the sorrow—noble suffering, grandly borne and courageously endured. (See Ex. 13–3.)

Handel's operas were generally stories of heroic personages. Meeting Handel's timeless characters reminds us of what heights humans are capable. Handel's heroes are ideal types. They speak in magnificent pronouncements with grandiose gestures. Handel ignores the everyday detail of confused emotions, uncertain feelings, and complex psychological problems. The reality of modern drama is missing. Only the music breathes real life into these characters, glorifying them and making them eternal.

Like Baroque music in general, operas were somewhat improvisatory. If an opera which had not been performed for some time was revived, the composer usually created new arias to suit the new singers. Handel tailor-made the vocal lines to fit each singer's capability. Singers also added their own flourishes and embellishments, and the harpsichordist improvised an accompaniment from a supplied bass part in a manner

Ex. 13–3. Handel: "If Thou Hast No Pity for Me," Cleopatra's aria from Giulio Cesare

similar to a contemporary jazz improvisation. Much of what a composer created was done according to his stockpile of formulas and techniques.

Arias generally express a pure mood, and Handel's arias were no

Peter Paul Rubens: The Garden of Love *(c. 1632–34). Museo Nacional del Prado, Madrid.*

Peter Paul Rubens painted in grandiose dimensions with masses of fundamental color. The lively, animated feeling of movement expresses the power and drama of his statement. To the left Rubens pictures himself, aided by a cherub, urging his wife to join the lords and ladies in happy companionship. The group gathers beneath a fountain topped with a statue of Venus, whose breasts flow with water. The women are plump and voluptuous. The joyous mood—directly and firmly stated—prevails everywhere. Ruben's boundless vitality and optimism introduced Baroque art in much the same way that Monteverdi ushered in Baroque music. The expansiveness and the expressive, unmistakable meaning communicated in his works marked the beginning of a new age.

exception. His brilliant vocal writing was unequaled. He employed tone painting to lend clarity to the text, but he painted with wide strokes and basic colors, much like Rubens.

Baroque opera had many problems. One problem was the wide use of what is called the *da capo* aria, an aria in A-B-A form. The *da capo* aria was not dramatically successful because of its nature of turning back upon itself. The circular form took the singer back to where he began, thereby impeding the forward momentum of the dramatic action. Another problem was the "star" system which was as prevalent in the Baroque era as it is today in the entertainment field. Each lead singer had to sing the same number of solos as every other lead singer, whether these were dramatically meaningful to the plot or not. Problematic, too, was the disjointed and fragmented structure of the operas which thwarted dramatic naturalness and prevented the accumulation of tension from scene to scene. Characterization could only emerge through the imposition of aria upon aria, mood upon mood.

Although the setting of texts in early operas was governed by reform and restraint, by the end of the Baroque era, the operatic aria had become an extremely florid musical form. Singers improvised, and embellishments were extremely elaborate. Indeed, the Baroque as a musical style is better defined in terms of its contrasts than its consistencies.

Even with all these difficulties, the best of Handel's forty operas offers the patient listener a treasure chest of melodies, superb craftsmanship, and daring originality. The present-day listener cannot recapture the original feeling of these operas entirely, but he can approach them with intellectual respect and understanding. The rewards are worth the effort.

Expectedly, the Italian opera of Handel, with its weighty subjects and artificial formal designs, fell out of favor of the English noble audience. Internal problems in the theater, social conditions, and John Gay's (1685–1732) *The Beggar's Opera* (1728) doomed Italian opera in England. *The Beggar's Opera* (in English) was a satire on the excesses of the Italian opera. It signaled a new era and a new style and sent Handel off to write oratorios and other works. John Gay's opera is a lusty work, not unlike the *Three-Penny Opera* of Bertolt Brecht and Kurt Weill (1900–1950), which was modeled after it. Gay's characters sang in the vernacular, and the subject matter was of an earthiness that

William Hogarth: The Beggar's Opera, Act III, Scene 11 *(1729). Collection of Mr. and Mrs. Paul Mellon.*

Hogarth, who shared John Gay's preference for authentic English subject matter, illustrated the most dramatic scene of Gay's opera. In this scene the highwayman-hero, Macheath, has been arrested and stands bound at center stage. His two sweethearts, Lucy and Polly, appeal to their fathers for his release. Macheath, who has pledged himself in marriage to both women, must now choose between them. Fashionable spectators in the eighteenth century often sat on the sides of the stage. The artist is barely visible behind the two gentlemen in the right-hand box.

must have had a startling impact after the stuffy and unreal themes of Italian opera. Mr. and Mrs. Peachum, for example, sing about their daughter Polly in explicit terms.

Ex. 13–4. Gay: "Our Polly Is a Sad Slut," from The Beggar's Opera

Polly defends herself with "Can Love Be Controlled by Advice?" (Ex. 13–5). These particular airs have been taken from Frederic Austin's revival of the work in 1920. The flavor of the original remains, even though

Ex. 13–5

the accompaniments have been rechorded. Compared with Handel's style, Gay's style might be viewed as folk-like, even antioperatic. Gay makes no attempts at vocal gymnastics, and the songs leave a direct and simple, but by no means artless, effect.

Italian opera, however, was not doomed elsewhere. Christoph Gluck (1714–1787) adopted more conservative practices and brought forth a new style Italian opera in the latter half of the eighteenth century. Gluck instituted reforms emphasizing a "more poetic" setting of the text, a music which responded to textual meaning, and a rejection of excessive embellishments. Gluck composed more than one hundred operas. Although his works influenced later composers, he did not establish a school of opera or have any immediate followers.

During this period comic elements developed. These began as interludes, called *intermezzi*, performed between the acts of a serious opera,

Ex. 13–6. Mozart: Don Giovanni

and later became a separate autonomous form, the Italian *opera buffa*. Reaction against the overstylized Italian opera effected a new style, known in Paris as the *opera comique* and in Germany as the *Singspiel*. Essentially, comic opera simplified the Italian form by speaking the recitatives and alternating the spoken drama with simple songs.

The development of English ballad opera, Italian *opera buffa*, French *opera comique*, and German *Singspiel* set the stage for Mozart. His operas represent the most successful combinations of operatic elements of the time. Mozart ingeniously solved the problems which plagued the earlier operatic composers. He was able to compromise the extremes. He balanced text, music, and drama in such a way that they serve a cohesive whole. Vocal and instrumental styles become one. Recitative and aria were neither totally monodic nor excessively embellished. Opera is no longer a series of recitatives, arias, dances, comic interludes, and choruses; it is a synthesis of proportionate elements portraying a coherent musical drama. The effect is not *drama per musica* (drama with music), it is music theater.

The Marriage of Figaro (1786), *Don Giovanni* (1787), and *Cosi fan tutte* (1790) are the most often produced of Mozart's comic operas. *Don Giovanni* is not comic in the sense of the other two. Although the adventures of the great lover do provide comic moments, the final retribution is pure drama. This scene, in which the statue of the Commandant, whom Don Giovanni has killed, seizes him and drags him through flames to hell, is only relieved by the short epilogue that follows. The *buffa* character returns briefly as the remaining cast joins in a closing moral.

Opera buffa, like contemporary musical comedy, assumes many shapes, including the combination of serious with *buffa* roles. It represents a striving for dramatic truth. In this sense, *opera buffa* is in keeping with modern dramatic style and contrasts sharply with Handel. Compare, for example, Donna Anna's aria "Or sai chi l'onore" (Ex. 13–6) with Cleopatra's aria from *Giulio Cesare* (Ex. 13–3). The music of *Don Giovanni* gives the feeling of reality and presence. Mozart's figures are earthly people, not the superhuman heroes of Handel. Yet in Mozart's opera there are moments that are not essential or real. Opera is still music, and beauty is not always functional.

The characterization in *Don Giovanni* is strong, and the drama logical and powerful. The opening measures of the overture, the cemetery scene, and the final scene demonstrate Mozart's dramatic, emotional style. The *Sturm und Drang* (storm and stress) literary movement and the Enlightenment are reflected in Mozart's thinking. These views anticipated the change in style brought about by Beethoven and helped usher in the Romantic era. Mozart's music reveals an impressive intensity that belies his image of simple elegance and grace. His orchestral writing is exciting, colorful, and convincing, with an abundance of beautifully wrought melody.

Mozart makes use of the *secco* (dry) recitative, a speech-like melody accompanied by occasional chords on the harpsichord. The *secco* recitative permits a rapid-fire repartee which moves the action and is conducive to humor. Mozart contrasts the *secco* recitative with the *accompagnato* (accompanied) recitative which employs the whole orchestra. The latter style uses instrumental color and richness to bring the necessary intensity to the more dramatic or emotional dialogue. The cemetery scene near the end of the opera illustrates both kinds of recitative. Don Giovanni and his friend Leporello find themselves before the statue of the Commandant, whom Giovanni killed. The part of the Commandant is set in *accompagnato* style, the others in *secco*. (See Ex. 13–7.)

Note the contrast between Leporello's burly bass and the higher,

Ex. 13–7. Mozart: Don Giovanni, *Graveyard scene, Act II*

more aristocratic voice of Don Giovanni. The final, dramatic scene in the banquet hall, when the statue appears and takes Don Giovanni to his retribution, is set in *accompagnato* style. The atmosphere created by Mozart's music gives credence to a completely unreal story.

Comparative Styles: Opera

	Baroque	*Classic*
	Handel (1685–1759), Julius Caesar	*Mozart (1756–1791)*, Don Giovanni
Expression	*Plots were based on myths, heroic legends, or the Bible. Dramatic reality and logic were less important than the need for each lead singer to have an equal number of arias. Little real character development. Elaborate stage machinery added interest.*	*Librettos were about real human beings. Greater dramatic impact resulted from a more logical approach to the story line. Characters were developed musically.*
Melody	*Each set piece (aria, duet, trio, chorus, etc.) was based on one or two short melodic ideas. Recitatives were highly repetitious.*	*Melodies borrowed the idea of development from the symphony. Melodies were altered in order to increase their expressive range.*
Rhythm	*One basic rhythm was usually exploited throughout each set piece. The text was made to follow a set rhythm.*	*Rhythm followed the natural enunciation of the words. Greater variety.*
Tone Color	*The orchestra is used in a secondary role to support the voices.*	*The enlarged orchestra gave more range of color. Instruments were used to set moods. The orchestral interludes are composed with dramatic assertiveness.*

	Baroque	*Classic*
Harmony	*Middle sections of an aria usually change to the related minor key or to the dominant key and return to the original key in the recapitulation.*	*Freer use of key changes. More accidentals added to the basic scale tones. Greater use of secondary harmonies and 7th chords.*
Dynamics	*Terraced. Whole sections on one level.*	*Sudden softs and louds were used for dramatic excitement. Crescendos and diminuendos permitted the singers to emote with the text.*
Structure	Da capo *aria became a common formula. Much repetition for the sake of unity. Individual set pieces were distinct entities. The orchestral overture was highly stylized.*	*Forms were invented to satisfy dramatic needs. Less use of* da capo *aria. The action proceeded more quickly. The same set pieces were used but were often run together for dramatic continuity. The overture sets the mood for the rest of the opera.*
Medium and Texture	*Castrati (high male voices—in the female range) were popular. Women sometimes sang men's roles.*	*Voice parts treated more realistically. The bass voice was given greater prominence.*

CANTATA, MASS, AND ORATORIO

Although the Reformation had its beginnings in the Renaissance, the music it inspired flowered in the late Baroque. The cantata and oratorio are typically Protestant forms. An oratorio is a musical setting of a sacred text that is scored for soloists, chorus, and orchestra. Although the oratorio was originally intended to be staged, it is usually performed in concert version today. The style of the music closely resembles that of opera. An opera or oratorio by Handel are similar musically but different textually.

Like the typical opera of the period, the oratorio is made up of recitatives, arias, small ensembles, choruses, and orchestral interludes. However, the oratorio emphasizes the chorus. The two most prominent composers of the oratorio in the Baroque era were Bach and Handel. The best known oratorios of these two composers are the Bach *Passions* and the *Messiah* of Handel. Bach did not restrict his sacred compositions to Protestant music. Although not a Catholic, his Mass in B Minor remains a monumental example of Baroque sacred music.

A new style of counterpoint reached its peak of perfection during the period of Handel and Bach. In contrast to the recitative, monody, and solo song, the choral works frequently included a type of harmonic counterpoint. Originally, musical forms in which melodies imitated each other and were interwoven were so composed that the harmony was secondary and more a result than a moving force in the music. In the contrapuntal writing of the late Baroque, harmony found an equal place with imitation and was not a *de facto* result. Counterpoint came to be created on a preestablished harmonic pattern.

The cantata is similar to the oratorio in form and content but less extended. J. S. Bach's Cantata no. 4, *Christ lag in Todesbanden* (*Christ Lay by Death Enshrouded*) is based upon a chorale melody dating from the sixteenth century and a seven-stanza poem by Martin Luther. Each verse is set separately as a movement. The melody appears in each movement but with a variation treatment that keeps each of the seven verses fresh and alive. The variety of tempos, accompaniment figures, rhythms, instrumentation that Bach invents provide interest at the same time that the repeated melody unifies the whole work. The symmetrical arrangement of the movements underscores Bach's architectural approach to composition. The movements very carefully balance one another as they pivot around the central fugue:

		Solo	*Fugue*	*Solo*		
	Duet	*Tenor*		*Bass*	*Duet*	
Chorus						*Chorale*
I	*II*	*III*	*IV*	*V*	*VI*	*VII*

The cantata begins with a short *sinfonia* scored for a quartet of strings plus continuo (usually harpsichord playing chords plus cello doubling the bass part), expressing the gloom of the sepulchre. Voices enter with the first verse proclaiming the joy of the resurrection, and

Ex. 13–8. Bach: Cantata no. 4, Christ lag in Todesbanden

build to whirling hallelujahs. Trumpets and trombones add to the excitement. Then the gloom returns to round out the first movement.

The second verse—a duet between altos and sopranos—expresses a quieter, more contemplative mood.

The third verse is again more exuberant. Tenors sing the tune while the violins play a rhythmic counterpoint. (See Ex. 13–8.)

The fourth verse is ornate with much canonic imitation in the voices. The voices are animated, sometimes entering in close succession.

The fifth verse for bass solo is sometimes sung by all the basses in the chorus. This time the melody is sung in triple rather than duple meter. The end of this movement is dramatically marked by the dropping of the voice on the word "death" (*Tod*):

Ex. 13–9

The sixth verse celebrates the disappearance of sin. Sopranos and tenors sing a duet to continuo accompaniment.

The final chorale blends all of the performers together in a simple but fully stated affirmation of faith.

If it is true, as Hindemith indicated, that Bach stood before the curtain that no one will ever draw aside, much of this veneration is due him because of his ability to interweave melodies and rhythms in such a way that they achieve a soaring beauty. Few composers can equal Bach's variation technique as demonstrated in his Cantata no. 4.

Bach's B Minor Mass is full of so many treasures that a lifetime could be spent in savoring each one. Listen to the mourning expressed in the harmonies and overlapping melodies of the "Crucifixus." Bach develops an emotional intensity as the voices reiterate the melodies and text, juxtaposing them in a surging wail. Underlying these parts is an ostinato figure, repeated throughout, which organizes and unifies the work.

Ex. 13–10

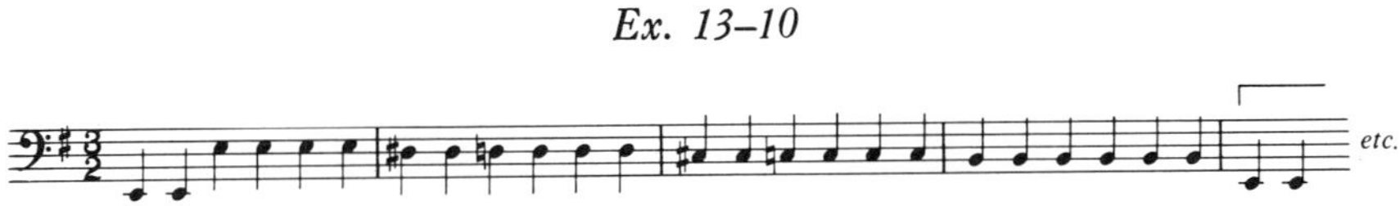

The uncontained joy of the "Gloria" is difficult to equal anywhere. The brightness is captured by the fast pace (*vivace*) and the use of Baroque or "Bach" D trumpets, a higher, more brilliant sounding instrument than the standard B-flat and C trumpets currently used in bands and orchestras.

Ex. 13–11

The "Sanctus" ("Holy") from the same work resounds like the swaying of gigantic bells. Some writers have compared it to "the swinging of censors before the starry throne," or "the sound of seraphim blowing their loud uplifted angel trumpets." The piece moves slowly (*largo*) and the voices break each beat into three pulses (triplets) so that the four-beat pattern becomes an undulating current of twelve pulses. The bass part, with its descending melodic figure, provides an undergirding of great simplicity and strength.

Ex. 13–12

The "Benedictus" shows a sweetness and restraint that is unusual in the Baroque period. It has only three parts (solo flute or violin, tenor solo, and continuo). The transparency of the texture belies its expressive impact and reveals the profundity and range of Bach's genius perhaps even better than his brilliant, thickly textured passages.

Ex. 13–13

Beethoven's Mass in D, the *Missa Solemnis,* joins Bach's Mass in B Minor as one of the greatest settings of the Mass in all music. One need only listen to the "Gloria in Excelsis Deo" to sense the power of Beethoven's conviction. The expanded orchestral resources (full orchestra without trombones) are wholly exploited. The chorus parts enter in succession, each singing the same theme. First comes the alto, then tenor, bass, and soprano. The upward, rapid thrust of the line (A), the vigorous shouts of "gloria" by the whole chorus (B), and the unexpected accents (C) combine in an ecstatic expression of praise (Ex. 13–14). Beethoven develops the "Gloria" movement with careful attention to the meaning of the text. The words, "adoramus te" ("We adore Thee"), for example, are treated with reverence and hushed humility. (See Ex. 13–15.)

Ex. 13–14

Ex. 13–15

The chorus alternates with the solo quartet as the text is explored. When the chorus sings the final "Amen," the end seems imminent, but Beethoven chooses that moment to begin a bold fugue.

Ex. 13–16

The soloists then join the rest of the singers and this section builds to a finale on repeated "amens." But even this does not satisfy Beethoven. He crowns the movement with a burst (*presto*) back to the original theme and ends the movement with a shout from the chorus. The structure is monumental and the accumulated energy is overpowering.

Other movements of the *Missa Solemnis* are equally worthy of study. Already deaf, Beethoven dedicated the "Credo" ("I believe") "To God, Who has never forsaken me." The movement is Beethoven's religious manifesto. Although inward at moments, he also reaches outward. The "Dona nobis pacem" (prayer for peace) is a universal expression that reaches across time. But the war-like interruptions remind us of mankind's thwarted quest for peace.

Ex. 13–17

The *Missa Solemnis* is dramatic, symphonic, and full of exultation and humility. This work, unlike the Mass in B Minor, was meant to be performed at an actual service, albeit a service of exceptional pomp. Today it is usually performed in the concert hall. Both of these masses are difficult to perform, but Beethoven's is particularly so because of the extreme range of the voice parts, the sudden shifts in dynamic level, and the rapid succession of notes. Although the voices are taxed to the fullest, the effect is always worth the effort.

The oratorio was developed in order to dramatize the Bible stories to an illiterate congregation. Oratorios resembled operas and made use of recitatives and arias. However, they relied much more on the chorus. During an oratorio, the chorus often portrayed townspeople, soldiers, an angry mob, or other roles.

The orchestra was employed in much the same manner as in other music. The thorough-bass or continuo was coupled with contrasting large and small groups, or solos. The instruments emphasized the strong pull and tension between the upper melody and the bass. This characteristic of Baroque style can be exhilarating. The orchestra in oratorio is more theatrical than ecclesiastical. Handel's orchestra generally consisted of less than forty players, and the chorus rarely exceeded twenty-five. Larger choruses often perform these works today. The full orchestra is usually reserved for the big climaxes.

Handel wrote more than twenty oratorios, of which the *Messiah* is probably the best known. As an oratorio, the *Messiah* is more akin to the German *Passion,* which dramatized the story of the death of Christ. It is not as typical an oratorio as others of his works, for instance *Saul, Judas Maccabaeus, Israel in Egypt,* and *Solomon.* The last work, composed in 1748, was one of the most elaborate oratorios Handel composed.

Solomon is more humanitarian in nature than religious. The work is full of pageantry and power, testifying to the triumph of peace over war. The text deals with the dedication of the temple, love in marriage, justice and mercy, material prosperity, and the sincere admiration of neighboring states.

Handel set the part of King Solomon for the female mezzo-soprano voice. The present-day listener should accept this in the same way that he accepts the high-voiced (falsetto) singing of the present-day male "pop" singer. In setting the part this way, Handel may have attempted to transcend Solomon's role as a man.

The choruses are on the grandest scale, many calling for eight parts sung simultaneously, as opposed to the usual four. One of the finest examples of this epic quality is the second chorus of Act I, "With Pious Heart."

Ex. 13–18. Handel: Solomon

The finale of this act, the nightingale chorus, exemplifies word-painting at its best. The "cooing" of the nightingale inspires Handel to some of his finest composing.

Ex. 13–19. Handel: "May No Rash Intruder," from Solomon

Act II describes in vivid tones the story of Solomon's wisdom in determining which of two women is the mother of a child that both claim. The true mother's air, in which she offers to surrender her child, is perhaps the most powerful and poignant depiction of motherly love in all music (Ex. 13–20).

Ex. 13–20. Handel: "Can I See My Infant Gored?"

Solomon announces his decision in the secco recitative that follows:

Ex. 13–21. Handel: "Israel, Attend"

In Act III Solomon entertains the Queen of Sheba with a choral masque, a short, dramatic court entertainment with music. He bids the musicians to perform a piece in "lulling" measure, a battle song, a song of hopeless love, and a song of calm after the storm. These choruses are examples of Handel at his best.

During the Baroque period composers found extreme contrasts dramatically satisfying: soft to loud, lyric to rhythmic, high to low, many-voiced to thinly-voiced, and contrapuntal to chordal.

The oratorio had its greatest flowering in the Baroque. The Classic composer turned more to instrumental forms as an ideal expressive media. Classic composers did, however, make a few notable thrusts into the oratorio arena. Haydn's *Creation* is an example.

The Classic composer took the old oratorio format but filled it in with his own instrumental and vocal style. Haydn opens his *Creation* with an orchestral "Representation of Chaos" that uses the orchestra in a dramatic and sophisticated way. The recitative that follows sets the tone for the work. (See Ex. 13–22.)

Recitative, aria, and chorus alternate to complete the design. The differences between Haydn and Handel are many. Haydn uses greater variety of coloration in the orchestra. His orchestra operates more independently of the voice parts. Compare "The Heavens Are Telling" of Haydn (Ex. 13–23) with Handel's "With Pious Heart" (see Ex. 13–18). Haydn carries the tone-painting much further and introduces a touch of humor. When God creates the fowl, for example, Haydn plays with the cooing of the dove (Ex. 13–24). Compare Haydn's cooing with the cooing of the nightingale in Handel's oratorio. (See Ex. 13–19.) Haydn also effectively depicts the lion and the worm. (See Ex. 13–25.)

Ex. 13–22. Haydn: The Creation, *"In the Beginning"*

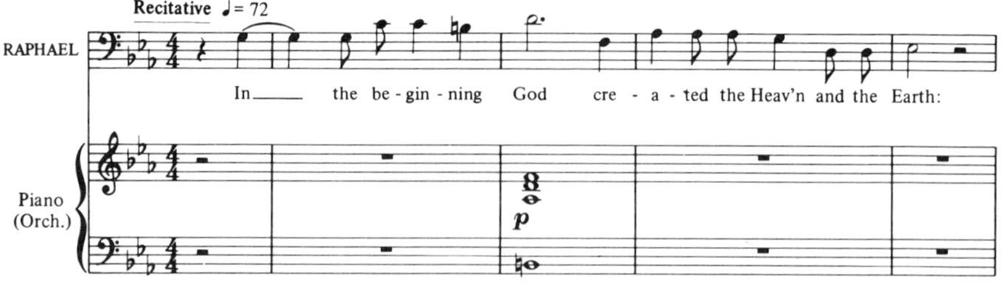

and the Earth was with-out form and void;
p
p
and dark - ness was up-on the face of the deep.
p
(Go on to Chorus)

Ex. 13–23

Chorus
Allegro ♩ = 116
Treble
The heav - ens are tel - ling the glo - ry of God,
Alto
The heav - ens are tel - ling the glo - ry of God,
Tenor
The heav - ens are tel - ling the glo - ry of God,
Bass
The heav - ens are tel - ling the glo - ry of God,
Allegro
Piano (Orch.)
f
mf
8va

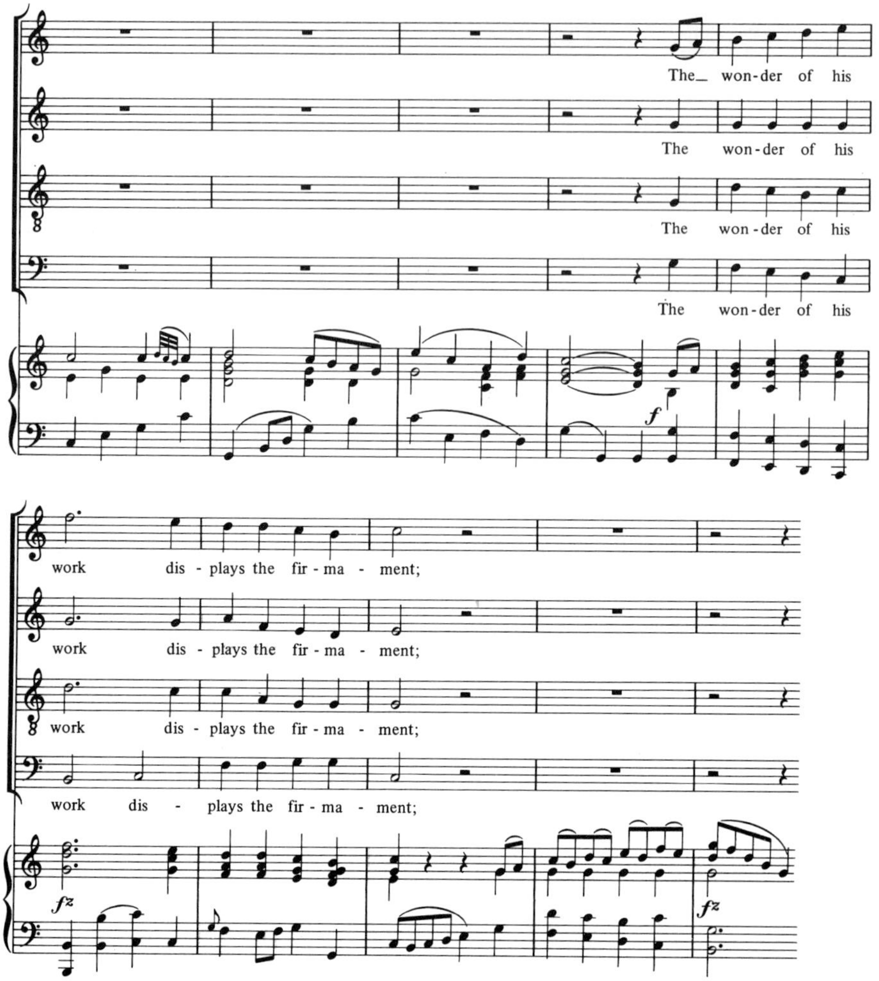

The_ won-der of his
The won-der of his
The won-der of his
The won-der of his

work dis - plays the fir - ma - ment;
work dis - plays the fir - ma - ment;
work dis - plays the fir - ma - ment;
work dis - plays the fir - ma - ment;

f

fz *fz*

Ex. 13–24. Haydn: "On Mighty Pens"

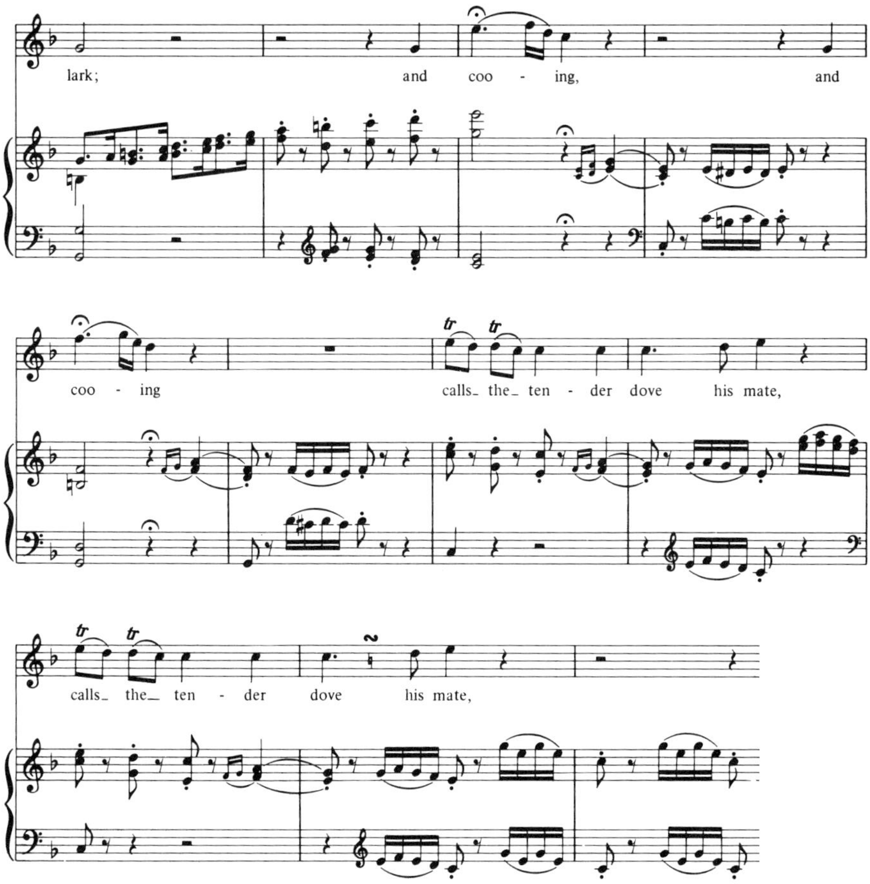

lark; and coo - ing, and
coo - ing calls the ten - der dove his mate,
calls the ten - der dove his mate,

Ex. 13–25. Haydn: "Straight Opening Her Fertile Womb"

Recitative
Presto ♩ = 152
RAPHAEL
... Cheer-ful, roar-ing, stands the taw-ny li-on.
Presto
Piano (Orch.)

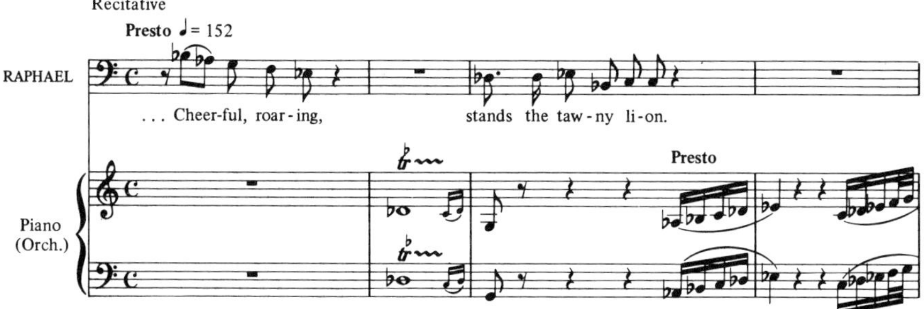

and bleat - ing
flocks.
Un - num-ber'd as the sands in swarms a - rose The
p
Adagio ♪= 88
host of in - sects.
In long di -
a tempo
men-sion creeps, with sin - uous trace, the worm.
fz
p a tempo

Perhaps one of the strongest choruses in the work is the second of the choruses, "Achieved Is the Glorious Work," which ends with a hallelujah rivaling Handel's, except that Haydn's hallelujah is more an expression of happiness than pomp.

Ex. 13–26

Comparative Styles:
Cantata, Mass, and Oratorio

	Baroque	*Classic*
	Bach (1685–1750), B Minor Mass	*Beethoven (1770–1827),* Missa Solemnis
Expression	*Full-bodied emotions are explored one by one at some length. Majesty, ceremony, and religious drama are the main themes.*	*Subtler emotions are expressed. Changes from one emotion to another can be abrupt with a variety of emotions being represented in one piece.*
Melody	*Highly developed sense of melodic flow and fitness of melody for a particular text.*	*More demanding and technical. Less is left to the improvisation of the singer.*
Rhythm	*One rhythmic idea often used as the basis for a complete piece.*	*Follows more closely the accents of the text. Greater variety.*
Tone Color	*Orchestra is used primarily to reinforce voices. Bass parts are almost always duplicated in the instruments.*	*The orchestra is given a more important, and independent role.*
Harmony	*Change of key to anything but the closest related keys is rare. Recitatives are often used between longer pieces as a bridge to the new key. Limited use of chromatics.*	*Far greater freedom in use of chromatics and keys. Harmony is used for its effect on the text.*

	Baroque	*Classic*
Dynamics	*Terraced. Sections at one dynamic level are contrasted with sections of similar length at another dynamic level.*	*Graduation of sound.*
Structure	*Much repetition. Phrases are often repeated many times. Form exists independent of text.*	*Form made to serve text. Melodies developed as in the symphony. Less repetition.*
Medium and Texture	*Extensive use of chorus. Thick textures are explored.*	*Chorus forms the core of the works. Works are less heavy in texture. Greater variety. Orchestra larger.*

GUIDE TO ADDITIONAL LISTENING

Opera

1. Giovanni Pergolesi (1710–1736), *La Serva padrona* (*The Maid as Mistress*, 1733).

La Serva padrona is a short two-act opera, originally written as an intermezzo. Each act was designed to be performed between one of the three acts of a serious opera. The two intermezzos are linked, however, and therefore can be performed together as a short opera. Notice the lack of overture and lack of contrast between aria and recitative. The opera requires three performers on stage, but only two singers. One performer is a mute. The plot involves intrigue, deception, and masquerade and is typical of Italian opera buffa. All ends well.

2. Jean-Jacques Rousseau (1712–1778), *Le Devin du village* (*The Village Soothsayer*, 1752). Overture only.

Compare the overture of *Le Devin du village* with the overture of *Cosi fan tutte.*

3. John Gay and John Pepusch (1667–1752), *The Beggar's Opera* (1728).

How does *The Beggar's Opera* begin? What is its spirit? Is its language unusual? How does its style differ from Italian opera? Notice the spoken dialogue. Compare with Gilbert and Sullivan's spoken passages.

4. Wolfgang Amadeus Mozart, *Cosi fan tutte* (*Thus do they all*, 1790), K. 588.

Cosi fan tutte was first performed about two years before Mozart's death. Listen to the overture, a recitative, an aria, and the ensembles. How do they reflect the mature Classic style?

Sacred music

1. Antonio Vivaldi, Gloria in D.

The setting to music of the "Kyrie" and "Gloria" portions of the Mass have been designated *Missa Brevis.* Vivaldi's Gloria in D is from such a setting. Notice the instrumental brilliance, the beautiful choral writing, and the contrast in expression. Compare the beginning "Glory be to God on high" and the "And on earth peace to men of good will." No exact date is available for this composition, but 1725 has been suggested. Sometimes recordings do not keep to the exact instrumental scoring of the original.

2. Johann Sebastian Bach, *St. John Passion* (1723).

Bach's *St. John Passion*, although originally in German, is usually performed in English in the United States. Listen to the way Bach expresses his moods. How does he differ from Vivaldi? Notice the alternation of chorus and recitative at the beginning. Contrast these styles with the first aria. How does the sound of Bach's orchestra differ from the sound of Vivaldi's? Notice the vitality of some of Bach's recitatives; the declamatory, dramatic style. Observe the expressive lyricism of the arias.

The *St. John Passion* depicts the drama and pathos of the death of Christ. The evangelist tells the story. Solo arias and chorales provide moments of reflection and contemplation. The chorus represents different groups: the angry crowd, the chief priests, the soldiers, and others.

3. George Frideric Handel, *Messiah* (1742–1759). Several versions exist.

Few works are as well known and as often performed as Handel's *Messiah*, the "Hallelujah" chorus in particular. Contrast Handel's sound and expression with that of Bach. Notice Bach's use of the sinfonia for the instrumental introduction, a form typical of the Italian opera. Handel's work, however, opens with a French overture: a two part form in which the first section is slow and the second a brisk fugue. Listen to the effects of the orchestra in the recitatives, arias, and choruses. Immediately after the overture, how does the orchestra set the tone for the words "Comfort ye," which follow? What is the effect of the repetition of text?

4. Wolfgang Amadeus Mozart, *Requiem*, K. 626.

In this choral work Mozart absorbed many Baroque traditions. The fugal subject in the "Kyrie" has the strength of a Handel subject. The dramatic outbursts of the "Dies Irae" are Baroque in flavor. Harmonically, Mozart is more imaginative than the Baroque composers. His own idiomatic style is best seen in the "Rex tremendae majestatis," the "Recordare," the "Confutatis," and the "Lacrimosa" (unfinished). Note especially the "Recordare"—one of the most effective and engaging movements Mozart ever wrote.

How does Mozart musically reflect upon death? Comment on the melodic and harmonic events which take place in the first minute of the short orchestral introduction. Listen, in addition, to the "Introit and Kyrie," and the "Sanctus." Which characteristics are Baroque? Which Classic?

5. Franz Joseph Haydn, *The Seasons* (1798).

Contrast Haydn's orchestral sound at the introduction of *The Seasons* with the other selections in this section. How does he express spring, summer, fall, and winter? Are there tinges of Romanticism in this work? If so, how are they manifested? Comment on the changing expression of the first recitative by Seniou, Lucas, and Janc. How does the orchestra prepare the listener for the first entry of the Chorus of Peasants? They, the peasants, sing, "Come, gentle spring . . ." How is "Come, gentle spring . . ." expressed musically? Select other sections and analyze the expressiveness.

Not all vocal works of the Baroque and Classic periods were lengthy. Below are a few shorter works.

Other vocal music

1. Heinrich Schütz (1585–1672): (a) "Tröstet, tröstet mein Volk" ("Comfort ye, comfort ye, my people"). Six voices and four instruments. (b) "Bringt her dem Herren" ("Give unto the Lord"). Solo voice and continuo.

The first work of Schütz, although German, displays a choral style similar to the chanson and madrigal. The second work, an accompanied melody, displays a monodic style.

2. Henry Purcell (1659–1695), songs: (a) "Hark! The Echoing Air a Triumph Sings." (b) "Musick for While".

Purcell did not score his songs for a particular voice. These songs fit the range of the countertenor, a high sounding male voice produced by special technique. Accompaniment is for organ or harpsichord and bass lute.

3. Johann Sebastian Bach, motets: (a) *Singet dem Herren ein neues Lied* (*Sing to the Lord a New Song*). (*b*) *Fürchte dich nicht, ich bin bei dir* (*Fear you not, I am with thee*).

Renaissance motets had Latin texts. Bach's texts are German. Each motet is for two choirs. What characteristics reflect the Renaissance? The Baroque?

4. Franz Joseph Haydn, *Te Deum.*

Contrast the *Te Deum* of Haydn with the motets of Bach, and the polyphonic work of Schütz. Compare the orchestral texture with the typical Baroque sound.

FOR DISCUSSION

1. Discuss why Handel's operas are seldom performed today. Why have Mozart's survived?
2. What aspects of John Gay's and Mozart's operas, when compared with Handel's, reveal the spirit of the Enlightenment

(reliance on reason, questioning of authority and traditional values, and the tendency toward individualism)?

3. Compare *The Beggar's Opera* with *The Threepenny Opera.* What has been retained? What has been altered? What has been added? Why?
4. Should opera be performed in its original language or in the language of the audience? How does translation affect the opera? How does it affect the reaction of the audience?

Baroque and Classic Styles: Instrumental Music

14

For instrumental music, the Baroque period represents a "coming of age." While much early instrumental music was derived from vocal music or served as an adjunct to it, during the Baroque period original instrumental forms were created that became as important as vocal forms. Baroque instrumental music achieved an independence, a variety, and an expressive power that had not yet been known.

Baroque style is often mistakenly thought of as the style of the late Baroque, when actually the early and late styles differ considerably. Baroque style also took on different characteristics in different countries. The German Baroque glorified counterpoint. It was music in the "grand manner"—colossal works of great energy and emotional range. The Rococo style of the French favored more delicate expression—

Jacques Germain Soufflot (architect): The Panthéon (Ste-Geneviève). Façade and floor plan (1764–90). Paris.

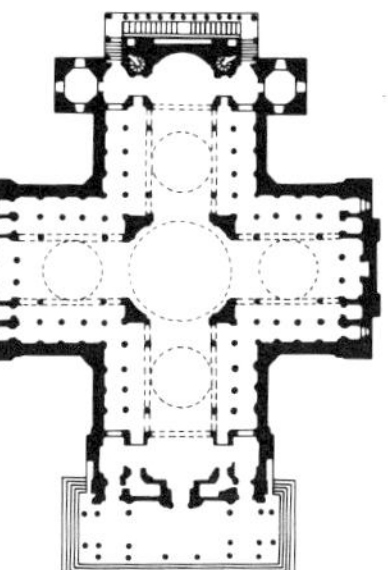

During the eighteenth century reason became the theme of man's life. It affected art as well as science and government. The Enlightenment brought knowledge of Greek architecture, a love of logic, and it brought clarity to art. The Panthéon in Paris represents a feat of brilliant engineering. The massive superstructure and domes are so ingeniously counterbalanced that the supporting piers seem delicate and light. Corinthian columns and moderate decoration, combined with the unbroken exterior walls, lend the building great dignity and power. The symmetry of the design, the ingenuity, and the restrained feeling are Classic characteristics. Circles, rectangles, and squares are the organizing forms. The feeling of simple serenity is the antipathy of Baroque art, repudiating both Baroque and Rococo extravagance. Lightness, regularity, simplicity, dignity, restraint, and logic were the ideals.

lightness, elegance, and grace. The Italians, influenced by the opera, developed a more fluid and lyric instrumental style.

The Classic style reflects a reaction to the overgrown artificiality of late Baroque style. Again there was retrenchment toward clarity and away from the intricacies of Baroque polyphonic music. Haydn, Mozart, and Beethoven incorporated some of the elements of Rococo style in more controlled and structured instrumental works during the Classic period. Classic forms were crystallized and were not subjected to the instability and evolution that characterized Baroque forms. Although the three principal producers of Classic music were born in Vienna, Salzburg, and Bonn, the style became international.

FROM HARPSICHORD TO PIANO

The harpsichord was essential to Baroque music both in the chamber ensemble and as a solo instrument. Although the piano had been invented in 1709 it was not taken up by Baroque composers, but became the principal keyboard instrument of the Classic period.

The essential difference between these two keyboard instruments is that the strings of the harpsichord are plucked by a quill, while those of the piano are struck by a felt hammer. The percussive action of the piano permitted a considerably louder dynamic range than that of the harpsichord where increased volume was achieved by coupling one "A" string to other "A" strings, so that when one key is struck many like strings are set into vibration. The piano mechanism also permitted the volume of sound and the manner of attack to be controlled by the performer's touch. In contrast to the harpsichord, where the plucked sound dissipated quickly, the piano tone could be sustained far longer.

To compare the two listen to the same music recorded on both, for instance Bach's *Inventions*, *Well-Tempered Clavier*, or *Goldberg Variations*. The differences between these two instruments interested composers and ultimately led to the development of different keyboard styles, forms, and combinations with other instrumental mediums.

CHANGES IN KEYBOARD STYLES AND FORMS

Johann Sebastian Bach and Domenico Scarlatti (1685–1757), both late Baroque composers, demonstrate different textural quality and musical form in their works. Bach's keyboard compositions were pri-

Fischer von Erlach (architect): Interior, Schönbrunn Palace (1694–1749). Vienna.

Rococo was more a modification of Baroque (the word may have been derived from Barocco, *Italian for baroque) than a repudiation of it. Graceful curves, gilded tracery, delicacy, lightness, and charm replaced the Baroque's ponderousness, pomposity, massiveness, and dramatic display. Violent contrasts are reduced to gentle ironies and witty repartee. Passion is subdued to wistful melancholy. The feeling was still luxurious and the buildings great in scale. There is still asymmetry, extravagance, and use of curved lines, but the feeling of Rococo is less worldly, more personal and intimate.*

marily inventions, preludes, fugues, and suites. Scarlatti structured his works in two-part form and called them sonatas. These works were actually forerunners of the sonata of the Classic period. Bach's multi-movement suites are collections of dances, while Scarlatti's sonatas are shorter works in one movement. The total effect of Scarlatti's texture is lighter and simpler than Bach's because of his emphasis on melody and harmony rather than counterpoint and design.

French harpsichord composers preferred the Rococo style. François Couperin was the key figure. The Rococo artists emphasized the simple but highly embellished melodic line. Their style was characterized by lightness, grace, and wit. The French made much use of a suite-like form called the *ordre* which consisted of various dances.

In 1700, Johann Kuhnau composed a set of programmatic pieces for harpsichord called *Biblical Sonatas.* They present interesting insight into the harpsichord's potential for program music. The sonatas carry titles such as *The Fight Between David and Goliath*, *The Marriage of Jacob*, and *Hiskias, Ill and Restored to Health.*

Two of Bach's sons, Johann Christian (1735–1782), and Carl Philipp Emanuel, who worked to establish a "singing style" on the piano, were leading figures in changing the style of keyboard music from the Baroque to the Classic. Some important keyboard pieces are presented below to give insight into the style and development of Baroque and Classic music.

Johann Sebastian Bach, Chromatic Fantasia and Fugue

This elaborate harpsichord piece is in two parts: a fantasy and a fugue. The fantasy is free. It includes rapid scale figurations, ornamentation, and chordal arpeggios and produces an almost harp-like rhapsody. The rhythmic events lack strict metrical impulse. The melody is not readily singable.

The structural unity is maintained through the movement of the harmonic events. The forward thrust results from the harmonic progression even though it is played in arpeggio (broken) style and not solid block-like chords. The elaboration of harmonic events adds brilliance, color, and vitality.

The first two measures resemble portions of scales.

Ex. 14–1

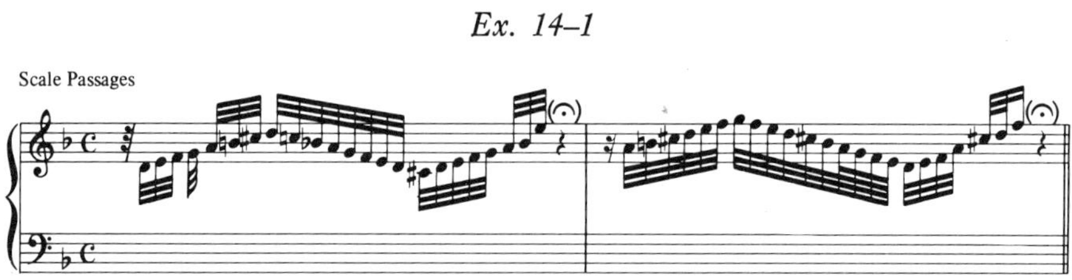

Although the eight notes in the blocks of sound in measures twenty-eight and twenty-nine look like chords, they are performed as arpeggios.

Ex. 14–2

A feeling of freedom and improvisation is conveyed, even though the fugue is tightly structured harmonically. The melodic subject is rather long and singable.

Ex. 14–3

As the rhythm develops it becomes regular and metrically controlled. The freedoms of the fantasia are followed by the strictness of the fugue.

Domenico Scarlatti, Sonata in C Major, Longo 104;*
Sonata in E Major, Longo 257; Sonata in D Minor, Longo 266;
Sonata in C Major, Longo 255

Scarlatti's sonatas, more than 150, were written during his later years, between 1738 and 1757. Contrasted with Bach's *Chromatic Fantasia and Fugue* they are short, reflect many expressions, and are generally lighter and less serious.

Scarlatti's sonatas vary in expression. His Sonata in C Major (Longo 104) is light in texture, has a lilting melody, and moves forward

* Allessandro Longo ordered and numbered all of Scarlatti's works, and his numbers have since been used in the standard references.

at a moderate speed with delicate rhythmic impulses. The Sonata in E Major (Longo 257) is slow, striving for expressiveness difficult to achieve on a harpsichord. The harmony and rhythm complement the decorative melody giving full expression to its lyricism. The Sonata in D Minor (Longo 266) is vigorous, somewhat fantasy-like, but has a steadily driving rhythm and clearly defined harmonic events. The movement is impetuous from beginning to end. On the other hand, the Sonata in C Major (Longo 255) is light and frolicking. Quite typical of Baroque style, these pieces express one mood throughout.

François Couperin, L'Arlequin (The Harlequin) *and* Les Barricades mystérieuses (The Mysterious Battlements)

L'Arlequin and *Les Barricades mystérieuses* are two short program pieces in the French clavecin (harpsichord) style. Each of Couperin's multimovement works, called *ordres* (orders), consists of many such pieces; more than Bach's suites. The *ordres* are collections of dances and pieces with titles such as:

Huitième Ordre des Pièces des Clavecin (Seconde Livre):

La Raphaele

L'Ausoniene: Allemande
Premiere Courante
Seconde Courante

L'Unique: Sarabande
Gavotte
Rondeau
Gigue
Passacaille
La Morinette

The dances have prominent melodies and bass lines. The slower moving simple bass lines contrast sharply with the ornamented melodies. Harmony and rhythm do not dominate. Repetition, recurrence, and variation are basic to the structure. The dances are meant to be a sophisticated composition for the ears of the aristocracy, and not functional as originally conceived. The same process occurs today when dance forms become "concertized." (Jazz used to be a dance phenomenon, but now it is more often heard in a concert.)

Johann Kuhnau, Sonata I: The Fight Between David and Goliath, *from* Biblical Sonatas

The forms of the various movements of this piece include the toccata, pastorale, fugue, and the dance. The *Biblical Sonatas* were to be six sonatas that illustrated biblical stories on the harpsichord. The eight movements of Sonata I express:

1. Goliath's boastfulness and bravado: A bold, thumping piece, with prominent rhythm.
2. The fear and trembling of the Israelites: A somewhat agitated chorale.
3. The courage of David and his desire to break down, with God's assistance, the arrogance of the giant: An expression of confidence, security. Classic style.
4. The battle, the throwing of the stone, the fall of the giant: Rhythmic activity; toccata-like structure; dissonance resolves into quiet, finally silence.
5. The flight of the Philistines: A fast, rhythmically moving fugue.
6. The rejoicing after the victory: A quiet song.
7. The praise of David by the women's chorus with kettledrums.
8. Loud dancing and cavorting with delight: A minuet-like dance.

Carl Philipp Emanuel Bach, Twelve Variations on the "Folie d'Espagne"

The *Folía* is a dance of Portuguese origin. The bass line of the Folía has been used as an ostinato for variations by numerous composers. Originally the dance was wild. But Bach's music is for the listener, not the dancer.

Folkways Records (no. FM3341) presents these variations on a piano built in 1810. Although it is not known whether Bach wrote this work for harpsichord or piano, piano seems the more logical. Comments on the style are based on piano performance.

The work exhibits characteristics of both Baroque and Classic style. The variations range from arpeggio and toccata-like to lyrical and chorale-like. The openness, control, and clarity of the Classic style are already evident. The rhythm is decisive and regular. The toccata-like passages fall within controlled metrical patterns. The harmonies vary from structural prominence to vapidness. Dynamic contrasts and the sounds of the different registers are exploited. Various tonal effects, created by the manner of striking the keys, are apparent. The musical events are ready to be molded into the piano sonata of the Classic period.

THE PIANO SONATA OF THE CLASSIC PERIOD

The Classic piano sonatas of Haydn, Mozart, and early Beethoven are solo works for the keyboard. Most sonatas are three movement works. A fast first movement, usually in sonata-allegro form, is followed by a slow, often lyrical second movement which is either a variation, a rondo, or a small A-B-A form. The final movement is usually spirited. It is the fastest moving, and is sometimes in sonata-allegro form, but is more often a lilting rondo.

Ideally the movements are related tonally, sequentially, and aesthetically to form a sustained, dramatic whole. Such works approach the spirit of a complete novel or drama rather than a series of short stories or one-act plays.

The melody of the Classic sonata becomes more controlled. The potential lyricism of the piano diminishes the importance of embellishments. The free style of the fantasia and toccata-like flourishes are rare after the Baroque.

Harmony may not change as frequently in the Classic sonata. It is often subservient to the melody in contrast to its dominant, frequently changing role in the Baroque, and especially in the German Baroque style. Recall, for instance, the strong chordal structures in the fantasia section of Bach's *Chromatic Fantasia and Fugue*. Although harmony sometimes functions as an important primary event, it most often underscores melodic clarity and lyricism.

Classic sonata rhythm imparts a sense of assured stability. The rhythms of the accompaniment often change with the design of the work, and the rhythmic contrasts of the movements–fast, slow, fast–help shape the entire musical expression of the sonata. The texture of the Classic sonata is more transparent than much of the late aroque style music and the melody is more clearly lyrical. The Classic style made more use of melody with accompaniment and less use of shocking harmonies. There are practically no sections that are totally contrapuntal.

In tone and dynamics, the change from harpsichord to piano gave composers an opportunity to express new meaning. Although the Classic piano sonata exemplifies clarity and control in contrast to the excesses of the late Baroque, still it modified and synthesized many of the niceties and affectations of the Baroque and Rococo styles within a new structure.

No one sonata could be recommended as wholly typical of a composer's style, but the following three sonatas, one by Haydn, one by Mozart, and one by Beethoven, represent Classic piano sonata style.

Franz Joseph Haydn, Sonata no. 31 in E Major ("Moderato," "Allegretto," "Presto")

This sonata, published in 1778, beautifully demonstrates Classic clarity. In the first movement, marked *moderato* rather than the usual *allegro*, arpeggio and scale-like melodies alternate with arpeggio and scale-like passages that embellish the strong, moving harmony. The rhythm is prominent and sometimes quite forceful. The contrast of chordal harmony with the arpeggios also provides rhythmic interest.

The short second movement is *allegretto*. Haydn usually wrote slower *adagios* for his second movements. Melodic and harmonic events, playing a dual role, offer a richness which set off the second movement from the first and third. Moderately quiet, the "Allegretto" flows evenly without strong dramatic developments. Tonal interest is increased by presenting the melody in different registers of the piano. The "Allegretto" is a pleasant interlude before the "Presto" finale.

The "Presto," a set of variations, is reminiscent of a Scarlatti frolic on the harpsichord. The melody, with its spritely embellishments, joins with the harmony and rhythm to become a colorful, vigorous finale.

Wolfgang Amadeus Mozart, Sonata no. 13 in B Flat Major (*K. 333*), ("*Allegro,*" "*Andante cantabile,*" "*Allegretto grazioso*")

In a discussion of Mozart, the term *eloquence* might well be added to the terms already used to describe the Classic piano sonata. Mozart's musical events have the sheen of a highly polished surface. The clarity, balance, and control are applied everywhere in a structural design that seeks aesthetic perfection. Let this not, however, imply dullness. Contrast, vitality, and dramatic expression are not diminished, but rather exist in the perspective of rational order.

Ex. 14–4

The first melodic theme of the "Allegro" (a.) flows with elegance and superb grace. The second (b.) offers some variety but the contrast is subtle (see Ex. 14–4).

Although different, the themes are melded into a cohesive exposition. The agitation of the development follows. Its harmony presses harder and the rhythm increases in intensity. The recapitulation brings the movement to a close, gently but with spirit. The quiet ending prepares the listener for the "Andante cantabile."

The song-like lyricism of the opening theme in the second movement follows with an almost inconceivable naturalness.

Ex. 14–5

Harmony and rhythm complement this lyricism to create a refined and almost mystical sense of warmth and security.

The third movement, a rondo, is fanciful and more carefree than the first two, but does not exhibit the rugged vigor and joy of Haydn's usual *presto* finales.

Ex. 14–6

The finale, however, makes strong use of dynamics and incorporates tonal and rhythmic surprises.

Mozart's sonata exposes the listener to Classic perfection. Melodies grow into and out of one another. Harmony supports and reinforces, but commands as well when necessary. Rhythm propels, retards, agitates, or calms. Dynamics become part of the total balance by being structurally important, not merely dramatically effective.

Ludwig van Beethoven, Sonata in A Major, op. 2, no. 2 ("Allegro Vivace," "Largo Appassionato," "Scherzo–Allegretto," "Rondo–Grazioso")

The Classic piano sonata was at its pinnacle of perfection when Beethoven was a young man. The titles of the four movements of Sonata no. 2 reflect change. Beethoven was moving from the Classicism of Mozart toward Romanticism. Beethoven's style tends to move from

Ex. 14–7. Beethoven: Sonata no. 2, op. 2
Opening Theme

Allegro vivace (♩ = 152)

clarity and eloquence toward development, with more dramatic and powerful expression.

In the first movement the melodies are motivic. They contain more inner contrasts and lend themselves to greater developmental possibilities. Compare the thematic idea in Example 14–7 with that of Mozart in Example 14–4.

The second movement, with its lyrical melody, harmonic strength, ostinato bass, variation, and use of dynamics, begins softly and gently, and ends in the same manner. Between its beginning and end it generates a wide range of expressiveness including a dynamic power beyond the scope of Mozart's Classicism.

Ex. 14–8

The third movement is a scherzo exhibiting grace, rhythmic surprise, and tenderness.

The fourth movement, a rondo, has many of the Classic stylistic elements. However, Beethoven makes use of variation, dynamics, contrast, and structure to move away from the eloquence and control of Classicism toward the broader range of expression associated with Romanticism.

ORGAN MUSIC

The organ style of J. S. Bach remains to the present day *the* organ style of the Baroque. His chorale preludes, fantasias and fugues, passacaglias and fugues, preludes and fugues, and toccatas number more than 150.

The chorale prelude *Christ lag in Todesbanden* was discussed as a variation form in Chapter 7. (See pp. 142–143 and Ex. 7–12 a, b, and c.)

The toccata and fugue combines two forms into one composition. The toccata section is free in form and contains elaborate, technical passages flourishing up and down the keyboard. The fugue section consists of controlled counterpoint written in the imitative fugue style discussed in Chapter 8.

Bach's Toccata and Fugue in D Minor for Organ is an excellent example of the organ style of the Baroque. "After Bach," according to Willi Apel, "organ music suffered a decline from which it did not recover until c. 1840."

Mozart did compose a Fantasia in F Minor for Organ, K. 608, but for the purposes of style comparison organ music of the Classic period is practically nonexistent.

Comparative Styles: Keyboard Music

	Late Baroque	*Rococo*	*Classic*
Expression	*Grand, exuberant, pompous.*	*Capricious, gay, witty, light.*	*Structured, controlled. A reserved combination of former styles.*
Melody	*Long passages. Elaborate motivic ideas in imitation. One melodic idea per movement.*	*Ornamental, embellished.*	*Structured. Clear and controlled. Greater variety within a movement.*

	Late Baroque	*Rococo*	*Classic*
Rhythm	*Great variety. Sometimes free. Gradually more regular and controlled.*	*Dance-like, light, airy, flexible.*	*Usually regular. Few rapid, frequent changes of pace. More subtle variations.*
Tone Color	*Little variety. Centered on plucked strings of the harpsichord.*	*Little variety. Centered on the plucked strings of the harpsichord.*	*Variety introduced through the flexibility of the piano.*
Harmony	*Frequently changing. Heavy and full. Often improvised but compatible with counterpoint.*	*Delicate, thin.*	*Balanced. No improvisation. Supports melody. Changes less frequent.*
Dynamics	*Terraced. Gradual increases or decreases impossible on the harpsichord.*	*Light. Little contrast.*	*Much contrast. Gradual increases and decreases of sound. Some sudden changes. Controlled.*
Structure	*Many large forms: suite, variations, sonata, rondo, fugue, fantasia.*	*Suites. Groups of dances or titled pieces. Short works.*	*Sonata form, including sonata-allegro, variation, A-B-A, and rondo. The idea of development is introduced.*
Medium and Texture	*Harpsichord, clavichord, organ. Textures vary. May be toccata-like, harmonic, or extremely contrapuntal.*	*Harpsichord. Thin texture, mostly melody and bass with sparse harmonic fill-in.*	*Piano. Homophonic melody with harmonic-rhythmic accompaniment. Little imitation.*

The precursor of Baroque chamber music was the "Sonata pian'e forte" (1594) by Giovanni Gabrieli. It was written for two groups of instruments and used the dynamic contrasts soft (*piano*) and loud (*forte*) for the first time. It also indicated for the first time the specific instrument to be used for each part. The specification of dynamic level and tone color ushered in the beginning of orchestration and probably the essence of instrumental ensemble music.

A detailed analysis of the variety of styles, the evolution of forms, the profusion of terms, and the general complexity of Baroque instrumental music is beyond the scope of this book. Many of the influences, relationships and history remain, today, a matter of conjecture and varying opinions.

Chamber music forms include the sonata da chiesa, sonata da camera, suite, sonata for harpsichord and one instrument, and trio sonata. These compositions usually required a chord-playing instrument such as the harpsichord which performed a part called the *basso continuo*. The basso continuo consisted of a bass line of single notes that indicated the harmonies. This continuo is called "figured bass" when numbers are placed under these notes to designate specific chords. The player "realized" these chords on the keyboard, reading the progressions from this system of musical shorthand. In addition, the bass line was often "doubled," that is, played by another instrument, usually a cello. A sonata for solo violin and harpsichord was performed, therefore, not by two performers but by three: a violinist, a harpsichordist, and a cellist playing the same bass part as the keyboard instrument.

The emphasis on chords and on their generation from a bass note is a significant stylistic development of early Baroque music—an achievement which served as the foundation of music for the next three hundred years. Chords, rather than counterpoint, functioned as the basic sounding substance of music. The vertical sonorities became as important as the horizontal flow of sounds.

Seven works are presented here as representative of the variety of styles, forms, and mediums of Baroque chamber music.

Giovanni Gabrieli, "Sonata pian'e forte" (1594)

The listener should note the two groups of instruments. (1) *Cornetto* and three trombones. (The cornetto is now no longer played. A precursor of the cornet and trumpet, it had a cup-like mouthpiece and was made of wood. Pitch changes were made by stopping open holes with the fingers; it did not have valves.) (2) *Violino* and three trombones. (The violino was a stringed instrument of either the viol or violin family.) These instruments, although capable of producing dynamic contrasts, did not produce the powerful sounds of their present-day counterparts. (The term sonata does not imply the present-day sonata.)

Dynamic and tonal contrasts are created by the alternation and combination of the two choirs. Melodies are relatively short and fragmentary. The lively rhythm creates a feeling of forward motion. The groups sometimes respond in an echo-like manner. The work does have some contrast in texture; homophonic sections vie and imitate each other. The counterpoint is not as developed as that of a fugue.

Arcangelo Corelli, Sonata no. 12 in D Minor, op. 5

This sonata is a set of 23 variations for violin, harpsichord, and cello based on the Folía theme, a fifteenth-century Portuguese dance. The variations are a study in contrasts. The sonata idea appears in the interplay among the instruments. A musical dialog develops between the violin and the harpsichord, and the violin and cello also contrast prominently. The lyricism of the violin is set against the plucked sound of the harpsichord. The changing moods of the variations are the result of the interplay of melody and harmony. Rhythmic contrast also adds to the change in mood. The texture is open and clear and without counterpoint. Fantasy-like passages are rhythmically controlled. Compare Corelli's sonata with C. P. E. Bach's *Twelve Variations on the "Folie d'Espagne"* (See pp. 323–24).

Georg Philipp Telemann (1681–1767), Trio for Recorder, Viola da gamba and Continuo in F Major ("Vivace," "Mesto," "Allegro").

Telemann's trio is, in fact, a sonata and was written in the late Baroque. The sonata idea is developed through contrasts in texture and dialog in the melody.

The bright first movement is followed by a slow movement, "Mesto" (meaning sad), which uses the musical device of imitation. The melody on the recorder is answered by the viola da gamba. These two instruments are then joined homophonically by the harpsichord. In the second half of the "Mesto" the recorder answers the melody stated by the viola da gamba. The third movement, a bright *allegro*, completes the form.

Antonio Vivaldi, Sonata for Oboe, Violin, Bassoon, and Figured Bass in E Minor (*"Adagio," "Allegro," "Gigue"*).

This colorful work displays especially interesting dialog among the solo instruments. The "Adagio" is an excellent example of a beautifully lyrical melody interwoven with counterpoint. An oboe melody enters above the opening moving bass line of the bassoon. The violin answers the oboe and the three parts join to form a quiet "conversation." The harmony is somewhat dissonant as a result of the interplay of melodies. The rhythm is slow but steady. There is little dynamic contrast and the supporting harmonies are subdued. Nothing interferes with the lyrical expression.

The "Allegro" is based on a long-note, short-note rhythmic pattern repeated throughout. The lively melodies are decorative and move above a prominent, active bass line.

The lyricism of the "Gigue" alternates with more rhythmically oriented patterns. Imitation adds vitality and increases interest. The fast triple meter changes to duple in an unusual way in the last section of the "Gigue."

François Couperin, Concert dans Goût théâtral, *no. 4 of* Les Goûts réunis (*"Overture," "Air," "Grande Ritournelle," "Air Leger," "Air Tendre (Roudeau)," "Saraband," "Air Leger," "Air Tendre," "Air de Bacchantes"*).

This nine-movement set of concert pieces is Couperin's musical answer to a courtly conflict over the relative merits of Italian and French styles. It contains abstract pieces, dances, and pieces with titles.

The "Overture" is in two sections: slow, followed by a spirited fugue. The "Grande Ritournelle" displays some of the contrasts of the concerto-grosso principle, the alternation of contrasting instrumental groups. The first "Air Tendre" has variations and delicate tone-color contrasts. The "Saraband," originally a rather lascivious dance of Spanish origin, has been stylized; Couperin's "Saraband" is stately and dignified. The second "Air Leger," or "light tune," is graceful, bright, gay, and light as the title implies. Oboe, bassoon, and flute are colorfully used. The second "Air Tendre" begins in a recitative-like fashion, but continues like an aria. The "Air de Bacchantes" is a festive, spirited, gay minuet.

Johann Sebastian Bach, Art of the Fugue

Bach's *Art of the Fugue* is a work consisting of thirteen fugues and four canons. In it, Bach tries to exhaust the contrapuntal potential of its one subject, which is used for all seventeen sections. Bach called these sections *contrapunctii.**

Ex. 14–9

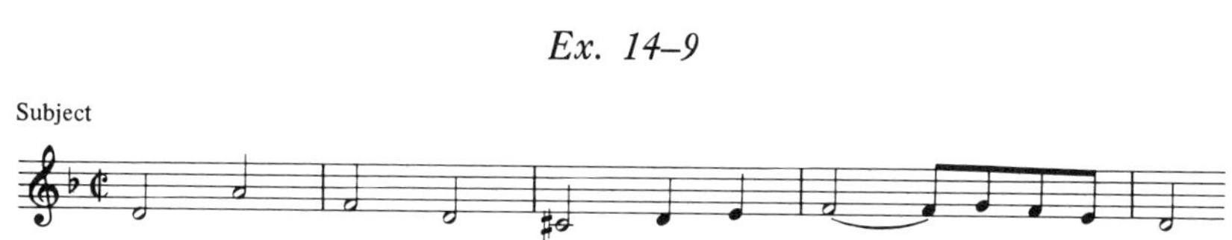

The original score does not specify instrumentation, tempo, or dynamics. Most of the work can be played on a keyboard instrument. The number of performers varies from two to four, depending on the section. The *contrapunctii* are, therefore, either duets, trios, or quartets. Due to its reputation as a masterpiece of counterpoint and the lack of directions in its original score, many versions are available: string quartet, woodwind quintet, harpsichord, piano, organ, orchestra, string orchestra, and others.

George Frideric Handel, Trio Sonata no. 2 in D Minor for Flute, Oboe, Cembalo (Harpsichord) and Continuo ("Adagio," "Allegro," "Affettuoso," "Allegro").

This work contains a considerable amount of thematic interaction between the instruments. The "Adagio" is characteristic of Italian lyricism but incorporates imitation. The "Allegro " is bright, sectional in construction, and uses interesting tone-color contrasts. The "Affettuoso" is again song-like, somewhat dramatic, and has some surprising

* Some references to the *Art of the Fugue* include an additional fugue and a chorale prelude, which are not related to the subject, bringing the total to nineteen pieces.

harmonies near the end. The final "Allegro" moves brightly at a rapid rhythm, making use of musical dialog.

In a process somewhat parallel to the evolution of keyboard styles and forms, chamber music flourished and stabilized in the hands of Haydn, Mozart, and Beethoven, and it underwent many of the same changes. The forms and mediums became fewer and more settled. The string quartet became the most important medium and remains popular today as a standard chamber-music medium. Other mediums, mentioned in Chapter 5, were established during the Classic period. They are the string trio, the piano trio, and the piano quintet, which became popular with nineteenth-century composers. The Classic period also gave birth to divertimentos and serenades. These works had no set structure or established instrumentation.

Five representative works of this period will afford the listener an idea of Classic chamber music style.

Franz Joseph Haydn, Quartet in D Major, op. 76, no. 5 ("*Allegretto,*" "*Largo* (*Cantabile e mesto*)," "*Menuetto* (*Allegro*)," "*Finale* (*Presto*)").

Haydn emerged as the leading producer of the string quartet, as it became increasingly more popular. His early quartets were little more than violin solos accompanied by a second violin, viola, and cello. However, as he experimented with the medium and the form, a new quartet style emerged in which all four instruments shared the thematic material.

The four-movement form is most common. The opening movement is in sonata-allegro form. The slow second movement is in A-B-A form or sometimes also sonata-allegro form. It is usually lyrical, being the most serious and dramatic movement. The third movement is a minuet and is followed, especially in Haydn's works, by a fast, gay finale, most often a rondo.

The Quartet in D Major opens moderately with a *siciliano*-like introduction that leads to a vigorous *allegro*. (The *siciliano* was a particular type of dance.) The instruments mix to some degree but are all separately distinguishable. Through Haydn the classic balance of harmony, melody, and rhythm emerges.

In the "Largo" movement, the cello becomes prominent, emancipating itself from being the bass-line reenforcement of the continuo. The work becomes a full quartet with harmonies alternating in prominence with melodies. The rhythm is steady. Dynamic contrasts are both gradual and direct. The lyrical, song-like sadness implied by the *mesto* is evident but not overdone.

The minuet is more stylized and polished than many of Haydn's minuets. Compare it with the minuet of Symphony no. 94 (*Surprise*), for example. The cello is prominent in the middle section. The minuet is not a mere "dance tune."

The fast, gay finale combines harmonic surprises, dialog, brightness, and rhythmic drive.

Franz Joseph Haydn, Divertimento no. 1 in B Flat Major ("Allegro con Spirito," "Andante–Chorale of St. Antoni," "Minuetto," "Rondo").

The divertimento is rarely played as originally orchestrated. Haydn scored it for two oboes, two French horns, three bassoons, and a serpent (obsolete bass cornet). The theme of the "Andante" is the basis for Brahms' *Variations on a Theme by Haydn*, op. 56a (see p. 144) and there is some doubt that the theme was originally by Haydn. A divertimento is characteristically less serious than a string quartet. Compare the Brahms and the Haydn.

Wolfgang Amadeus Mozart, Quartet no. 20 in D Major, K. 499 ("Allegro," "Minuetto (Allegretto)," "Adagio," "Allegro").

The sudden mood changes give this quartet an operatic feeling. The opening unison passage of the "Allegro" is soon followed by a musical dialog. The different dynamic levels and changes in key (from major to minor) are responsible for some of the mood changes. Some changes are sudden and surprising. The canon is used as a textural device. The moods range from *mesto* (sad) to lively. Note that the minuet and the slow movement ("Adagio") have exchanged places.

The minuet has a stately character, almost a heaviness. The individuality of the separate instruments plays an important role.

The "Adagio" is dramatic, with prominent contrasts in expression. Voices other than the melody are important. The melodies are lyrical, sparingly embellished, and have a singable quality. Harmonies are meaningful, and not thin and light as in some Baroque styles.

The fourth movement moves along brightly but not as consistently bright as the finale of Haydn's quartet. There is much "working-out" among the instruments and effective use of dynamic contrasts. Serious mood changes appear, and the finale does not express continuous gaiety although it is bright and moving.

Wolfgang Amadeus Mozart, Quintet in E Flat Major, K. 452 ("Largo: Allegro moderato," "Larghetto," "Allegro").

Mozart's quintet is scored for a diversified group of instruments: piano, oboe, clarinet, French horn, and bassoon. The contrasts in tonal coloring in the dialog among the instruments give the work its special character. Note the sonority of the piano and winds. If Mozart had scored the voice parts of an opera for instruments, the result might have been something like this quintet. The lyric French horn is reminiscent of the tenor voice, the bassoon of the bass, and the complete ensemble of the chorus. Other instruments function similarly.

The piano's opening lyrical melody is accompanied by chordal harmony in the winds. The piano then harmonically accompanies the dialog of the wind instruments. The dramatic harmonies give the work a serious feeling. The "Allegro" resembles the repartee of an operatic "ensemble finale" in which all participants are "having their say."

The slow movement reminds the listener of an aria or a slow, stately dance. The rondo finale is colorful and rhythmic. It begins like a folk tune, and then alternates with more serious sections. A contrapuntal cadenza-like section including all five instruments surprises the listener just before the close.

Ludwig van Beethoven, Quartet no. 6 in B Flat Major, op. 18, no. 6 ("Allegro con brio," "Adagio, ma non troppo," "Scherzo (Allegro)," "La Malinconia (Adagio; Allegretto quasi allegro)").

The six quartets of opus 18 are considered Beethoven's "early" quartets. Many passages from them are in the Classic tradition of Mozart. Beethoven soon began to order musical events in new ways. Even these early quartets show signs of change. The sixth quartet is a transitional piece.

The first movement, "Allegro con brio," begins with freshness and clarity, periodically displaying the operatic quality common in Mozart's works. Freshness and clarity gradually give way to greater involvement, tension, and intensity. The operatic lyricism turns emotionally dramatic. Beethoven incorporates greater dynamic contrasts, expanded use of crescendo and diminuendo, and sudden stops in the music. He employs vigorous dialog among the instruments, sudden shifts from major to minor keys, and vivid thematic contrasts. The sounds of the quartet diminish to a dramatic silence before the Mozart-like recapitulation.

The second movement expands the classic openness to include inner turmoil. A new, drawn-out seriousness confronts the listener.

The lyricism of the violin melody, which is harmonically accompanied, is soon complemented by the other instruments. The return to lyricism is accompanied by motivic figuration, rather than the previous straightforward harmonies. Beethoven makes dramatic use of all the instruments playing in unison and the second contrasting theme results in a drastic change of mood. Dynamic contrasts are effective, dramatic, and often quite surprising. The theme fragments at the close of the movement are resolved by two pizzicato chords. But an air of restlessness pervades which demands the continuation of the quartet.

The intriguing rhythm of the scherzo is a dominant feature. Rapid, joyous, and playful, it moves with a sense of "trickiness." The B section of this A-B-A form offers tonal and rhythmic variety. The entire scherzo is filled with accents and rhythms that confuse the meter. The scherzo movement replaces the conventional minuet.

"La Malinconia" (sadness) provides a unique opening to the fourth movement. The music is in keeping with its title. The serious expression of the entire quartet results from an exploitation of powerful harmonies and gentle rhythms. An exclamation, almost of despair, by the cello follows. Dissonant harmonies reenforce the statements. "La Malinconia" fades away and the "Allegretto quasi allegro" changes the mood. It is joyous in the style of a slightly fast minuet, but the mood is not maintained. As major and minor keys fluctuate and the rhythmic activity subsides the melancholy returns, alternating with the dance-like mood. The listener wonders which will dominate. Beethoven answers with a flourish of fast bright sounds, closing the quartet.

The previous chart comparing the Baroque and Classic styles of keyboard music is also an accurate reflection of the style differences in chamber music in the categories of expression, melody, rhythm and harmony. The following chart indicates the contrast between Baroque and Classic chamber-music styles for tone color, dynamics, structure, and medium and texture.

Comparative Styles:
Chamber Music

	Late Baroque	*Classic*
Tone Color	*Strings and harpsichord predominate. Flute and oboe provide added contrast. Characteristically, continuo doubles bass part on cello. Keyboard instrument always included.*	*Less variety. Piano is developed but used only when specifically called for. More attention to sonority of instruments, rather than contrast and competition.*
Dynamics	*Terraced. Even wind instruments follow the terraced plan of the harpsichord but with a little more freedom.*	*Use of crescendo and decrescendo. Bigger sounds, especially when the piano was included.*
Structure	*Much variety. Forms adapted to musical content. Sometimes no difference between suite and sonata. Fugue widely used.*	*Established forms. Emphasis on structural control. Musical events made to fit into structure.*
Medium and Texture	*Variety of mediums. Texture ranges from lyrical, expressive melody with accompaniment, to strict counterpoint.*	*String quartet and trio, piano quartet and quintet, serenade and divertimento. Melodic, homophonic texture. Counterpoint rare.*

THE CONCERTO GROSSO AND THE BAROQUE SOLO CONCERTO

The previous discussion of the concerto (Chapter 12) defined the concerto in terms of two mediums, at times contrasted and "pitted" against each other while joined during others. The concerto grosso sets a small group of solo performers against a larger ensemble or full orchestra. For example, the solo group might be two violins and a cello, the larger ensemble a string orchestra. In Bach's Brandenburg Concerto no. 2, a concerto grosso, the solo group consists of a flute, oboe, violin, and trumpet, while the larger ensemble is a string orchestra. The effect is reminiscent of the "Sonata pian'e forte" of Gabrieli. The two groups produce expressive contrasts in medium.

In comparison, the solo concerto contrasts one solo instrument with the larger ensemble. In the true concerto style the larger ensemble is not merely an accompaniment. The two forces, solo instrument and ensemble, whether a solo group or an individual, work in cooperation.

The following works of Corelli, Telemann, and Bach are representative of the Baroque concerto grosso.

Arcangelo Corelli, Concerto Grosso in F Major, op. 6, no. 12 (*"Preludio–Adagio," "Allegro," "Adagio," "Sarabanda–Vivace," "Giga–Allegro"*).

Corelli and Vivaldi are credited with establishing the concerto grosso form. The larger ensemble employed by them, called the *ripieno*, is a string orchestra; the solo group, called the *concertino*, varies. Corelli's solo group (two violins and a cello) was favored by many composers. Composers varied in their use of other mediums for the concertino.

The "Preludio" is based on a lyrical, embellished melody set against a prominent moving bass line. The inner harmonic voices are thin, and the texture is light and open. The contrast between ripieno and concertino results in terraced dynamics. The movement is emotionally expressive.

The "Allegro" begins with two short phrases and afterwards continues with persistent, regular rhythm. The movement is repetitious, making use of key and mood changes.

The "Adagio" is an immediate contrast. This short movement is propelled by the harmony and slow rhythm and provides little or no melodic interest. The last three chords lead to the lively "Sarabanda" and "Giga," both dances. The dance movements are a contrast in spirit. The speed and meter change, the melodies are light, and the harmonies are thin.

Georg Philipp Telemann, Concerto in D Major for Three Trumpets, Timpani, Two Oboes, Strings, and Continuo ("Intrada: Allegro," "Largo," "Vivace").

The title of this concerto grosso immediately suggests the potential for variety in the concertino. Telemann exploits these tone-color possibilities. The work reflects many aspects of Baroque style: the long-short rhythmic figure at the beginning (characteristic of the opening of French overtures), terraced dynamics, recitative-like passages for oboe, aria-like passages, varying textures, and contrasts.

The small, high-pitched trumpets have no valves. Their sound is brilliant. The players were virtuosos.

The "Intrada" includes fanfare-like trumpet passages, decorative oboe figurations, an oboe recitative, and a contrapuntal section. The short "Largo" opens harmonically, as do many slow movements, and the harmonies support the lyrical oboe aria. The brilliance of the trumpets returns in the "Vivace" with its rhythmic movement and counterpoint. Telemann finishes the concerto with a "fast and fancy" spectacle of sound.

Johann Sebastian Bach, Brandenburg Concerto no. 2 ("Allegro," "Andante," "Allegro assai").

The concertino of this second of six concertos is trumpet, flute, oboe, and violin. The trumpet is again the valveless variety mentioned in the Telemann concerto and the flute is the present-day recorder.

Bach's first "Allegro" is a display of brilliant sound, rhythmic vitality and instrumental virtuosity. The concerto effect is heightened by the interplay between the two groups, the tone colors, and the resulting terraced dynamics. Solid harmonic movement adds to the vitality.

The "Andante" is an immediate contrast. It is slower and more gentle, scored for flute, oboe, violin, keyboard, and continuo only. The violin states the theme quietly. The oboe and then the flute respond with the same melody. The three instruments develop a lyrical melodic counterpoint that becomes a pinnacle of quiet emotional expression.

The closing "Allegro" is a fugue of spirit and vitality. The subject, stated by high trumpet, is answered by oboe, violin, and finally the flute. After the exposition, the counterpoint continues to the end. The larger ensemble joins the concertino group periodically, adding an additional contrast as the two contrasting groups join in a concerted effort.

The solo concerto (or simply concerto) discussed in Chapter 12 was also a popular form during the Baroque. The two examples below are representative.

Antonio Vivaldi, Concerto in E Minor for Bassoon and Strings ("Allegro poco," "Andante," "Allegro").

In addition to composing various concerti grossi, Vivaldi leads the field in writing solo concertos. His bassoon concerto is one example.

An orchestral introduction, which seems to forecast some of Mozart's operatic–orchestral style, leads to the entrance of the soloist. The passages for bassoon vary from song-like to passages with fast runs and embellishments. The orchestra gives rhythmic and harmonic support. Contrast between the two mediums is stark, with only a little uninvolved dialog. A quiet ending leads to the "Andante," which begins with orchestral harmonies that set the tone for what is actually an aria for bassoon. The orchestra provides light harmonic accompaniment.

The third movement is rhythmic, almost gypsy-like. The triple beat, in the style of a fast minuet, gives new contrast. The movement is sectional with solo passages, aria-like ones, and some variation. The orchestral parts supply rhythmic movement and harmonic propulsion. The interplay of mediums is in a state of evolving into the Classic concerto. The expression is more like a solo with accompaniment even though there is some dialog.

George Frideric Handel, Oboe Concerto no. 8 in B Flat Major ("Adagio," "Allegro," "Siciliano (Largo)," "Vivace").

This oboe concerto, one of eighteen by Handel, provides another example of a Baroque solo concerto. The "Adagio" is a beautifully lyrical oboe passage with orchestral accompaniment, primarily harmonic. Some dialog and imitation occur but they are not pursued. The movement ends with a flourish. The dance-like "Allegro" resembles a hornpipe (a step dance). The quiet third movement is like an operatic aria. The repetition of the flowing "Siciliano" rhythmic figure adds a sense of unity. The "Vivace" is dance-like in the style of a minuet.

THE CONCERTO IN THE CLASSIC PERIOD

The concerto grosso vanishes entirely in the Classic period and is succeeded by the solo concerto. The great variety of instruments which served as solo mediums in the Baroque concerto are almost entirely replaced by the violin and the piano.

The concerto form became more standardized and similar in structure to the keyboard sonata and the symphony. It is usually in three movements. (The minuet of the symphony is omitted.) Sonata-allegro form dominates the first movement. Second movements vary. They may employ A-B-A, variation, or rondo form. Third movements are usually, although not exclusively, rondos.

The sonata-allegro design, when used, was modified. It was given two expositions: an orchestral exposition serving as an introduction followed by the soloist's exposition. The two are not identical. The soloist may have thematic material of his own which was not exposed by the orchestra.

In addition, the larger ensemble of the Baroque was usually a string orchestra while the larger ensemble of the Classic period was the symphony orchestra of Mozart and Haydn. (See Chapter 4.) The concerto also became longer.

The following works of Haydn and Mozart are representative of the solo concerto style of the Classic period.

Franz Joseph Haydn, Concerto in E Flat Major for Trumpet and Orchestra ("Allegro," "Andante," "Allegro spiritoso").

Most of Haydn's concertos are rarely performed. Although the violin and piano became the principal solo mediums, his trumpet concerto continues to command attention. In this work Haydn is no longer limited by the older Baroque unkeyed trumpet.

Note the orchestral exposition, the exposition of the solo trumpet, and the joining of forces at the close. Observe the interplay of soloist and orchestra as the two mediums combine to "work out" the development. The recapitulation culminates with a cadenza for the soloist. After the cadenza, the coda by the orchestra alone closes the "Allegro." Note also that this orchestra is a symphony orchestra, not the string orchestra that usually formed the ripieno in the Baroque period.

In the "Andante" the soloist sometimes soars melodically, accompanied by the orchestra. The melody is lyrical but does not have the operatic flavor of the Classic aria. The embellishment is more suited to the trumpet than to voice. On occasion the trumpet blends into the harmony.

The rondo "Allegro spiritoso" is in Haydn's jovial style. Repetitions of the A section of the rondo are interestingly varied. There is concerto-like dialog as well as concerted efforts by soloist and orchestra. The soloist is given ample opportunity to exhibit his virtuosity at embellishment and in improvising two cadenzas. Both forces, solo and orchestra, join for the ending.

Wolfgang Amadeus Mozart, Concerto in C Minor for Piano and Orchestra, K. 491 ("Allegro," "Larghetto," "Allegretto").

Mozart succeeded in all the forms and mediums he touched. His piano concertos are no exception. Mozart's style in this concerto goes beyond the polished eloquence of the compositions previously referred to in this chapter.

The "Allegro" is more than an opening movement. The clarity and elegance do not leave, but a certain amount of turbulence is added, reminiscent of the intensity, moodiness, depth, and involvement of the Beethoven String Quartet, op. 18, no. 6.

The orchestral score is full and rich in terms of the Classic orchestra: strings, flute, two oboes, two clarinets, two bassoons, two French horns, two trumpets, and timpani.

The orchestral exposition, the piano exposition, and the subsequent interplay of the two mediums again reflect Mozart's ability to synthesize. The piano is a solo medium, but the orchestra and piano combine to form an expressive whole.

In this concerto, the outpouring of emotional feeling reaches unusual heights for a classical piece. Lyrical melodies abound, as do rich harmonies and rhythmic subtleties. Tone colors are exploited, and key changes are more frequent than is customary in other works by Mozart.

The "Larghetto" leaves the turmoil and complexity of the "Allegro" behind. The restfulness is welcome. The work is not, however, simplistic. Observe the effect of the piano alone at the beginning of the movement. Contrast the piano opening and the orchestral passage that follows. Note the short passage for piano with accompaniment before the dialog with the bassoon and later with the flute. Observe Mozart's exploitation of the tone colors of the woodwind instruments and their role in the dialog. Note also the joining of the woodwinds in a unison passage with the piano.

Most of Mozart's final concerto movements are rondos. This "Allegretto" is a theme and eight variations followed by a coda. The piano takes no part in the statement of the theme but is always part of the variation. The theme and variations give a more serious expression to the conclusion of the concerto. The concerto does not end with a lilting rondo, which would have been out of place.

Concerto expression, harmony, melody, and rhythm underwent the same modifications in evolving from Baroque to Classic as did keyboard music and chamber music. The contrasts in tone color, dynamics, structure, and medium and texture are indicated on the following chart.

Comparative Styles:
The Concerto

	Late Baroque	*Classic*
Tone Color	*Based on contrast. Keyboard always included.*	*Greater contrasts from a more fully instrumented orchestra. Keyboard included only as solo instrument.*
Dynamics	*Terraced. Wind instruments followed the terraced dynamics of the harpsichord but with a bit more freedom.*	*Wider range. Greater use of gradual change in volume. More sudden contrasts.*

	Late Baroque	*Classic*
Structure	*Variety of movements. Use of fugue. No set number of movements.*	*Established forms. Emphasis on control of structure. Events made to fit into the structure.*
Medium and Texture	*Variety of mediums. No set pattern. Texture ranges from lyrical, expressive melody with accompaniment, to strict counterpoint.*	*Ensemble becomes full orchestra. Emphasis on solo concerto. Violin and piano are principal solo instruments.*

THE SYMPHONY

The symphony might be defined as a sonata for orchestra. Its roots are in the instrumental music of the Baroque. Its development parallels that of the chamber music sonata and the solo sonata.

One of the roots of the symphony is the *sinfonia.* Sinfonias (notably composed by Alessandro Scarlatti) are introductory instrumental pieces for operas. They were structured in three parts: fast, slow, fast. Subsequently these and similar three movement instrumental works were performed independently as concert pieces. A minuet was later inserted between the middle and the last movement (the pattern adopted for the Classic sonata) making the symphony a four movement work: fast, slow, minuet, and fast.

In addition to its structural development, the symphony had to undergo stylistic development. It had to assimilate the various stylistic characteristics of the period, particularly those of the orchestra which was becoming a colorful, highly polished, technically efficient performing ensemble. These changes developed through the efforts of the pre-Classic symphonists and reached fulfillment in the symphonists of the Classic period.

THE PRE-CLASSIC SYMPHONY

In the middle of the eighteenth century the symphony interested composers as an instrumental form. In Italy, Giuseppi Tartini included numerous symphonies among his instrumental compositions, and Giovanni Battista Sammartini (1701–1775) composed more than twenty-three. William Boyce (1710–1779), an English composer, composed eight. Active symphonists in Germany and Austria were Johann Gottlieb Graun (1703–1771), Carl Philipp Emanuel Bach (although Bach's keyboard sonatas and concertos were far more important), Georg Christoph Wagensiel (1715–1777), and Franz Xaver Richter (1709–1789).

The center of activity, however, was at Mannheim led by Johann Stamitz (1717–1757). Other composers, and later his son, Carl (1745–1801), also participated but did not achieve the fame of Johann.

In addition to his symphonies Johann Stamitz gained a reputation for his work with the symphony orchestra at Mannheim by demanding excellence in performance. He was evidently meticulous about dynamic control, bowing styles, and other techniques, demanding a perfection in orchestral playing not previously encountered.

Symphonies by Bach, Boyce, Stamitz, Wagenseil, and Richter are representative of the various styles of symphonies of this period.

Carl Philipp Emanuel Bach, Symphony in D Major ("Allegro di molto," "Largo," "Presto").

Bach uses an orchestra of two flutes, two oboes, bassoon, two French horns, strings, and continuo in this symphony. This work and related works liberate the symphony and the symphony orchestra from other mediums and forms.

In the style one can hear the influences of J. S. Bach, Corelli, Vivaldi, and Handel, and anticipate Mozart and Haydn. One can also hear the essence of the sonata and the concerto grosso.

The "Allegro di molto" is fresh and spirited. The exposition clearly contrasts thematic ideas. The movement then moves dramatically into a development section which is not as involved as those of later symphonies. A recapitulation brings the movement to a rather surprising slow and quiet ending, almost as if a cadenza were expected.

The "Largo" is harmonically rich and expressive. The pizzicato adds newness and variety. The texture is full, thick, and without counterpoint.

The "Presto" moves rapidly but includes changes of mood. It forecasts a synthesis of styles.

Johann Stamitz, Sinfonia (à 8) in D Major ("Presto," "Andante non Adagio," "Minuetto," "Prestissimo").

Stamitz' style also anticipates the Classic. He demanded precise performance, vigorous contrasts, "singing" soft passages, and attention to detail. The performance technique adds to the clarity and openness of the style.

Although he lived at the same time as Carl Philipp Emanuel Bach, Stamitz' symphony style is less Baroque in flavor than the Bach D Major Symphony.

The "Presto" has a driving rhythm and emphasizes thematic contrast, sudden dynamic change, crescendo and diminuendo, decorative harmonies between thematic ideas, and the development of thematic ideas.

The "Andante non Adagio" is not as heavy as Bach's "Largo." The movement is basically light but includes some dynamic contrasts which give it a dramatic flavor.

The "Minuetto" exploits tone colors, giving alternating prominence to the winds and strings.

The "Prestissimo" is almost Mozartean, as if from an opera buffa. It displays lyrical melodies, episode sections, and dance-like passages using full orchestra, strings, and winds in concerto style. It also makes use of dynamic and tone-color contrasts.

THE CLASSIC SYMPHONY

Both the symphony orchestra and modern symphonic form originated in the late eighteenth-century music of Haydn, Mozart, and early Beethoven. Their symphonies, like the other works of these composers, became part of the Classic international style. In the Classic symphony the sonata-allegro form was adopted for the first movement. It was exploited, perfected, and made more interesting. The double theme was emphasized and the contrast maximized. The contrast was considerably more focused if the tone-color and key were made different. The composer's inventiveness in developing one or more of these themes took on new importance. The total resources of the orchestra were brought into play, and the sonata-allegro form became musically exciting.

The second movement could be a rondo, variation, song form (A-B-A), or, on occasion, also a sonata-allegro form. Its expression was usually serious and dramatic rather than depending on the excitement of the first movement. The longer, expressive melodic lines were a reflection of the opera aria. The harmonies were often more prominent because of the slower pace and played a primary role in the dramatic expressiveness. The expressive lyricism gave commanding depth to the music. The second movement is the breath-holding movement, the "intensifier."

The minuet moves the listener to the relaxed, emotionally untaxing freedom of the dance. This movement served as a release from the serious second movement.

The fourth movement—finale, *presto*, *allegro*—gave the symphony the excitement of a rapid, moving, climaxing close. This movement consummated the symphony.

The Classic symphony is not a series of four contrasting pieces. It is a complete entity expressed by an orchestra. Haydn and Mozart absorbed, united, and assembled within their works all the facets of Baroque style at their disposal. They brought the excessive outpourings and overdone melodic embellishments under control. They changed the effect of harmonies, frequently using them in an accompanying capacity but depending upon them for dramatic effect and expressiveness. They eliminated the improvisatory nature of inner parts, bringing harmony into control and making the inner voices more prominent and important.

The rhythmic freedoms of the fantasia and prelude were traded for the precision and clarity of rhythmic regularity. Allowances were made, however, for flexibility in the performance of parts calling for lyrical expressiveness. But rhythm was not restricted to a redundant dullness. Mozart and Haydn both created some surprising and effective rhythmic events. The surprise, the off-beat accent, the nuance, and the sudden unexpected silence were their tools. In short, rhythm was carefully planned.

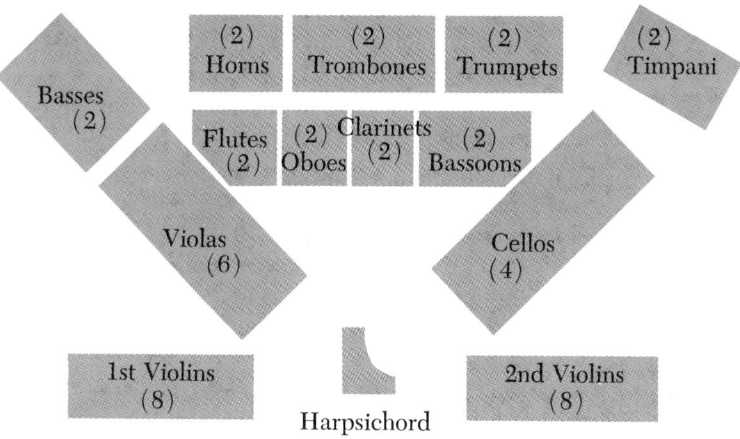

The Classical Symphony Orchestra.

One possible seating arrangement and instrumentation for the Classical symphony orchestra. The Classical symphony varied in size and instrumention just as the contemporary symphony orchestra may vary. In the early symphonies, the harpsichord filled in and elaborated on the harmonies and was generally played by the conductor. The harpsichord's role in the Baroque and Classical orchestra was called the continuo.

Dynamic events were brought into balance. In a sense, they functioned structurally. The first movement was usually loud or moderately loud. The lyric second movement was soft and moderate but forceful and strong when the dramatic expression so demanded. The third movement was moderate. Although the fourth movement usually ranged from very soft to loud, the symphony usually ended with a firm, loud statement.

The Classic symphony became an international form. It incorporated musical characteristics from the sinfonia, the dance, the suite, the fugue, the opera, and the cantata, and integrated musical influences from England, France, Italy, and Germany. The following symphonies by Haydn and Mozart are typical of this new international Classic style.

Franz Joseph Haydn, Symphony no. 104 in D Major (London) (*"Adagio-Allegro," "Andante," "Minuet (Allegro) and Trio," "Allegro spiritoso"*).

The slow introduction to the first movement is fanfare-like with dynamic contrasts and mood changes. It centers on the opening rhythmic figure. It begins in D minor but leads to the principal theme of the "Allegro" section in D major.

The "Allegro" is vigorous, generally following sonata-allegro form. Its development is based on a fragment from the second theme. After it builds up to a dynamic climax, it surprises the listener with a sudden silence. The recapitulation closes the movement vigorously.

The "Andante" is a rondo. The strings open quietly in the style of a slow, stately dance. The expression is neither spirited nor lyrical in an operatic fashion. It is not in the mood of one of Haydn's gay rondo finales, but rather somber. Some themes give the impression of being developed, and restatements are subjected to variation. The range of dynamic contrast is wide. The expression is neither restful nor dramatic.

The "Minuet" has the full sound of an Austrian *Landler* (a slow waltz). It displays contrast and some surprises, and becomes more stylized after the first section.

The "Allegro spiritoso" is based on two themes. The first is folk-like, the second, contrasting. Both themes are developed. The movement is in sonata-allegro form.

The symphony is scored for two of each of the winds, flutes, oboes, clarinets, bassoons, French horns, trumpets, timpani, and the full complement of strings.

Wolfgang Amadeus Mozart, Symphony no. 41 in C Major, K. 551 (Jupiter) (*"Allegro vivace," "Andante cantabile," "Menuetto (Allegretto)," "Finale (Allegro molto)"*).

The *Jupiter* Symphony of Mozart is a masterpiece of combined musical elements and styles.

The first movement begins with a short vigorous motive (Ex. 14–10).

Ex. 14–10

This motive is followed immediately by a short gentle motive.

Ex. 14–11

After each is repeated, the full orchestra enters in a fanfare. The two motives return and another melody is superimposed on them. (See Ex. 14–12.) These elements set the beginning pace for a vigorous first movement in sonata-allegro form. A contrasting, more lyrical theme stated at the end of the exposition includes still another theme. The statement, development, and restatement of the themes give vigor to the movement.

The second movement is a beautiful expression of dramatic lyricism. The harmonies are bold and the rhythm interjects an air of

Ex. 14–12

restlessness. The entire movement reflects the conflict of peace and agitation.

The third movement is an elegant minuet. It is based on a chromatic theme and follows conventional external minuet form. Internally the form is extended. In one section, Mozart treats the theme in the fashion of a canon.

Ex. 14–13. Theme

Ex. 14–14. Imitation

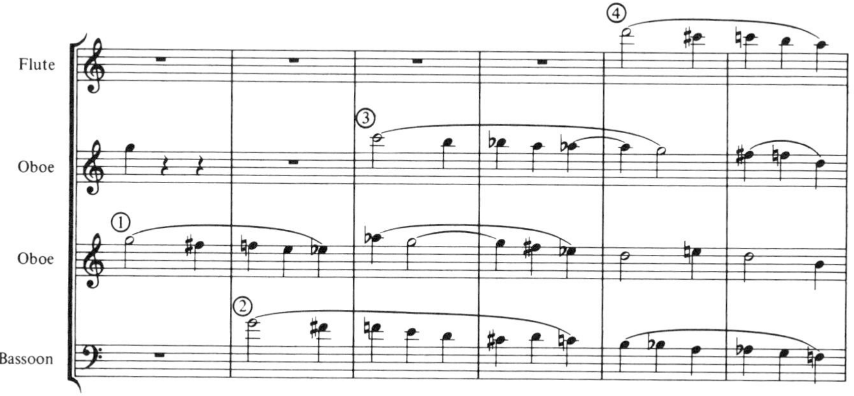

In the "Finale" Mozart uses all of the following melodic ideas.

Ex. 14–15. Thematic Idea I

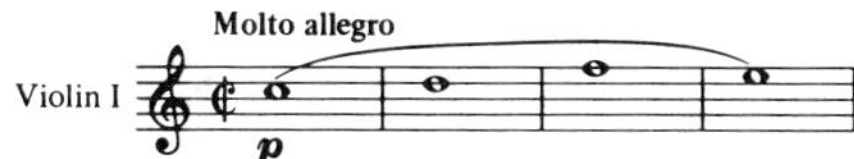

Ex. 14–16. Thematic Idea II

Ex. 14–17. Thematic Idea III

Ex. 14–18. Thematic Idea IV

The whole-note theme is treated contrapuntally.

Ex. 14–19. Thematic Idea I—Imitation

To understand this movement, the listener should try to remember each melody since each appears frequently. Listen for each of them. Try to experience them by themselves as primary elements and mixed together.

Much of this last movement, in sonata-allegro form, is contrapuntal. However the total effect is Classic. The elegance, openness, clarity, symmetry, and balance remain. Melody, harmony, rhythm, tone color, variety of texture, and dynamics are united in a balanced perspective.

In the coda, the four themes appear simultaneously (Ex. 14–20).

Ex. 14–20. The four thematic ideas superimposed

A SUMMARY OF STYLES: BAROQUE AND CLASSIC

Above all the Baroque style is dramatic. New forms proliferated and strove to embrace a wide range of moods. The Baroque composer, far more than his predecessors, wanted his audience to respond to the music. He created sharp contrasts: terraced dynamics, large versus small groups of instruments, alternating tempos, varying rhythms between movements, and contrasting moods. The emotional meaning of the texts is expressed musically. The Baroque composer sought clear and forceful musical statements to stun the listener. Each piece focused on one basic rhythmic or melodic idea; each created one mood that was sustained and intensely explored.

Melody and bass are as important as counterpoint to the texture of the music. Pieces were sectionalized with such distinct contrasts that the listener's attention was assured. The multisectional structure of Baroque vocal music, its quilt-like pattern, was a logical result of the subordination of the music to the text. The music alters to convey the changing emotional content of the words. The Baroque composer was interested in the verbal message. Even though the operatic plots were often grandiose and aloof, the music was emotionally direct. The Baroque composer recognized the power of spontaneity and incorporated improvisation and a seeming freeness of style into his music.

Exuberance characterizes the Baroque period. Exaggeration, a tendency for overstatement, is as much a part of the music of the period as it is of the architecture. As the Baroque period progressed, composers moved from the simpler chordal style to a musical style that wed harmony with counterpoint. The culmination of this synthesis is heard in Bach's complex and powerful works.

In contrast, Classic style is more rational and controlled. Emotion was not permitted to burst the musical forms, to change and distort them for dramatic effect. The forms were proscribed and maintained; the composer was content to use given outlines to structure his expression, to preserve coherence, balance, and clarity. In instrumental music the Classic composer made the symphonic form all-encompassing. While the Baroque composer achieved this range of expression with vocal forms, the Classic composer achieved it with instrumental forms. The Baroque composer had emancipated instrumental from vocal music; the Classic composer released instrumental music to new heights of expression. He slowed chord changes and permitted the various instrumental sonorities to speak. He found new ways to achieve cohesiveness in his compositions and invented development to build musical tension.

The Classic composer preferred more earthy operatic plots; his music is more emotionally subtle than the Baroque composer's. Musical moods flow into each other with smooth transitions. Applying development to opera permitted building emotional tension to highly charged points of release, an effect not quite possible in Baroque music, which is dependent on the accumulation of individual blocks of energy.

The Classic style is calculated, but it is not cold. Economy, subtlety, and restraint of musical expression often resulted in the emotive high points achieving a more powerful impact. More important, however, the Classic style is intimate, directed more towards the individual than an audience. The music was intended not as spectacle or pageantry, but as an art of personal dimensions. Wit, not eloquence, fine details rather than large, were predominant. The gulf that separated the Baroque style from the Classic was enormous, even though there were continuities in the musical language that reached back for centuries.

GUIDE TO ADDITIONAL LISTENING

Keyboard music

1. Johann Sebastian Bach, *French Suites for Harpsichord.*
2. Domenico Scarlatti, Sonata in G Major (Longo 335); Sonata in G Major (Longo 302).
3. Wolfgang Amadeus Mozart, Sonata for Piano, no. 10 in C Major, K. 330.
4. Ludwig van Beethoven, Sonata for Piano in F Minor, op. 2, no. 1.

Contrast the sound of the harpsichord with the sound of the piano. What are the limitations and potentials of each? Contrast the varieties of structures in Baroque with the lesser number of forms in the Classic period. How is this difference significant? Observe the differences between the suite and the sonata. Observe the musical development from Bach to Scarlatti to Mozart.

Chamber music

1. Johann Sebastian Bach, Suite no. 2 in B Minor for Flute and Strings.
2. François Couperin, *Concerts royaux.*
3. Arcangelo Corelli, *Sonata da Camera for Two Violins and Basso Continuo.*
4. Antonio Vivaldi, Sonata no. 1 in B Flat Major for Bassoon and Continuo.
5. George Frideric Handel, *Trio Sonatas.*
6. Franz Joseph Haydn, Quartet in C Major, op. 76, no. 3; Divertimento in F Major.
7. Wolfgang Amadeus Mozart, Quartet no. 21 in D Major, K. 575; Quintet in A Major for Clarinet and Strings, K. 581.

Observe the changes in style which differentiate Baroque and Classic chamber music.

Concerto

1. Arcangelo Corelli, Concerto Grosso, op. 6, no. 8.
2. Antonio Vivaldi, *Concerto for Flute, Oboe and Bassoon; Concerto for Trumpet and Violin; Concerto for Two Trumpets; Concerto for Two Oboes, Two Clarinets, and Orchestra.*

Vivaldi has written solo concertos for a great number of mediums. The listener can choose from bassoon, cello, flute, guitar, mandolin, oboe, piccolo, recorder, or viola d'amore. Most of these instruments (as well as others) have been used in his concerti grossi in combination with each other and with strings. A few examples are provided above.

3. Johann Sebastian Bach, Brandenburg Concerto no. 3 in G Major; Concerto no. 2 in E Major for Violin and Orchestra.
4. George Frideric Handel, *Concerto for Two Oboes, Two Horns, and Srting Orchestra; Concerti grossi,* op. 3.
5. Franz Joseph Haydn, Concerto in D Major for Cello, op. 101.
6. Wolfgang Amadeus Mozart: Concerto in A Major for Piano and Orchestra, K. 488; Concerto in D Minor for Piano and Orchestra, K. 466.

Compare the concertos in terms of melody, harmony, and texture. Observe the change in overall length. What are the most interesting features of the concerto grosso? Does Bartók's *Concerto for Orchestra* (see pp. 248–51) reflect the concerto grosso? Which instrument do you prefer as a solo instrument?

Symphony

1. Franz Joseph Haydn, Symphony no. 88 in G Major; Symphony no. 94 in G Major (*Surprise*); Symphony no. 100 in G Major (*Military*); Symphony no. 101 in D Major (*Clock*); Symphony no. 103 in E Flat Major (*Drum Roll*).
2. Wolfgang Amadeus Mozart, Symphony no. 35 in D Major, K. 385 (*Haffner*); Symphony no. 38 in D Major, K. 504 (*Prague*); Symphony no. 40 in G Minor, K. 550.

Note that the symphony orchestra and the symphony as a form are the product of the late eighteenth century. Assembled into the Classic symphony are the many diverse styles, mediums, and forms of the Baroque. Observe how the symphonic form penetrates the many different mediums. The solo sonata, the concerto, the string quartet, and the symphony have much in common. The medium of each, however, allows it to create its own unique expressiveness.

FOR DISCUSSION

1. Why is the Classic style considered international?
2. Johann Sebastian Bach has been accepted as the towering figure in Baroque music. Why are his works performed so much more than those of Corelli, Vivaldi, Couperin, Scarlatti, and Telemann?
3. Handel is probably best known for his *Messiah*. Are other works of his of equal stature?
4. The music of the Baroque and Classic periods lives today on record and in the concert hall. What present-day music will be "alive" 200 years from now? What gives music immortality?
5. What similarities do you see between the Romantic and Modern periods and the Baroque and Classic periods?

Medieval and Renaissance Styles

15

The music of the Ancients still echoes in the music of today. Early experiments with melody, with rhythmic flow, with the difficulty of indicating sounds by symbols on paper, and with the subsequent problem of combining several sounds simultaneously form the foundation of the whole approach of sound and notation in later centuries. Medieval music was highly sophisticated, even if it seems limited by contemporary standards. The beauty of the music need not be obscured for present-day listeners by its remoteness in time. The religious chants reach across centuries, resonating in the interiors of modern churches to touch the listener as they did a thousand years ago.

VOCAL MUSIC

Monophony

Early Christian music consisted of psalms, hymns, and spiritual songs. It is supposed that the first ordered collection of Christian music

Donatello: Mary Magdalene *(1454–55). Baptistry, Florence.*

Renaissance art is often dramatic and expressive, and here the religious fervor is overpowering. Mary Magdalene, after her conversion, had become a hermit saint. This wooden sculpture shows her late in life; she had taken off her clothes to pray, and God took pity and clothed her with hair. There is a certain fascination with the aesthetics of the ugly.

was assembled by Pope Gregory the Great (540–604). The "plain-songs" which formed this collection were afterwards called Gregorian chants. In its pure form Gregorian chant is monophonic vocal music, neither harmonized nor accompanied, and sung only by men. The text is the liturgy of the Roman Catholic Church. Chant melody is extremely fluid. The range of the melodies is narrow and the rhythmic flow irregular, devoid of the steady pulsation characteristic of later music.

Three kinds of melodies exist: syllabic, neumatic, and melismatic. Syllabic chants have one note of music for each syllable of text. Neumatic chants have from one to four notes of music per syllable of text. Melismatic chants were sung on highly festive occasions and are florid.

Ex. 15–1

a. Syllabic

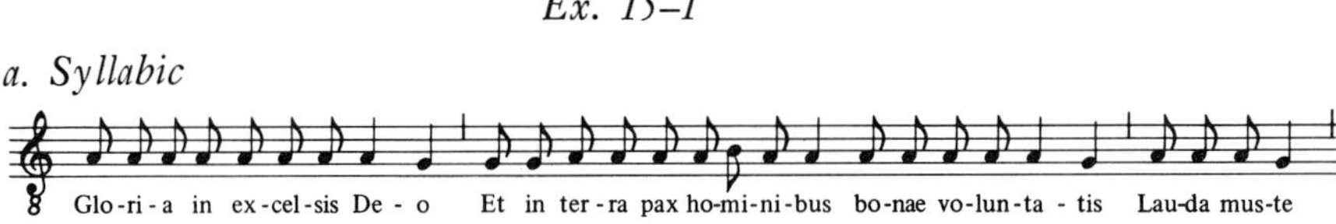

b. Neumatic

c. Melismatic

The chanting priest is answered by the men's chorus, providing alternating tone colors. Hearing a Gregorian chant in a cathedral can be a mystical experience. There are separate chants for each day of the year. A collection, the *Liber Usualis,* approximately 2000 pages in length, contains the entire body of liturgical chant.

Secular music was also written during the middle ages. Over 1000 Latin, French, English, German, and Spanish secular songs from this period exist. These songs are attributed to traveling knights, minstrels, and scholars, who wandered throughout Europe in the eleventh, twelfth, and thirteenth centuries. The texts deal with moral codes, praise of the deeds of noble men, love, and satire. Some are quite serious, others frivolous and light-hearted. Still others are unashamedly sensual.

The melodies are similar to the chant melodies but it is believed that the meter was performed in more pronounced fashion. Text aside, however, the overall sound was different and did not appear liturgical or chant-like. Singers often accompanied themselves with a stringed instrument. Some songs were through-composed; some had repeated musical passages.

The following is a medieval French secular song. Observe the form of the music: A-B-A-A. The first and last lines of the text are the same.

Ex. 15–2. Trouvère Song: 12-13th century. Virelai, "Or la truix."

Polyphony

In addition to monophonic music, the Middle Ages saw the beginning of polyphony—the source of the sophisticated polyphonic writing of the High Renaissance and Baroque eras.

Giotto: Meeting of Joachim and Anna at the Golden Gate (*c. 1305*). *Arena Chapel, Padua, Italy.*

The Middle Ages yielded outstanding mosaics, stained glass, vaultings, book illuminations, and frescos such as those of Giotto di Bondone (1266–1337). This work, one of a series depicting the story of the Virgin, illustrates the moment when the Virgin's parents meet with ecstatic news of the coming birth of Mary. The two figures form the symbolic arch of love, echoed in the sympathetic tenderness of the enraptured bystanders and in the arch above. This arch and the line of the footbridge relate the two groups of figures. The figure in the light-colored robe marks the exact center of the painting, radiating light and controlling the delicate balance of the two groups. The figures are monumental and powerfully expressive. The gestures of the husband and wife greeting each other communicate their personal understanding.

The earliest polyphony was called *organum.* A second voice, called *vox organalis* (the organized voice), was added to an existing chant melody. The two voices sometimes merely proceeded in a parallel motion except for the first and last few notes. (See Example 5–1, p. 67.) In another example the upper voice rather than the lower voice is the "organized" voice. The words "Benedicamus Domino" were originally set to a few notes. In the polyphonic version these notes are held for a longer duration while an elaborate "organized" voice is composed above the modified original voice. (See Ex. 5–3, p. 69.)

Other forms of medieval sacred music, rarely performed today, include the liturgical drama, songs for ceremonial processions, passion plays, and Christmas plays. Several medieval liturgical dramas have been revived in recent years. One of them, *Daniel,* has been performed throughout the United States.

Léonin (late twelfth century) and Pérotin (thirteenth century) became the first identifiable composers in Western civilization. The idea of fixed meter became established. Most accepted measured rhythms were based on a meter of three. In the early fourteenth century a theorist, Philippe de Vitry (c. 1291–1361), wrote a treatise called *Ars Nova.* Although Vitry did not "invent" duple meter, his treatise was a first step in its sanction. In the *Ars Nova,* Lang explains, ". . . he [Vitry] meant the logical and consequential application of a reformed system of music and of musical notation. Besides triple time, the *Ars Nova* recognized duple or binary divisions, heretofore prohibited in the realm of official art music." The fourteenth century is now referred to as the *Ars Nova* and the thirteenth century the *Ars Antiqua.*

In small steps, music progressed toward the High Renaissance. However, this intervening period is more important historically than musically.

The Mass

All of the Gregorian chants in the *Liber Usualis* are monophonic. All the music is liturgical and designed for the Roman Catholic service. The text of the "Ordinary" of the Mass, with the exception of the Mass for the dead, remains the same for all occasions. Other portions, called the "Proper," change from day to day. The "Ordinary" consists of the following sections: "Kyrie," "Gloria," "Credo," "Sanctus," "Agnus Dei," and "Ite missa est" (not always included).

Guillaume de Machaut (c. 1300–1377) was the first to compose (c. 1337) a complete polyphonic setting of the "Ordinary" of the Mass: *La Messe de Notre Dame*. From this time the Mass has remained a principal musical form.

Machaut's most common techniques are his use of a *cantus firmus* (fixed song) and a device called isorhythm (fixed rhythm). The cantus firmus is usually a melody from a monophonic chant which is combined with the isorhythmic principle and a text and sung by the tenor voice.

Ex. 15–3. Machaut: Messe de Notre Dame, *Kyrie I*

The contratenor (baritone voice), motetus (alto), and triplum (soprano) are written as contrapuntal parts to the cantus firmus. The isorhythmic technique may or may not be applied to all voices. Since the contratenor has no text, it is generally assumed that this part was intended to be instrumental.

Present-day listeners may find Machaut's *Mass* rather dull aurally. The expression is limited, the range of the voices is narrow, dynamic contrasts are nil, rhythmic movement is monotonous, the harmonies are not dramatic, and there is little contrast in tone-color. This *Mass*, however, is a masterpiece when viewed in historical perspective. The craftsmanship of Machaut's composition is unexcelled in its time. Unfortunately, however, it is dwarfed by the musical monuments of later centuries. The *Mass* has, nonetheless, a relationship to some contemporary sounds. The use of modes rather than major and minor scales, the stark intellectualism, and the openness and clarity of parts—all are reminiscent of twentieth-century music. A comparison of Machaut's *Mass* with the *Mass* of Stravinsky is interesting.

Eighteenth- and nineteenth-century composers wrote principally symphonies, sonatas, and operas; fifteenth- and sixteenth-century composers wrote Masses, motets, chansons, and madrigals. Renaissance settings of the Mass range from works for one choir (soprano, alto, tenor, and bass) to works for several multivoiced choirs. They are usually sung *a cappella* (without accompaniment) although instruments may have been used on some parts, especially in the early Renaissance. The Renaissance Mass makes use of the device of imitation. The parts are extensively interwoven both melodically and rhythmically. Careful listening will enable the listener to hear the simultaneous singing of several melodically related lines, interwoven in a continuous smooth-flowing pattern. Each melody is basically chant-like. The separate voices rarely begin or end simultaneously except at the end of a section of the Mass. Harmony results from the vertical convergence of melodic lines and does not project as a prominent event. The rhythm is measured, flowing, and decisive, and is sometimes a prominent device. Dynamic contrasts are slight. The little variation there is results from the natural flow of individual melodic lines. In the fifteenth and sixteenth centuries, polyphonic settings of the Mass became one of the highest forms of musical art.

In contrast to our knowledge of the early Middle Ages when Léonin and Pérotin were the only two known composers, composers in the Renaissance flourished in the courts of Europe. The origins of the cantus firmus were expanded to include popular secular and freely composed tunes. Eventually both the cantus firmus and the isorhythmic technique were discontinued. Music began to be more freely composed and all musical events became the original ideas of the composer. The vocal range was widened with the addition of a bass voice. Occasionally, harmonies became homophonically meaningful rather than being simply the result of counterpoint. Intricate canonic techniques were explored. Composers achieved a perfection in lyrical counterpoint that resulted in the sixteenth century being called the Golden Age of Choral Polyphony.

The popular tune, absorbed into the cantus firmus, lost its identity within the polyphonic texture of the Mass. The Mass, nonetheless, was named after the original song, and many composers used the same tune. One of the popular tunes of the period was "L'Homme armé" ("The Armed Man"). Numerous masses are entitled *Missa L'Homme armé*. The *Missa L'Homme armé* by Guillaume Dufay (c.1400–1474) is an example.

In his *Missa Pange lingua* Josquin Des Prés continues the practice of borrowing from the chant. To lend continuity to his work Des Prés uses

Ex. 15–4

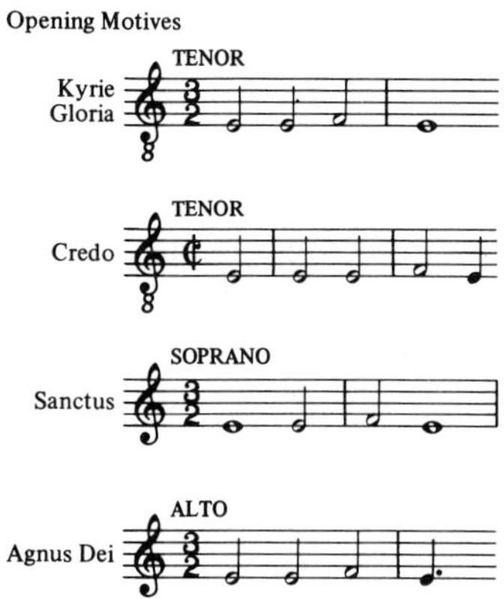

the theme of the borrowed cantus firmus to open each section of the Mass—in principle the same cyclic technique employed by some nineteenth-century symphonic composers. The example above shows the opening motives of each section. Thematic ideas are initially recognizable but get lost as they continue into the texture of interwoven melodies. The listener may be more intrigued by the interweaving of voices than by the statements of a subject and its answers. The Renaissance composer does not complete his subject as Bach does.

The music of Giovanni da Palestrina, while conservative and not totally representative of sixteenth-century polyphony, has been recognized by some as the purest Renaissance sacred vocal polyphony.

His *Missa Papae Marcelli*, which some consider less interesting musically than works of Des Prés and others, is reflective of his style. The greater portion of the Mass is scored for six voices: soprano, alto, two tenors, and two basses. Palestrina includes two "Agnus Dei" sections. The second one is scored for eight parts, adding an additional soprano and a second tenor.

The "Kyrie" begins with stretto-like imitation, each voice sounding, but at varying pitch levels. These entries, which are not bold, blend immediately into the texture. They do not speak with the authority of Bach's fugue subjects. Other motivic ideas are also imitated, however, always within the perspective of the fluent and serene interwoven melodies. (See Ex. 15–5.)

Ex. 15–5

Kyrie
S.
Ky - rie e - lei - - - son, Ky - rie e - -
A.
Ky - rie e - lei - son, Ky - rie e - lei -
T.
Ky - rie e - lei - - - - son, Ky - rie e - lei - - - - -
Ky - rie e - lei - - -
B.
Ky - rie e - lei - - - - son,
Ky - rie e - lei - -

Ex. 15–6

Gloria
S.
Et in ter - ra pax ho - mi - ni
A.
Et in ter - ra pax ho - mi - ni-
T.
Et in ter - ra pax ho - mi - ni-
B.
Et in ter - ra pax ho - mi - ni-
Credo
S.
Pa - trem o - mni - po-
A.
Pa - trem o - mni - po-
T.
Pa - trem o - mni - po-
B.
Pa - trem o - mni - po-

The "Gloria" and "Credo" have more passages of a homophonic texture necessitated, no doubt, by the longer texts of these movements. Set in contrapuntal style, these sections could run on at a length impractical for the church service. While the "Gloria" begins homophonically, contrapuntal texture appears in the third measure. (See Ex. 15–6.) The text, "Qui tollis," begins homophonically, and again the counterpoint enters in the third measure. The texture fluctuates but counterpoint predominates.

Ex. 15–7

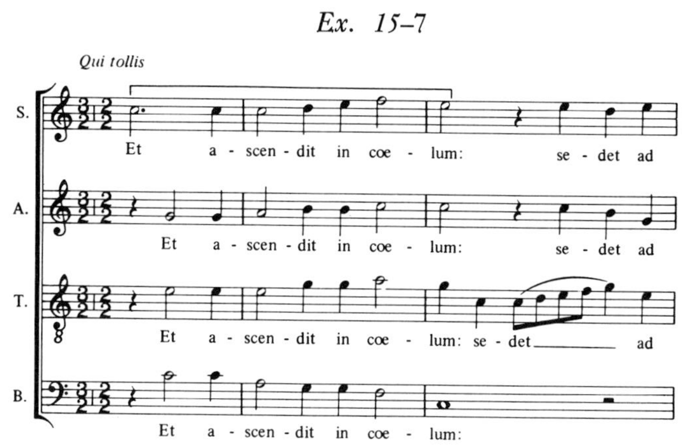

The "Sanctus" is a treasure of motivic ideas, all of which are spun into the contrapuntal fabric. Five motives from the opening section are shown in Ex. 15–8. The first statement of the "Hosanna" is set harmonically, the same as "Et in terra" at the beginning of the "Gloria."

The first part of the "Agnus Dei" begins with the same opening motive as the "Kyrie." It continues differently but with the same contrapuntal principles. In the second part of the "Agnus Dei" the first basses and the second altos sing a canon. This canon also begins with the opening motive of the "Kyrie." (See Ex. 15–9.)

Whether or not it commands modern attention, the *Missa Papae Marcelli* exhibits a craftsmanship not likely to be surpassed. The numerous melodies are fluent in their movement. No single melody reaches fulfillment. Each is always related to other equally important melodies.

Ex. 15–8

S.
San - - - - ctus, San - - - - - -
A.
San - - - ctus, San - - - - - ctus, San-
T.
San - - - - - ctus, San - - -
San - - - ctus, San - ctus,
B.
San - - - - - ctus, San - - -
San - - - ctus, San - - - - - - - - - - -
S.
ctus, San - - - - - - - - - - ctus,
A.
- - - ctus, San - - - - - - - - -
T.
ctus, San - - - - - - - - - ctus, San - - -
San - - - - ctus, San - - - - ctus, San - ctus,
B.
- - - ctus, San - - -
ctus, San - - - - ctus, San - ctus,

Ex. 15–9

Harmonies, for the most part, are sixteenth-century contrapuntal "happenings," resulting from the interplay of melodies and only occasionally prominent. The rhythm also serves the melody. It does not become independently prominent. Likewise the dynamics. The tone color is a function of the voices used. Blending is very important, and contrasting vocal color is minimized.

In total expression, the *Missa Papae Marcelli* does not compare to the outpouring of sound and emotion of later Masses. It is highly disciplined, creating more awe than excitement, more calm than turmoil, and more reverence than joy. To some it may be dull and boring; to others, spiritual and inspiring.

The motet

Medieval motets (derived from the French *mot,* meaning word) emerged when additional words were added to the upper voice of the organum. Occasionally, in three-part writing one voice would sing a French text, sometimes profane, and another would sing a sacred Latin text. The musical styles are based on the isorhythmic principle. Machaut followed Pérotin as the leading motet composer. Their works are rarely performed.

The motets of present-day repertory stem primarily from the Renaissance. They are one-movement choral works based on sacred nonliturgical Latin texts. It is difficult to distinguish a motet from a movement of a Mass by the musical style. The difference is the text. Composers recognized for their Masses were also the principal writers of motets. In general, their styles remain the same.

Dufay set the "Ave Regina coelorum" to music twice: once about 1420 and once about 1465—forty-five years later. The first is scored for three parts: alto, and two tenors. Its texture is light, primarily homophonic and typical of motets written without the complete range of voice parts. The second setting for soprano, alto, tenor, and bass moves toward the more mature Renaissance style.

Des Prés' *Ave Christe, immolate,* a four-voice motet, is in the style of his *Missa Pange lingua.* Another motet, *Salve Regina,* translates its text into beautiful musical terms and is an excellent example of Renaissance musical style employing a cantus firmus. The word *salve* is set to four notes as the soprano, tenor, and then the alto enter.

Ex. 15–10

Cantus Firmus

S. Sal - - - - - ve

A. Sal - - - - ve

T. Sal - - - - - ve

Set against these are melodies from the second alto and bass.

Ex. 15–11

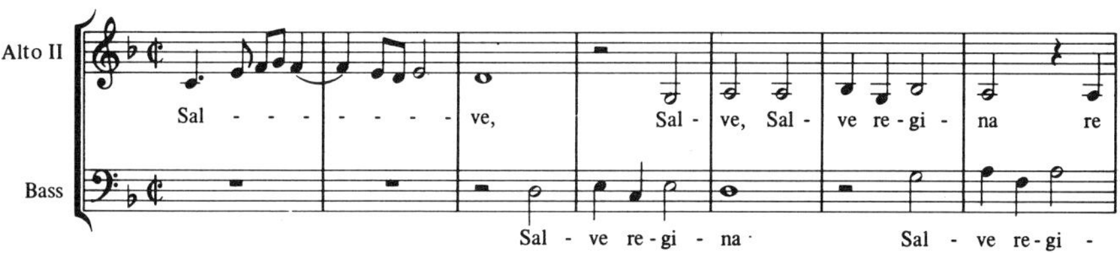

The "salve" theme continues in the alto voice, reentering at regular intervals in ostinato fashion. Just before the end, the tenor restates the theme also. Other parts are woven into the usual contrapuntal melodic texture. The effect is exciting, and the motet becomes a counterpoint of text as well as of music.

A four-part setting of *Salve Regina* by Orlandus Lassus (1532–1594) is in High Renaissance style. It has no cantus firmus. All of the voice parts were the original work of Lassus.

Raphael: Marriage of the Virgin *(1504). Pinacoteca di Brera, Milan.*

The Renaissance painter was concerned with how to represent three-dimensional reality on a two-dimensional surface. Perspective, form, light, shade, color, and line were studied for the visual truth they could convey. Many technical problems were conquered in the early Renaissance, and the solutions were passed on to such geniuses of the later Renaissance as Raphael. Here the monumental simplicity of the building in the background creates an atmosphere of great dignity for the foreground group. The work is generally symmetrical—the wedding ring is the central focus of the whole work. There is a Classic feeling in the entire approach—balance, restraint, dignity, and precision of detail. The rejected suitor symbolically breaks the staff at lower right.

Burgundian chanson

In the late fifteenth century the Burgundian chanson replaced the French monophonic secular song of the Middle Ages. The chanson was polyphonic, but not as complex as the sacred music. Homophonic texture was occasionally prominent. Most chansons are composed for three parts: a solo voice and two accompanying parts. The accompaniments are thought to be instrumental because they had no text, and were often of a sustaining nature. Textless interludes in the upper voice may also have been instrumental. These instrumental interludes were decorative and were probably improvised.

The chansons are not melodically complicated. Harmonically they are light. The rhythms are somewhat complicated, and cross-rhythm patterns give the pieces the effect of mixed meter. The dynamic range is narrow. Chansons were often plaintive in nature and the musical phrases corresponded to the poetic patterns. The mixture of voice and instruments accounted for tonal variety and contrast.

The leading composers were Dufay, Gilles Binchois (c. 1400–1460), Antoine Busnois (d. 1492), and John Dunstable (c. 1370–1453) from England. The forms follow the text and the music often reflects the mood of the text. The chansons are charming pieces and can be a delightful listening experience.

"Adieu m'amour" ("Goodbye, my love") by Dufay is a rondeau written for three parts, two of which have text. It has a light contrapuntal texture and some imitation.

A chanson by Binchois with the same title, but not the same poem, is also a rondeau. It is scored for solo voice and two accompanying parts but is without imitation. The melody is straightforward and includes instrumental interludes. Binchois' work is less complex than the "Adieu m' amour" of Dufay.

"Filles à marier" ("Marriageable Daughters"), a short (less than a minute) chanson by Binchois, is a bright, gay musical commentary warning girls of the problems of marriage. It is written for two voices and two instruments.

'Bel Acueil," a rondeau by Busnois, is written for solo voice and two instruments. It displays an interesting contrapuntal texture. These chansons are a refreshing contrast to the large body of monumental and serious music of the past.

The sixteenth-century polyphonic chanson

In the sixteenth century the chanson became more sophisticated. It was scored for various numbers of parts, and the counterpoint became more complex than that of the Burgundian chanson. The rhythm was usually in duple meter. Melodies and rhythms reflected the spirit of the texts, which dealt with the delights and sorrows of love and were often frivolous and risqué. Although these chansons are performed a cappella today, they may have been accompanied by instruments doubling the voice parts.

Three prominent composers of the polyphonic chanson were Josquin Des Prés, Clément Jannequin, and Orlandus Lassus.

Two chansons of Des Prés display unusual texts and unusual musical approaches to the popular song. In "Bergerette savoyene" ("Little Shepherdess"), the singer begs for the love of a little shepherdess:

Watching sheep in the fields,
Tell me if you will be mine,
I will give you shoes
I will give you shoes
And a little cape
Tell me, will you love me
When you rest to eat your meal?

Each line of text is begun with a new pattern of melodic imitation. Voices sometimes enter in pairs, sometimes individually. The rhythm of any one part is not complex, but the imitation and counterpoint create an interesting rhythmic interplay.

"Parfons regretz" ("Deep regrets") expresses a more serious mood.

Deep regrets and mournful joy,
Come to me wherever I may be.
Make haste, with no dissembling
And with dispatch lay low my heart,
That it may drown in mourning and tears.

The counterpoint is similar to that found in a motet. The rhythm is less spirited. The music reflects the attitude of the text.

The sixteenth-century polyphonic chanson reflects the secularization of Renaissance man. It is in strong contrast to the spiritual Mass and motet. The leading composers wrote in both styles.

The Italian madrigal

The Italian madrigal is the Italian counterpart to the French chanson. The musical style was similar to that of the motet except that the music often reflected the mood of the text. The texture was primarily contrapuntal. However, composers occasionally included homophonic sections. Solo madrigals, which led to opera, appeared in the late sixteenth century.

Three madrigals are illustrative of the Italian madrigal although all reflect a somber mood. "Voi ve n'andat' al cielo" ("Ye go heavenward") by Jacob Arcadelt (c. 1514–c.1567) is about a loved one lost in death. The music has alternating contrapuntal and homophonic sections. The composer uses a technique called word-painting. The style of music changes to suit the thought conveyed by each line of text.

"S'io parto, i' moro" ("This Parting Now Kills Me") by Luca Marenzio (1553–1599), although displaying some counterpoint, is quite homophonic in style. The text, again concerned with parting lovers, is reflected in the mood of the music. The madrigal employs some word-painting, but it is more subtle than that of Arcadelt.

"Io pur respiro ("In Anguish I Breathe") by Carlo Gesualdo (1560–1613) is contrapuntal and imitative. The imitation occurs in rapid succession, similar to the Britten example from the *Ceremony of Carols*. (See pp. 161–2.) For his time, Gesualdo was individualistic and daring. His use of dissonance is a "modern" touch that makes his madrigals sound less like sixteenth-century music than those of his contemporaries.

The English madrigal

During the last decades of the sixteenth century, English composers were fascinated by the Italian madrigal. In 1588, Nicholas Yonge (d. 1619) edited and published *Musica Transalpina*, a collection of Italian madrigals with English words. Subsequently, the English composed their own madrigals, and the form became exceedingly popular in England. The popularity of madrigals persists in present-day choral repertory.

Most English madrigals are fairly short, unified compositions, almost folk-like in nature, scored for three to six voices. Textures include alternating contrapuntal and chordal passages. Rhythms tend to be lively, and the music has a sprightly quality.

Prominent composers of the English madrigal were Thomas Morley, Orlando Gibbons (1583–1625), and Thomas Tomkins (1572–1656).

INSTRUMENTAL MUSIC

Medieval instrumental music is of little consequence to the present-day listener. It was restricted to accompaniments, processionals, and dance melodies. There were no specific instrumental composers and few of the musical forms were indigenous to instruments alone. Most forms were derived from vocal forms.

Renaissance instrumental forms grew out of the vocal forms. The idea of instrumentation slowly materialized, and instrumental ensembles began to develop. When King Henry VIII of England died in 1547, he left behind him a collection of three hundred and eighty-one instruments: 78 cross flutes, 77 recorders, 30 shawms, 28 organs, 25 cromornes, 21 horns, 5 cornets, 5 bagpipes, 32 virginals, 26 lutes, 25 violas, 21 guitars, 2 clavichords, and 3 combinations of organ and virginal. Of these the recorder, organ, virginal (a form of harpsichord), lute, and viola are the most representative Renaissance instruments. Recorders (the flutes of the period) came in various sizes: soprano, alto, tenor, and bass. They are played in a vertical position rather than transversely as the present-day flutes are played. They produce a woody, mellow sound. Renaissance organs were in principle the same as present-day pipe organs, although the mechanisms and the sound possibilities were different. Lutes are guitar-like instruments played by plucking. The most frequent number of strings is six or seven. Strings, however, were sometimes doubled, vibrating sympathetically under the basic strings.

The instrumental music of the Renaissance consisted of accompaniments for solo songs and vocal ensembles, dance music, music derived from vocal forms, and some music written especially and solely for instruments. The latter was an important development for it was the first acknowledgement of the concerted power of instruments as a separate and distinct vehicle for musical expression.

Early in the sixteenth century, instrumentalists who had often doubled the parts of vocal compositions began to play these same pieces without singers. The players modified the lines, as necessary, in order to adapt them to the limitations of their instruments. This was the beginning of chamber music and of pieces composed especially for instruments. Forms such as the fantasia, canzona, ricercare, and sonata came into being and provided the background for the trios, quartets, and sonatas that were to flourish in the Baroque and after.

Canzona

At first, when instruments accompanied several voice parts they did not play independent parts; instead, they doubled the vocal lines. Gradually these pieces came to be played without the singer. A vocal piece, for example, might be played by a soprano recorder, a cromorne (a reed wind instrument), a bassoon of the period, and a trombone of the period. This practice ultimately lead to "instrumental pieces" called canzonas.

Giovanni Gabrieli composed brilliant canzonas for brass choirs and double brass choirs. These made extensive use of counterpoint. Gabrieli modeled his instrumental works after his vocal works. An opening motive is stated, imitated, and dissolved into the contrapuntal melodic texture. Another motive appears and the process is repeated. These motives give the canzona a sectional form, each new idea representing the beginning of another section. His Canzona per sonare no. 2 is an excellent example. It opens with a rhythmic motive:

Ex. 15–12

The imitation follows:

Ex. 15–13

The style continues using several different subjects. Gabrieli uses the same style in his Canzona septimi toni no. 1 but includes more lyricism. This work is to be performed by two choirs. The interaction of the two creates dynamic and tone color contrasts. The canzona for brass is a brilliant show piece and remains such in today's repertory.

Fantasia

Renaissance lutanists and keyboard performers sometimes played modified versions of chansons, Masses, and motets. The modified forms were usually embellished versions of the vocal works set to music. The principle is no different than that of a present-day performer improvising on a popular tune. Such improvisation and embellishment led to the fantasia, a freer form often spontaneously improvised. Many music anthologies contain fantasias by numerous composers. It is uncertain, however, whether they were performed first and then written down, or the reverse. Thomas Morley in an early lute instruction book states:

> In this way more art be showne then in any other musicke, because the composer is tide to nothing but that he may adde, deminish, and alter at his pleasure.

The following example illustrates the embellishments applied to a chanson by a lutanist.

Ex. 15–14. "Quando penso il martire"

Later the composed fantasia became the free-styled section that customarily precedes the fugue.

Ricercare

Instrumentalists developed an indigenous contrapuntal form called a *ricercare.* The ricercare was a composition played by lutanists, organists, keyboard players or instrumental ensembles. It was usually constructed in sections, and similar to the instrumental canzona in sound and style.

Sonata

Renaissance instrumental pieces called sonatas were not sonatas as currently defined. They were instrumental pieces, to be sounded (sonare), rather than sung (cantare). One famous Renaissance sonata is the "Sonata pian'e forte" by Giovanni Gabrieli. (See Chapter 14, p. 332.)

During the Renaissance man invented musical instruments, striving to extend the range of his expressive capacities. He created new musical forms to encompass a broader range of instrumental communication. Musical developments are the counterpart of the scientific advances of the age.

Comparative Styles: Medieval and Renaissance

	Medieval	*Renaissance*
Expression	*Ranges from the spiritual mysticism of the chant to earthy secular song.*	*Gradual glorification of spiritual mysticism. The change in philosophy from concern with the hereafter to concern with the present is felt in the music.*
Melody	*Monophonic. Melodic styles vary from plainsong style to popular style. Modal. Fluid.*	*Lyrical. Melodies interwoven in counterpoint often are treated imitatively. Motivic ideas anticipate fugue and symphony.*
Rhythm	*Varies from free textural rhythm to measured meter, usually in three.*	*Regular. Not dominant in sacred works. More metrical in secular works. Sometimes quite complex. More use of duple meter.*

	Medieval	*Renaissance*
Tone Color	*Monophonic men's voices for sacred music. Limited range. Variety of instrumental sounds. Weak winds and strings. Use of plucked and fretted stringed instruments. Not reflective of present-day homogenized sound.*	*Voice ranges are defined and part writing ranges from bass to soprano. "Consorts" of instruments are developed that span the same range as voice. Instruments used for tonal contrast as well as blend.*
Harmony	*Contrapuntal. Composers think horizontally rather than vertically.*	*Contrapuntal. Evolving. Some harmonically oriented passages.*
Dynamics	*Little contrast. Instruments did not produce a "big" sound.*	*Terraced dynamics. More contrasts but not a major event until late Renaissance.*
Structure	*Sacred vocal music followed liturgical text. Secular music organized around poetry. Few instrumental forms.*	*Evolving. Vocal work textually oriented. Music adopted the poetic structure. Canzona, fantasia, ricercare, and sonata develop.*
Medium and Texture	*Voice, monophonic, and polyphonic. Instrumentalists not formed into organized ensembles.*	*Chorus reaches its first "Golden Age." Polyphonic sounds move toward organized harmony.* *Instrumental ensembles formed. Lute, virginal, and forerunners of present-day wind instruments develop. Bowed stringed instruments still nonresonant.* *Great developments in brass polyphony.*

A SUMMARY OF STYLES: MEDIEVAL AND RENAISSANCE

From the sixth century to the end of the sixteenth century musical expression moves from the simple, monophonic melody serving a function (whether sacred or secular) to a complex music of many parts and tone colors designed to enlarge the palette of human expression. Within this framework music moves from serving God and glorifying man's life after death to both serving God and enriching man's earthly life.

In the late Renaissance early sacred monophony culminates with a sophisticated understanding of the expressive possibilities of various combinations of voices and instruments. Early medieval secular monophonic songs were limited in range and expression. In text and musical style the Renaissance saw the development of a secular style that expressed the human essence of man: his sufferings, his joys, his hopes. During this period the gamut of musical expression expands—it ranges from plainsong to a glorious Mass, a simple hymn to a complex motet, from a shepherd's plaintive song to exquisitely composed chansons and madrigals.

GUIDE TO ADDITIONAL LISTING

Most compositions of the Middle Ages and Renaissance are short. They usually are recorded in collections and historical editions. The following are some of these.

1. Archive Production (History of Music Division of the *Deutsche Grammophon Gesellschaft*):

   I Research Period: Gregorian Chant;
   II Research Period: The Central Middle Ages (1100–1350);
   III Research Period: The Early Renaissance (1350–1500);
   IV Research Period: The High Renaissance (sixteenth century).

2. *The History of Music in Sound* (RCA Victor):

   Volume II, Early Medieval Music up to 1300;
   Volume III, Ars Nova and the Renaissance (c. 1300–1540);
   Volume IV, The Age of Humanism (1540–1630).

3. *Masterpieces of Music Before 1750* (The Haydn Society, Inc. in conjunction with W. W. Norton and Co.). An anthology of music examples from Gregorian chant to J. S. Bach.

4. *Voices of the Middle Ages* (Nonesuch).
5. *Music of the Court of Burgundy* (Nonesuch).
6. *Renaissance Vocal Music* (Nonesuch).
7. *Isaac, Des Prés, DiLasso* (Nonesuch).
8. *Renaissance Music for Brass* (Nonesuch).
9. *Court and Ceremonial Music of the Sixteenth Century* (Nonesuch).
10. *English Madrigals* (Westminster).
11. *Madrigals and Instrumental Music* (Everest).
12. *The Golden Age of Brass* (Unicorn).

FOR DISCUSSION

1. In the Renaissance the composers of Masses, the highest form of musical art at that time, also composed popular music. Compare this with practices in the twentieth century.
2. Does the Renaissance Mass appeal to you? Is it somewhat academic and uninteresting? In either case, why?
3. Compare an unadorned chanson with a version embellished by a lutanist. Comment in terms of present-day improvisation.
4. How do the texts of Renaissance popular music compare with texts of contemporary popular music? With those of the 1930s?
5. What effect might the concert setting have on the enjoyment of Medieval and Renaissance music?
6. The exact performance traditions of Medieval and Renaissance music are a matter of some conjecture. Why? How are performance traditions preserved in later music: Bach's, Wagner's, the Beatles'?

Additional Stylistic Dimensions

16

Although the historical contrasts between styles are fundamental to musical understanding, they are by no means the only stylistic considerations that are useful to the listener. Up to this point, the reader has been invited to compare Romantic and Modern style, Baroque and Classic, and Medieval and Renaissance. However, more

Jacques Louis David: The Oath of the Horatii *(1784). Clichés Musées Nationaux, Paris.*

Themes from antiquity were frequent inspirations for art works during the Classic period. This painting by David (1748–1825) was inspired by a play of Corneille's presenting the tragic theme of lovers whose families were bitter enemies. But form is the essential consideration: the triple arch in the background is repeated by the group of three sons on the left; the father, the center of importance, subtle stylistic differences can also be studied with profit—differences that are not based on historical change. These extrahistorical contrasts include comparisons between the styles of composers within the same historical period, between one composer's early, middle, and late styles, between the styles of two or more settings of the same idea or text, between national and international styles, between the styles of different performances, and between the styles of different mediums. Such comparisons often reveal the special flavor of a style, the distinctive perceptions and insights of a composer, and the incisive meaning of a musical composition.

CONTRASTS WITHIN A PERIOD

Perhaps at no other time in the history of music was there a greater homogenization of style than in the Classic period, particularly in the time of Mozart (1756–1791) and Haydn (1732–1809). Yet perceptive listeners can distinguish the differences between these composers' styles.

One might expect differences. Mozart was born twenty-four years after Haydn and lived only thirty-six years. Mozart was a child prodigy and developed rapidly. Haydn matured slowly. In his first thirty-six years he composed few important works. Although these two men became steadfast friends and learned from each other, the difference in age probably benefited Mozart. He always had models to follow.

Mozart's phrases are regular in length, produced within the limits of standard formulas, and his work employs the sonata-allegro form in a conventional way. Haydn, on the other hand, digresses into remote keys. He fills his work with unexpected rhythms, and the phrases are irregular in length. Haydn's work appears to violate all the rules. Mozart's sym-

---

forms a rectangle with the group of his sons. All the arms, legs, and swords form harsh angles. The weeping women at the right form another rectangle of similar proportions but smaller; here inner lines are graceful, in keeping with the feminine subject matter. Masculine courage is contrasted with feminine foreboding. Such dependence on form is more similar to Haydn than Mozart, while the emotional content anticipates the Romantic era and such expressive works as Beethoven's Eroica *Symphony.*

phony demonstrates his great ease in handling counterpoint. The effect is brilliant. Haydn's melodies tend to sound more spontaneous and folk-like than Mozart's. The effect of Haydn's melodies is immediate and clear. Mozart's melodies convey moods that seem more varied, more complicated, subtle, and psychologically profound. Haydn clearly marks the ends of phrases and sections. Mozart often interjects contrapuntal connecting material that ties the parts together. However, these stylistic differences are only incidental details. They do not account for the true difference between the two composers.

The fundamental stylistic difference between the genius of both Haydn and Mozart lies in the focus of their innovation. Haydn invented the sonata-allegro form. His originality of melody, his freedom in development, and his variety of ideas were largely determined by his concentrated rounding-out of the overall form. Mozart, and for that matter, Beethoven, borrowed and adopted the sonata form. They never used it like the originator. Instead of balancing odd length phrases and carefully molding the various sections to create a subtle perfection of form, they concentrated on content. Mozart generally wrote in eight-measure phrases and conformed to the general outline of the sonata form. He expanded the form and experimented with it only when the content seemed to dictate the need for a different formal approach. Although Mozart was more rigid than Haydn in his use of the sonata form, he "says" more to us than Haydn. The "language" may be the same and the formal outline similar, but the content is not. Mozart expresses his own individual world of feeling and attitude. He does so with such aplomb and polish that his expression, however subtle, is always lucid. In Mozart's music, the drama is deeper, and the listener who is familiar with it can usually identify it without difficulty.

Styles of composers from other periods who lived at the same time can sometimes be distinguished more easily than Mozart from Haydn. J. S. Bach (1685–1750) and George Frideric Handel (1685–1759) contrast much more sharply; so do Richard Wagner (1813–1883) and Johannes Brahms (1833–1897); Claude Debussy (1862–1918) and Maurice Ravel (1875–1937); Gustav Mahler (1860–1911) and Richard Strauss (1864–1949); and Samuel Barber (1910–) and Elliott Carter (1908–). Such contrasts can bring clear understanding of a composer's style and his position within the general style of a historical period.

For further study

Choose two composers from the same period and characterize the differences and the similarities in their style after listening to several of their works. Attempt to establish characteristics that enable a listener to identify positively each composer upon hearing a piece of his music.

CONTRASTS WITHIN A COMPOSER'S STYLE

The whole body of a composer's work is a continuum of stylistic development: from youth, to maturity, to old age. If Verdi's later operas, for instance, *Otello* (1887) and *Falstaff* (1893), are compared with his earlier works, like *Il Trovatore* (1853), the listener immediately becomes aware of Verdi's maturing sense of drama. The composer has developed a continuity of action and a perfection of expression that far surpasses his earlier style. His melodies in later works are long-spun, infinitely varied, and sensitive. They are supported by an orchestra that is used to fullest advantage.

Arnold Schoenberg composed his string sextet, *Verklärte Nacht* (*Transfigured Night*), op. 4, in 1899. Like his symphonic poem *Pelléas und Mélisande*, op. 5 (1902) and his gigantic cantata, *Gurrelieder* (*Songs of Gurre*) (1900–11), which employs the mammoth orchestra of the Strauss-Mahler period, these works are clearly in the Wagnerian-Romantic spirit. However, Schoenberg's somewhat later works, for instance his *Three Piano Pieces*, op. 11 (1909), *Erwartung* (*Expectancy*) (1909), and *Pierrot Lunaire*, op. 21 (1912), demonstrate his development toward a more classic orientation. These works tend to replace harmony with counterpoint, melodic outpourings with thematic logic, full-blown utterance with economy, large forms with small forms, tonality with atonality, and Wagnerian vocal writing with extremely complex, instrumental-style vocal writing.

From these works the evolvement of Schoenberg's style into twelve-tone technique was natural. The *Five Piano Pieces* of op. 23 (1923), which ushered in the twelve-tone method, sounds little different from the earlier atonal compositions. The new technique enabled Schoenberg to organize longer works than in his atonal phase. His *Quintet for Flute, Oboe, Clarinet, Bassoon, and Horn*, op. 26 (1924), his String Quartet no. 3, op. 30 (1926), and his *Variations for Orchestra*, op. 31 (1927–

28) are other examples of this new style. Compare the latter with *Verklärte Nacht.*

Schoenberg's final period (during which he lived in the United States) brought refinement to his twelve-tone technique. In some of his works, he employed the system in a freer, more expressive manner, not letting it control his composing. His *Piano Concerto* (1942) mixes tonal elements with twelve-tone style. Other works, for instance his *String Trio*, op. 45 (1946), still used the system strictly, but with profound effect.

In summary, Schoenberg went through three periods: the first in which he imitated and assimilated, the second in which he was innovative, and the third marked by refinement and maturity.

Many other composers went through three similar periods. For example, Beethoven's piano sonatas, string quartets, and symphonies, which he continued to write all of his life, are excellent indicators of his changing style. His first works were composed in the Classic tradition established by Mozart and Haydn. His piano sonatas of op. 2, nos. 1–3, op. 7, and op. 10, his string quartets of op. 18, nos. 1–6, and his first and second symphonies are excellent examples.

His second period is characterized by freer use of forms, expansion of development sections, more successful use of counterpoint, use of unifying rhythmic and tonal motives, and exploration of the tonal resources of instruments and voices. His piano sonatas, op. 27, no. 2 (*Moonlight* Sonata), op. 53 (*Waldstein*), op. 57 (the *Appassionata*), the *Razumovsky Quartets*, and symphonies three through eight are illustrative.

Beethoven reaches his greatest height in his last period. Compare the piano sonatas, op. 101, 102, nos. 1 and 2, and op. 106, 109, 110, and 111 with the earlier sonatas, and the string quartets op. 127, 130, 131, 132, 133, and 135 with his first quartets. The Ninth Symphony, op. 125 and the *Missa Solemnis*, op. 123 are monuments equivalent to the Egyptian pyramids, so great is the grandeur, eloquence, power, and clarity of their design and emotional statement.

For further study

1. Compare early, middle, and late works of Stravinsky.
2. Compare an early and a late work of one form by a composer.

Consider treatment of melody, rhythm, use of instruments and voices, harmony, counterpoint, emotional impact, and economy of expression.

SETTING VERSUS SETTING

Stylistic individuality can also be revealed by comparing different musical settings of a particular text. Even if composers work under the most similar circumstances, their works are bound to be different. Holding the setting a constant, then, is another technique of differentiating characteristics of composers' styles, particularly where stylistic differences might be difficult to hear, for instance, when both composers wrote during the same period.

Prokofiev was forty-five years old when he completed his rather lengthy score to *Romeo and Juliet*, op. 64, in 1936. The work moves away from the cool Classicism of the early twentieth century and absorbs some elements of Romantic expression. Because the work is scored for ballet, it encompasses a strong, athletic, rhythmic drive. In this work Prokofiev employs his characteristic lyric elements: simplicity, the standard diatonic scale, and boldness.

Considering the Romantic subject matter, the work may appear somewhat cold and cheerless. Prokofiev's music suggests the tragedy; still it is emotionally restrained. The work might serve other subject matter equally well. Prokofiev expresses feeling without histrionics.

David Diamond's setting of *Romeo and Juliet* (1947) is not a ballet but a concert suite for chamber orchestra. The Romantic element here is far more clearly in evidence. Yet the work also displays the tight, economical forms associated with the Classic.

Diamond's work is not brashly modern; in fact, the dissonance is rather gentle. Written when Diamond was young (thirty-two) it is somewhat academic and certainly not as compelling as his later works or the work of Prokofiev.

Two earlier works have also been composed on the subject of *Romeo and Juliet.* Peter Ilyich Tchaikovsky's overture-fantasy *Romeo and Juliet* was completed in 1868 when the composer was twenty-eight years old. This setting opens with clarinets and bassoons, depicting Friar Lawrence. The feud between the Montagues and Capulets follows. The love music, marked by muted violins and the English horn, is an unmistakably Romantic theme.

Ex. 16–1

The fighting returns followed by love music again. Then all the themes follow in succession, culminating in a fierce crash, ending with a roll of the kettledrums.

This symphonic poem is typical of Tchaikovsky's instrumental style. It overflows with a program of melodrama and sentiment. At times, Tchaikovsky exhibits such an abundance of personal feeling that the listener is flooded. The raw emotions, the extreme exaggerations, and the orgy of sequences are precisely what Modern music protests against. Yet this piece is solidly conceived.

The work is structured in three large sections (presentation, development, restatement) and follows the general outline of sonata form. Tchaikovsky does not attempt to depict the drama in detail. Instead, he treats three images: gentle Friar Lawrence, the feud of the Capulets and Montagues, and the lovers. The chords of the first section create a medieval atmosphere. The brisk rhythms and sweeping runs of the second section express explosive action. The third section displays a long-lined love theme, played by the English horn and muted violas. The development section employs mainly the second theme, referring only briefly to the Friar Lawrence music. The recapitulation begins with the feud theme but is followed by the love theme which is expanded into waves of voluptuous sound which build to an overwhelming climax. A short epilogue closes the work with a dirge of muffled drums and a return to the opening chorale.

In 1839, twenty-nine years before Tchaikovsky's work was written, Hector Berlioz completed his dramatic symphony *Roméo et Juliette*, op. 17, scored for solo voices, chorus, and orchestra. This work consists of twelve sections, each representing a particular scene—"House of Capulets," "Romeo in the Garden," "Dance," "Love Scene," and so on.

One of the most exquisite sections is the "Queen Mab" Scherzo. "It lives," Lang claims, "in the memory of every musician as bold music of eternal freshness." The simple melody assumes an intense life in this compelling depiction.

Ex. 16–2

In the love scene, Berlioz expresses the pure beauty of innocent love. The dialogue of the lovers is suggested by the contrast of violas and cellos (Romeo) with oboes, flutes, and clarinets (Juliet).

Berlioz explores the details of the story with all the resources of color, harmony, melody, and form. He employs great contrasts, ranging from voluminous, massive effects to frail whispers.

The old Classic symphony style is obliterated and the tone poem is well on its way. Berlioz completely renounces form. When form is secondary or largely repudiated, composers depend on the programmatic content to harness the sounds. It is no accident that Classic music is almost devoid of literary and poetic references; form was well established.

Although Berlioz' and Tchaikovsky's versions of *Romeo and Juliet* are both Romantic, the former is more detailed, bold, segmented, free, and original, while the latter is more solidified, generalized, unified, magnanimous, and sweeping.

For further study

Compare the Berlioz setting of the "Dies Irae" from his *Requiem* with Verdi's.

War and peace have been the subject of much music. Find two twentieth-century compositions on this subject and explore the differences in treatment.

Compare the *Don Quixote* of the German Baroque composer Georg Philipp Telemann (1681–1767) with the cantata of the same name by the French Baroque composer Courbois (first half of the eighteenth century). Compare these with Richard Strauss's tone poem *Don Quixote*, op. 35.

What are the special stylistic characteristics of Jules Massenet's (1842–1912) opera *Don Quichotte*, in Manuel de Falla's (1876–1946) *El Retablo de Maese Pedro*, and in *The Man of La Mancha*, the contemporary Broadway musical version?

Compare Ravel's three songs, *Don Quichotte à Dulcinée*, with Ibert's songs from *Don Quichotte.*

NATIONAL VERSUS INTERNATIONAL STYLE

Since the sixteenth century there have been English, French, Flemish, German, Italian, and Spanish schools of music, each individual in character, particularly in the case of secular music. Church music tends to be more international. In the twentieth century all arts have adopted an international style as a result of the greatly increased communication between nations and the disillusionment with nineteenth-century nationalism. Nevertheless, some national traits do emerge in the work of some composers. We can hear Russian influences in Shostakovich, Prokofiev, and even Stravinsky. Heitor Villa-Lobos (1887–1959) makes clear use of Brazilian rhythms and sonorities. Ernest Bloch (1880–1959) sometimes employs Hebraic themes; the works of Manuel de Falla

(1876–1946) exude a Spanish flavor, and there are many other examples.

To study the differences between a national and international style we might contrast the works of Charles Ives (1874–1954) with those of Walter Piston (1894–   ). While Ives' music incorporates elements of Americana, Piston's strikes a more neutral, international tone.

Piston's Symphony no. 4 (1950) is a finely-wrought representative of neo-Classic style that is comparable to the absolute music of many nations. Piston believes in a universal beauty and has little shrift for those who incorporate so-called "national" elements into their music. "The composer," he ventures, "cannot afford the wild-goose chase of trying to be more American than he is." American music "is music written by Americans." It does not depend on integrating folk melodies, jazz idioms, Indian tunes, Negro spirituals, or poetic descriptions.

He strives to balance elements of form and expression by working out the various sound events. His neo-Classic style is an international approach, as readily understood in Germany and France as in the United States.

Charles Ives's American roots are echoed in every one of his musical compositions. His New England heritage of square dance fiddlers, hymn tunes, town parades, popular ballads, and minstrel music are the sources of his particular style. Ives wrote completely what he wanted to write and remained free of European or, for that matter, of American models. Listen to his *A Symphony: Holidays* (1904–1913). In this work, Ives recollects four major holidays in a Connecticut country town: Washington's Birthday, Decoration Day, Fourth of July, and Thanksgiving Day. Here is American nationalism at its best: honest, straight-forward, and enthusiastic. Its contemporary, progressive quality, and innovative style have won Ives international acclaim as a forerunner of modern musical expression and as an indigenously American composer.

For further study

Listen to the following compositions and determine what musical events lend the music a national sound.

1. Heitor Villa-Lobos, *Bachianas Brasileiras no. 5* (1938 and 1945); Brazilian.

2. Aaron Copland, *Appalachian Spring* (1943–1944); American.
3. Ernest Bloch (1880–1959), *Schelomo* (1916); Israeli.
4. Serge Prokofiev, *Lieutenant Kijé* Suite (1934); Russian.

By way of contrast, listen to the electronic music of Varèse, Stockhausen, Babbitt, and Ussachevsky and identify the international elements.

PERFORMANCE VERSUS PERFORMANCE

The number of recordings of the same musical selection produced today offers ample opportunities for comparing performances. One might take several performances of Beethoven's Fifth Symphony, for example. Note the tempo and length of the movements, the clarity of the details, the expressiveness and spirit of the playing, the interpretation of the various melodies, the rhythmic intensity, and the beauty of the tone. The listener will soon be able to distinguish between performances. Preferences for certain qualities will develop with increased listening.

In order to hear the difference that interpretation can make in a performance, listen to Glenn Gould's recording of Mozart's *Piano Sonatas*, Vol. I (Columbia MS-7097) and Gieseking's recording of the same work (Angel 35069, 35070, 35072, and 35074). The performer's personality exerts an enormous influence over the music, as does his philosophical approach. Gieseking interprets Mozart in terms of Rococo elegance, refinement, and charm. Gould's interpretation is more closely allied with the *Sturm und Drang* (storm and stress) literary movement in Germany that took its cue from Rousseau. Rousseau believed that man's spontaneous natural instincts and feelings were a reliable source of truth. Gould's rhythmic liberties, percussive accents, impulsive tempos, and florid embellishments give these sonatas a remarkably different style.

Gieseking's approach is, however, more customary, although his rendition of the sonatas may seem pallid by comparison. This interpretation is not angry, but gentle. There is simple perfection in the graceful flow. Initially this performance may not appear to reveal as profound a Mozart. Repeated listenings, however, convey other levels of feeling. Gieseking conveys a wistful mysticism that underlies the delicate, almost frivolous surface. Gould's originality leaves little to the listener's interpretation; Gieseking reveals the multidimensional Mozart, a composer of such subtlety and depth that each listener can tap his own deepest resources in coming to understand his music.

Which performance is more authentic? Probably Gould's. In the 1770s the piano, although not as full-toned as today's instrument, was capable of reproducing the crescendos, diminuendos, and all the dynamic nuances and shifts that characterized the early orchestral style. Mozart's youthful enthusiasm, his vigorous expressiveness, his sprightly exuberance, and his occasional boisterousness are all indigenous to this style. Yet, these qualities are seldom expressed in modern performances. Gould exploits these qualities in a performance that reveals a forceful, if unexpected, side of Mozart.

For further study

1. Compare Pierre Monteux's interpretation of the third movement of Haydn's Symphony no. 94 (*Surprise*) (LSC 2394) with that of Carlo Maria Giulini (LON 6027).
2. Compare the Swingle Singers' version of J. S. Bach's "Air" from his Suite no. 3 in D for Orchestra with the version by Ernest Ansermet conducting L'Orchestre de la Suisse Romande.
3. In a recent edition of *Records in Review* (Wyeth Press: Great Barrington, Mass.) or other review of recordings, locate a review of a recording at hand and determine to what degree the review was helpful, harmful, correct, incorrect, complete, incomplete, objective, or subjective.
4. Read a sample of record reviews. What kinds of information do they convey? What do reviewers see as their purpose? Do all reviewers have the same aim?
5. Read a variety of record jacket covers. What information do they provide? Who prepares this information? How accurate is it? Does it assist the listener in understanding the music?

MEDIUM VERSUS MEDIUM

Does the listener notice a difference when a ballad intended to be sung by a woman is performed instead by a man? Substituting one medium for another permits performances of works with the forces at hand. Without such flexibility, many works would go unperformed. In the Middle Ages and Renaissance a score was adapted to the instruments and voices that were available. The practice is still common today. Piano pieces are adapted for the organ, harpsichord pieces are played on the piano, orchestral pieces are transcribed for band, ballets are arranged in suites for concert performance, and arrangements are made of popular music for many combinations of voices and instruments. Such adaptations affect the nature of the music, what it conveys, and also the listener's reaction to it.

For further study

1. Compare any of the works on the recording *Switched-on Bach*, by Walter Carlos (Columbia–ML 7194), with other recordings of the same compositions.
2. Compare two recordings of Bach's *Chromatic Fantasy and Fugue*, one for harpsichord (Wanda Landowska, Angel Records–COLH 71), and the other piano (Rudolph Serkin, Columbia–ML 54350).
3. Compare Verdi's "Grand March" from *Aida* (Act II, Scene 2) as performed in a recording of the opera with a recording by the Carabinieri Band of Rome (Angel Records–35371).
4. Compare the Beatles' recording of "A Hard Day's Night" with that of the Boston Pops (RCA Victor–LM 2827).

FOR DISCUSSION

1. Does a listener's musical preference change from youth to middle age, and from middle age to old age? What evidence do you have?
2. On what fair basis could one compare Bernstein's *Mass* with *Jesus Christ Superstar?* On what unfair basis?
3. Is it helpful to compare your reaction to a performance with another listener's reaction? Why?
4. Why doesn't the music of other ages fulfill the needs of today's composers? Audiences?
5. Is there what might be called an "international style" in today's popular music field?

Part Four

MUSIC IN THE HUMAN ENVIRONMENT

Musical Value

17

Each age and each culture produce music in a particular style. The philosophical rationale of people living in a particular era creates the climate that results in that era's musical language. Haydn and Mozart provide a good example of how composers from the same period and general cultural background draw on similar resources and use equivalent concepts of organization. The overlapping of their styles points to a common base—a set of traditions—that governs musical craft, in this case, the music of the Classic period.

Stylistic characteristics and traditions are manifestations of the

Yen-Tz'u-yü: Hostelry in the Mountains, *Album leaf (late 12th century). Courtesy of the Smithsonian Institution.*

The Chinese considered calligraphy and painting the supreme forms of art. They were fascinated by the beauty of line. Their art is intended to portray an inner reality rather than an outward likeness. The same themes are repeated endlessly. The Chinese painter seems to ask, "Does the singer need to make up new songs? I want to show how well I can sing an old song." A traveler on horseback, accompanied by his servant, is depicted crossing a bridge on his way to a village. But the aesthetic impression has as much to do with rocks and trees and movement, suggested by the rising mists, as it does with the traveler and the village. The thought is simple and direct; the art, subtle and decorative. Works from other cultures and eras, viewed on their own terms, provide thought-provoking alternatives to our modern modes of life.

musical values of composers and periods. These characteristics often provide clues to the meaning of the music. Musical value is nothing more than the relevance that these musical works can have for those who hear them today.

STYLE AND VALUE

Artists react to their times, expressing consent or criticism, acceptance or rejection, seeking to communicate present meaning or interpret anew. The composer's overt or implied reaction to his environment, which he expresses in his music, provides the listener with a stylistic feeling for the composer's times. Mozart does not communicate the experience of his culture so much as his attitude toward it. His style, in effect, becomes synonymous with the character of a particular age and people. The capacity of music to convey the essence of a culture or era is one of its most remarkable qualities. Several examples demonstrate how style invests music with special meaning.

In the seventeenth century, scientific and religious upheavals created an atmosphere of heightened emotion that is clearly reflected in the art of the Baroque. Man's religious foundations were shaken by the Protestant reformation and the Catholic counterreformation, and scientific findings caused him to abandon the idea of a fixed and unchangeable universe. The telescope enabled man to see that the universe was far more extensive and complex than anyone had believed. The ornate richness of Baroque art, the expansiveness of its forms, the emotionalism of its content, and the keen interest in personal religious expression are directly related to this change of outlook about the world.

In a similar way, contemporary music is an expression of twentieth-century rationale. Today man's mind is persuaded by the pace of change, by the mechanization of life, by the continual threat of war, and by the ever-present bomb. The "nothingness" of human life as viewed in the philosophy of existentialism, and doubts concerning Christianity and God, and the growing distrust of science as the arbiter of the "good life" have infected the age. Music expresses the tenor of modern times in many ways. Let us examine, for example, chance music. As science moved away from total dependence on the time-honored principle of cause and effect, musicians such as John Cage began to look to happenstance as a fundamental approach to creating music. Cage also believed that all sounds are potentially musical. By combining these two principles Cage produced a new art, free of restriction and of human error, and also void of musical form and meaning in the usual sense.

Although he carefully notated the music for his piece *Music for Changes* (1951), the succession of the sounds is governed by a game of chance. The kaleidoscopic patterns are so complex that continual variation is assured. Such a piece is not memorized or interpreted by the performer. Space and silence set off the sounds, and Cage invites the listener to lose himself in the emptiness. His *Music for Carillon* (1958), says Wilfred Mellers, "is strangely beautiful: like a tolling of Japanese temple gongs dedicated not to a god, but to nothingness."

If Cage expresses the dehumanization of the times, other composers have acknowledged the loneliness of man in the infinity of the universe. Varèse's *Poème Électronique* expresses the struggle of man against the empty reaches of space, but strives to help him come to terms with it.

The same rationale that governs science has now come to govern music. Just as science came to realize that man often imposes his own order on nature, composers such as Schoenberg and Boulez sought a system of organization which they could impose upon sounds. Others, like Stockhausen, used electronic sources of sound in predetermined, intricately planned works. Unlike Babbitt, Ussachevsky, and many other electronic composers, Stockhausen's music does not try to express anything except, perhaps, the order that he has created.

The anguish, anxiety, and alienation of present day life are evident in contemporary music. So is modern man's changed sense of pace. The onrush of events sometimes allows little opportunity to look back or to repeat. Events pile on events in an overpowering buildup. Life at such times is all development: live *now*, keep going. Contemporary music sometimes consists of complexes of sounds and rhythms that leave us confounded and perplexed. It encompasses the simultaneity of superimposed events in life, the frantic uninterrupted movement, and the freak incomprehensible speed of successive events.

Just as man has discovered that he can in large measure control his own evolution and destiny, he has also learned that he is not bound to a steadily recurring beat and pulsation. The long-dominant strict rhythmic structure of music has been overthrown and with it, the concept of history as an irreversible, cause-and-effect progression. Sounds in contemporary music often command their own particular space. Motion is a secondary concern. Whereas time in traditional music is defined in terms of recurring pulse, measured movement, and inevitable evolution, in electronic music time is a matter of filling space (measured distances along the tape) with the flow of sounding substances. In electronic music there is usually no equivalent to basic beat, meter, measure, or balanced rhythmic structures.

But if contemporary music shows a tendency toward unpredictability and discontinuity, it also expresses demoralizing repetition. Like machines turning in endless revolutions, contemporary music can drone on, repeating and repeating while it gathers momentum and tension. Contemporary popular and classical music both reflect this tendency.

However, lest it appear that contemporary music expresses only the nihilism of the times, one need only listen to a wide selection to see that it also affirms life. Although music is not impervious to man's tortured history, it does confirm man's optimistic faith in the future.

As we have already noted, the way a society lives and the way it thinks will find expression in the arts. The New Guinea lullaby probably sounds more like a screech to the uninitiated listener who is accustomed to the musical traditions of Western culture. Although music often provides clues for understanding a culture, the opposite may also be true. One must sometimes understand a culture in order to understand its music. The Manus child in New Guinea learns through a system of imitation. However, it is the adult who imitates the child. The child is brought into a consonant relationship with reality by *hearing* that the environment is in step with him. At first the adult imitates the birth cry, later transforming it into a lullaby that rises in steady crescendo until it drowns out the child's cries. Unless Western ears understand the cultural phenomena, the New Guinea lullaby cannot be understood or appreciated. Emotional response is culturally determined. It depends upon attitudes, mores, and tastes that are inherent in a society and passed on from generation to generation.

The fact that all cultures have some form of music does not mean that music is universally understood. Whether music is "the universal language of mankind" depends on the definition of "language." If language implies communication, then a universal language would be understood transculturally. However, we have already seen that much musical meaning is bound up in its cultural style. The listener's expectations in music depend upon stylistic "norms." For this reason, music that is in a totally unfamiliar style tends to be meaningless.

Our first task is to understand our own musical culture. How does music serve man's needs in contemporary American life? What role does music play in social life? What role should or could it play? What are the responsibilities of each citizen toward maintaining and improving musical culture?

MUSIC IN CONTEMPORARY SOCIETY

In the wake of wars, riots, crime, starvation, poverty, racial violence, and other social unrest, music does not seem to command much priority in American society. One might well ask, "Shall we fiddle while Rome burns?" In a society shaken by rapid flux and social crises, the musician is in a precarious position. Should the composer seclude himself with his art, or should he engage in the social affairs of his fellow men? If he chooses the latter course, won't his music suffer from superficiality? Can music ever be socially effective?

Obviously, music is useful in some ways. We need music in the churches and synagogues, as background for motion pictures, for dancing, and to help us fill nonwork time. Such uses tell us little, however, about music's real thrust in contemporary life. Abraham Maslow, the psychologist, tells us that all humans strive for "peak" experience–moments of transcendent ecstasy. The two easiest ways humans have found of achieving peak experiences, Maslow claims "are through music and through sex." The result of peak experience is "cognition of being." Music serves as a trigger for such experience.

Man's psychological needs are also served in other ways by music. A person's state of mind can be altered by sounds. Moods can be changed or heightened. Music can induce a sense of well-being and happiness. Going to a concert makes us feel good. Listening to music on the car radio can bring us into comfortable touch with our inner selves at the same time that it creates its own pleasant environment. In this sense music serves as an arbiter of good feelings. It is a mediator between reality and man, modifying life to more tolerable dimensions.

In a highly controlled and mechanized society, outlets for man's pent-up anxieties are an essential need. Music is a medium for expressing the irrational as well as the rational, for emotional outpouring as well as calculated restraint, for surprise as well as expectation, for innovation as well as tradition, for subjectivity as well as objectivity, for intuition as well as intellect. It may reflect the computerized environment and, at the same time, offer a means of escaping it. In its totality, music expresses that broad range of alternative values that is encompassed by man's mind and spirit.

Music is a social art. Among its values is its capacity to bring people together. Concerts are an obvious example, as are the growing number of amateur choruses, bands, and orchestras. The social protest song is an effective solidifier of group feeling. Background music, however amorphous, washes over people, immersing them in a community of sound. It tends to unify people by unifying the environment.

The composer who creates art for art's sake, who is content in his ivory tower, may find that when he serves up his creation, it is rejected by the audience. The alienation of the composer in contemporary society, however, is not a one-sided affair. Listeners, too, can fail to listen with interested eagerness. New sound formulations may threaten accepted and stabilized conventions. However, it is precisely this unconventional, spontaneous element which can be an essential ingredient in the musical experience.

The use of music for recreation, as a morale builder, as an historical and cultural index, and as an educational enterprise, are all nonaesthetic or peripheral values. Music also has aesthetic value. A listener can become completely absorbed by the pure fascination of the music itself. Perceiving fully the intrinsic character of music can be the central focus and value of musical experience. Some of the finest music, we must acknowledge, has no practical or functional value, unless one interprets "function" broadly enough to include serving man's aesthetic needs. In this sense, self-expression, sensitivity, awareness to beauty and perfection, might be considered "functional" values of music. Man can learn from music that feelings, as well as facts, constitute reality. The understanding, control, and use of feelings together with facts is of signal importance in a world where an imbalance of either can be manipulated for the destruction of mankind.

PAYING THE PRICE

If it is true that humans value anything to the extent they sacrifice in its behalf, music does not command much regard. Musicians, like other artists, have been forced to accept economic crisis as a way of life. Among composers and performers poverty has a history that traces a path from Bach and Mozart, to Beethoven and Berlioz, and on to Schoenberg and Bartók. Few musicians today can sustain themselves solely on the proceeds from their work in music. Most resort to supplementing their income from occupations removed from their profession. In describing the performers' plight, a recent two-year study of the economic dilemma of the arts found that, "exhausting tours, high professional expenses, frequent unemployment with its accompanying uncertainty, the rarity of paid vacations and the frequent lack of provision for retirement, all add up to what most of us would consider a nightmare world."

Nor are performing organizations in any better financial state. Deficit budgets are commonplace among symphony orchestras and opera and dance companies. The economic problem has become severe, because new sources of private subsidization of the arts have failed to materialize in proportion to the population increase and the artistic demands of the burgeoning middle class. At the present time the arts have accumulated a $25 million debt that will double by 1975. Ticket prices have not kept pace with rising production costs. There is some evidence that if ticket prices continue to increase, even larger segments of the population will be excluded. The box office is not a likely place to find the needed funds. Nor can labor-saving breakthroughs be expected in the area of live performance. It still takes four musicians about forty minutes to perform Schubert's String Quartet no. 14 in D Minor, just as it did in 1824 when it was written. It still takes one hundred men and women to play most symphonic literature. Performers spend almost as much time rehearsing as they did decades ago. Wage increases in industry are partially offset by increases in productivity. Raises in musicians' salaries simply lead to higher undefrayed costs. In addition, the costs of artistic productions are increasing.

Where will the necessary support come from? If the public does not meet the rising costs at the box office, the deficits can only be eliminated by private (generally corporate) philanthropy or by the local, state, and federal governments. The individual donors and the support of corporations, foundations, universities, and the government have not met the need.

Expanded interest in electronic music and the proliferation of recordings offer some alternative to dependence solely on live performances. If live musical performance is to survive and flourish, and if performers and composers are to achieve a respectable status as members of the community, direct and vastly increased subsidization is essential. The musical arts have never been self-supporting, nor can they ever hope to be.

The federal government is presently providing less than four percent of the subsidies. Annual federal appropriations for the arts are disproportionately low, particularly when they are compared with the total national budget. High quality musical performance is costly. The Rockefeller Panel Report recommended that "the artistic goal of the nation be the day when the performing arts are considered a permanent year-round contribution to communities throughout the country, and our artists are considered as necessary as our educators." If Americans believe that the musical arts are worthy of survival, they will have to find a way to pay the price. The increasingly abundant American economy could provide the funds to pay the mounting bill, if Americans are determined that it do so. The future of music as a performing art depends upon the strength of that determination.

FOR DISCUSSION

1. Why have young people invented their own musical culture, given it wide support, and avoided the concert establishment that the older generation values? Who supports the present-day *concept* of the symphony concert?
2. Why was Charles Ives largely ignored by the public during most of his lifetime? What factors are contributing to a change?
3. Does understanding the life of a composer and the times in which he lived help the listener understand his music? Give illustrations.
4. What do the letters of Mozart or Beethoven contribute to understanding their music? Do Stravinsky's writings help the listener to understand his music?
5. Why have musicians such as Bartók and Schoenberg had such difficulty supporting themselves in the United States? Are conditions different today?
6. How do other countries attempt to solve the problem of financial support for their music?

Musical Taste

18

Musical tastes are developed and "learned" in much the same way that other knowledge, habits, and attitudes are acquired. As children we are bombarded by musical sounds every day and surrounded with the expressed and implied musical tastes of our family and friends. Like the rest of the culture men fall heir to, music is handed to the younger generation in a definite, although selected and often limited, form. One mother turns off the symphony concert, preferring the current hit parade, while another listens to a wide variety of recorded literature and plays Chopin and Schumann on the piano. One father encourages his children to study a musical instrument, while another is interested only in sports. A teen-ager buys the same "pop" recordings that his friends do.

Each person gathers haphazardly a set of musical values that constitutes his taste. These preferences and priorities continually shift and alter according to the environment and one's personal disposition. At any particular moment we generally know what we like. This is not to say that if we possessed different musical tastes we would not make more satisfying choices. To extend the range of one's musical taste is, after all, to extend pleasure. Do we confine our taste generally to one particular realm of music, or do we exercise more cosmopolitan choices? Do we allow our musical choices to be socially motivated, or do we seek a more reasoned approach? Musical entertainment comes in many forms and many levels of sophistication. The plurality of American tastes is served by a plurality of musics. Different kinds of music offer different sorts of satisfaction.

Audience of 300,000 at the Woodstock Music and Art Fair. New York, August 1969.

POPULAR AND CLASSICAL

Popular and classical music have often been pitted against each other and thought of as enemy camps. Comparisons between the two have generally tended to downgrade one in favor of the other. The concert artist may condemn popular music; the teen-ager, classical. A person's tastes control his attitudes. Is one type of music truly better than another? What are the differences between popular and classical music?

The term "popular" refers to the current music on the hit parade and the juke boxes. It includes jazz, love ballads, folk music, protest music, ragtime, blues, gospel, swing, soul, country and western, rock and its various offspring, and all kinds of social dance music. "Classical" refers to the music of the concert hall and the so-called "master" composers. It includes orchestral music, chamber music, opera, art songs, and choral works.

The qualitative difference between musical works is more often a matter of content rather than of kind. Musical works (both popular and classical) are generally either conservative or innovative. Conservative works utilize elements already present in other compositions. They tend to be past-oriented, enjoyment-focused, stereotyped, lucrative, and deindividualized. They require little or no effort on the part of the listener. At their worst they may be static and dull. At their best they can be soothing and emotionally gratifying. Much popular music falls into this category, ranging from the predictable arrangements of Guy Lombardo, Lawrence Welk, and Muzak, to the more vibrant Henry Mancini, the Ray Charles Singers, or The Young Americans. A large portion of classical music also falls into this category: from the less-inspired works of Rossini, Johann Strauss, Mendelssohn, and Grieg, to the best works of Vivaldi, Dvořák, Liszt, and Rachmaninoff.

Although conservative music appeases and reassures us, innovative music challenges the accepted mode of musical expression. Innovative musical works may be difficult to understand, demanding effort on the part of the listener because they are future-oriented. Their unusual qualities make them stimulating, even disturbing. The listener is forced to respond in his own way. The uniqueness of such works may ensure their endurance, but will tend to make them more costly than conservative art, simply because they will have more restricted appeal. Innovative works are pacesetters, revolutionizing and revitalizing musical forms, modes, and expression.

Popular music has had many innovators. During the 1950s Stan Kenton was such a progressive. But there are others, for instance Louis Armstrong, Frank Sinatra, Ella Fitzgerald, Bob Dylan, and Simon and Garfunkel. Among the more radical are the Beatles, James Brown, Cream, John Coltrane, the Rolling Stones, and the Paul Winter Consort. Many classical composers have been progressive in their day: Beethoven, Wagner, and Hindemith, for example. Others have been more revolutionary: Gesualdo, Monteverdi, Berlioz, Debussy, Stravinsky, Schoenberg, Ives, and Varèse.

Popular and classical styles do not differ on the basis of traditional versus progressive, nor can they be contrasted on the basis of categorical mediocrity versus excellence. Some have offered the thesis that popular music is designed to entertain, whereas classical music is intended to edify. In the broadest sense all music is designed to entertain. The degree to which the mind of the listener is engaged differs as much with classical as with popular music.

The Grateful Dead.

This San Francisco rock and roll group pioneered in multimedia special effects with light, combined with electrified organ, guitar, bass, and percussion. Many such rock groups appeared during the sixties, distinguishing themselves by the originality of their music and their sound.

There are, however, genuine differences between popular and classical music. Stylistically, popular music employs its own rhythmic, harmonic, and melodic "language." Its instrumental color and usage is also distinctive although considerable cross-fertilization has occurred in recent years. Vocal color is one distinguishing factor. In popular music the vocal quality must be natural, even rough-hewn and often deliberately unpolished. A nasal twang might lend just the desired bite and spirit to "pop" expression. In contrast, classical singing maintains its own traditions of polished sound. The voice range is extended and the projection increased so that amplification is unnecessary. Coloration is classified, and singers train their voices to produce the desired characteristics. Technically, the voice must be able to execute rapid successions of notes, sing long phrases on one breath of air, control dynamic shadings, and express a wide range of moods.

The younger generation employs much popular music as dance music. Because its meaning is largely dependent on the lyrics, popular music is essentially a vocal art. Classical music, on the other hand, is intended to engage the interest of contemplative listeners in the concert hall. It is generally more abstract in character. Both forms of musical art command their own ritual, with appropriate customs of dress, attitudes, and responses.

The most fundamental difference between popular and classical music is in content. The harmonies, rhythms, and forms of popular music are less complex and varied than those of Classical music. Phrases, melodic ideas, and overall length are generally shorter and simpler. Popular music depends on immediate and continuous effect. It sometimes achieves spontaneity through improvisation. It generally displays fewer "events" such as changes of key, changes in meter, and variations in orchestration. Popular music usually expresses one particular emotion or mood in each piece. Classical music may present many emotions in the course of a composition, continually transforming them. The variety and development of musical ideas in classical music has the effect of postponing gratification. For this reason the finale of a classical work can produce a more profound and moving feeling than is to be expected from most popular works. The final outcome and unraveling can carry with it a greater feeling of release because of its evolutionary struggle to "arrive." There are exceptions; *Jesus Christ Superstar* builds as much emotional tension as a classical oratorio.

Classical music is not necessarily a more "serious" music. The finest composers of popular music often demonstrate the same sincere, earnest, and energetic posture as the best of the composers of classical music. Leonard Bernstein, Andre Previn, and Dave Brubeck have helped the old distinctions and divisions to fade. Musicians can learn to communicate in both realms using each whenever necessary and appropriate. Listeners, too, can enlarge their range of enjoyment to span music of both types.

Although genuine differences in style and content exist between popular and classical music, the two realms are not mutually exclusive. Both function as important vehicles of musical communication and both express fundamental human feelings. Only sheer snobbery and stupidity classifies all popular music as "inferior," or all classical music as "dull."

MUSIC AND THE MASS MEDIA

The United States is bombarded by the mass media. The arts have undergone great expansion through the mass communications media of radio, television, the phonograph recording, the movie house, and the paperback book. However, the immensity and voracious appetite of the mass media forces the development of an art designed for mass production and mass consumption. Media music is everywhere—in the grocery store, the elevator, on the street—a ubiquitous and inescapable fact of modern life. An omnipresent loudspeaker encircles us, lulling and soothing tensed nerves, or jarring and numbing our senses by its invasion of privacy. Shall music be an escape, or an entrapment from which humans must eventually retreat?

Music can unquestionably stifle the din of life in the electronic age, but not for everyone, and not all the time. This is especially true when the choice is not ours, and the selection of music is unsuitable to the surroundings and to our disposition. The dangers of musical saturation are clear. Sensitivity can be bruised. Aural nerves can atrophy.

One's taste may also be so persuaded by the bulk of commercial music that it will be won over to it exclusively. The media have enormous influence over public taste, particularly with the young. The influence and persuasion of the mass media on the young is tantamount to artistic dictatorship. When music is furnished to millions of people, the media try to serve a common denominator of musical tastes. The advertisers who support radio and television broadcasts usually pay to reach the largest number of people. If music is a part of the program content, it is generally selected on the basis of what will "sell" to the largest possible number of listeners. In the world of the mass media, the listener has become the consumer, and music is a product to be sold.

Both popular and classical music have their valuable qualities and special virtues. What happens to these qualities when music is produced for and disseminated by the mass media? Turning out huge quantities of music can force a composer to resort to formulas. He may reuse the same sequence of chord patterns and rhythms with new but unimaginative melodies. Instrumental color can become standardized. A formal pattern can be repeated endlessly in song after song. Such music is sterile and dull, attracting transient attention because of promotional efforts, a temporary fad, or the current popularity of the performer. It is usually little more than a highly stylized, traditional caricature of music.

The quantity of music required by the mass media of necessity lowers artistic standards. Rapid consumption leads to disposable or "throw-it-away" music. The composer who works within this system is apt to bend to market demands. He begins to "manufacture" music to meet the fads and fancies of the moment. He aims for a "hit," accepting that it will be shortlived. For the listener, these products offer distraction from, rather than revelation of, life.

The media also have the effect of mixing together music of all styles and qualities to the point that listeners can no longer distinguish between them. Tastes become homogenized. Complex music and complex sections of music are avoided, so that everything begins to sound alike. Bach is candied, Mozart is condensed, and Tchaikovsky is simplified.

Happily, not all mass media music succumbs in this manner. Mass distribution can have a salutary influence on musical taste. The growth in the production and sale of classical phonograph recordings is one example. Stereophonic radio broadcasts of fine music are widely heard and continue to increase in number. Although a disproportionately small portion of time is devoted to classical music on television, the media has not neglected it altogether. Television brings operas, symphony orchestra programs, and other concerts into millions of homes. If more composers chose to work in the media, an increased amount of care and craftsmanship would raise the artistic level of music for mass consumption. However, a more demanding public taste coupled with a greater public consciousness on the part of those who own and control television and radio are necessary pre-conditions for improvement.

Opening night of The National Symphony Orchestra (September 9, 1971). Concert Hall of the John F. Kennedy Center for the Performing Arts, Washington, D.C. Photograph by Fletcher Drake.

Built with public contributions and government funds, this first official national center gives new stature to the performing arts in America.

THE ELITE, THE AVANT-GARDE, AND THE CONNOISSEUR

Musical taste is a personal matter. One person may favor the classics, another only popular music, still another may be completely satisfied by the poorest fare on the mass media. As in any field, music has its so-called "elite," a small minority of people who have developed specialized tastes and discerning musical judgment. Among the elite are composers who create what has been called "high" culture. They do not particularly care about the audience. Their interest is solely artistic—art for art's sake. Their musical creations may be so difficult to perform or interpret that a limited audience is a foregone conclusion.

Also among the "elite" are composers who produce esoteric music only part of the time. They may do this for reasons similar to those of the painter who paints quaint paintings for the tourists for a month so that he can afford to live and to paint for himself for part of that time. Composers sometimes accept commissions to compose pieces for particular occasions and particular performing groups. They are not always free to create what they themselves would prefer.

Some listeners also possess "elite" tastes. A person might, for example, savor seventeenth-century recorder or lute music, or chamber music, or relish only "progressive" jazz. Such people have gained a musical understanding, at least in one area of music. Elite taste is prized by those who feel they possess it because they have expended considerable effort in acquiring it. The professional critic often considers himself in this group. Unfortunately, such highly-developed tastes can become unreasonable and snobbish. Elite taste is given to egotistical self-promotion instead of being used as a means to greater musical enjoyment. Such snobbism occurs when one lauds one's tastes over the tastes of others.

One of the special areas of music that requires elite taste is avant-garde music. Music that is on the forefront of change is difficult to evaluate by usual standards of taste. Because the music is experimental, unorthodox, and original, new untraditional tastes are required of those who attempt to understand and enjoy it. Electronic music and aleatory music are examples of contemporary music that make special demands on their audience. When one becomes accustomed to the bizarre, of course, such modern music is no longer extreme. Understanding avant-garde music requires the listener to bring it into his own frame of reference. He must make it customary. Repeated listenings are necessary to bring such (initially) strange sounds into personal focus. One has to "get to know" the stranger before one can judge him.

When a person becomes an expert in some special phase of music, he is a musical connoisseur. As a listener, the connoisseur understands at least one particular kind of music in depth and is competent to act as critical judge. He appreciates the subtleties and is sensitive to musical detail. The connoisseur is a person who possesses educated tastes and discriminates with keen insight and sensitivity. He distinguishes where others fail to distinguish. He enjoys in depth what others shun. He exercises musical preferences where others express only ignorance or uncertainty. The connoisseur enjoys intelligently. He may or may not possess elite tastes. He may love *all* operas but be able to separate the strong from the weak. He may be an expert at rock-and-roll, being able to differentiate between the mundane and the unique, or he might prefer classical Baroque music. To be a connoisseur is the aim of any good musical education. To be a connoisseur is to focus taste and to extend the horizon of enjoyment. The musical connoisseur, like the expert wine taster, enjoys the best. He sorts it out, selects it, and demands it when he can.

FOR DISCUSSION

1. What effect do recordings have on musical taste?
2. Should people be subjected to music on elevators and in grocery stores, or is this an invasion of privacy?
3. What can the listener do to improve the musical fare on television and radio?
4. What is the range of the ideal record collection?
5. Categorize current popular artists and groups that you know as either conservative or innovative, and provide examples to illustrate your decision.

Musical Judgment

19

Every man is by necessity a critic forced to distinguish between true and false, good and bad, beautiful and ugly, meaningful and superfluous. No man accepts everything. In music, evaluation is a continuing process. The composer evaluates his own world as he creates. The performer judges the craftsmanship of the composer as well as his own performance. The audience evaluates the quality of both.

It has been said that in the realm of the aesthetic, the public generally gets what it deserves. Generation after generation of Americans are aesthetically indoctrinated to be hypnotized conformists. Musical quality depends upon a discriminating public, a public independently responsible for its own standards. Such a public possesses the means to evaluate judiciously. How does the listener know if what he has heard is "good"? How can he distinguish between the great performance and the mediocre?

Aesthetic judgment—a person's ability to select and enjoy—is a subject of much conjecture and debate among audiences, artists, and philosophers. Many theories and approaches have been advanced, from Plato and Aristotle to John Dewey and Santayana. An acquaintance

Buna Hicks, Beech Mountain, North Carolina, plays her fiddle with an intensity, dedication, and self-expression that could rival any concert violinist. The fact that she is part of the American folk tradition demonstrates that what is ordinary and what is exotic is largely due to where you happen to be standing. Photograph by Arthur Tress.

with aesthetic concepts can provide a foundation for the development of one's own outlook.

A person's musical judgment functions first in terms of preference, then in terms of selection. Musical judgment is the exercising of one's musical taste. It is often influenced by such factors as physical well-being, momentary mental state, and the ability to concentrate. Prior judgments and experiences provide each person with a set of musical preferences that he expresses as a reaction to the musical work at hand. A person's approach to musical judgment may be subjective, objective, relative, or universal.

SUBJECTIVE JUDGMENT

To the subjectivist, a work of art is beautiful when he feels pleasure. Beauty exists in the experience of the spectator. Since it is not an objective property, quality varies with the spectator. What one person calls beautiful, another may judge ugly. Beethoven may be one man's peak musical experience and another man's boredom. Folk music and rock may be "the greatest" to one person and an aural insult to another. "Taste" is what one likes or dislikes. Good taste means my taste, or a taste that I admire and wish to be identified with. As such, taste cannot be proved or refuted. Beauty is a quality conferred on an object by a perceiver according to his personal system of values. The argument follows the logic of the philosophical question as to whether, in the absence of a perceiver, there is sound in the forest when a tree crashes down. To the subjectivist beauty depends on his presence and his reaction. Since the listener confers beauty on an object, he can also withdraw it and withhold it indefinitely. A piece of music may be judged a masterpiece today and rejudged an ineffectual exercise tomorrow. In a similar manner, a performance may be called "great" because it was a profoundly moving musical experience, or mediocre because it was dull and uninteresting. Again the judgment holds only for the individual making it.

This personal, intuitive evaluation of music is a legitimate approach to artistic judgment because it is based on an accumulated, though often unarticulated, value system which is real to the individual. The inadequacy of the subjective view is that it fails to provide adequate means to substantiate judgments and communicate them to others. Although personal preference may constitute an adequate value system for the individual, judgments based on mere liking make no provision for growth and cultivation of taste. Criticism becomes arbitrary when, in the process of communication or the attempt to persuade, the value system and criteria remain unidentified. The subjective view can be a very intense and compelling means of aesthetic judgment for the individual, although usually not sufficiently delineated to serve as a convincing musical evaluation for others.

OBJECTIVE JUDGMENT

The objectivist believes a person liking a piece of music actually likes certain features of it; that taste is governed by the properties of the work itself. While the subjectivist believes that there is no authoritative opinion concerning musical greatness and beauty, the objectivist believes that there are tangible distinctions between good and bad. When we evaluate music objectively, we are not so much interested in the feelings of another person, but *why* he has these feelings. The objective view tries to fortify chance feeling with reason.

In theory, the objective critic maintains that the properties of an object exist within the object independently of the viewer: aesthetic "truth" is nonrelative, and the beauty of an object remains even if we do not look at it. The mind of the listener cannot affect a work's aesthetic worth.

Although most objectivists believe that aesthetic quality can be identified and defined, there is a group which believes that quality cannot be defined at all. According to this group, aesthetic values are grasped directly without reason. Since we perceive beauty, we cannot doubt its existence. The difference between this view and the subjective view is that the former maintains that aesthetic qualities are irreducible properties of the art work. Because such intuition is self-certifying, there can be no appeal to discussion, analysis, and evidence. One cannot define beauty and perfection. These qualities are what they are. The composer, performer, and listener either hears and understands them or he doesn't. Intolerance, authoritarianism, and the dictatorship of the individual critic are allies of this position.

Most objectivists, however, do believe that aesthetic criteria can and should be defined. Properties of the work such as form or harmonic movement are often pointed out to justify aesthetic value. The objectivists may say a piece of music is beautiful because of its melody, or that it is exciting because of its rhythmic interest and drive. They may say a performance was outstanding because of the performer's brilliant technical skill and expressive phrasing. We substantiate our value judgment, not by defining beauty or the perfect performance, but by evaluating the properties which accompany these phenomena. Such substantiation permits discussion and possibly the settling of disagreements.

The objective approach may, however, lead to a cold, mechanical, theoretical view of music. Systems and rules, set up to determine if a work achieves excellence, may become rigid and insensitive to the emotional effects of music. The evaluator might try to fit the musical work into a straitjacket of preconceived notions. We see this to some degree in the classification of works by genre. Categorization of a piece of music according to the intention of the work—folk song, symphony, advertising jingle—influences expectation. New formulations could be rejected immediately. Flexibility should be maintained. The evaluator must ask both how well the artist fulfills his intentions and what unique approaches he employs.

Laws and rules are valuable only insofar as they permit greater understanding of what the artist is trying to say. The objective critic believes in the existence of absolute, ultimate standards that lie outside the person. He believes that there is only one correct taste. The widespread reaction against objectivism stems largely from its tendency to support absolutism. American society today has little patience with an aristocracy which dictates what one ought to like.

Nevertheless, the search for objective criteria serves a useful purpose. Aural and visual analysis of the components of the musical score can provide substantiation for subjective reactions. The main difference between the subjectivist and the objectivist is the distinction between emotional liking and rational reflection. To the former, the value of a musical work lies in the momentary mark it makes upon the individual consciousness; to the latter, the value of the musical work lies in the music itself.

RELATIVE JUDGMENT

While the objectivist seeks the intrinsic value of a piece of music, wholly ignoring personal reaction, and the subjectivist turns completely to individual feeling, wholly ignoring the support of reason, the relativist strikes a middle course. He sees aesthetic experience as relative; as the result of the interaction of the listener and the properties of the music.

A fair judgment of a work is dependent upon the function and purpose of that work in terms of the society for which it was created. Every culture breeds its own artistic attitudes and its own characteristic standards. Relativism recognizes that values are largely conditioned by, and relative to, specific cultural variables. Value judgments are therefore valid only for the society within which they are formulated. As societies differ, so will evaluations. Stolnitz contends that relativism teaches us not to ask, "What is the true interpretation of the symphony?" The listener, instead of resisting several interpretations, should welcome them, for they provide the means to find diverse values in a piece of music. There is no "one way." Truth to the relativist is not absolute. Aesthetic evaluation is subject to change. There may be several correct standards by which an object may be measured and several correct evaluations.

This viewpoint takes into consideration the functional aspects of music. Popular music according to the relativist is equally as good as classical music. Both are legitimate forms of musical art. Under the relativist system, Mozart would not be rated better than Muzak. The Indian *raga* may mean little to Western ears, in the same way that a string quartet might evoke little sympathetic response from an African tribesman. However, this lack of understanding does not imply that one culture's music is any better than another's. The relativist tolerates and respects individual differences.

In evaluating a work of art, the relativist studies the relationship between music and history, society, and psychology. For instance, he seeks to discover Mozart as he was viewed in Vienna in 1780. When encountering a work from the past he tries to "adjust to its pastness." He alters his expectations according to the period, the style, and the purpose of the composition. The tonal resources in Mozart's time were far less diverse than in today's electronic music. Study of the tonal "norms" of Mozart's day can help us to experience his music on its own terms and to judge it accordingly.

Although the relativist does not like to admit it, his theory often leads to a reluctance to take a firm stand, to become committed to a viewpoint, and to have convictions about what values are worthwhile. This viewpoint tends to treat art simply as a matter of fashion.

UNIVERSAL JUDGMENT

The three viewpoints thus far presented contrast sharply. Subjective evaluations are binding only for one person and at one particular moment; objective evaluations are binding universally for all time; relative evaluations are binding for a particular group of people during a particular time. The relativist does not recognize common values, nor is he able to favor one cultural approach over another. The universalist, on the other hand, does not believe either in personal, absolute, or relative values. The universalist welcomes the challenge of taking a position based on evidence collected from every source and defending that position. He enters into free discussions with others of varying opinions, criticizing and being criticized, and willing to alter his viewpoint in the light of new evidence.

Strangely enough, primitive art led to this new approach to evaluation. The discovery of classical qualities in the works of primitive peoples demonstrated a certain universality of human needs, perceptions, and emotions. The African chant and the Polynesian carving, reveal transcultural continuities. In all cultures, in every period of history, there is evidence that man has sought to impose a pattern of order on the chaos of life. Through the study of widely diverse cultures, and the analysis of their music, we know that form is a universal value. Similarly, there is evidence that the human response to rhythm also constitutes a universal element.

The universalist does what the relativist cannot: he *uses* comparisons to establish not only differences but similarities. He uncovers strengths and weaknesses. He discovers which is the most successful approach. He makes judgments in spite of the relative worth of two systems.

Each person has a commitment to a particular outlook. The folk singer may say, "Bach is fine, but I am committed to folk singing. To me it is more important than Bach, more worthy of my energies, because I have interest and ability in it. These are the values I can communicate." The listener may say, "I like pop music on the dance floor and as background music while I'm conversing with friends, but it is not something I want to hear in the concert hall." The jazz artist and the symphony orchestra performer may differ in what they value in the arts. Each has his place and his purpose. But one may have a more compelling message than the other. Some men, after all, are more effective creators than others. They invent more ingenious solutions and combinations. The persuasion of a musical work, and the power of a musical composition to move the listener, is often decisive in judging its value.

Fairness requires that we do all we can to understand the artist's aesthetic orientation, and also understand our own artistic perspective and taste. The confrontation of our taste with the composer's taste often exposes us to what our own taste really is. One of the primary functions of art is to assist in determining, clarifying, and interpreting our own perspectives. In this clash with the composer our own tastes change and evolve.

The universalist is free to prefer one interpretation of a symphony over others. He substantiates his belief by all the means that he can command: his personal reaction, his knowledge of the score and the composer's style, and his knowledge of the social milieu in which the piece was created. He does not search for the true Mozart in the eighteenth century. He knows that we view Mozart through twentieth-century ears. He does not search for what Bach meant in his own time, but for his worth seen in twentieth-century perspective.

The universalist does not adopt the laissez-faire attitude of the relativist. He recognizes that this philosophy carries tolerance to extremes. Relativism leads to vacillation and paralysis of judgment. Universalism seeks conviction. The relativist believes in the old Latin expression, *De gustibus non est disputandum.* (There is no disputing taste.) The universalist believes that while each person has the right to like what pleases him musically, there are tastes that are more discriminating, knowledgeable, and rewarding. By using knowledge from every source to study music, not only will the differences between various musical works be recognized, but the successes and failures, the naïve and profound, the noble and mundane. The broad study of music reveals universal values in musical art, and at the same time, the unique musical values of specific works, including those of one's own society. Such insight into one's own musical heritage may induce a commitment to better choices and higher-quality aesthetic surroundings.

THE ROLE OF CRITICISM

All people are critics to the extent that musical criticism is a means of understanding a musical work. By synthesizing every bit of information he can gather about a piece of music—the "sense" and feeling of the piece, the style of the period in which it was produced, the individual style of the composer, the elements and processes employed by the composer, the function of these in the whole work, and the effectiveness of the performance—the listener can make a fair judgment of "what this work means to me." Communication is a two-way street—composing and listening, informing and being informed, comprehending sensitivity and sensitively comprehending. Criticism can explain to the listener his emotional reaction to the music.

If we do not personally have the faculties of artistic perception, knowledge of style and of musical elements, and emotional sensitivity, we may have to rely on the professional critic. Such reliance is often helpful, but should never deteriorate to the level where people read the newspaper to know what they think and feel. Only independence of judgment prevents us from subjecting ourselves to a derivative, second-hand world. Considering the barrage of musical stimuli that daily floods our lives, people need to exercise their right to discriminate and to select. Indoctrinating tastes leads only to the formulation of a tepid, stereotyped, and debased musical art. Musical taste is individual and self-evolving. Only independence can produce a dynamic, varied, and continually evolving musical art now and in the future.

FOR DISCUSSION

1. Analyze your own approach to musical criticism. Are you a subjectivist, an objectivist, a relativist, or a universalist?
2. Is there a way of measuring the exact aesthetic worth of a musical composition? Why or why not?
3. Select a cross section of writings by various critics in this month's newspapers and magazines. What effects could these specific writings have on the public's musical tastes? Do any of the critics try to help the reader understand the music better? Should they?
4. Why is it more difficult to judge the merits of contemporary musical compositions than pieces written many years ago? Can listeners like or dislike contemporary music, or should they withhold judgment?
5. Query friends and acquaintances about their attitudes toward symphony concerts and opera. How many have experienced live performances? Why do they like or dislike either or both? Are their attitudes based on reason or emotion? What could change negative musical attitudes?

Glossary–Index

Absolute music. Music that is nonreferential and abstract in meaning. 15–17, 30–32, (examples) 34–35, 55
compare *program music* *
Abstract music. 15, 16–17
see *absolute music* *
A cappella music. 46, 57, 369
Accelerando. To gradually increase the tempo.
Accent. The greater stress or emphasis given particular tones. 76–77, (examples) 101
Adagio. Slow; frequently used to indicate a slow movement of a *symphony,** *concerto,** or *sonata.**
Aesthetic criteria. 429–30, 431
Aesthetic experience. A highly concentrated emotional, intellectual, spiritual, and often creative human response. 4, 6
Africa, music of. 199
Aleatory music. 174, 177, 179, 424
see *chance music* *
Allegretto. Quite lively in tempo; faster than *andante,** slower than *allegro.**
Allegro. Fast; also used to indicate a fast movement of a *symphony,** *concerto,** or *sonata.**
"All Through the Night." 115
Alto voice. 45
see also *contralto voice* *
"America." 74, 87, 156, 157, 184, 185, 186
American Metaphysical Circus. 62
Amplifiers. Electronic devices for increasing the dynamic level of sound.
Analysis. The technical and studied approach to understanding a musical score.
Andante. Moderate speed; sometimes used to indicate a movement of a *symphony,** *concerto,** or *sonata.**
Antecedent phrase. 112
Antheil, George. 256, 265
Ballet mécanique. 256, 265
Antiphonal. Book containing music for the Office of the Roman Church; also, multidirectional sounds; live stereo.
Apel, Willi. 330
Arcadelt, Jacob. 380
Aria. An accompanied, usually elaborate air, song, or melody sung by a solo voice, as in an *opera* * or *oratorio.** 279, 281–82, 287, 292, 299
compare *recitative* *
Aristotle. 427
Armstrong, Louis. 141, 169, 170, 419
Arpeggio. Playing the tones of a chord in succession rather than simultaneously. 325
Art song. Song in which the emotional intent of the text, the melody, and

*Asterisk indicates a cross reference.

Chamber music (continued)
Baroque and Classic, 332–40, (examples) 360
ensembles, 51–53, (examples) 58–59
Romantic and Modern, 256–59, (examples) 270
Chambonnières, Jacques Champion de. 118
La Drollerie, 118
Chance music. Music in which chance—happening—is involved in the composition or performance. Also called *aleatory* music.* 167, 174–79, (examples) 180; 408–9
Chanson. French song. 378–80
Chanson, Burgundian. French song and musical style prevalent in the Court of Dijon, Burgundy, in the first half of the fifteenth century. 378
Chanson, polyphonic. 379–80
Chávez, Carlos. 59
Toccata for Percussion, 59
Chopin, Frédéric. 53
études: op. 10, no. 3, 35; no. 6, 15, 22
Fantaisie-Impromptu, op. 66, 260–61
Fantaisie in F Minor, op. 49, 261–63
Nocturne in F Major, op. 15, no. 1, 120
piano music, 260–63
Polonaise no. 6 in A Flat, op. 53, 61
Prelude no. 20 in C Minor, 103
Préludes, op. 28, 270
"Valse," op. 64, no. 1 ("Minute Waltz"), 125
Chorale. An early German Protestant hymn tune.
Chorale prelude. An *embellishment* * or *variation* * on a hymn tune scored for organ. 137, 142–43, (examples) 146–47
Choral music. 46–49
a cappella * (examples), 46–47, 57
with instrumental accompaniment (examples), 47, 57
in *opera,** 48–49
in *sacred* * compositions, 47–48
types of, 46–49
see also *cantata,* mass,* oratorio* *
Chorus.
in *opera,** 48–49
in *oratorio,** 299
Chromatic scale. The half-step, half-tone, or twelve-tone scale that occurs when all the different black and white keys on the piano are sounded in consecutive order. 80, 83
Chromaticism. A style, usually nineteenth century, in which tones of the chromatic scale are indigenous to the composition. 80
Classical music. 431
comparison with popular music, 418–21
Classical symphony orchestra. 351
Classical musical style.
dates of, 276
see *Baroque and Classic musical styles* *
Clavecin. French word for harpsichord.
Clavichord. Keyboard instrument; one precursor of the piano.
Coda. Structural ending of a composition. 162
Codetta. Small coda; a structural ending of an internal section of a composition; sometimes the structural ending of a relatively short work. 190
Cole, Nat "King." 171
Coloratura soprano voice. 43
Coltrane, John. 419
Combo. A small group of performers—trio, quintet—usually in reference to *jazz* * or *popular music.**
Comic opera. 287
see also *opera buffa,* opera comique* *
Communication, musical. 4–5, 13–23, 37
Composer-performer relationship.
in chance music, 177, 179
in improvisation, 172–73
Concertino. The part of the *concerto* * performed by a solo instrument or small group of soloists, which alternates with the larger ensemble or *ripieno.** 120
Concertmaster. The lead player in the first violin section who represents all the musicians in the orchestra and prepares them for the conductor.
Concerto. Structural form; usually a work in several movements, for soloist or solo group and orchestra. 53–54, 247–48

Concerto (continued)
Baroque, 343–44
Baroque compared with Classic, 346–47
Baroque and Classic (examples), 360–61
Classic, 344–46
Romantic and Modern, 247–51, (examples) 268
Concerto grosso. Structural form; solo group and orchestra. 120
Baroque, 340–43
Connoisseur, musical. 424–25
Consequent phrase. 112
Consonance. Sounds that seem to require no resolution, suggesting repose and lack of tension. 93
compare *dissonance* *
Contemporary music. 408–10
see also *Romantic and Modern musical styles* *
Contemporary society, music in. 411–12
Content, of an art form. 17
Continuo. An accompaniment, usually "realized" from a bass part provided with figures indicating the chords, performed by harpsichord with a cello or other low-stringed instrument doubling the bass. 293, 296, 299, 332
Contralto voice. 45
see also *alto voice* *
Contrast and recurrence (examples). 123–24, 126
in extended musical forms, 117–22
in simple musical forms, 109–12
Copland, Aaron. 168
A Lincoln Portrait, 233
The Red Pony, 29
Rodeo, 27
Symphony no. 3, 268
The Tender Land, 235
Twelve Poems of Emily Dickinson, 33
Corelli, Arcangelo.
concerti grossi: op. 6, no. 1, 34; no. 8, 360; no. 12, 341
Sonata da Camera for Two Violins and Basso Continuo, 360
Sonata no. 12 in D Minor, op. 5, 333
Countermelody. A *contrapuntal* * part added below the principal melody. 158
Counterpoint. The combination of two or more independently moving parts. 95, 157–60
Countersubject. A contrasting melody juxtaposed against the subject in a *fugue.**
Countertenor voice. 45
Contrapuntal. A technique of composition resulting in two or more melodies sounding simultaneously and usually involving *imitation* * between the parts. 95, 157–60, 277
Country and western music. 418
see also *popular music* *
Couperin, François. 14, 320
L'Arlequin, 322
L'Art de toucher le clavecin, 61
Les Barricades mystérieuses, 322
Concert dans Goût théâtral, 334–35
Concerts royaux, 360
Huitième Ordre des Pièces des Clavecin, 322–23
Cowell, Henry. 60, 270
Ostinato Pianissimo, 60, 270
Cream. 180, 419
Creative process. 13, 25–35
Crescendo. Gradual increase in the dynamic level of the music. 79
Criticism, role of. 433–34
Culture, relation to music. 410, 430
Cunningham, James. 30
Suite in the Form of a Mushroom, 30
Cyclic. Works in which the same musical idea is used in more than one movement as a unifying device. 122, 243

Da capo. Return to the beginning; a method to indicate an ABA form: play A, then B, return to the beginning and repeat A. Also, an aria in ABA form. 282
Dance music. 26–27, 33, 66, 256, 418
Daniel. 367
David, Jacques Louis. 391
The Oath of the Horatii (painting), 390, 391
Davidovsky, Mario. 264
Electronic Study no. 1, 100–101, 271
Davis, Gene. *Dr. Peppercorn* (painting), color insert

Recitative (continued)
tell the story. 277, 279, 287, 288, 292, 299
accompagnato recitative. Recitative with a more elaborate accompaniment scored for full orchestra. 288, 289
secco recitative. A recitative with a simple, usually chordal, accompaniment on harpsichord. 288
compare *aria* *
Recorded versus live performance. 9–11
Recordings. 10–11
Recurrence after contrast. (examples) 123–24, 126
in extended musical forms, 117–22
in simple music, 109–14
Refrain. Recurrence of the same text and melody of a hymn or popular song. 112, 113
compare *ritornello* *
Reif, Paul. 238
Five Finger Exercises, 238
Religious music.
see *sacred music* *
Renaissance musical styles.
see *Medieval and Renaissance musical styles* *
Renoir, Auguste. 212
Repetition (examples). 122–23, 126
in extended musical forms, 117–22
in simple music, 107–9
Respighi, Ottorino. 254
The Pines of Rome, 14
Rest. The notational sign for silence. 75
Retrogression. Altering a melody, subject, or *motive* * by reversing the order of the *pitches,** playing it backwards. 156–57
compare *inversion* *
Rhythm. 65–77
alteration of as developmental technique, 185
Richter, Franz Xaver. 348
Riegger, Wallingford. 165
Canon and Fugue in D Minor for Strings, 165
Riley, Bridget. 3
Current (optical art), 2, 3
Rimsky-Korsakov, Nicholas. 16, 269
Russian Easter Overture, 269
Scheherazade, 16
Ripieno. The part of the *concerto* * performed by the larger ensemble of instruments, which alternates with a solo performer or solo group, called the *concertino.** 120
Ritardando. Growing gradually slower in tempo.
Ritornello. The returning section of an instrumental composition. 112, 114, 120
compare *refrain* *
Ricercare. 384–85
Rock music. 53, 66, 80, 418
improvisation in, 171
motives in, 90
Rococo musical style. 317, 318, 319, 320, 325, 330–31
see also *Baroque and Classic musical styles* *
Rolling Stones. 419
Romantic and Modern musical styles.
instrumental music, 241–72, (examples) 268–71
vocal music, 201–39, (examples) 233–38
Rondeau. 120
Rondo. An instrumental form in which the leading *theme* * recurs, alternating with new thematic material. 120–22
Rorem, Ned. 228–32
Poems of Love and the Rain, 228–32
Rossini, Gioacchino Antonio. 418
Round. A type of imitation form in which all the parts perform the same melody but begin at different times, so that the parts overlap and harmony results. 151, 160
Rousseau, Jean-Jacques. 312
Le Devin du village, 312
Rubens, Peter Paul. 281
The Garden of Love (painting), 281
Ryder, Albert Pinkham. 45
Forest of Arden (painting), 44, 45

Sacred music.
Baroque and Classic, 291–312, (examples) 313–14
Medieval, 363–64, 367
Romantic and Modern, 218–24, (examples) 236–37
"St. Louis Blues." 141

Sonata-allegro form (continued)
the beginning and a *coda* * at the close. 188–92, (examples) 191, 194
Song cycle. A group of poems given individual settings so that together they form a musical entity. 226
Soprano voice, types and examples of songs for. 43, 45
Soufflot, Jacques Germain. 317
the Panthéon, 316, 317
Soul music. 418
Sousa, John Philip. 123
"King Cotton," 100
"The Stars and Stripes Forever," 66, 76, 158
"The Thunderer," 50
Spirituals; Negro. 113
Sprechstimme. Singing in a speech-like manner. 214, 215
Staccato. Direction indicating that the tones are to be performed in a detached and disconnected manner; also indicated by a dot over a note.
compare *legato* *
Stamitz, Carl. 348
Stamitz, Johann. 348
Sinfonia (à 8) in D Major, 349
Stanza. Verse.
Starer, Robert. 59
Five Miniatures, 59
"Star Spangled Banner." 74, 82, 84, 87
Stockhausen, Karlheinz. 264, 409
Mikrophonie II, 55, 271
Stolnitz. 431
Strauss, Johann. 418
"Emperor Waltz," 100
Strauss, Richard. 39, 254, 393
Ein Heldenleben, 30
Salome, 29
Stravinsky, Igor. 157, 168, 212, 399, 419
Cantata (1952), 86
Chorale Variations on Bach's "Von Himmel hoch," 35, 146–47
Dumbarton Oaks, 269
The Firebird, 269
The Flood, 29–30
L'Histoire du soldat (*Tale of the Soldier*), 73, 94, 100, 252–54
In Memoriam Dylan Thomas, 60
Mass, 47, 219, 222, 223–24, 368
Le Sacre du Printemps (*The Rite of Spring*), 27, 256
Stravinsky, Igor (continued)
symphonies, 243–45; *Symphonie de Psaumes,* 222–23; *Symphonies of Wind Instruments,* 245, 268; *Symphony in Three Movements,* 244, 245, 246–47
Three Pieces for Clarinet, 61, 95, 103, 271
Stretto. A technique in imitation in which successive entries appear in rapid sequence, resulting in a more concentrated overlapping of the subject. 150
Stringed instruments.
in orchestra, 39, 40
in string quartet, 52, (examples) 58
in string trio, 51
see also *chamber music* *
Strophic. A song form in which each stanza of the poem is set to the same music. 27
compare *through-composed* *
Sturm and Drang (literary movement). 288, 401
Style. The distinguishing characteristics—the personality—of a composition, determined by the choice of musical resources and the manner in which they are used.
see *musical styles* *
Subject. The main theme, melody, or *motive* * on which a composition or movement is based. 88, 89
Suite. A multimovement musical composition consisting of a series of dance forms. Earlier suites have four main divisions: allemande, courante, saraband, and *gigue,** with other dances, such as the bourée, *gavotte,** minuet, passepied, etc., introduced at will. The contemporary orchestral suite is more like a *divertimento.** 251–54, (examples) 269
Swing. 168, 169, 418
see also *big bands,** *jazz* *
"Swing Low, Sweet Chariot." 81
Syllabic. A type of chant in which each syllable or text is set to an individual tone. 364
compare *melismatic,** *neumatic* *
Symbolism, musical. 14–15

Symphonic poem (tone poem). 254–55, 269
Symphonic wind ensemble. 50
Symphony. A generally lengthy orchestral composition in several movements, usually four, the first movement spirited and in *sonata-allegro form,** the second slower and in contrasting mood, the third a *scherzo* * or minuet, often in lighter mood, and the fourth fast and often in *rondo* * form. 347–57
Classic, 349–57, (examples) 361
Pre-Classic, 348–49
Romantic and Modern, 242–47, (examples) 268
Syncopation. A jazz feeling achieved by shifting the *accent* * on certain melody tones so that they precede the strong beats.

Taj Mahal. 182, 183
Tango. Dance form from Argentina.
Tartini, Giuseppi. 348
Devil's Trill Sonata, 25
Taste, musical. 417–25
Tchaikovsky, Peter Ilyich.
ballets: *Nutcracker,* 66, 101, 126; *Romeo and Juliet,* 269, 396–98, 399; *The Sleeping Beauty,* 27; *Swan Lake,* 27
chamber music, 257
Concerto no. 1 in B Flat Minor for Piano and Orchestra, 202, 250–51
1812 Overture, 14, 95, 265
and sonata-allegro form, 191
symphonies: no. 4, 40, 79, 87, 101, 122, 126, 136–37, 188; no. 5, 102, 268; no. 6 (*Pathétique*), 72, 122
Variations on a Rococo Theme for Cello and Orchestra, 143
Telemann, Georg Philipp. 333–34, 342
Concerto in D Major for Three Trumpets, Timpani, Two Oboes, Strings, and Continuo, 342
Trio for Recorder, Viola da gamba and Continuo in F Major, 333–34
Television shows, incidental music for. 29–30
Tempo. The rate of movement of a piece or passage. 66–67, (examples) 98, 100
Tenor voice, types and examples of songs for. 45
Ternary. Three-part form. 115–16, 118, (examples) 120, 125
Tessitura. The range of a particular part; how high or low all the notes seem to lie.
Texture. The character of the interweaving of various tones or lines as they sound together. 65, 95, (examples) 103
Theme. 88, 89
alteration of to develop musical ideas, 184, 186–88
in *sonata-allegro form,** 189–91
see *motive* *
Theme and variations. A set of variations based on a fully stated melody, usually in *binary* * or *ternary* * form. 137, 142–47
Thompson, Randall. 57, 233
Alleluija, 57
The Testament of Freedom, 233
Thomson, Virgil. 29
Louisiana Story, 29
The Plow that Broke the Plains, 29
Thorough-bass. A musical shorthand in which chords are indicated by figures written over a bass part. 299
see *continuo* *
"Three Blind Mice." 151
Through-composed. A song form in which there is no thematic repetition. 27
compare *strophic* *
Timbre. Tone color; the character of the sound. 43, 46, 56, 186
Toccata. A showy keyboard composition in free form, usually with rapid scale passages and *contrapuntal* * sections.
Toch, Ernst. 28–29
Geographical Fugue, 28–29
Tomkins, Thomas. 381
Tonality. *Tonic,** the central organizing mode of a composition, and all the harmonies related to it. 136, 212, 245
see also *modulation* *
Tone color.
see *timbre* *

THE WADSWORTH MUSIC SERIES

MUSIC LITERATURE

English Folk Song, Fourth Edition by Cecil J. Sharp
The Musical Experience, Second Edition by John Gillespie
The Musical Experience Record Album by John Gillespie
Scored for the Understanding of Music—Supplemented Edition by Charles R. Hoffer and Marjorie Latham Hoffer
Scored for the Understanding of Music Record Album by Charles R. Hoffer
Talking about Symphonies by Antony Hopkins
The Search for Musical Understanding by Robert W. Buggert and Charles B. Fowler
The Understanding of Music, Second Edition by Charles R. Hoffer
The Understanding of Music Enrichment Record Album by Charles R. Hoffer

MUSIC FOUNDATIONS

Basic Concepts in Music by Gary M. Martin
Basic Resources for Learning Music, Second Edition by Alice Snyder Knuth and William E. Knuth
Foundations in Music Theory, Second Edition with Programed Exercises by Leon Dallin
Introduction to Musical Understanding and Musicianship by Ethel G. Adams
Music Essentials by Robert Pace

MUSIC SKILLS

Advanced Music Reading by William Thomson
Basic Piano for Adults by Helene Robinson
Intermediate Piano for Adults, Volume I by Helene Robinson
Intermediate Piano for Adults, Volume II by Helene Robinson
Introduction to Ear Training by William Thomson and Richard P. DeLone
Introduction to Music Reading by William Thomson
Keyboard Harmony: A Comprehensive Approach to Musicianship by Isabel Lehmer
Keyboard Skills: Sight Reading, Transposition, Harmonization, Improvisation by Winifred K. Chastek
Master Themes for Sight Singing and Dictation by Winifred K. Chastek
Music Dictation: A Stereo-Taped Series by Robert G. Olson
Music Literature for Analysis and Study by Charles W. Walton
Steps to Singing for Voice Classes by Royal Stanton

MUSIC THEORY

Harmony and Melody, Volume I: The Diatonic Style by Elie Siegmeister
Harmony and Melody, Volume II: Modulation; Chromatic and Modern Styles by Elie Siegmeister
A Workbook for Harmony and Melody, Volume I by Elie Siegmeister
A Workbook for Harmony and Melody, Volume II by Elie Siegmeister

MUSIC EDUCATION

A Concise Introduction to Teaching Elementary School Music by William O. Hughes
Exploring Music with Children by Robert E. Nye and Vernice T. Nye
Music in the Education of Children, Third Edition by Bessie R. Swanson
Singing with Children, Second Edition by Robert E. Nye, Vernice T. Nye, Neva Aubin, and George Kyme
Teaching Music in the Secondary Schools, Second Edition by Charles R. Hoffer